FITZWILLIAM DARCY

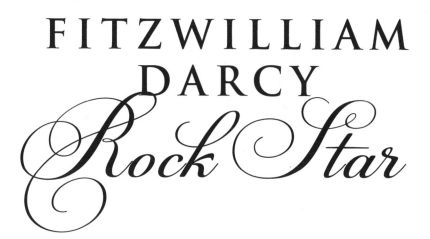

HEATHER LYNN RIGAUD

Published by Sourcebooks Landmark, an imprint of Sourcebooks, Inc.
P.O. Box 4410, Naperville, Illinois 60567-4410
(630) 961-3900
FAX: (630) 961-2168
www.sourcebooks.com

Library of Congress Cataloging-in-Publication Data

Rigaud, Heather Lynn.
  Fitzwilliam Darcy, rock star / by Heather Lynn Rigaud.
      p. cm.
  1. Darcy, Fitzwilliam (Fictitious character)—Fiction. 2. Rock musicians—Fiction. I. Title.
  PS3618.I39378F58 2011
  813'.6—dc23
                              2011026417

            Printed and bound in the United States of America
            VP 10 9 8 7 6 5 4 3 2 1

Dedicated to my mom, Grace,
who would have been so proud,
and to Abigail, without whom
this book never would have happened.

AUTHOR'S NOTE

THIS BOOK WAS ORIGINALLY written just for fun, and because I didn't plan on publishing it, I used popular songs for the music the characters performed. This gave the story another element to enjoy and led to some fun discussions about how the songs fit into the story.

Fast forward to now, I find myself with the rare and wonderful opportunity to publish my little book. This is very exciting, but it means the songs have to go away to avoid violating copyright law.

I've now written new songs, so everything you read here is 100 percent my work. But I wanted to include a list of the original inspirations, so readers can enjoy them, too.

In general, you will find that Jane sounds a lot like Michelle Branch, and Lizzy bears a striking resemblance to Sheryl Crow. Slurry most closely resembles Puddle of Mudd.

Here is the list:

Chapter 1: Jane is singing "Everything" by Michelle Branch.

Chapter 2: Slurry's song is "Breathe" by Seven Channels.

Chapter 3: Lizzy sings "Steve McQueen" by Sheryl Crow, and Slurry plays "Drift & Die" by Puddle of Mudd on *TRL*.

Chapter 4: Slurry opens its concert with "Crawling in the Dark" by Hoobastank.

Chapter 6: Lizzy plays "If It Makes You Happy" by Sheryl Crow.

Chapter 8: Jane plays "Everything" by Michelle Branch to Charles.

Chapter 9: Jane dances to Slurry playing "Control" by Puddle of Mudd.

Chapter 10: Lizzy plays "Soak Up the Sun" by Sheryl Crow.

Chapter 11: Lizzy's video was made to "Steve McQueen" by Sheryl Crow.

Chapter 12: Long Borne Suffering and Slurry play "The Game of Love" by Michelle Branch and Carlos Santana.

Chapter 13: Slurry plays "She Hates Me" by Puddle of Mudd.

Chapter 14: LBS plays "Good-bye to You" by Michelle Branch, and Slurry plays "Blurry" by Puddle of Mudd.

Chapter 15: Lizzy plays "I Shall Believe" by Sheryl Crow.

Chapters 16 and 17: Darcy's classical playing sounds very much like John Williams.

Chapter 19: Richard sings "Somewhere Out There" by Our Lady Peace.

Chapter 20: Lizzy sings "I Shall Believe" again by Sheryl Crow.

Chapter 21: Darcy sings "Hanging by a Moment" by Lifehouse.

PROLOGUE

Narrator: "This week, on *Inside the Music*: Slurry was the brainchild of enigmatic virtuoso guitarist Fitzwilliam Darcy, but it wasn't until he teamed up with outgoing front man Charles Bingley that the group began their meteoric rise to fame. Tonight we will learn the story of one of the most successful rock bands on the road today. We will look at the band's history, at the tragedies that spawned it, and the curious blend of personalities that make up the group."

Cut to each band member in turn.

Charles Bingley (smiling happily): "This is better than any dream I have ever had. I have a great life. I get to do something I love, every day, and I'm getting paid to do it. It's incredible."

Richard Fitzwilliam (looking rumpled, like he just rolled out of bed): "Will's gonna tell you it is all about the music, and he's right, on one level. But you know, everyone has a story, and everyone has a song. It takes something more to be interesting, to be a success. I don't know what it is, but we seem to have it."

Fitzwilliam Darcy (staring at the camera): "You have this audience of millions of people and you want to ask me questions about my *hair?*"

Cue theme music.

Narrator: "The story of Slurry begins with the story of Fitzwilliam Darcy."

Photo of Darcy, looking broody.

"In 1982, world-famous classical guitarist and artist Anne Fitzwilliam married business mogul Walter Darcy."

Wedding picture.

Stephen Fitzwilliam, uncle: "When they got married, everyone believed it would never last. There was a general feeling that this relationship was doomed. They came from different worlds. Walter was very serious, very conservative, very committed to his work, and Anne was this wild free spirit and people said that she would never fit in." *He pauses.* "And in a sense, she never did, but that didn't matter to Walter. They loved each other so deeply that they felt the rest of the world, and the world's opinion, didn't matter."

Narrator: "In March of 1983, the couple had their first child."

Fitzwilliam Darcy (looking thoughtful): "My parents had a relationship of equals. They believed very firmly in this. It was the foundation of their marriage. This belief was so strong that they named me, a product of their joining, by joining their two names, Fitzwilliam and Darcy."

Narrator: "Fitzwilliam Darcy had a golden childhood. He was raised in the family's elegant SoHo apartment and was exposed to a wide range of cultures and people. However, not everything was perfect."

Richard Fitzwilliam: "My aunt was very focused on her career for as long as I knew her. When Will was born, she continued to tour and record, relying on nannies to care for him. And his father, he was always gone. He was very, very committed to his work. I always felt that Will was very lonely as a child. We would spend summers together, he and me and George, but he was always a very solitary person."

Narrator: "Things changed for the family in 1993, when the Darcys had their second child, a daughter named Georgiana."

Stephen Fitzwilliam: "When Georgiana was born it was like a new beginning for the family. She was such a beautiful child, and indeed, she has become a beautiful woman, but back then everyone immediately fell in love with her, and Walter and Anne found a new focus. It was like a second marriage with each other."

George Wickham: "Will has always been devoted to Georgie; we all are. But you can't deny that it was when she was born that his folks suddenly became much more interested in being parents. I'm sure that hurt Will deeply." *He pauses, shrugging.* "But he never blamed Georgie or took it out on her. They were always as close as they could be."

Narrator: "With the birth of their daughter, the focus of the Darcy household changed. Anne Fitzwilliam drastically cut her touring schedule, and Walter reduced the time he was away from the family."

Photo of the Darcy family with a baby Georgiana.

"In an effort to reestablish her relationship with her son, Anne began teaching him classical guitar at the age of ten. Darcy proved to have a natural talent for the instrument and quickly became a prodigy."

Photo of an eleven-year-old Darcy holding a slightly oversized classical guitar.

Richard Fitzwilliam: "Oh, once Will began the guitar, that was it. He played all the time! Hours! Every day! That was all he wanted to do."

Narrator: "Anne was extremely proud of her son's talent, and the bond between them became closer through their music."

Clip of Anne and a gawky thirteen-year-old Darcy in formal dress playing at a concert in 1996. Fitzwilliam has a huge smile on his face, as his mother embraces him. Freeze on that image.

Narrator: "Then, in the spring of 1997, tragedy stuck. Anne Fitzwilliam was diagnosed with cancer, which ravished her body and left her dead just seven weeks after it was discovered."

Stephen Fitzwilliam: "The cancer, it was just devastating. It was so quick, it just stole her away." *He shakes his head, clearly still stricken.* "That was thirteen years ago, but I can still remember it perfectly. It was like we got the diagnosis and the next day she was gone. It was that fast, and we were all, all devastated."

Richard Fitzwilliam: "When Aunt Anne died, it destroyed Will. It was the one thing he could just not handle, and he retreated into himself."

Narrator: "Darcy put his guitar away and entered the prestigious and demanding Phillips Academy Prep School. He channeled his grief over the loss of his mother into his studies, graduating at the top of his class in 2001."

George Wickham: "Will retreated into himself and really cut himself off from his family. He would come home for holidays and summer, of course, but emotionally, he was never really there. I think he was still grieving over his mother."

Narrator: "During the summer of '01, Walter Darcy decided to focus on his children to try to improve his relationship with them. He took a leave of absence from his professional duties and took his family on a tour of Europe. The trip was a success. It was during that time that the Darcys were able to overcome their lingering grief and grow closer."

Photo of a teenage Darcy with his family on a ship.

Richard Fitzwilliam: "Europe changed everything. That was the first time that I think my uncle and Will ever had a good relationship. When Will was a boy, his father was always working, and then, when my aunt died, they were both so depressed. It took them that long to really find each other and develop a relationship."

Fitzwilliam Darcy (remembering, his face softening slightly): "That summer was critical to me and my development as a person. I am grateful I had that chance to really get to know my father as a person, not just a parent. That trip gave me some of my best memories, ever."

Narrator: "Recharged from the trip abroad and secure in his improved family relationship, Darcy entered Brown University in the fall of 2001, immediately going to the top of his class. Along the way, he made an important friend: Charles Bingley."

High school graduation picture of Charles Bingley.

"Bingley was studying business a year behind Darcy. The two soon became fast friends, despite their differences.

"Charles Bingley was born in 1984 to a prosperous family. He lived a carefree childhood in California, dividing his time between the sun and the shore."

Pictures of Bingley rock climbing and surfing.

"While Darcy thrived on the academic challenge of Brown, Bingley faltered, eventually transferring to the Rhode Island School of Design, where he graduated with a degree in graphic arts. Despite being at different schools, Darcy and Bingley maintained their friendship.

"Then in November of 2004 tragedy struck again. Walter Darcy suffered a massive heart attack and died hours later. Darcy was once again devastated."

George Wickham: "Oh man! That was a nightmare. I remember getting the phone call from my mom, and I just couldn't believe it. It was impossible for me to accept it. Mr. Darcy had always been so strong and vital a person and just like that"—*makes a gesture with his hand*—"he was gone." *Shakes his head and looks away.*

Richard Fitzwilliam: "I thought that was *it* for Will. I really didn't think he would survive that. He had just found his father, had just connected with him, and then he lost him. It was his mother all over again.

"I really think it was Georgiana that kept him alive. I think if he hadn't had the responsibility of caring for her, he would have been gone."

Narrator: "With the loss of his father, Darcy threatened to once again retreat into depression. However, his twelve-year-old sister needed him, and he rallied for her."

Photo of Darcy and Georgiana, both looking haunted.

"He focused himself on his remaining time at Brown, graduating in May of 2005 with dual degrees in business and literature. While he was completing his studies, Darcy turned back to the guitar that his mother had left him to try to express the grief he was feeling."

Fitzwilliam Darcy (introspective): "I attempted to play the classical music my mother had taught me, but it wasn't enough. I was hurting and angry and I needed to release that somehow. Then George suggested I let go of my mother's music and try writing my own."

Narrator: "That was the key. Unlike the sophisticated, elegant style of Anne Fitzwilliam, Darcy's own music was anguished hard rock. In the spring of 2005, Darcy gathered together his childhood friend, George Wickham, and his cousin Richard Fitzwilliam to form a band he called Slurry."

Richard Fitzwilliam: "I did it as a lark at first, really. I had nothing better to do with my time, and I said, 'Hey, why not?'" *Shrugging*. "Plus my family wanted me to keep an eye on Will, so, you know, I figured it was good as anything else."

Narrator: "Richard Fitzwilliam was born in Boston, Massachusetts, in 1980."

Stephen Fitzwilliam, father: "Oh Richard, his mother and I knew even when he was a baby, that boy would be trouble." *Laughing*. "He was always fearless, wanting to try everything, and always getting his friends into trouble with him."

Narrator: "Fitzwilliam grew up in a wealthy home and loving family. Blessed with a charming and easygoing manner, he had perused a number of interests, including college, but had never stuck with anything until Slurry. When Darcy was forming his band, he called on his cousin to play drums."

Richard Fitzwilliam (laughing): "I was never a serious musician like Will. I had studied drums as a kid in school, mostly because it was a good way to meet girls." *Laughs some more*. "And it's still a good way to meet girls!"

Narrator: "For vocals, Darcy sought out his childhood friend George Wickham. Wickham's father had been a close friend to Walter Darcy, and the two families had spent much of the boys' childhood together."

George Wickham: "Will was like a brother to me. I mean, for the longest time, we were practically brothers. Neither of us had any other siblings, and so we bonded." *He smiles brilliantly at the camera*.

Fitzwilliam Darcy (in a light tone): "George and I were very close as children, until my sister was born. Then my family relocated and we spent less time together with the Wickhams, but we would still spend summers together. For most of my life, George was my closest friend."

Narrator: "Slurry began humbly, as nothing more than an outlet for Darcy to express the music he was writing to deal with his grief. Eventually Wickham pressed for the group to begin performing publicly. The harsh, loud music and stark performance style struck a chord with audiences, and by the beginning of 2006, Slurry had a devoted following in Providence.

"Then Darcy made a life-changing decision."

Fitzwilliam Darcy: "I realized that a part of me that I thought was long gone was still alive. I found that the music, which I had started as a hobby, had become more important to me than anything else I was considering doing, and I realized that this was what I wanted to.

"It was very hard for me to walk away from my father's companies. All throughout college, I had planned on working with him. The plan had always been for me to take over when he retired." *He looks away and shrugs.* "But that clearly wasn't going to happen. I decided the band was what I had to do."

Narrator: "Darcy moved the band to New York City, so he could be with his sister Georgiana. Soon the band had dates playing local clubs."

Photo of the band, all looking very young, onstage.

"It was then that they were discovered by De Bourgh Records."

Anne de Bourgh, A&R, De Bourgh Records: "I remember seeing them and knowing, right away, that this was a serious group and that they were going right to the top. These guys weren't just fooling around. They were professionals."

Narrator: "Their self-titled debut album was released in October of 2006, after several grueling months in the studio."

Picture of the album cover.

Richard Fitzwilliam (remembering): "That was a really tough time, because Will wanted to go one way, and George wanted to go another way. And those ways were not the same. The album took much longer than it should have because George and Will could not agree on anything. That was when I started to realize we had trouble."

Narrator: "The trouble did not stop once the album was released."

John Willis, *Spin* magazine: "You can tell that the band was divided when you listen to that album. All the elements are there, all the pieces, but like a puzzle, it never comes together. There is a great drum section here and some really strong vocals there, but it never meshes into a whole. It was no surprise to anyone when the breakup came."

Narrator: "Slurry had one moderate hit off their first album that made it to thirty-seven on the top forty, but it was becoming clear to Darcy the band had reached its limit, and he started to feel frustrated."

Fitzwilliam Darcy: "I wanted to be doing more, but it was like we could just never come together. I had all these ideas, and I could hear, in my head, what I wanted. But we just couldn't do it. It was a very difficult time."

Narrator: "The band went on tour in late fall of 2006, leaving the comfort zone of their fan following in New York City to introduce themselves to new audiences. With every concert, the tension between Darcy and Wickham grew."

Picture of an angry-looking Darcy standing next to a grinning Wickham.

Richard Fitzwilliam (angry, frowning): "That was the tour from hell. It was a *beep*-ing nightmare, and it was all George's fault. It should have been a triumph, our first tour and all! And George turned it into a tragedy." *Hits his fist on the couch while looking away.* "Bastard!"

Narrator: "The tension had reached the breaking point when the band played the Ramsgate Festival on the Fourth of July weekend. While no one was willing to say exactly what happened"—*Darcy glaring coldly at the camera*—"that weekend was the end of the relationship between Fitzwilliam Darcy and George Wickham."

Fitzwilliam Darcy (icily): "We had artistic differences that prevented us from being able to continue to work together."

George Wickham: "What did Darcy say?" *Listens for a moment to a voice off camera.* "Artistic differences?" *He smirks.* "Yeah, I guess you could call it that."

Narrator: "Darcy and Fitzwilliam returned to New York City following Ramsgate, while Wickham fled to Florida. For a while the future of the band seemed to be in question."

Richard Fitzwilliam: "I thought we were done. Darcy was so angry and disgusted; I really thought we were just done."

Narrator: "Then an old friend entered the picture. In September, Charles Bingley joined Darcy in New York City for a visit. Bingley was surprised to learn about the band's existence, but he quickly auditioned for the role as lead singer."

Fitzwilliam Darcy: "I knew Charles could sing, but I never realized he was so talented. What's more, he could understand what I was trying to do and add to it. It was when Charles joined us that everything came together. I felt I was finally able to express what I wanted to artistically."

Richard Fitzwilliam: "Oh, Bingley came in and just like that"—*snaps fingers*—"everything was better. It was like every difficulty, every stumbling block that we had had with Wickham never existed."

Charles Bingley: "It was like love at first sight, you know?" *Smiles.* "As soon as Darcy told me about the band, I got really excited. I just knew I wanted to be a part of it, that it was where I belonged."

Narrator: "Charles Bingley was the missing piece that the band needed. Like a phoenix, Slurry was reborn—a completely new band, and its potential was seemingly limitless."

Anne de Bourgh: "As soon as I heard Charles singing with the band, I knew that this was what I had been waiting for. They were electric. They were on fire. It was like holding a lump of plutonium in your hand. You could feel the energy there, ready to be released. We threw out all the old material and sent them right into the studio."

Narrator: "That proved to be a wise decision. In the studio Darcy took over writing all the songs, a task he had unsuccessfully shared with Wickham in the past. The result was a collection of twelve songs, recorded in a blistering five weeks. The CD was titled *Crush,* and when it was released in February of 2008, it debuted at number ten in the charts."

Charles Bingley (smiling): "Yup. Right away we had a hit, and you know that felt great!"

Narrator: "'Searching in the Dark,' Darcy's brooding song about uncertainly and self-direction, was the first single from the CD. It peaked at number one."

John Willis: "It is amazing when you listen to *Slurry* and then compare it to *Crush.* You knew in *Slurry* that the talent was there, but it's not until *Crush* that the band found its balance. As soon as I heard 'Searching in the Dark,' with that opening guitar riff"—*humming*—"I knew that these guys were going right to the top."

Clip of the video for "Searching in the Dark."

Narrator: "Slurry's success came hard and fast. Three more number one hits followed, and the band supported the album with nine months of touring.

"But Charles Bingley brought more that his powerful vocals to Slurry; he also brought his twin sister, Caroline, who became the band's tour manager."

Caroline Bingley, tour manager: "Charles called me up and said, 'Come out to New York; I need you.' So I did and off we went."

Narrator: "Caroline proved to be a quick study, taking the reins of the tour and leaving Darcy free to focus on his music. Another album, *Polish*, followed, which went platinum. The band supported these albums with tours, spending most of the last four years on the road. They continued to gain fans and number one singles.

"By the beginning of 2009 Slurry looked unstoppable. Their albums had sold over ten million copies, and their tour was selling out larger and larger venues. But trouble was just around the corner."

Richard Fitzwilliam: "We were having a blast. We were rock stars, and we were everywhere. Everything was going our way. We were on TV, we were on the radio. Everyplace we went, there were girls screaming at us. It was a trip, and I was going to enjoy that party."

Narrator: "But the party soon got out of control. Richard Fitzwilliam had always been a casual drug user, but while on tour he developed an addiction to alcohol."

Picture of Fitzwilliam with a bottle.

"Darcy and Bingley were only starting to become aware of the problem when, on January 28 of 2009, Fitzwilliam was arrested for DWI."

Picture of Fitzwilliam in handcuffs being led away by police.

Caroline Bingley: "I had my suspicions that something was up with Richard, but he never got ugly. Yes, he always had a beer in his hand, or later on, a bottle, but it's not like he was getting into fights or passing out or messing up shows. And he was always so happy, I never thought he could be having a problem."

Ronaldo Faust, lighting engineer, *Polish* Tour: "I was working with the band during the fall leg of that tour. I remember watching Fitzwilliam, and every day he just looked a little more tired and a little less in control. He always had a drink in his hands, always: before the show, during, and after."

Fitzwilliam Darcy (troubled): "It was my fault. I blame myself. I was so obsessed by what was going on with the music and the details of the tour, I lost sight of what really mattered. I lost sight of my cousin and my friend."

Charles Bingley (looking surprised): "I had no idea he was in trouble. He never said anything. It completely caught me off guard."

Caroline Bingley: "Once Darcy became aware of what was going on, when Richard was arrested, he stopped everything. He brought us all together, the band and the staff, and he told us that nothing was as important as the people here. So that night the tour ended. There was never any talk about getting a replacement drummer. It was over."

Narrator: "Fitzwilliam was ordered by the courts to enter a rehab program as part of his sentence, and Bingley and Darcy joined him there."

Richard Fitzwilliam (in a matter-of-fact tone): "It was the oldest story in the book. I told myself I could handle it, and I couldn't. I was stupid and I had lost control of it." *Shrugs.* "But I was lucky. I was damned lucky the night I got arrested, because I couldn't hide from it anymore. And I got help."

Charles Bingley: "Will and I decided that we were going to hang together on this. We are like brothers, the three of us, and what we have together is too important to let die. So we fought for it and for Richard."

Narrator: "When Fitzwilliam was released in May of 2009, the band went back into the studio. Inspired by their experience, lightning struck again and their next album was recorded in less than eight weeks."

Richard Fitzwilliam (laughing self-deprecatingly): "We seem to thrive on abuse. Hit us again and we will just swing back harder."

Narrator: "On their fourth CD, *Grind*, Slurry expanded their talents. Bingley and Darcy collaborated on several of the songs, and the tone shifted from dark and brooding to a wider expression of emotions. The CD was released in September of 2009 in the top five, and it continues to rank in the top twenty, five months later.

"The first single from the CD, 'Bound,' released August of 2009, went straight to number one and remained there for three weeks. It was followed by 'Lost Myself' and 'Feel Me,' which both hit number one."

Clips of the respective videos.

"The band toured in Europe and Asia during the second half of 2009 to record crowds. Now they are preparing for the North American leg of their tour, scheduled to begin in March."

Footage of the band onstage.

"Although critics have viewed the album as a success, the band is still trying to overcome their reputation for trouble on tour."

John Willis: "The band is good, no doubt about it. I've seen the show, and it's brilliant, but… the fact remains, of the four tours they've started, they've only completed"—*holds up one finger*—"one. The question is, are the fans and De Bourgh going to support them if they have any more problems? After all, there's a lot of money invested in this."

Narrator: "Through adversity, Slurry has managed to not only keep its edge but come back even stronger. The band has so far achieved startling success, and on the eve of their next tour, they show no signs of slowing down."

Charles Bingley (grinning confidently): "People keep asking me, 'Are you ready for this? It's a big show.' Let me tell you: We are ready to go. Let us out there!"

Richard Fitzwilliam (winning smile): "Do I know where we are going? Hell no! I'm here for the ride, baby. But it's a good ride, and it's not going to be stopping for a long time." *Laughs.*

Fitzwilliam Darcy (thoughtful): "I hope the band will continue to expand our style and our talents. For me, it is all about the music. That is why I'm here. My job is to make music, and the rest of it—the fans and the videos and the money—they're nice, but they're not what matters.

"Ten years from now I want us to be able to look back and be proud of our work and not say, 'Oh, that was just a phase or a trend.' I want our work to have lasting value. That is what I am trying to do."

Closing credits.

CHAPTER 1

I T WAS LONG AFTER 9:00 p.m. when the black GMC Denali pulled into the club's crowded parking lot. The engine shut down, the doors opened, and three men and a woman exited the vehicle. The parking lot was full of cars; the sign announced that this was the Meryton Public House. The building had once been a chain restaurant of some kind but had long ago been converted to a nightclub and had numerous additions built. It was currently attempting a southwestern style of decor, but the result was simply shabby.

"Such an exotic location, Darcy," the woman murmured softly over the shoulder of the tall man in front of her. "Are you quite sure we will be safe?"

Fitzwilliam Darcy turned his head, and his dark eyes fixed hers with a look.

Caroline allowed herself a brief smile before they were interrupted by the sharp staccato of high heels clicking across the asphalt.

"Christ! Are you people ever on time?" Anne de Bourgh swore through clenched teeth. She was a small, slender woman, with short dark hair and a stylish yet severe suit of black leather.

"Sorry, Anne." Charles Bingley was the only one who felt obliged to reply. Not because he was the driver, rather that he was the only one who cared at this point.

"Caro, who are we seeing tonight?" Darcy asked, his boredom evident.

Caroline Bingley smiled inwardly, while shaking her head slightly. It didn't matter that she had emailed all this information to the boys already. They hadn't read it, just as she knew they wouldn't. They were so predictable. "Tonight's band is called Long Borne Suffering," she said as brightly as possible.

"Some kind of Goth group?" Darcy asked dryly.

"No, actually, it's a girl band. Two sisters and a friend." Caroline consulted her notes. "Here we are: Jane and Elizabeth Bennet and Charlotte Lucas."

"Can we just go?" Anne snapped.

The group followed the shorter woman to the club's entrance. There was no need to comment on Anne's behavior; they were all feeling the pressure that was provoking her. It was a ridiculous situation they found themselves in. Slurry, the hottest ticket across the country this summer, had a problem, a serious one. Their opening act had left following the Asian leg of the tour, and no amount of begging or threats had been able to bring them back. This was the third act Slurry had lost, and the group had gained a reputation in the process. The word was out that Slurry was impossible to tour with. Rumor had it that they were arrogant, demanding, and out of control. Consequently every act on their "A" list was suddenly unavailable.

Hence they found themselves in the wilds of northern Westchester County, New York, looking at the best of the "B" list: groups that were good enough but hadn't broken through yet and were hungry enough to risk the trauma of touring with Slurry.

This was the third band in as many nights they had auditioned, and the situation was getting critical. The tour resumed in just two weeks, barely enough time to get a new act ready. Besides that, the press was starting to notice the problem. They all knew that the last thing Slurry needed was more bad press.

Anne's title was Artist and Repertoire Executive for De Bourgh Records, but in fact, her sole duty was Slurry. Slurry was the company's biggest band, with revenues that outpaced every other act. It was her job to see that nothing happened to the prize cash cow.

As the group followed Anne de Bourgh through the doors of the nightclub, they knew the real reason for her temper. It wasn't the wrath of the media that was keeping her awake at night. It was her mother, the Gorgon. Lady Catherine, owner of De Bourgh Records, had been made aware of the situation and if it was not resolved very soon, she would become *involved*, which was something they all wished to avoid.

Muffled music throbbed through the walls of the small lobby. A short man pushed himself off the wall he had been leaning on and approached Anne. He was balding, overweight, and wearing a tan turtleneck sweater that emphasized the olive in his complexion.

"Ms. de Bourgh," he enthused, taking Anne's hand and pumping it. "What a delight it is to see you again!"

"Yes, of course, Mr. Collins," Anne replied without returning his excitement. She stood silently, waiting until the lack of conversation had gotten distinctly uncomfortable. Then with a look at her companions, she sighed and addressed him again. "Mr. Collins, this is Caroline Bingley, Slurry's tour manager," she indicated the tall woman who was wearing her professional smile. "Mr. Collins is the A and R for Long Borne Suffering."

Collins laughed at Anne's words. "Yes, I'm her counterpart, as it were. She is the executive for Slurry, and I, well, have my own little flock to tend."

Caroline fought off the discomfort she felt as his clammy hand clasped hers and he waited expectantly. Caroline looked at Anne, who glanced at the men and spoke up. "You do understand, I really can't introduce you in this setting, Mr. Collins. Security and all that."

Collins's eyes flared. "Oh, of course!" he assured her anxiously. "Certainly. I completely understand. Please let me escort your *friends* inside." He winked broadly, but he was moving and that was all she wanted.

Caroline shared a quick smile with Anne as she passed by. Security was not really a problem. The lobby was empty and the boys were "incognito," as Charles liked to say. That meant that Charles's long blond hair was in a ponytail and tucked into the collar of his shirt. Richard was dressed in a button-down shirt and gray slacks, which covered all of his tattoos. Darcy was actually wearing a shirt and did not have his sunglasses on, sufficiently altering his appearance from his onstage persona. The three tall and attractive men would stand out anywhere, but it was unlikely anyone would recognize them for the rock stars they were.

The music became clear as they entered the nightclub. It was large, and the group was careful to skirt the sides of the room, getting close enough to watch the band and yet remain in the shadows.

"Of course, I'm sure you have listened to the girls' CD. We're very proud," Collins fluttered at Anne.

She shook her head once. "We don't care about the CD, Mr. Collins. We just want to know if they can play."

Darcy turned his attention away, glad that for once Anne was doing her job and keeping that buffoon from him. He turned to his right to comment on the full house to his closest companion and stopped.

His expression immediately darkened as he beheld Charles Bingley's face. He knew that look. Charles's attention was locked on the stage, although Darcy doubted he was listening to the music. "Charles!" he said loudly into his ear.

Bingley broke away from his stare to focus on his friend.

"What do you think?" Darcy demanded.

Charles's face broke into a huge grin. "She's an angel."

Darcy looked up to the stage to see who the object of worship was this time. For once he was not disappointed. The subject of Charles's rapt attention was the singer. Of course, Darcy generally didn't think of angels as wearing white leather corsets, but she was quite beautiful. Tall and slender, she moved with an easy grace as she sang. Under the corset, she wore a pink filmy skirt that exposed her shapely long legs. Her hair was elegantly arranged into an almost '40s-style arrangement and in a most intriguing shade of pink. Her features were stunning, with large blue eyes and high cheekbones. Her expression was pleasant, and Darcy was impressed by her ability to interact with the crowd watching her.

Her voice sailed easily over the energetic crowd as she played the keyboards to accompany herself.

The guitarist moved closer to stand beside her and sing along with the chorus. Darcy saw them share a matching smile and knew that these were the two sisters.

"Well, at least they can play," he sighed to himself. It was a clear improvement over the last two bands. The guitarist, he noticed, could actually play quite well. She was not anywhere as attractive as her sister, but she was not bad looking by any means. If she were standing alone, he reasoned, he would consider her pretty. She was not as tall as her companion; Darcy guessed she would be about average height. Her arms were exposed by the black silk tank top she wore, and he could see she had the unique muscling there of a committed guitarist. She wore low-riding jeans that hugged the curves of her hips. Her face was turned down to her instrument, hiding her features, except for her long brown hair, which was captured in a ponytail.

Of the drummer, he could see nothing more than a pair of flailing arms and the top of a head.

He looked over at Caroline and indicated Bingley. She took in her twin's expression, understanding it as well as Darcy did, and rolled her eyes in response.

"Well at least they can play," Richard echoed Darcy's own thoughts in his ear. "You want to talk to them?"

Darcy nodded once, and Richard gave Anne the sign. They would meet with the band after the show. As he leaned against the vibrating walls, Darcy hoped they weren't making a mistake.

∞

Elizabeth smiled joyfully at the crowd. She waved and blew kisses as she exited the stage with her sister and friend. The Public House was their "home base," where they had played more times than anywhere else. The crowd there was their devoted following and had supported the band for years.

As they reached the backstage area, Alex was waiting and kissed them each in turn. It was a ritual. Alex always saw them out onto the stage and received them when they got off.

Elizabeth noticed the gleam in his eyes as he looked at them. "What?"

"You had some special guests tonight," he replied mysteriously. "A band is here to make a very interesting offer to you. Go get cleaned up and then there are some people you should meet."

The women looked at their manager questioningly until he motioned them away with his hands. Then they broke into wide grins and separated.

Elizabeth shrugged and went to do what she always did after a show: take care of her guitars. Her younger sisters teased her that she was in love with them, and she was. The shining instruments, one electric, one acoustic, were her constant companions. She was cleaning the electric when she sensed someone behind her.

"What brand is that?" a deep voice asked her.

She finished wiping the black body down and laid it in the case before answering. "It's a Guild Guitar Bluebird." She turned around to look into the deepest pair of dark eyes she had ever seen.

The eyes held her captive, completely unaware of anything else until the voice asked, "May I try it?"

That jolted her out of her daze. She looked down and then back up again, a refusal on her lips, when recognition, quickly followed by surprise, blessed her fine features. "You're Fitzwilliam Darcy," she said in a soft, puzzled tone.

"Yes I am," he acknowledged with a matter-of-fact tone. "May I try your guitar?" His long arm reached toward the instrument.

"Yes, certainly," she replied.

He picked it up and carefully positioned the strap. Hefting it, he looked at her. "It's very light," he observed.

"That's because it's chambered," Elizabeth explained.

She watched as Darcy's long fingers moved gracefully up and down the neck of the guitar, a classical scale left softly in his wake. Slowly he moved away from her, listening intently to the instrument, his face blank with concentration until she believed he had forgotten her presence. He was tall, maybe six foot, three inches or so, Elizabeth guessed. His eyes, which she had always seen hidden behind sunglasses, were large, dark, and intense—eyes that were like a weapon, dangerous. He had short black hair that curled tightly around his head. His nose was long and straight and he had full lips that were pressed together as he played.

Finally he stopped and looked up at her. She had large, intelligent eyes that were watching him, filled with questions. "It has a great sound," he complimented her sincerely.

"Thanks," she replied, pleased, puzzled, and a bit uncomfortable. "Um, I'm Elizabeth Bennet." She was slightly annoyed that she had been reduced to introducing herself.

"Oh, yes." He paused. "Nice to meet you," he responded belatedly. He released the strap on the guitar and presented it to her.

Holding the instrument like a shield, she asked, "Why are you here?"

❧

Jane Bennet was sipping warm water as she hummed softly to herself.

"Hi," a soft voice spoke behind her.

Jane turned to find herself in the company of a tall, handsome man with white blond hair, tan skin, and dark blue eyes. "Hello," she replied.

"I'm Charles Bingley," he said, smiling.

Jane smiled brightly back and held out her hand, "I'm Jane Bennet. It's nice to meet you."

"It's nice to meet you too," he replied, delighted by her touch. "I really liked your song. Did you write it?"

"Yes, I did," she blushed becomingly. "Thank you."

With every second, Charles was becoming more bewitched. The angel named Jane was dressed like a siren. He took in every detail, from her finely arched brow, to her bare shoulders, to her delicate hands, and he desired her body. Yet her every word and look was completely open and innocent. Her expression was warm and her laugh infectious. A mixture of sex and purity had come together in a package that was swiftly becoming irresistible.

"Did you write it about someone?" he asked openly, incapable of guile.

Jane shook her head slightly. "No, I wrote it more about wanting an ideal so much that it becomes an obsession. I've never been in love that deeply, and I'm not really sure it's possible, but I've dreamed about it." Her eyes met his shyly, as if she suddenly realized how openly she was sharing herself. "Do I know you, Charles? You seem very familiar."

Charles blushed slightly. "I sing too."

"Oh," Jane nodded. "Is that where I know you from?"

"Yes." He grinned. "Let me take down my hair." He moved his hands and a moment later a blond, wavy cloud surrounded his face.

"Oh, yes," Jane smiled playfully. "Slurry, right?"

"Yes," he smiled back. "Would you like to sing with me, Jane?" he asked shyly.

⁂

Charlotte was standing by the stage door, enjoying her post-show cigarette. She smiled as she inhaled lightly. *Better than sex.* Or at least any sex that she'd ever had.

Footsteps on the cement floor alerted her to a man approaching her. He was tall and handsome, in an easy, casual way; long brown hair falling in loose curls, blue eyes, strong shoulders, and a trim figure. Charlotte couldn't help but smile at eye candy like that. He walked up to her and held out his hand. "Hi, I'm Richard Fitzwilliam."

"Charlotte Lucas," she replied, carefully shaking around her cigarette. "Do you mind?" she asked.

"No, not at all," he assured her easily. "Mind if I join you?"

Charlotte nodded and made room for him by the door. As Richard lit up, he took a moment to study her. She was average in most ways. Average height, average build, average looks. The only thing that really stood out was her hair, which was short and spiked, with white-gold tips, showing up against the light brown of the rest of it.

"So, I heard you play," he said easily after a moment. "You're very good."

"Thanks," Charlotte smiled. She'd recognized his name and was puzzled why a major rock band was here but was willing to let the man tell his story.

"So, my band is on tour and we need a warm-up act." He looked at her slightly sideways. "Would you be interested in that?"

Charlotte watched the way one half of his mouth curled up and mentally drooled. *Oh yeah, baby.* "Really?" she replied aloud. "I would be very interested. But you'd have to work it out with our manager."

"Yeah," Richard assured her. "Caro is talking to him now."

"Caro?"

"Caroline Bingley," he explained. "She is our tour manager. Everyone calls her Caro. You'll like her."

Charlotte took another drag and nodded easily. "Sounds good."

❧

Alex Lucas listened impassively to Caroline Bingley. The woman was very friendly and professional, and the offer she was making was very good—too good.

"We start up the tour again in two weeks. Your group would have that time for rehearsal. We have arranged for practice space, a choreographer, and a stylist to get them ready."

"What would be expected from the band?" Alex asked.

"They will be expected to perform a thirty-minute set at the start of each show. Generally that would work out to be six songs. They will also be expected to participate in any promotions that are done for the shows."

Alex bristled inside but was careful not to let it show. He had been managing bands for ten years, and he knew how many songs were in a thirty-minute set. He pushed his annoyance down. This was far too important a deal to lose his temper over.

As Caroline continued selling her deal, Darcy, Bingley, and Richard stood together, talking softly.

"Do you really think they can do it?" Richard asked.

"What choice do we have?" Darcy said blackly. "They can play and they're available."

"I think they are wonderful," Charles objected.

"You think the girl is wonderful, Charles."

"Isn't she gorgeous?" he asked, not perceiving the acid in Darcy's tone.

Elizabeth was carrying her instrument cases to her truck, oblivious to the negotiations as she passed by. Then she heard Darcy's voice rise above the murmur, catching her attention.

"Let me make this clear to both of you. If these girls come with us, they're there to play. They are not going to be anyone's personal playthings, got me?"

"Darcy!" Charles replied, his voice echoing the shock Elizabeth felt.

"No, Charles! Listen, these girls are just starting out. They're not prepared for what's going to happen to them. Christ! They don't even have people to set up and break down the stage for them.

"When they get on this tour, they're going to get a taste of a completely different world. Once they do, they'll try to do anything to hang on to it—and that would definitely include us." His tone was flat and ugly. "So I'm only going to say this once: keep your dicks clean."

Elizabeth was shocked beyond words. The breath left her lungs as she was stung by what she had heard. Silently she moved away from the trio and back into the dressing room where Jane and Charlotte were packing and excitedly discussing their visitors.

"Lizzy!" Charlotte exclaimed upon seeing the flabbergasted look on her face. "What happened?"

Elizabeth repeated Darcy's warning verbatim, causing Jane to gasp in shock and Charlotte to swear under her breath.

Elizabeth just shook her head in amazement, trying to understand why that man would say such an outrageous thing about them. Then the absurdity of it struck her. Elizabeth covered her face, which was quickly getting red, with her hand. "Damn it, they think we're whores!" she squeaked between her fingers until she could no longer control herself and broke out in laughter. "Charlotte! Don't you get it? They think we're morally loose women who are a threat to them! *Them!* Slurry! The bad boys of rock and roll with the worst reputation in the business and *we* are going to somehow corrupt them!" She had to stop as her laughter became too strong to continue.

"Well, you know, we are just so hot! We could totally make them our slaves," Charlotte took up the charge. "Because, after all, we're only here for their money!"

"And their drugs!" Jane piped in loudly. "I don't know about you, but I want some of those party drugs they are all doing, right?"

All three of the girls were laughing so hard that they were holding each other up when Alex knocked on their door and asked them to come out. It took them longer than it should have for them to compose themselves, mostly because they would start laughing again whenever anyone made eye contract. Eventually, they regained control and filed out silently.

The others were all there: Alex and Bill Collins on one side and Caroline, Anne, and Slurry on the other side.

Elizabeth quickly realized she would not be able to look at Darcy without laughing, so she carefully looked at anything else.

"Well, ladies," Caroline said brightly, "I'm pleased to say we have reached an agreement. In two weeks you will be joining Slurry on the *Grind* tour!"

Jane grabbed Elizabeth's hand and squeezed it tightly as she said, "Thank you very much! We're so excited and happy to be joining you."

Elizabeth didn't trust herself to speak but nodded in agreement, while Charlotte added, "I'm sure this'll mean great things for all of us." This caused Elizabeth to bite her lower lip to keep from giggling.

"Oh," Jane said excitedly. "Perhaps we could invite you to our house next weekend for dinner. It would give us all a chance to get to know each other before we leave, and you could tell us what to expect."

Caroline and Charles exchanged looks. "Are you sure?" Caroline asked.

"Definitely. I'm sure our families would like to meet the men we are going to be spending the next eight months traveling with," Jane assured them with a bright smile.

"That is, if we're not too dangerous to you," Elizabeth said softly.

Darcy's eyes locked on hers, and she was able to meet his gaze with frank inquiry. She realized that despite her laughter, his warning still stung badly.

"I think that is a lovely idea," Charles said agreeably. "Next Sunday then?"

"That would be great," Charlotte replied.

"We'll send you the directions and the time," Jane glowed.

"I look forward to it."

"Good night then; it was nice meeting you," Anne said formally as she began leading the group away. Darcy left with a cold feeling in the pit of his stomach, which turned colder as he heard Elizabeth's laughter at his exit.

∽

"For MTV News, I'm Mark Cole.

"The rock band Slurry has finally announced the warm-up act for the North American leg of their *Grind* tour, squashing the rumors that had been circulating about the band following the resignation of their last opening act, Dead Man Walking.

"The new group is called Long Borne Suffering. Relatively unknown, the band recently released their debut CD, *First Impressions*, on De Bourgh's Rosings Park label.

"That's all for now. Stay tuned for more MTV News, every ten minutes of the hour."

CHAPTER 2

THE WARMTH OF SPRING filled Elizabeth as she sat down at the kitchen table to enjoy the peace of the morning. She cherished this time, before she remembered everything she had to do and the pressure of expectations forced her to move. For now she could just enjoy her coffee and biscotti and not worry about anything yet.

A sudden burst of female laughter broke Elizabeth out of her daze. Lydia called out to her, "Lizzy! Come here! You gotta see this!"

"Do I?" she asked her father as she got up and started moving to the other room. A week of long rehearsals had left her sore and numb. She found her youngest sibling in front of the desktop in the living room. On the screen were three naked women, their faces turned away. "What the heck is this?" Elizabeth blurted to Lydia's peals of laughter.

"Watch!" Lydia commanded and moved the mouse. As the cursor passed over each body, a name appeared. With a sinking feeling Elizabeth saw the names were "Lizzy," "Charlotte," and "Jane."

"What the hell?" she asked, rubbing her forehead.

"It's Long Borne Suffering, d'uh!" Lydia replied.

"*Where* did you find this?" Elizabeth asked.

"Ever since you were on the news, stuff like this has been popping up," Mary observed from the couch, where she was reading.

Elizabeth read the title of the website: "Long Borne Suffering: NUDE." She was surprised and a little shocked, but her good humor quickly overcame it. "I had no idea my hips were that small," she quipped. "And when did I get a racing stripe?"

The girls all laughed together, then Lydia offered to show Lizzy her other finds. The girls sifted through a pile of sites, each more lurid than the last. Elizabeth was especially amused by the web page that proclaimed them "*Slurry's Bitches*" in large type. "I can't believe all these things they've written about us. So many wild stories."

"What about all the stories about *him*?" said Kitty as she entered the room.
"Who?"

"Fitzwilliam Darcy, of course," answered Lydia. "I've heard he keeps three hot blonde masseuses to travel with him."

"Well, there's a lot of tension on the road," Elizabeth joked to Mary.

"I've heard he does a lot of drugs," Kitty said.

"I think they all do," Lydia confirmed.

"Did you hear about the lawsuit?" Mary asked.

"No, what?"

"I heard that he is so big," she lifted her eyebrows to indicate what she meant, "that he put a girl in the hospital and she is suing him, because she can never have babies because of him."

"Ewwwwwwwwwwww!!!!" the sisters chorused.

"Could a guy really do that?" Lydia asked.

Elizabeth shrugged. "I guess, but he would have to be the size of a friggin' oak tree."

"Girls! Girls!" Their mother's sharp voice interrupted their discussion. "Look at the time. Our guests will be here in an hour and the house is nowhere near ready!"

Exchanging guilty looks, the women separated to their various tasks. Elizabeth put on her grungy sneakers and went outside to begin mowing.

❦

Darcy pulled his car off the Taconic State Parkway, following the directions from his GPS. His mouth was set in its familiar frown. He couldn't believe he was going to meet the girls' families. He was hiring a band, for Christ's sake, not asking them to the prom. He felt stupid, a feeling he hated.

Caroline had succeeded in getting him to go by reminding him that they had lost three acts already in the last year and that if they wanted to keep this one there would have to be some changes. Always sensible, Caroline pointed out the girls would be much less likely to ditch if Slurry had actually made the effort to meet their parents.

Darcy knew she was right. He was glad he had Caroline around. She seemed to understand people much better than he did, and she could make reasonable suggestions. The last thing Darcy wanted to do was spend a rare Sunday off doing something work related, but he knew that it was for the best.

Charles had been completely delighted with the idea. He'd called Jane Bennet personally to get the details and, according to Caroline, had spent over an hour on the phone. It seemed that Darcy's advice to his band mates had been ignored. Darcy would be keeping an eye on Bingley today, trying to keep things from getting out of hand, but the sinking feeling in his gut told him it was already hopeless.

He was twenty minutes early when he pulled his jade green Mercedes-Benz CL65 AMG coupe into the driveway of the Bennet home. The house was modern, large, and clean, but that was the most that could be said for it. It was a colonial style on a large lot that was surrounded by trees.

As he shut off the motor, he could hear the whine of a lawn mower nearby. He exited the car and immediately saw the source of the noise: Elizabeth, the guitarist from the other night, was wearing a pair of faded jeans and a ragged T-shirt as she operated the mower. She seemed oblivious to him, and Darcy took a moment to study her.

She was not beautiful, he concluded again, she was simply pretty. Her figure was not perfect; her waist was too short and her hips and breasts too large to be perfect. Yet she was very attractive, he had to admit, as he watched the sweat dripping off her chin to land between her breasts.

He wondered, not for the first time, what she had meant the other night: "*That is, if we're not too dangerous to you.*" Had she overheard his warning to his friends? An uncomfortable feeling hit his stomach at the idea of getting caught, but he overcame it quickly. It was unlikely she had heard his remarks, he reasoned, and even if she did, she just had to deal with it. He was Fitzwilliam Darcy, and he did not have time to worry about every little thing he said that might be taken the wrong way by someone who was working for him.

He was right, after all; Slurry was too important to have Josie and the Pussycats hanging off their coattails. This was a business transaction between two companies and that was all. Today is just a business meeting, he reminded himself.

Even he was aware of the hypocrisy of telling himself this as he was staring at Elizabeth Bennet's ass. Before he could stop himself, he was caught as she looked up and saw him.

ༀ

She stared for a moment, and then with an indifferent shrug, she kept going. Elizabeth had been startled to see Darcy standing there. He was so still, like a ghost just watching her. She couldn't make out his eyes, which were once again hidden behind his trademark dark sunglasses, but it was clear he was watching her, and by the set of his mouth, he didn't seem too pleased by what he saw. Nevertheless, Elizabeth was not going to make any apologies to him for her behavior, and she continued with her work.

Feeling awkward, Darcy approached her. She was struggling to turn the mower when it stalled. He took advantage of the quiet to speak.

"Good morning, Elizabeth."

Elizabeth wiped her forehead with the back of her hand. "Good morning..." She paused, frowning, not at all sure how to address him.

"Most people call me Darcy," he offered.

"Good morning, Darcy." She quickly decided she would be perfectly polite to this rude man. It was the only way she could remain civil. "You're a little early. I'm not finished here yet, but if you go inside, I'm sure Jane can introduce you to everyone and get you something to drink."

"Thank you," he replied automatically. He turned to the house, then turned back to watch Elizabeth pulling on the start cord to the mower.

Elizabeth looked up to see a puzzled expression on Darcy's face. "Is something wrong?" she asked.

"Why are you doing this?" he asked flatly.

"Mowing?" Elizabeth exclaimed, surprised. "Because I waited all week for the mowing fairy to come and she missed our house." She answered in a straight tone that belied the stupidity of the question. *Well, so much for being polite.*

Darcy frowned at her as he took her meaning. "I meant, doesn't your father have someone he hires to do this?"

Elizabeth was losing control of her expression. "Why should my father pay someone good money when he has five able-bodied daughters at home?" She returned her attention to the pull cord, ignoring her observer.

"Is that hard?" he asked.

A thought dawned on her then that she immediately realized must be true. "You've never mowed a lawn, have you?" she asked incredulously.

He didn't answer her, but by the way he locked his jaw she knew she was right. "Do you require assistance?" he asked stiffly.

Elizabeth almost laughed out loud at the idea of a multimillionaire guitar god mowing her lawn. Luckily she was saved by the arrival of the black SUV carrying the two Bingleys. "Thank you, but I can finish this. Why don't you go inside with the others; I'll be along shortly."

Silently Darcy left her and joined his friends. Elizabeth gave the Bingleys a friendly wave and directed them to the house, then started the mower. In the white noise of the mower, she was able to lose herself to her thoughts. What a strange man! Elizabeth felt the distance between them as she thought about all the other things he had probably never done: never cleaned out a garage, never scrubbed a toilet. Hell, the man had probably never even pushed a vacuum cleaner. She couldn't help but feel the vast differences in their lives.

Elizabeth had certainly never been poor. The Bennets had always been comfortably middle class, but the girls were no strangers to work either. They had always been expected to help out around the house as they were growing up. Now that her father was approaching sixty and had a weak heart, Elizabeth felt that helping out with the yard work was the least she could do.

She continued to puzzle over her mysterious guest until the lawn was done. Elizabeth put the mower away in the shed, and then slipped in the back door, hoping to avoid the company until she had a chance to get cleaned up.

As luck would have it, she walked right into her mother giving the house tour. "Lizzy!" her mother scolded, making sure that everyone saw her.

"Excuse me," Elizabeth said softly as she sprinted for the stairs.

Fifteen minutes later, showered and freshly dressed, Elizabeth returned to the party. Charlotte and Alex had arrived in the meantime and greeted her warmly. Then she turned to the other guests.

"Elizabeth?" The tall blond man smiled sincerely and offered his hand. "I don't think we have been introduced. I'm Charles Bingley, everyone calls me Charles." He shook Elizabeth's hand. "It's nice to meet you."

Elizabeth was charmed. "It's nice to meet you, Charles. I'm sorry I was busy when you arrived."

"Oh, don't think about it." He dismissed her apology with a wave of his hand. "I used to have to mow the lawn at my parents' house. Remember, Caro?"

Caroline Bingley joined the couple and laughed, "Oh God! Don't remind me. I hated that!" She addressed Elizabeth. "I'm Caroline Bingley. It's nice to meet you again, Elizabeth." She shook her hand warmly.

"Our father would make us do the lawn—to build character, he would say," Charles explained.

"And you have to realize that every other house in the neighborhood had a lawn service," Caroline continued.

"So we tried everything to get out of it."

"But it never worked. Remember that time we had to mow by flashlight?"

Elizabeth watched in amusement as the twins jointly told their story, one picking up the other's lead without thinking about it. She was impressed by the openness and good manners of the Bingleys. They seemed the polar opposite of Darcy, who was standing apart from everyone, studying the content of the bookshelves.

"Where is your other band member? Richard?" Elizabeth asked as she noticed his absence.

"Oh," Caroline flicked a quick look at her brother, "he had a previous commitment. But you will get to meet him on Thursday."

"What's Thursday?"

"Slurry is going to watch our rehearsal on Thursday, Lizzy," Jane volunteered as she joined the group. Elizabeth watched as Charles flashed her a bright smile and moved to allow her room beside him.

"Actually, now that you are here, and before we eat, why don't we all sit down, and I can brief you on the plans?" Caroline asked in a warm tone that softened her professional words.

As the group assembled on the two couches, Elizabeth was glad to see her younger sisters had disappeared. Some snacks were sitting on the coffee table and everyone had drinks, but there were no signs of her family, besides Jane, for which Elizabeth was both relieved and grateful.

"Okay," Caroline said as she flipped through a leather-bound clipboard. "How has rehearsal been going?"

"Wonderful," Jane smiled. Elizabeth and Charlotte agreed.

"That's great," she smiled, her eyes briefly meeting Darcy's. "Let's go over the schedule. We'll be in to see you on Thursday, then on Friday we are leaving from Kennedy. You need to be at the airport by 9:00 a.m. Don't be late. Then we will be flying to Austin for three shows. Now,

I know you haven't had a lot of time to prepare, but we are going to hit the ground running, and we need you all to be ready, right?"

Elizabeth nodded. "We're ready."

"Good. After Austin we will be traveling on the buses. Here is a list of the dates and locations for the next few months." She passed over a packet several pages long. Elizabeth could feel the excitement growing inside of her as the reality that next week they would be touring settled upon her awareness. She shared a look with Charlotte that told her Charlotte felt it too. Years worth of dreams were coming true.

"There's something else, girls," Alex said softly. "On Thursday we will be shooting footage for a video."

"What!?!"

"The label is putting 'Everything You Are' into heavy rotation, and they are going to rush a video together." He smiled happily. "They believe that with the increased exposure of the tour, you are going to be getting a lot more attention to your songs."

"What kind of video?" Jane asked.

"It's just going to be a simple performance shoot from the rehearsal," Caroline answered. "They want something fast, and you all are pretty enough you don't need any fancy gimmicks."

"I always knew my girls would be famous!" Elizabeth cringed as she heard her mother's voice from the doorway. Chance would have it that she had been looking at Darcy when her mother spoke. "Are you ready for dinner?"

Caroline looked over at Alex, who nodded, and turned to Mrs. Bennet. "Yes, I think we are pretty much done here."

Francine Bennet was an attractive woman in her late forties. She was very proud of all of her children and had no problem showing it. Without stopping her monologue on the natural talents and gifts of Jane and Elizabeth, Mrs. Bennet led her guests into the large dining room she had designed and had built many years ago to accommodate her love of entertaining. The long rectangular table had been fully extended to seat all the Bennets and their guests. Elizabeth wasn't surprised to see Charles sitting next to Jane but was surprised to see Darcy directly to her left.

"Thank you so much for making the potato salad, Caroline," Jane said graciously as she passed the serving dishes.

"You made potato salad?" Darcy dryly asked the woman sitting to his left.

"Of course, Darcy. It's a barbecue," she replied lightly. "Don't you think I can cook?"

Darcy shrugged indifferently.

"Caroline, can I put the tour dates on the band's web page?" Elizabeth asked.

"Of course," Caroline nodded.

"You manage your band's website?" Darcy asked quietly.

"I created it," Elizabeth answered easily.

"Elizabeth has a degree in software design," Jane explained pleasantly.

"Did you see all those new web pages up about us?" Charlotte asked excitedly.

The sisters all laughed as they acknowledged they had. "My favorite is '10 Reasons to Hate Long Borne Suffering,'" Elizabeth smiled wickedly.

"I saw that!" Charlotte exclaimed. "Reason number ten is Jane's hair!"

Jane winkled her nose and turned, grinning, to her neighbor. "You're reason number two, Charles."

Bingley laughed. "That's not too bad. Where's Darcy?"

"Number one."

Darcy smiled in a distinctly satisfied way while Caroline quipped, "The power of those Darcy fans. You gotta love it."

"Will," Lydia spoke up, her voice louder than it needed to be. "Are any of the rumors about you true?"

Elizabeth couldn't believe her ears. She looked down at her plate and hoped that Lydia would realize how rude she was being and stop.

"What rumors are those?" Darcy asked slowly, his eyes unfriendly.

Any other person there would have backed down, but Lydia was blessed with an unfortunate mixture of presumption and cluelessness that enabled her to completely ignore all the signals Darcy was giving off.

"Like, is it true that you have a private chef on tour with you?"

Jane caught Elizabeth's eye, and they silently breathed a sigh of relief that the question had been so safe.

"No, I don't have a private chef on tour with me," Darcy answered, his voice short.

Kitty, never one to be outdone by Lydia, followed up boldly, "What about the masseuse?"

"You have a masseuse, Will?" Charles teased. "You've been holding out on me."

Darcy lifted one side of his mouth in dark amusement and shook his head. "No masseuse. And before you ask, the lawsuit isn't real either."

Lydia and Kitty looked at each other with eyes as wide as saucers while Jane quickly redirected the conversation.

The meal continued pleasantly; however, Elizabeth could not help but notice how quiet her neighbor was. He contributed almost nothing to the conversation, except to answer her sisters' questions in a way that made it clear what he thought of them. While in contrast, the Bingleys were delighting the table with their stories. Elizabeth wondered if her family really offended Darcy, or if he was just quiet by nature.

When the meal was over, Elizabeth escaped onto the rear deck to enjoy the spring day. She was still tired from her past week and craved some quiet time alone. She sat down on her favorite Adirondack chair and listened to the sounds around her. She could hear Mary playing the piano in the living room, entertaining the guests.

Her mind was drifting when she heard footsteps come onto the porch. "May I join you?" Darcy's voice asked formally.

Go away, she thought. "Certainly," she answered politely.

Darcy took a seat beside her. "Your sister is very talented," he said softly.

"Thank you," Elizabeth replied, careful to hide her surprise. "She is studying at Juilliard. We're very proud of her."

"You should be. That must be quite an accomplishment for your family." He studied her face a moment. "Is everyone in your family musically talented?"

Elizabeth smiled politely. If she had a quarter for every time she had been asked this… "Not everyone. My mother, Lydia, and Kitty aren't musical at all."

"What about your father?" Darcy asked, his voice low and indifferent.

"My father is the one who started it all. He is a music professor at Vassar."

A flash of surprise passed Darcy's face and quickly disappeared, but Elizabeth had seen it. Inwardly she grinned. *Not quite the hicks you thought we were, hmm, Darcy?* "Yes, he encouraged all of us in our careers. He's been very supportive."

"You're quite fortunate," Darcy observed woodenly. His words were interrupted by a loud crash from the kitchen, which was immediately followed by angry screams from Kitty and Lydia.

Elizabeth's lips tightened as she grew embarrassed by the display. Her mother's voice joined the fray, and she was relieved when the yelling stopped a second later.

"Lizzy?" her mother called out to her, and she joined her a moment later on the porch. Mrs. Bennet observed that her daughter wasn't alone and softened her tone as a result of it. "Sweetheart, your sisters had a little accident with the cake. Could you run to the store and get some dessert?"

"Sure, Mom," Elizabeth answered easily and stood to get her purse.

"Elizabeth," Darcy's voice stopped her. "I think my car is blocking yours. Could I give you a ride?"

Recognizing she was trapped, Elizabeth agreed, but she wasn't fooled for a moment as to why Darcy was offering to help her. She had seen it in his face the moment her mother had asked her to run out. He didn't want to be stuck with her family a second longer than he had to. The Bennets were simply too suburban middle class for the world-famous Fitzwilliam Darcy.

Elizabeth was simmering inside but was determined not to show it as she followed Darcy to his car. Ignoring the luxury automobile around her, Elizabeth gave directions to Darcy. Then she asked the first thing she could think of. "So, why did you cut your hair?"

Darcy's eyes were hidden behind his sunglasses, but she could see the annoyance in the set of his lips. "You know," he said softly, "I have written seven number one songs. I have traveled over four continents. I have performed before hundreds of thousands of people. I have met both the Pope and the Dalai Lama, and still, do people ask me about any of that?" His voice had risen slightly, "No, they ask me about my hair."

Elizabeth was slightly embarrassed, but she wasn't going to let him know that. "Yes, but everyone has hair. Conversation is as much about the things we have in common as it is about the experiences that make us unique."

Darcy turned his head to stare at her for a long beat, and then turned back to the road. "I cut my hair because it was becoming more important than my music. I don't want people to associate my name with my appearance. I want to be known for what I play."

Elizabeth was impressed by his answer. "I can understand that. It really pissed me off that none of the record companies would meet with us, or even respond to us, until we started including our picture with our demo tapes."

Darcy nodded once. "It's harder on women musicians. There is much more focus on your appearance."

They pulled up to the store. Adam's was a combination garden center and gourmet market. Elizabeth hung a shopping basket over her arm and looked at the produce section. "Do you like strawberries?" she asked, eyeing the first harvest of the season.

"Yes," he replied, slightly surprised. "But Caro is allergic to them," he recalled.

Elizabeth nodded and passed by the rest of the fruit. She moved on to the bakery and chose a fruit tart and a chocolate cheesecake. "That ought to satisfy everyone," she smiled to her companion.

Darcy walked with her to the register and offered to pay. Elizabeth assured him it wasn't necessary, but he insisted. She shrugged and waited in line. While waiting, she noticed the checkout girl watching them closely. When Darcy handed the girl his credit card, she giggled and blushed, but quickly processed the transaction. Darcy took the card back with a confident smile and warmly thanked the girl, which produced even more giggles.

"Does that happen often?" Elizabeth asked as they walked back to the parking lot.

"What? Being recognized?" He shrugged. "Not very often."

"Do you mind it?" She was annoyed somehow by his behavior with the girl, and she realized she was now trying to provoke him.

"Not when people are polite about it. I hate it when people I don't know stand and talk at me like I'm their best friend or something."

"Hmm," Elizabeth said noncommittally as she got into the car.

"Elizabeth, you better get used to this. Once your video hits MTV, your private life is over. You'll have to be able to handle it."

"You seem pretty sure we'll be a success."

"I believe you will be," he answered. "You are a talented band, and you are going to have the label marketing supporting you." He didn't sound too convinced, but Elizabeth was willing to take him at his word.

"Can I ask you a question?" Darcy said softly.

Elizabeth snapped out of her thoughts. "Of course."

"Why 'Long Borne Suffering'?"

Elizabeth smiled ironically. "It's actually a joke about my mother."

Darcy looked at her, willing her to continue.

"My mother will sometimes go on these rants, complaining about things, the way everyone does, I guess. She always ends with 'You don't know how I suffer!'" Elizabeth grinned. "When we were putting the band together that seemed like a funny joke, so we picked it and it stuck." She shrugged. "It's too late to change it now. Why 'Slurry'?"

"It's just a name," his deep voice said darkly.

Elizabeth didn't believe that for a moment, but she also recognized that he didn't want to talk about it. She had clearly reached the limit of questions she was allowed to ask for the day.

They rode the rest of the way in silence. Darcy stayed for the dessert and then left quickly afterward. Elizabeth, for her part, was glad to see him go. She spent the rest of the afternoon enjoying the company of her family, the Lucases, and the Bingleys, forgetting about Darcy and his coldness.

CHAPTER 3

THE BLONDE WHO WALKED out of the loft on Broone Street was not exceptional in appearance. She was attractive, but not so much that it would draw anyone's attention. That was just how Rebecca Nelson wanted it. She walked out, her blue eyes carefully inspecting the street on that rainy morning. Seeing that it was clear, she raised her hand, and two men and a woman exited the building and entered the black limo that was waiting at the curb. Rebecca was the last to enter the limo, and it pulled swiftly away.

"Why are you here, Rebecca?" Fitzwilliam Darcy asked as he sipped his mug of green tea.

"Why, to guard you, Darcy," Rebecca replied frankly. "Hence the term 'bodyguard.'"

Darcy looked at the woman sitting opposite him. Rachel Brown was tall, leggy, and gorgeous. Unlike Rebecca, it was not in her job description to be unremarkable, something Rachel was quite pleased with. Her long legs flowed out of her short skirt, covered by the long jacket she wore over it. Her hair was long, dark, and wavy and her eyes were the color of a stormy ocean. Darcy asked his personal assistant in a tired voice, "Why is Rebecca here?"

Before Rachel could answer (not that she planned to) Rebecca gave up. "Okay, I'm here for two reasons. One: because you are going on tour tomorrow and you are out of practice moving with your security detail." Rebecca ignored the way he rolled his eyes. "And two: because you are going on Fuse this afternoon."

"*What?*"

Top 20 Countdown was the afternoon program on Fuse that consisted of a pair of affable hosts interviewing music stars and charming fans while counting down top music videos. Darcy hated the program and the hosts for their banality.

Rachel took a deep breath and suggested that they go over his schedule for the day.

"Yes, perhaps we should," Darcy snapped and took another sip of his tea.

Rachel consulted her BlackBerry and began. "We are going to the studio now to meet with Caro and Charles. Caro has some papers for you to go over. At eleven you are going to see Long Borne Suffering perform. Charles has suggested that the two bands do lunch together."

"He would," Darcy muttered to himself.

"At one thirty you have to be at the Fuse studios. Slurry is going to be the first act on *Top 20.*"

"Did you know about this?" Darcy asked Richard, who had been watching him with amusement.

"Oh yeah. Caro told me Monday," he nodded.

"Are we scheduled to perform?" Darcy asked Rachel.

Rachel had had enough. "No, you and Juliya are going to glare at each other on live TV for twenty minutes."

"That's not funny."

"No, it's not," Rachel answered him flatly. "You are booked to play 'Lost Myself.'" Charles and Richard will handle all the talking; you can brood in the corner."

Darcy grew silent for a moment as he thought. "We need a violin for 'Lost Myself.'"

"Caroline's hired Kay," Rachel answered efficiently.

"Kay?"

"She played for the recording and will be at the studio all day for *rehearsal*," Rachel answered without looking up.

"How could you forget Kay, Darcy?" Richard said, amazed. "She was that hot redhead. She plays violin and she's a yoga instructor?"

"And didn't she totally reject you, Richard?" Rachel asked.

"And that's why I'm so glad I will get to see her again," Richard replied, grinning. "She can't say no to me forever."

Darcy was spared listening to any more of this by their arrival. The Studio, as it was called, was a large building that Darcy owned in the middle of 54th Street between 9th and 10th avenues. It was his home base, where he created the music that had made him famous and housed the offices that managed the business of the band.

Darcy waited impatiently until his security expert gave him the okay; then he marched into the building, his long black leather coat flaring out around his tall frame.

Caroline was waiting for him in the offices, examining papers on her desk. As he entered, she looked up and said firmly, "Good morning, Darcy. You *are* going on *Top 20* today. Don't try to get out of it."

Darcy resembled an annoyed cat as he growled, "I hate *Top 20*. I hate the Juliya. I hate Allison. I hate performing like a monkey before all those drooling teenagers."

"And they hate you," Caroline replied, then she smiled, "but you are going." She saw his face settling into his usual sulk and returned her attention to her papers.

"Where is Charles?"

"Watching LBS rehearse," Caroline answered, expecting the question. "Slurry might want to rehearse as well, being that you haven't played in three weeks."

He gave her his trademark glower and walked into his office without comment. Twenty minutes later, Rachel left the office and Caroline was called in. Darcy's office decor was purely functional. This was where Darcy the businessman reigned. It was a side of him he did not enjoy, so he spent as little time as he could in it. The premium equipment contained in the office was modern and expensive but entirely without soul.

"You have some papers for me?" he said without looking up.

Caroline passed a few folders over. "When are we expected to see the band?" he asked as he flipped through the documents.

"They will call for us when they're ready," Caroline answered. She watched him as he worked, waiting. Whether he was being Darcy the businessman or Fitzwilliam the artist, it was her job to wait on him, which she did with a loyalty that went beyond her job description. Luckily for her, Caroline was patient. She would wait for him forever.

The ringing of the phone interrupted her musings. Caroline reached across the desk for it when she saw that Darcy wasn't moving. "Yes? Okay, we will be right there."

She hung up and told Darcy, "They're ready for us."

He nodded and led the way to the next floor. They stopped at the smaller studio, where they found Richard talking to a beautiful petite woman holding a violin. "Will," he said, a charming smile on his face, "you remember Kay, don't you?"

In fact, Darcy did not remember her at all, although he did have to admit she was quite beautiful, and he found the knowledge that she taught yoga momentarily intriguing. He shook the lady's hand then led Richard away to the larger studio. He found Charles waiting by the door. "Will! Richard! Wait till you see them; they're wonderful!" he bubbled and led the way into the large rehearsal area.

Darcy found it difficult to credit Charles's objectivity, but he had confidence in the band. He turned to look at them and blinked. For a moment he hadn't recognized the trio.

Jane was the least altered, and it was she whom Darcy latched onto first. Her hair was now platinum blonde and her makeup was improved, with dark red lipstick, pale skin, and highly arched brows. On her left wrist she wore a length of rhinestone bracelets, her right arm free to play her instrument. She was wearing a red halter top that showed off her fine shoulders and her flat stomach. Her hips were circled by a white belt that was holding up a pair of low-slung jeans, which were peppered with rhinestones.

Charlotte was behind her drum kit, but Darcy could see her from where he stood. Her hair was even shorter now and had been dyed a dark turquoise blue, so it looked more like the feathers of an exotic bird than hair. Her makeup was dark, emphasizing her eyes. She wore a white tank top and black plastic bands around her wrists, exposing the colorful tattoo on her upper right arm.

But Elizabeth really captured Darcy's attention. He dimly heard Charles announce, "Ladies and gentlemen, Long Borne Suffering," as he watched her. She flashed a coy smile to the small audience and she began playing her acoustic guitar. She was wearing black leather pants that laced closed and a vibrant red shirt that clung to every curve. Her hair, which Darcy was sure he had never seen down before, was long and loose around her shoulders, its soft waves showing off the red highlights in the rich warm brown. It looked like she wasn't wearing any makeup at all, but her eyes were huge and vivid and her lips full and red. The only jewelry she wore was a large silver pendant that hung between her breasts.

As striking as her appearance was, his attention was totally captured when she started to sing. Her voice was dark, rich, and full. Low and sexy, he wasn't sure he had even heard the lyrics. Darcy found himself trapped in her eyes. They were so large and bright, challenging him with intelligence; he realized she was staring straight at him as she began her next verse.

Darcy could tell she was singing to him and he could not withdraw from her. His eyes devoured every inch of her as she strutted confidently over the stage area, her body swaying in a way that spoke of both sexuality and self-possession. He remained perfectly still until the song was over, when Jane immediately started the next one without a pause.

Hearing Elizabeth's sister broke his trance, but he watched her still, fascinated. Darcy was struck by the differences in the two women. Jane's voice expressed innocence while Elizabeth's spoke of experience. Elizabeth played along with Jane's singing, adding her voice for backup but completely comfortable with sharing the spotlight. Back and forth between the two women the performance went, ending thirty minutes later with Jane's "Everything You Are."

When they were done, Darcy approached Elizabeth directly. "You can sing," he said in a tone of disbelief.

"Yes," Elizabeth replied, her voice puzzled. "I sing and play guitar."

"I had no idea," Darcy said softly.

"Didn't," Elizabeth frowned and started over, "didn't you hear us perform at Meryton?"

"Yes, but you didn't sing there."

"Yes I did!" she protested. "If you missed me, you must have come really late to the show."

Darcy began to get the uncomfortable feeling that he was making a fool of himself. Stiffly he replied, "Yes, we were late that evening."

"But didn't you listen to our CD?"

"No, I did not," he answered her haughtily. "Frankly, it doesn't matter to me what you sound like in a studio. We needed a band who could play live."

"And what do you think?" Elizabeth asked him, her eyes demanding an immediate answer from him.

He stared at her for a beat. "I've told you before, Elizabeth, you're very talented."

"Darcy! Elizabeth! We're going out to lunch to celebrate." Elizabeth jerked, as if startled by Charles's voice. She looked away from Darcy to the safety of her friends.

"No, Charles, I'm going to stay here," he demurred. "I want to practice."

"Will!" Richard protested. "Come on! We're going to get Indian."

Darcy refused, despite the protests of his friends. Finally, Caroline offered to bring him back something and the group moved out in a noisy cheerful mass.

Darcy shut the door, opened the case to his Paul Reid Smith, and plugged it in. For the next forty minutes, he played without thinking, processing emotions he didn't care to examine or understand in the way he knew how. He felt troubled and frustrated, and he sought release of these feelings in the privacy of his music. His eyes closed and his breathing grew deeper as he focused on the sensations in his hands. His fingers moved of their own volition, without thought. They gently loved the instrument, caressing the strings, squeezing them tightly then releasing them, his fingertips dancing over the frets to cause the silver strands to vibrate at the rate he desired. The music that came out of this communication between man and guitar would never be heard by another soul. It was his alone. It was a song of yearning, but even he could not name it as such. He just knew the music was him at that particular moment in time.

He stopped, slightly dazed, when the door opened and Caroline walked in. "I knew I would find you here," she said indulgently. She placed a white paper bag on the table. "The others will be back in a moment. Now unplug, eat, and get changed."

Darcy looked at her, his eyes expressing the gratitude his words never would. "Thank you, Caro," he said simply.

With a nod, Caroline left the room, satisfied.

It was twenty minutes after one when Darcy walked into the office area. He was wearing skintight black leather pants, a loose white linen shirt that was left mostly unbuttoned, and boots. "Where's Charles?" he asked, looking around.

Caroline could just see the edge of the tattoo on his left breast. "You are wearing a shirt?"

"Are you disappointed?"

"I'm heartbroken."

Darcy's eyes expressed annoyance. "Caroline." She grinned when he used her full name. "Despite what you and every other woman in this building thinks, I do not go shirtless for your viewing pleasure."

Caroline tilted her head skeptically and folded her arms across her chest.

"It's very hot under the stage lights and I hate having anything binding my arms when I play," he said in a low tone that was not to be challenged.

Caroline resisted the urge to comment on the fact that Darcy didn't seem to mind having anything on his arms when he was rehearsing and moved on. "Sorry, Darcy. Charles is probably watching the video shoot."

Darcy regarded her carefully and then shut the office door. "What do you think of them?"

She had been expecting the question. She valued her role as Darcy's confidant and made a rule of being prepared for anything he might ask. "LBS?" she shrugged indifferently. "I like them. I mean, they *are* green and a little young—"

"They're our age," he disagreed calmly.

"You know what I mean. Jane invited us for Sunday dinner, for goodness sakes," she grinned and shook her head. "Still, they're smart and professional. I haven't had a single complaint from them. They aren't whiny divas or anything. You can't know until we are on the road, but I think they're going to work out."

"Have you been watching them?" he asked softly.

"Oh yeah."

"Are they clean?"

Caroline nodded. "Cleaner than we are, at least," she shrugged.

"What about Charles? He's all over them."

"I wish I could tell you that it's just Charles being friendly."

"What about Jane?"

Caroline sighed. "Yeah, I know. I don't know what we can do about it. Just have to hope…" Her voice trailed off, leaving all her worries unspoken. "Frankly, I'm surprised. She's not really his type. He usually goes for high-maintenance exotics."

"Don't remind me," Darcy frowned, tiredly. "All right, we need to get going."

"Have a great time. I'm not coming," Caroline said simply.

"Why not?" Darcy asked suspiciously.

"Faust just called from Austin. It seems one of the big lighting boards has gone missing."

"Do we have a backup?"

"Of course. But Faust is really hoping we can still find it. According to him, the house manager down there couldn't find his asshole with a flashlight."

"Faust would never say that."

"He didn't, but that was the general message," Caroline shrugged. "If we have to use the backup board he will be up all night programming it. The backup board belongs to the house and our software won't talk to it. I need to stay here and man the fort."

"Will you have to fly down early? Should I cancel *Top 20*?" he asked hopefully.

"No, Faust can handle it. My going down a day early won't help anything, and I need to stay here and make sure you do what you're supposed to," she added with a meaningful look.

The phone rang. Darcy knew who it was and was moving toward the doorway even as she hung up. "That was Rebecca. They are waiting for you out front."

"Bye, Caro," he sulked as he left the room.

Caroline grinned privately to herself as she went back to work.

❧

Elizabeth looked at her bags. They looked disturbingly small, considering how long she was going to be away from home. Her personal belongings had been packed into two suitcases and a carry-on that she would be living out of for the next three months.

Her costumes and instruments were already packed on the plane. Her beloved guitars had been taken from her arms and were now part of the Grind Tour freight. It bothered her to not have her babies where she could see them. She longed to hold her Taylor acoustic. It would soothe her nerves to play it.

Although she knew she should be trying to sleep, Elizabeth was simply too unsettled to lie down. Every day this week had brought completely new experiences to her; at times it had been overwhelming. The long train ride home each day had been her time to examine and process her thoughts and calm herself. Jane and Charlotte had seemed to understand, sitting quietly on the train beside her.

But today had been different. Perhaps it was the performance for Slurry or the video shoot, but today the train ride had not been enough to quiet her mind. She was a wild mixture of emotions inside:

excitement and pleasure being periodically dampened by a swirl of fear, worry, and anger.

A hiss escaped from her chest as she remembered again her conversation with Darcy. *Arrogant prick!* First the jerk stared at her throughout the whole concert, so much so that even Charlotte noticed it from the other side of the room, then he came down on her because he didn't know she sang? *What the hell was his problem?* She clenched her teeth together as his brooding face appeared before her eyes.

Jane entered the room through the open door, sat on the bed, and said in a singsong voice, "I know what you're thinking."

Elizabeth exhaled in an annoyed snort, then grinned. She was grateful that Jane understood her so well. "What did I ever do to him?" she asked with genuine curiosity mixed with the annoyance in her voice.

Jane shrugged. "Charles said he is just uncomfortable around strangers," she replied kindly as her hand absently played with her hair.

Elizabeth let go of her anger and switched tracks in her mind. She smiled at Jane. "You and Charles seem to be spending quite a bit of time together. Tell me about him."

Jane's forehead creased in thought. "You have been there every time we've met," she paused, and then grinned, "except the first time."

"And when you two picked up lunch for everyone on Wednesday, and the tour of the studio he gave you on Tuesday, and…"

"All right!" Jane conceded Elizabeth's point with a smile. "We have been talking, but it's not like we have been sharing any big secrets. He is just so nice and charming. I really like being around him."

"And he's cute," Elizabeth teased.

"Oh, he's gorgeous! What do you mean cute?" Jane objected playfully. "Lizzy, he is so beautiful," she moaned wistfully. "But so far, he has just been friendly around me, that's all."

Elizabeth did her best "worried mother" impression. "Oh-ho! You'll see. Just wait. He's waiting till he can get you alone on the tour. Then he's going to sully you and leave you desperate and ruined on the side of the road!"

Elizabeth and Jane laughed at the very idea. Then Elizabeth grew quiet and looked at her sister thoughtfully. "Be careful, Jane," Elizabeth said quietly. "You tend to see only the good in people. I don't want you getting hurt."

Jane hugged her sister tightly. "No one is going to get hurt! Nothing is going to happen between Charles and me, Lizzy. He is a famous rock star and who am I?" She released Elizabeth to look in her face. "Besides, we have each other, you, me, and Charlotte. We're going to look out for each other and have a wonderful time. Right?"

Elizabeth nodded. "Right. I'll see you in the morning."

"'Night, Lizzy," Jane said softly as she left the room.

Elizabeth crawled into her bed. She forced herself to stop worrying about last-minute things she might have forgotten to pack, resolving that whatever she had left behind, she would either get new on the road or have sent to her.

To distract her mind, she thought about her performance. In her mind, she went over the songs she had drilled over and over again for the last two weeks. But her thoughts betrayed her attempts to settle them, quickly giving way to the tall man who had been watching her today. Even his intensely good looks were not enough to soften her feelings about him. He rankled her, like an itch she couldn't reach to scratch, mostly because she couldn't figure him out. Elizabeth had always prided herself on her ability to read people, but Darcy simply confused her. He was nothing like his reputation for a wild man. In fact, she was certain she had never met a more uptight, arrogant man in her life. If there was going to be any trouble on the tour, it would be coming from him.

CHAPTER 4

I T WAS THE PLANE that did it. Getting up early, saying good-bye to her parents and sisters, even the limo ride to the airport all had a vague, hazy, surreal sensation. But when Elizabeth saw the large jet sitting alone on the tarmac bearing the name *De Bourgh* on its side, she knew it was real. She was really doing it. A desire, an ambition she had held for longer than she could remember was coming true. She smiled at everyone in the car and squeezed Jane's hand.

The black limo pulled up beside the plane and stopped. As Elizabeth exited the car and walked around to the trunk to get her bags, another limo pulled up beside her own.

Like a warrior, Darcy strode out of the car, his black sunglasses shielding his eyes from the early morning light, his long coat protecting him from the chill. Without acknowledging anyone, he walked purposefully to Rebecca, waiting at the bottom of the ramp.

"Good morning, Darcy," she said, her eyes making only the briefest contact before returning to their constant scanning.

"Are we ready to go?" he asked, his face turning to the others, who were moving toward the ramp.

"Almost."

Darcy turned his head and stared at Rebecca, his expression displeased.

"Charles and Caroline aren't here yet," Rebecca said by way of explanation.

In a flash Darcy snapped open his cell phone. He punched a button and held it to his ear. "Caro, where are you?" he demanded.

"Five minutes, Darcy," her voice replied apologetically.

"Caro!"

"Seriously, Darcy, we will be there in five minutes."

"You know, Caroline, generally it is the job of the tour manager to call the artist, not the other way around," he snarled.

"I'm sorry," she repeated, sighing.

He looked up. "Damn!" he swore softly but emphatically.

"What? What's wrong?"

Darcy's eyes swept over a third limo, just pulling up along his. "The bitch is here."

"Who? Which bitch?"

"The one who owns the plane," he growled, "and her stooge." As he watched, Anne de Bourgh exited the limo and walked toward Darcy and Rebecca. He snapped the phone shut and put it away.

"Darcy," Anne said coldly as she passed by him and climbed up the ramp. Darcy nodded once in acknowledgement.

"Mr. Darcy," ogled Bill Collins, his hand extended. "It is such a pleasure to really meet you at last."

Darcy ignored the bubbling fat man and addressed Rebecca. "Is everyone else here?"

She nodded. "As soon as the Bingleys arrive, we can go."

❧

Elizabeth watched the interaction as she gathered her bags. She wasn't really eavesdropping, because Darcy had made no attempt to hide what he was doing. She stumbled slightly as she climbed the steps of the ramp, unbalanced by her bag. She was relieved to feel a strong hand on her shoulder steadying her.

"Easy there. You okay?" Richard Fitzwilliam asked.

"Yeah, thanks," she smiled embarrassedly and made her way into the plane.

It was a large jet with a custom interior. Instead of the normally cramped seating, larger seats were installed. Halfway into the cabin were four tables with chairs around them, clearly designed for workspaces. The front of the plane contained more seats and another smaller work area just behind the cockpit.

Elizabeth was surprised at how crowded the plane was. The seats in the rear were filled almost entirely with people Elizabeth had never seen before, despite her time at the studio. She stopped to look for a seat when Richard again came to her aid.

"This is where the crew sits. Our seats are up in the front," he said kindly from behind her.

"Oh, thank you," Elizabeth said softly and moved forward.

There were empty seats in the front of the plane, just as Richard had said. Elizabeth sat down with Charlotte, Jane taking a seat in the row in front of them, and Alex across the aisle. As she settled in, Elizabeth watched Anne de Bourgh stride to the front of the plane and sit down. Darcy followed her a minute later, taking the other front seat across the aisle from her, stretching out his long legs. Collins ignored Long Borne Suffering and instead followed Ms. de Bourgh and took the seat directly behind her. Rachel took her seat behind Darcy. Elizabeth could see that clearly the battle lines were drawn.

Five minutes later, running feet were heard and Charles, Caroline, and Rebecca entered the plane. Darcy, his sunglasses removed, gave Caroline a black look as Rebecca moved to the cockpit and spoke to the pilots before sitting down beside Caro.

Charles, for his part, took the seat next to Jane, and attempted to begin a conversation as the plane taxied forward. "Good morning," he grinned. "I hope you weren't waiting too long. We can never seem to get out on time, you know?"

He waited a moment for a response, then receiving none, tried again. "How was your trip down?"

Silence was his only answer. He leaned forward to see Jane's face very pale and her eyes looking large and nervous. Her hands were tightly clenched together in her lap as she bit down hard on her lips.

"Jane?" Charles asked, concerned. "Jane? What's wrong?" He touched her arm lightly and felt her trembling. "Jane? Are you okay?"

When she felt his touch on her arm, Jane looked at him. Her beautiful blue eyes were anxious and desperate. "Jane," Charles asked worriedly, "are you afraid?"

Jane could only shut her eyes and nod nervously.

Charles's heart immediately went out to her. She was plainly terrified. He ran his hand along her arm and spoke softly to her. "It's okay, Jane. It's okay." She opened her eyes to look at him weakly. "Can I help?" he asked, his eyes full of concern.

His kindness broke through the thin barrier she had created to hold in her feelings and she started crying softly.

In a flash he lifted the armrest between them. He moved closer to her, taking her ice-cold hand and holding it firmly. "Jane, can you look at me?"

he said in a low, calm voice. When she turned slightly, he continued. "That's good. Now listen to me carefully, *we are going to be okay*. I won't let anything happen to you, Jane. I promise. The plane is perfectly safe."

He could see the panic rising in her eyes as she thought of a hundred things that could go wrong. "No, no, shhhh, Jane," he said soothingly as he rested his forehead against hers. "Jane, trust me."

"What if something happens?" she said in a tiny voice.

"Nothing is going to happen. Rebecca has been here for hours. She oversaw the inspection of the plane herself and triple-checked the pilots."

"Are you certain?" she asked in an even softer voice.

He pulled her close and pillowed her head on his shoulder, his arm slipping around her shoulders and his other hand holding her hand tightly in his. "I'm certain. It's going to be all right."

"Thank you," she murmured brokenly. "I know I'm not being sensible. I just suddenly got so afraid. I know it's foolish; it's just, I have no control over the plane, and it terrifies me for some reason."

"It's not foolish. I totally understand."

"You aren't afraid," she challenged him weakly.

"I used to be," he spoke softly in her ear. "I was so afraid of flying I couldn't travel." He grinned for a moment. "And for a California boy, that's no good. I knew I had to beat it, so I took flying lessons. Even got my pilot's license." He shrugged against her. "It helped me feel not so out of control."

"Really?" she asked as she pulled back enough to look at his face.

He grinned. "Really, that's why I told you to trust me. I won't let anything happen to you, Jane." He stared into her eyes for a long time, until the plane started moving again and Jane's face turned white with fear.

Charles pulled her close and held her tightly, his head beside hers. "We are just getting into position and waiting for the signal to take off. Once we are up and cruising, you won't be so scared." His voice was calm and reasonable. "Now I want you to talk to me. Tell me anything you want to about yourself, and I will listen, completely fascinated. I promise."

Jane closed her eyes and even chuckled once, which produced a relieved grin on Charles's face. "Have you always sung, Jane?" he asked, his voice soft and warm in her ear.

"Yes," she whispered into his ear, "always. Even when I was a little girl, my father would play piano and I would sing duets with him."

Charles nodded, rubbing her back and encouraging her to go on. "When did you start writing songs?"

"When I was in middle school." She told him in a low voice about how she would write songs to deal with her frustrations with her mother and her schoolmates. "What was that?" she asked suddenly as the plane started moving abruptly.

"We are going to take off now," Charles explained calmly. "Hold on tight, and, remember, I won't let anything happen."

Shutting her eyes, Jane wrapped her arms tightly around Charles as he held her close and he rubbed her back, making soft, reassuring noises in her ear. It was crazy, but somehow he did make her feel better. She believed him. Somehow he would keep her safe. Holding on to him with a death grip, she let herself focus on the sound of his voice and the scent of his skin as the ground dropped away and the plane climbed.

"Oh, Jane, you're doing fine," he whispered to her, his voice warm with admiration.

"Don't let go," she gasped raggedly.

Charles smiled to himself. "Never," he promised to both of them. When the plane leveled out, Charles could feel her relax slightly. Only then did he loosen his grip. "Are you okay?" he asked softly.

Jane nodded, her head still close to his. "I'm sorry. I've never had a panic attack like that before. It was just like, all of a sudden, I was so afraid and I didn't know what to do." She looked at him gratefully, uncertain if she should say anything more.

"I'll stay with you and be you for the landing too, if you need it," he said, his emotions flaring into a need to protect her.

"Thank you, Charles. You are very kind."

He smiled, tilting his head and touching her soft cheek. Without thinking about it, he leaned close and kissed her lightly on the forehead. As soon as his lips touched her, a circuit was made. He was suddenly fully aware that he was holding a beautiful woman in his arms. Slowly he pulled back, his eyes fixed on hers.

Jane flushed, her breathing shallow and her heart racing from something other than fear. She closed the short distance between them and kissed him.

Words left him as he kissed her gently. Jane filled his senses. She was all he had dreamed: sweet and giving, yet more; there was a spiciness and heat to her that he never had expected that stole his breath away. He pulled back with a look of wonder on his face and pulled her close to him again. She snuggled against his shoulder: safe, relaxed, and amazed.

❧

"Why is Charles kissing Jane?" Darcy asked as his eyes glared at the pair of blond heads that were joined at the lips.

Rachel looked at Caroline, who said, "I know it's been awhile, Darcy, but even you must remember something about boys and girls."

Darcy fixed her with a look that told her she was still in trouble for being late and said crisply, "Let's begin."

❧

Elizabeth watched as Darcy snapped at the two women before him. Rachel got up and sat with him at the small table and began going over notes and papers with him. "What do you think he is doing?" she asked Charlotte.

Charlotte had been drumming her fingers on the tray in front of her and looked up, distracted, when Elizabeth spoke. "Who? Darcy?" she shrugged, unimpressed. "Looks like paperwork to me."

"It's the morning routine," Richard volunteered from behind them. "See, every morning, Will has a meeting first thing with Rachel. She goes over everything happening with his business and any other personal stuff he has to deal with."

"The family business? Darcy Technologies?"

Richard nodded distractedly. Elizabeth suspected he was still half-asleep. "I thought he left that. Turned away from it all to be an artist and all that."

"Oh, he did." Richard frowned. "As much as Will is able to. He isn't the president of DT, but he still owns the company. Rachel has a counterpart who stays at DT, and they work together so that Will is always up to date on what the company is doing. But he doesn't interfere with how it's run, usually." He rolled his eyes.

"Hm," Elizabeth snorted. "Sounds like he's got some control issues."

"Issues?" Richard said sarcastically. "Liz, he's got a whole subscription."

Elizabeth laughed softly. "I noticed he doesn't seem to like Ms. de Bourgh too much."

"Will doesn't like anyone who tries to tell him what to do," he said as he looked over at the tiny woman in the severe black suit. "Anne doesn't make it any easier by challenging him every chance she gets."

"So she provokes him?"

"Oh yeah. That's our Annie," he nodded. "See, poor Anne is stuck under her mother. She is always trying to prove she is good enough, and the only job Anne has is Slurry. So consequently, she is always trying to prove she can manage Will." He shook his head. "It's what you might call *a bad situation*."

As Elizabeth watched, Rachel went back to her seat and Caroline moved forward to the table. "What's this?" she asked Richard, who was lying back across his seat and drumming on his chest.

He sat up to look over at what Elizabeth had indicated, then laid back down. "That is just Caro's morning meeting. She always goes after Rachel. Caro handles all the tour business with Will."

"Do you do any of the business work?" Elizabeth asked him archly.

"Nope, I leave all that to Will."

"How come?"

"Well one: because he actually cares, I don't, and two: because he's better at it than me."

Elizabeth looked at him skeptically.

"Believe it, Lizzy, I'm just along for the ride."

With a mental shrug, Elizabeth leaned back in her seat and opened her laptop. The trials and tribulations of Slurry were interesting in a morbid kind of way, but she had work to do.

❧

The afternoon passed in a blur. Starting with their arrival at the airport, then meeting the press for pictures of Long Borne Suffering, it ended with the trip to the arena, where they spent the afternoon doing sound checks, rehearsing, and waiting.

Elizabeth was amazed at the amount of work done around them. Technicians were everywhere, doing final checks on lights and sound and preparing their instruments. Caroline Bingley was moving at a constant pace, always speaking into her headset, making sure everything was perfect. LBS experienced their most exhaustive sound check ever, then were dressed, groomed, and wired for sound.

At seven, the girls participated in their first meet-and-greet with Slurry. About fifty people from the area, winners of tickets from the local radio stations, were brought backstage to meet the bands. Although Elizabeth was a little nervous about the experience, her natural charm got her through it. The fact of the matter was that while everyone was polite to LBS, they were really there to see Slurry.

Elizabeth expected Darcy to be rude and glare at everyone, but to her surprise he was completely unlike the arrogant, brooding grouch she had seen at the studio. This was the Darcy she remembered from the grocery store. He was completely approachable. He shook hands, signed autographs, and even posed for pictures. She was surprised by this change in his demeanor but suspected it was simply a role he performed as part of the job.

While their fans distracted them, Elizabeth had a chance to observe Slurry. Darcy was dressed in his concert attire: black leather pants and black sunglasses. His long torso, broad shoulders, and long arms were completely bare. From her close position, she could see clearly the tattoo on his chest. It was a lyre, strangely enough: an instrument that would be more at home in the hands of an ancient Greek than a rock god. It was finely done; Elizabeth could even see the individual strings on the skin just to the left of his heart. He had another tattoo of a black spiral over his right shoulder and going down his arm.

Richard was simply dressed in a pair of jeans and boots. With his broad chest and powerfully built arms, he didn't need a shirt. Elizabeth could not count all his tattoos in one sitting without being obvious. She started with his back, where a large Celtic knot was centered over his spine and spread out to his shoulder blades, the top just brushed by the tips of his long curls. For a full minute Elizabeth entertained herself by watching the tattoo move as Richard's muscles flexed. Just above the waistband of his jeans, at the base of his spine, was a small blue-black scarab. The Fitzwilliam family crest in all its glorious color adorned his right upper arm, and a blue sun sat on his right forearm.

Charles wore tight jeans and a royal blue T-shirt. The shirt matched the color of his eyes. His blond curls flowed over his collar and rested on his shoulders.

Once the meet-and-greet was over, the girls had thirty minutes before they were to begin the show. Elizabeth thought she would burst from the excitement and nervousness burning inside her, but she kept control of her passions. She was away from the others, tuning her Taylor one last time and mentally rehearsing her song, when she realized with a start that Darcy was standing in front of her.

"Can I give you a word of advice?" he said softly.

Elizabeth nodded, her neck stretched up to look at him.

"When you get out there, don't look at the crowd at first. It's too much. Get on your mark and as soon as the others are on theirs, *just start playing*. Don't look around, don't think, just play." He lifted a shoulder in a shrug. "Your music is programmed inside of you. Trust it. You know what to do; play, and it will be all right."

Elizabeth nodded, not quite sure what to say. She was disturbed by the intimacy of his voice and the intensity of his gaze. "Thank you. I'll try to remember that."

"Good luck," he said quietly and stepped away.

Charles called her over, "It's time, ladies." He smiled brightly. "You all look great! If you are ready, I'll walk you out."

Charlotte frowned. "But Alex always walks us out."

Alex's voice came over their earplugs. "Char, I'm right here." They looked up to see him wave from the control station. "I'm going to be watching you on the monitors with Caro." Caroline waved distractedly. "Let Charles walk you out tonight, okay?"

"But what about our kiss?" Elizabeth asked in a tone of amusement mixed with concern.

Alex smiled, came around the control desk, and quickly kissed the three women. Charles then led them through the dark maze of cables, curtains, and consoles until they reached the edge of the stage.

"Ready?" Charles grinned. "You will be great, don't worry, okay?" He kissed each girl, lingering over Jane slightly, when Alex's voice in their heads commanded them to take their positions on the stage.

The words "Long Borne Suffering" filled the hall, lights flooded the stage, and Elizabeth started her opening riff. Four bars later Charlotte and Jane joined in on their instruments and she started her song. She lost herself in the words and dance she had drilled for two weeks solid. It was only when her song was over and Jane was singing "Wanted" that Elizabeth allowed herself to look at the huge arena. It was full of thousands of faces, many of which were ignoring the band, but still more were smiling and nodding slightly with the beat. A sense of euphoria filled her as they ended the song and paused for applause.

Their set was over in a shorter time than they could have imagined, and they left the stage to warm applause. A roadie led them back to the green room, where Alex was waiting.

"Wonderful!" he exploded, kissing the girls and hugging them tight. "You were perfect!"

They laughed, each a little giddy and speechless from the experience. "Oh Alex!" Jane said, remembering something. "Where can we watch Slurry from? We want to see their show."

"Where are they anyway?" Charlotte asked.

"Right here," Charles answered. Elizabeth turned to see all three men standing together. "We just wanted to tell you how great you were."

"You girls rocked," Richard grinned.

"Did you want to watch the show?" Darcy asked.

"If you don't mind," Jane answered. "We've never seen you perform," she smiled happily.

The men shared a look, and Richard said slowly, "We prepared for this." He grinned and pulled out what looked like a credit card. "Private skybox, number twelve," he said, passing over the card.

"Or you could watch from the side of the stage," Charles offered, teasing. "But we thought a box would be more comfortable."

"And then the speakers are facing the right way," Richard added, joking.

"Thank you," Jane said, astonished, speaking for them all. "This is so thoughtful."

"You're welcome," Darcy said softly, his eyes again masked by his shades.

"Thanks for coming on tour with us," Charles added. "You might want to go up now. See you after the show." The men moved off with Caroline for their final check.

Rebecca hurried up with a man beside her. The man was of average height, but with a powerful build. He wore a black T-shirt that had "Security" printed across the chest in red block letters. "Girls, this is Tommy. When you are ready, he will take you up to your box."

Elizabeth nodded and with the help of a couple of sound techs, their microphones, receivers, and the accompanying wires were removed from their bodies. As soon as she was free, Elizabeth hurried to where the instruments were being kept and found her beloveds waiting to be cleaned.

Darcy was there, with Ronnie, the guitar tech, doing a final check on his Paul Reid Smith. He looked at her, surprised. "We're about to start, you're going to miss the show."

Elizabeth shook her head. "Guitars first, show later," she replied lightly. Carefully she put the Guild in its case and moved on to the Taylor.

"You know, Ronnie can do that," Darcy sounded amused.

"I know," Elizabeth said coolly, taking offense at his tone. "But these are my babies. I missed not having them last night and I need to take care of them."

Understanding crossed his features and he crouched down beside her. "You can keep your guitars with you, if it would make you feel better."

Elizabeth looked up into his face, feeling quite small and insignificant next to him. "Thank you," she said softly.

Darcy nodded once and rose while Elizabeth put the acoustic guitar in its case. She didn't see Darcy move off to go onstage as she thanked Ronnie and ran for her friends. Joining them, Tommy quickly led the three women and Alex to the elevator, which took them to a private, lush hallway. After a short walk, skybox number twelve appeared before them and Tommy directed them to stay there until the show was over, when he would come and walk them backstage.

Smiling, they entered the small room to find two surprises. The first was a small spread of food on a table along the back wall. The second was Bill Collins, standing in front of the glass wall, stuffing his face.

He turned with a start and smiled beneficently, "Oh, there you are! Just in time!" he said loftily as he licked his fingers then held out his hand to the girls. "I can't tell you how proud of you I am. You girls put on a lovely little show. Even Ms. de Bourgh was impressed."

Elizabeth was horrified, but by quickly getting a drink from the mini-bar she was able to avoid touching Collins. A silent yet urgent conversation, conducted only with looks, got Alex to sit between Collins and the girls. They just settled down into their seats when the intro tape ran out and the arena grew silent.

Darcy's flawless guitar flooded the room. Elizabeth's jaw dropped as first Richard's drums and then Charles's bass exploded with a crash of lights and pyrotechnics. The crowd roared as the lights came up and the show started. Elizabeth sang softly along with Charles, smiling at Jane and Charlotte, who were singing as well. They all knew the words so well:

words about searching in the dark, trying to find answers, trying to know what one's life path is.

As Elizabeth watched, her hair swinging unconsciously back and forth to the beat, she considered that Darcy probably wrote those words as well. They seemed so doubtful and questioning, from a man who seemed so secure and in control. The enigma of it challenged her mind and she watched him, trying to reconcile all she knew about this puzzling man. Try as she might, she could come to no conclusion about Darcy. She resolved to find out more about him and allowed herself to enjoy the show.

Slurry was tight and masterful in their playing, but there was more to it. They did more than simply play music; they knew how to communicate with the crowd, to move it and control it. It was amazing. Elizabeth was impressed not only with the music but with the whole experience. She watched the thousands of people below her, laughing, singing, and dancing. It was only when the band broke for intermission that she realized that she had not been still once during the entire set.

"*Wow!*" Charlotte said as Elizabeth and Jane smiled and nodded in agreement. "Oh my God!" She laughed, giddy. "That was so intense!"

"They're extraordinary," Elizabeth observed, grinning in spite of herself.

"Hey, don't sell yourself short!" Alex objected. "You girls rock too, you know."

"Alex, thanks, but we are nothing like that," Jane gently disagreed.

"I wouldn't be so sure about that," their manager objected. "Seriously, I really think you have as much talent as them." He nodded toward the stage. "You just need a chance."

Elizabeth smiled gratefully. "Well, this is certainly going to be our big chance." She looked at the crowd. "And I'm going to do everything I can to succeed."

"I'm so pleased to hear that, Lizzy," Collins said silkily. "That's the kind of attitude that is going to get you places. Stay focused on your goal."

Elizabeth nodded, but she didn't like the way he was looking at her. As quickly as she could, she turned back to the stage, to watch the band begin the second half.

The crowd was deafening as they screamed at Slurry's return. Charles smiled broadly and waited a moment for the crowd to quiet down, and then he spoke easily over them. "Oh man!" He laughed. "You're all so great!" The crowd cheered back for him. "So, let me ask you something."

He paused and the crowd roiled in anticipation. "What did you think of our new act?" Screams filled the air.

Elizabeth turned to Jane and Charlotte her mouth hanging open. "Yeah, we like them too," Charles grinned conspiratorially. "Give it up for the ladies of Long Borne Suffering, Charlotte, Liz, and Jane!"

Elizabeth cynically suspected that Charles could have told them to "give it up" for the T-shirt venders out front and the crown would have gone nuts, but that didn't stop her from grabbing her band mates in a huge hug as they squealed and jumped up and down excitedly.

"But I know you came to see us," Charles continued once the crowd quieted, "so let's get back to work." He winked and the band started the riffs for "Bound."

As Charles sang about domination, Elizabeth found herself again watching Darcy. He seemed entirely focused on his playing, his expressive eyes hidden behind those dark glasses, but Elizabeth could see he was subtly communicating with his band, and even more fleetingly, with the audience: a nod, a glance, even a rare grin. The crowd ate it up; the tiny flashes of attention he showed them only made them long for more.

She had to admit he was startlingly handsome. His skin had a soft sheen of sweat over it at this point. His arms were pumped up, his muscles bulging. He radiated sex, danger, and talent, a combination Elizabeth found very arousing.

The concert finally ended after 10:00 p.m. As they waited for Tommy, Jane caught her eyes and grinned knowingly.

"Okay, you are right; he's gorgeous," Elizabeth said sotto voce, recalling their conversation from the night before.

Jane nodded happily. "I'm in love," she sighed half-mockingly.

Sooner than she expected, LBS and Slurry were loaded into limos and whisked away to their hotel. Rebecca brought them straight through the lobby to the waiting elevators. Once inside, she passed out keycards to each of them. The girls would be sharing a three-bedroom suite, while the men each had their own room. Charles was, as usual, standing next to Jane, and Elizabeth saw him whisper something into Jane's ear, which caused her smile to drop. After a moment, Jane responded with a tiny nod.

Charlotte was oblivious, drumming on the side of the car, Darcy was silent and withdrawn behind his glasses, and Richard was talking softly to a pretty young woman with long dark hair.

Charlotte, Jane, and Elizabeth were delighted to find that their luggage had been brought up and arranged in their bedrooms. The suite was large, light, and luxurious. Elizabeth doubted that every band lived this high when they were on tour, but she also suspected that LBS was being handled with kid gloves. It was a strange situation, but she was willing to take advantage of it.

A knock on her bedroom door preceded Jane's entrance. "Can I talk to you, Lizzy?" she asked worriedly.

"What's wrong, Jane?" Elizabeth's eyes reflected the concern she felt.

"It's Charles," she said softly. "He asked me to come to his suite," Jane explained bluntly. "I said I would, but now I'm not so sure." Her eyes were troubled. "I mean, he is so nice and a good kisser and everything, but I worry. We are going to be working together for a long time, and I don't want any bad feelings between us."

Elizabeth motioned for Jane to sit on the bed beside her while, unbidden, Darcy's warning came back to both of them.

"Lizzy, do you think he thinks I'm throwing myself at him?" Jane asked worriedly.

Elizabeth frowned. "I don't know, Jane. I know you are not, but he doesn't know you," she shrugged. "How do you feel about him, really?"

Jane looked at the floor and whispered, "I'm crazy about him." Once she got that out, it seemed easier for her to speak. "I know it sounds like a stupid fangirl crush, but I've been thinking about him nonstop since we met. It really feels like there is something between us, and then this morning," she sighed and laid back on the bed, drawing up her knees. "If we weren't working together, Lizzy, I'd be all over him."

Elizabeth sighed and lay down on her side next to her. "No, you wouldn't, because you wouldn't know him."

Jane nodded. "You're right. Oh Lizzy, I wish I hadn't kissed him! What must he think of me?"

"What are you going to do?" Elizabeth asked.

"I don't know!" Jane fretted. "If I go to his room, I'll look easy, and I don't know what will happen, but if I don't go, he might think I'm playing with him or he might be angry. I just don't know." She looked at her sister. "What do you think I should do?"

Elizabeth was interrupted by a knock on the door. Thinking it was only Charlotte, she sat up and called out, "Come in."

The door opened and Charles walked inside. "Hi," he said awkwardly. "Charlotte told me you were in here." He eyed the two sisters on the bed with embarrassment. "Am I interrupting something?"

Jane closed her mouth, sat up, and smiled nervously. "No, we were just having a talk."

"Oh." Charles eyes widened. "Girl talk, right, sorry; I'll leave."

"No," Jane exclaimed. "I mean, please don't leave. I just wasn't expecting you." She got up and moved closer to him.

"Uh," he said uneasily. "I thought about what I said before, and I realized I might've given you the wrong impression, asking you to come to my room like that." He looked away a moment. "I was wondering if instead we could hang out here, with your friends."

Jane's lips pressed tightly together as she realized what he was saying. Then she smiled and nodded. "I'd like that very much." She took a step closer to him. "Would you like to sit in the living room?" she asked politely, suddenly at ease again.

"Sure," he smiled back.

"Charles," Elizabeth called out before they left. "Do you know if the pool is still open?"

"I know it is," he said, looking back. "Are you going for a swim?"

"Yeah, it helps me to unwind."

Charles nodded and closed the door behind him as he left. Elizabeth quickly changed into her suit and threw a pair of running pants over it and her shoes.

When she exited the suite Charles and Jane were curled up on either ends of the couch, talking and laughing softly while Charlotte was watching TV. She passed through with a friendly wave and went to the elevator. Riding it down alone, she took a moment to reflect on the ground she had covered in one day. Austin was such a long way from Meryton, where she had slept the night before.

Even further was the distance she had traveled in her career. Years of practicing, dreaming, and rehearsing had paid off. All those rejections she had suffered through were finally answered. She had done it. She had successfully performed in front of a larger crowd than she had ever done before. A milestone had been reached, a challenge completed. It was with a small smile of self-satisfaction on her face that she entered the pool.

The area around it was empty, but she could hear someone in the pool itself. Looking closely, she saw a lone swimmer doing laps. With a single glance she knew who it was, the black spiral on his shoulder a dead giveaway.

Fitzwilliam Darcy was in the pool. For a heartbeat, she considered turning around, but then she thought, *to hell with it*, draped her towel over a chair, and took off her pants and shoes. She watched Darcy as she approached the side. His long, lithe body stretched out on the surface of the water, his long powerful arms were pulling him forward, and his feet were kicking a foamy trail behind him.

He must have been spotting for his turn when he looked up and saw her. Their eyes met and he stopped, his chest surging out of the water as he stood. "Do you mind?" Elizabeth asked, not sure of what else to say. He just shook his head in response, his eyes watching her. Elizabeth dived off the side and started her lap, ignoring the way he was studying her body. She knew her figure wasn't perfect. She would never be gorgeous like Jane, but Elizabeth was strong and in shape. She didn't feel ashamed, despite the critique she saw in his eyes.

❧

Darcy's eyes were still burning from the sight that had greeted him when he looked for the wall. She wore a plain racing suit, he noticed. Irrationally it pleased him that she chose something designed for speed, not attractiveness. Nevertheless, the suit fit her body in a way that left little doubt what was underneath it. It was a revelation he enjoyed.

The suit and her shape suggested to him what her dive confirmed: Elizabeth Bennet was a swimmer. Like him, she had the signs of someone who had trained and swum competitively. He suspected that it had been in school, because while she was good, she wasn't particularly fast.

Suddenly, he realized he had been staring at her for an unforgivably long time and began a new lap.

❧

Elizabeth finished her twentieth lap. Her arms and lungs were burning. As she looked up for the wall, she saw Darcy still there, waiting for her on the side. *Why wouldn't he leave?* she snapped in annoyance to herself.

She realized that he was not going to leave without her and that the embarrassing encounter she was hoping to avoid was inevitable. Giving up her attempt to outwait him, she came out of the pool, forcing herself not to reveal how tired she was.

He handed her a towel, which she accepted with a polite smile. "Did you race in college?" he asked quietly.

Elizabeth stared at him a long moment, stunned by his perception, then answered, "No, just in high school. But I worked as a lifeguard and taught during college." She dried herself off as she walked away. Deciding that a little payback was in order, she asked, "What about you?"

"High school and university," he answered. "But I was never really serious. It was mostly a way to work out."

Elizabeth nodded in understanding. She sat down on her chair and started pulling on her pants. "So you swim every night?"

Darcy shook his head. "No, most nights I'm on the bus. But I swim when I can." Elizabeth saw that he already had a T-shirt and shoes on. He was wearing plain swim trunks at least; she hated men wearing Speedos outside of competition. "If you want to swim with me, it would be nice to have the company," he said quietly.

"Thanks," Elizabeth said noncommittally.

"What did you think of the show?" Darcy asked as they exited the pool area.

Elizabeth repressed her initial reaction. "It was very impressive. You're excellent performers. I really enjoyed it."

"And the box?"

"Oh yes!" She remembered his kindness with a flash of embarrassment for her coolness toward him. "Thank you, and thanks for the refreshments. That was great."

He acknowledged her thanks with a nod as they waited for the elevator. "You were good too. I watched you on the monitors." He looked at her, his eyes observing her closely.

"Thanks," Elizabeth said sincerely. She didn't understand his look, but she was determined not to let him fluster her again. "This is a big step forward for us. It's a challenge. Considering Slurry's track record, there's no guarantee we'll make it through the tour."

"I believe you will," he said sincerely. "I think our bands work well together."

"That's good to know," she said cheekily, not quite able to look at him. "You signed a pretty big contract to have us here."

He looked at her meaningfully. "Contracts are just about money, Elizabeth. I can assure you, if you weren't good enough, you would not be on my tour."

Elizabeth's jaw dropped as the doors to the elevator opened. She could not believe he had just said that. With an ice-cold "good night" she moved off to her suite, rigid with anger.

When she got through the door, she found Jane sitting alone on the couch, staring at nothing and smiling to herself. Elizabeth stood stock-still, clenching her fists, and counted to ten.

"What did he do this time?" Jane asked easily.

Elizabeth took a deep breath and released it noisily. Then she looked at her sister. "How did you know?"

"Charles told me," she answered with a smile. "He said that Darcy has the hotel open the pool for him after concerts. That's how he knew it would be open when you went downstairs." She grinned. "So, what did he say this time?"

"Oh, forget about that, Jane," she said with an aggravated snort. She sat down on the couch beside Jane. "Tell me about Charles."

Jane glowed with a smile that lit up the room, "He was wonderful. We sat and talked and laughed. He's very smart. Did you know that?" Elizabeth grinned and shook her head. "And he is so nice. He is the nicest person I've ever met." Jane sighed and leaned back against the couch. "Did you see how he came to me, Lizzy?" Her voice was soft with a happy disbelief.

"I saw," Elizabeth assured her, "and I have to say, I was impressed."

"And he never tried to kiss me, not even once."

Elizabeth frowned, "Jane? Are you sure he's not gay?"

Jane shook her head with a wicked grin. "*I* kissed *him* good night, and yes, I am quite sure he is not gay."

The sisters laughed together, then Jane took Elizabeth's hand and insisted that she tell her what had happened with Darcy. Elizabeth related the whole story, including his remark in the elevator.

"Maybe he was trying to compliment you, Lizzy. Maybe he is just awkward with words."

"Or maybe he was threatening me and letting me know if we don't play up to snuff, we will be out on our asses!" Elizabeth snapped. She stopped and sighed. "Oh, I'm sorry. I'm not mad at you. It's just that man!" she hissed. Elizabeth got up and paced the room angrily. "First he was staring at me at the pool."

"Oh, and I'm sure you didn't look at him," Jane challenged her gently.

"Yes, but—" She stopped and frowned thoughtfully. "It's different when he looks at me. I always feel like I'm not good enough or something." She remembered she was angry and resumed her pacing. "And then he has to go and be so insulting like that in the elevator. *Ohhhhhhhh,* he makes me insane!"

"Do you think you might be overreacting, Lizzy?" Jane frowned. It was unlike her sister to get this upset over anything.

"Oh, if you could have heard him, Jane, you would know I'm not. He was so snide about it, so superior." She kicked a sofa pillow. "Arrogant prick!"

Jane smiled kindly. "Come on, Lizzy, we need to go to bed." She rose and gestured for Elizabeth to follow her.

Elizabeth agreed. She was tired and her body was aching. She took a hot shower, letting the water carry away the rage and the chlorine from her body, and tucked herself into the strange hotel bed. Within minutes, the arrogant Fitzwilliam Darcy was forgotten, and she was asleep.

CHAPTER 5

"Lizzy!" Elizabeth Bennet felt herself being shaken. "Lizzy, wake up!"

Elizabeth opened one eye to see Alex sitting on her bed, smiling at her. "Go away," she grumbled and attempted to roll over.

"Oh no, Lizzy. You gotta get up. You have breakfast in a half hour. Now up!" He pulled the blankets off her with a flourish.

"Fuck!" she swore. "Jesus, Alex, can't a girl have some privacy?"

"Oh, like it's anything I haven't seen before?" he questioned her mockingly. "I'm serious, Lizzy, you need to get up now."

Elizabeth sat up, rubbing her face, and gingerly opened both eyes. She was cold now, wearing only a T-shirt and boxers. "I hate you," she growled.

"Then it's probably a good thing we broke up. Let's go, Liz!" he replied cheerfully as he headed for the door.

"Gah," Elizabeth moaned, expressing her view of the world at the moment. Elizabeth Bennet was not a morning person.

Thirty-five minutes later found Elizabeth, Jane, and Charlotte entering a private dining room filled with large round tables and a buffet to one side. Elizabeth made a beeline for the coffee and found herself next to Caroline, who was refilling her cup.

"Good morning, Lizzy," she said brightly.

Elizabeth covered a yawn and nodded, reaching for a cup. "Good morning, Caroline."

Caroline smiled. "You can call me Caro. Everyone else does." Elizabeth nodded her thanks. Caroline waited for Elizabeth to get her coffee and then walked with her toward the table. "Did you girls have a good time last night?"

Elizabeth wasn't sure what Caroline meant. At her confused look, Caroline added, "At the show?"

Elizabeth took a big sip of coffee. "Oh yes! Thank you. We had a great time." Her enthusiasm died when she realized that she had followed Caroline to a table where Darcy was already seated.

Their eyes met for a moment; Elizabeth's were uncertain, Darcy's patient, then Alex came up beside her, distracting Elizabeth. "Push over one, Lizzy. I need to talk to Caro," he said, planting a quick kiss on her cheek. Elizabeth shifted over a seat, finding herself between Jane on one side and Alex on the other.

Elizabeth focused on her coffee before she could face the question of food. She struggled to pull herself together, letting the caffeine banish the fuzziness from her brain and increase her awareness. As she sipped, she let her eyes wander the room, taking attendance. Almost everyone from the tour was there.

"Where are Mr. Collins and Ms. de Bourgh?" Elizabeth asked Alex, as she realized they were missing.

"Gone," Alex answered easily.

"The studio people don't have a whole lot to do with the tour, Lizzy," Caroline explained. "They only come down to observe or if there's a problem."

Elizabeth nodded at the explanation and went back to her coffee. She noticed Richard, standing in the doorway kissing the girl from the elevator last night. As she watched, he handed the girl something and she left with a walk that would have done Jane Russell proud. "Who was that?" she asked quietly.

Caroline looked up from her notes and answered briefly, "That's the flavor."

"Flavor?"

"Flavor of the Day," Caroline said with a meaningful look.

"Her name is Lissa," said Richard in a voice that was loud enough to carry to Elizabeth but not be overheard by the other tables. "And since she is coming to the show tonight, she has moved out of the 'groupie' category into 'short-term relationship,' thank you."

Elizabeth was taken aback. Not by the fact that Richard had one-night stands with his fans, she was too experienced in the business for that to faze her, but by the matter-of-fact way he talked about it. "Oh," she said dumbly.

"Don't let him get to you, Lizzy; that's just the way Richard is," Charles said with a reassuring smile. "He has no shame."

"And why should I?" Richard asked as he returned with a plate of food and coffee. "If a lady and I wish to have a meaningless physical relationship, and we are both consenting adults, what is the problem with that?"

Darcy seemed to be deliberately ignoring the conversation and focusing on his food, periodically casting surreptitious glances at Elizabeth.

Charles just laughed and shook his head. Elizabeth felt like she was watching a discussion that had been repeated numerous times before. She left the table to get a plate of food. As she returned, Caroline rose and moved to the front of the room.

"Since everyone is finally here," she flashed a look at Richard, "let's begin. Last night was good. I was very impressed with LBS." She looked at the girls. "Nice work, ladies, welcome to the tour." There was a brief smattering of applause. "Today is an easy day. I want everyone to relax and try to catch up on sleep; the rest of the week is going to be tough. Tonight and tomorrow we are at the arena. Everything is packed up Sunday night, and we go to Houston. The crew will be leaving with the stage, but the artists get to spend one last night in this fine hotel." There was a wave of laughter at her sarcastic comment. "Enjoy it; we will be on the buses for the rest of the week. Monday night is Houston, Tuesday night is Shreveport, and so on from there. Any questions or problems?" She looked around the room. "Okay, have a good day, and we'll be meeting again for breakfast tomorrow, as usual," she concluded and returned to her seat.

Caroline took a sip of coffee, turned to Lizzy and Jane, and said in a quiet voice, "I'm serious what I said, girls, about taking it easy today. Starting Monday we are going to be sleeping on the buses and performing for eight days straight. I want you to do whatever you have to do to get your heads on straight today, because it's going to be rough."

"Thanks, Caro, we will," Jane answered, touched by her concern.

"Would you like to see the city today, Jane?" Charles asked warmly. "Just you and me?"

Jane smiled delightedly at his suggestion.

Elizabeth had been idly looking in Darcy's direction, and she noticed his brows come together at Charles's offer. She knew Darcy didn't like Charles spending time with Jane; after all, Jane was clearly just using him to get what she could from him. The taste in her mouth turned bitter, and she took a gulp of coffee to wash it away.

The next two days quickly passed into routine for Elizabeth: breakfast meetings, quiet afternoons, shows at night, followed by late-night swims, and bed. She ignored Darcy as much as possible, being formal and polite to him when she could not.

Monday morning found her getting up even earlier than usual (not a pretty sight) and dragging herself down to breakfast and the buses.

A trio of buses waited for them. The first was the domain of Slurry, the second was for Darcy's top staff, and the third would be the on-the-road home of Long Borne Suffering. Richard casually informed her that three more buses carrying the crew had left the night before, with all the sets and equipment on trucks.

Elizabeth couldn't repress her smile as she climbed up into the bus, her guitars in each hand. The bus was like a huge, elegantly appointed motor home: two sets of bunks on the right side, a dinette and kitchen area on the left, and couches in the back. Spontaneous laughter bubbled up out of the three women over the novelty of the experience.

"I'm glad you like it," Alex observed as he climbed up the steps, "because you are going to be here for a while."

"It's great, Alex," Elizabeth grinned as Charlotte loudly announced the discovery of a deluxe entertainment center in the back.

⸙

Tour life settled into a routine as well. The novelty of the bus wore off quickly, but the girls' spirits were kept up by their nightly performances.

Each morning the tour had breakfast together, at a restaurant either on the road or in the city where they would perform that night. After breakfast, the two bands would often mingle. Charles was a frequent visitor to the LBS bus, and he and Jane would talk and entertain each other for hours. Charlotte and Elizabeth would sometimes visit the Slurry bus, usually to hang with Richard, or he would visit them. An easy camaraderie developed between the groups as they learned more about each other. They learned that Elizabeth was a complete bitch in the morning until she had her coffee; that Jane was as sweet as she appeared; that Charlotte was the least romantic woman on the planet; that Richard was easygoing and had a self-effacing joke about everything; and that Charles would do anything for a friend. Only Darcy remained apart.

When she wasn't talking to her friends or rehearsing, Elizabeth spent her time balanced between writing songs, playing her guitar, and working on her computer. She noticed that the amount of hits to the LBS website had increased greatly during their first week on tour, and she was answering more fan email than ever before.

Tuesday was the first night they were not performing, and the girls relished not only the time off but also the idea of sleeping in a bed that was not traveling down the highway. As they settled into the luxurious suite, Caroline invited the girls to go out that night with her, Charles, and Richard. They agreed happily.

"Why isn't Darcy coming?" Elizabeth wondered out loud after Caroline left.

"He probably doesn't want to get snarled at by you," Charlotte said bluntly as she carried her bag to her room.

"I do not snarl," Elizabeth objected.

"Oh no. *Never*," Charlotte called out sarcastically. "Just like you never stare at him either."

"Lizzy," Jane said gently to Elizabeth's surprised and questioning look, "I know you don't snarl, but the fact of the matter is that someone who doesn't know you as well as we do might think you are being a little short with Will."

"I have been perfectly polite."

"Yes, you have, but we all know that you are only 'polite' with people you dislike." Jane turned to her bed and opened her suitcase. "It's possible that Will has noticed this, too."

"Since when have you called him *Will*?" Elizabeth asked, amazed.

"Lizzy," Charlotte began as she reemerged from her bedroom, "I don't know what you have against him, but maybe you should try being a little nicer to him."

"You don't know?" Lizzy repeated incredibly, her exasperation rising. "Charlotte, I told you what he said to me; you heard what he called us when he met us!"

Charlotte rolled her eyes.

"And have you seen the way he looks at Jane and Charles? It's clear that he hates the fact that they are getting close."

Jane looked away, embarrassed.

"Are you telling me you know what he's thinking, Lizzy?" Charlotte asked quietly.

Elizabeth stopped short, her mouth hanging open.

"Look," Charlotte continued, "I'll be the first to admit, he's not Mr. Congeniality, but you are not even giving the man a chance, and that's not like you."

Elizabeth looked puzzled at her friend, then to her sister. "Jane? Have I been rude to Darcy?" she asked in a doubtful voice.

"No," Jane assured her, "you are never rude. But you haven't made him feel accepted either, and I think it's possible that this is why he isn't joining us tonight."

Elizabeth stood still for a moment, thinking. Had *she* been the one being standoffish? She had always blamed it on Darcy, but perhaps she hadn't given him a chance. She remembered the night of the first show, when he gave her advice about performing. Their interaction had been odd, but still it was good advice, and she hadn't thanked him for it. She realized if Charles or Richard had done the same, she would have made a point of thanking either one of them afterward.

As soon as she realized her friends were correct, she was resolved to try to amend her behavior. She didn't like it, but she was determined to try to mend fences with Darcy. Setting her jaw, she walked out of her suite and knocked on the door to Darcy's rooms. It was only afterward, when it was too late, that she questioned her impulsive behavior. What if they were wrong and Darcy was staying in for other reasons? She wondered if perhaps he wasn't alone in his room, when the door opened.

His eyes flared for just a moment in surprise when he saw her. Elizabeth screwed up her nerve and pushed forward. "Hi," she smiled. "Do you have a moment? I'd like to talk to you."

Without a word, Darcy opened the door wide and stood aside. Darcy's rooms were similar to her own. The living room was empty, except for his guitar resting on the couch. Elizabeth walked to the sitting area and asked uncomfortably, "Were you doing something?"

Darcy shook his head as he sat down on the couch, drawing the guitar back into his lap. "I was just playing," he answered softly, looking down at his instrument and then fixing her eyes with his gaze. He indicated the love seat next to the couch where he sat and once she was seated, asked, "What's on your mind?"

Elizabeth stared at his fingers, which were instinctively curling around the neck of the guitar. "I, um," she stopped and looked down. Then started again. "I'm sorry; this is a little difficult for me. I realized today that I have been pretty rude to you, and I apologize. You have been trying to be friendly and I've been blowing you off and that's not like me, really." She shrugged uncomfortably. "So, I came to say I'm sorry."

She paused. Darcy waited, silently. Then she continued, "I heard you aren't coming out with us tonight, and I hope that isn't because of me." She realized how egotistical it sounded and wondered again about making a fool of herself. "I would like for you to come. Charles said something about an eighties karaoke party, and anyway, I'd like to try to get to know you better." Realizing she was babbling, she finished as gracefully as she could.

Darcy stared at her long enough to make her nervous. She was convincing herself that she was not only a fool but about to get thrown off the tour when he finally spoke. "Thank you for coming here," he started. His eyes broke away, as he looked down for a beat, before traveling back to hers. "I had wondered if I had offended you," he spoke slowly, and Elizabeth realized with a flash of insight that he was embarrassed. "I didn't mean to, and I'm sorry if I did." He watched her again, waiting for her reaction.

Elizabeth had nothing to say to that, so she smiled uncomfortably and waited. "I'm not coming out tonight because, truthfully, I hate clubs. Too many people and too much noise." He shrugged and flashed a quick smile. "I'm something of a homebody, I'm afraid."

Elizabeth was speechless. This was the last thing she had expected from the imposing Fitzwilliam Darcy. She questioned how much she did know about this man she had been working with for two weeks. She realized he was staring at her, expecting a response, and quickly said the first thing that came to her mind. "Oh, well, I'm glad it's not me," she smiled nervously. "But I do hope we can be friends, Darcy." She said his name uneasily.

"My friends call me Will," he said, his deep voice warmer than she had ever heard it.

Elizabeth smiled genuinely and held out her hand. "And mine call me Lizzy."

As Darcy shook her hand, she noticed his palm was warm, his touch firm, and she could feel the roughness of his calluses scraping against her own. A flash of something like desire bolted through her as she had a sudden vision of that rough skin against her most tender parts. Looking quickly away, she rose and moved toward the door. Darcy followed her silently.

"So I'll see you tomorrow then, Will?" she asked pleasantly as she opened the door. Darcy nodded and took the door as she passed through it. "Bye," she waved.

Darcy watched as she blithely returned to her suite and then slowly shut the door.

❧

Four nights later found them in Pensacola, Florida, for a one-night show. This was one of the smallest houses they had yet played, a large civic center rather than a stadium or arena. Jane commented on how she was looking forward to performing in a more intimate setting. Elizabeth really couldn't see how eight thousand was more intimate than twenty, but she wasn't going to argue.

Before they went out, Alex informed the girls that their video would debut on MTV on Tuesday. Excited by the news, they took the stage, ready to play their hearts out.

The set progressed flawlessly until they reached Jane's second song, "Good-bye." Elizabeth was focused on her playing when suddenly she knew *something* was wrong. Jane abruptly stopped singing and fell to the floor. Elizabeth froze in shock until she saw the blood pouring out of Jane's forehead and pooling on the stage.

Then her guitar was on the ground and she was pulling Jane onto her lap, saying her name over and over again. Jane was unconscious, her face very white against the bright red blood running into her hair. Elizabeth looked up, feeling very small and alone, wondering what to do, when suddenly Charles appeared.

❧

Darcy was standing where he always stood during her performance, watching her at the bank of monitors. He didn't know why. At first, it had been just to make sure she was good enough, then to make sure she was okay. But she had long since proven herself. Darcy knew her act by heart, still, every night he was there, watching her and listening to her songs. It was like he was bewitched.

Charles stood beside him, as always. At least Charles had no doubts, Darcy reflected in annoyance. Charles was absolutely clear why he was there. He wore his Jane smile, and Darcy wondered who was trying to fool whom. It was clear that Charles was completely hooked on Jane. It had only been dumb luck and separate tour buses that kept them apart. He didn't object to his friend's romance with Jane in principle. Jane seemed like a nice person. The circumstances were the problem. With only two weeks into the tour and another seven months to go, all their lives could become a total hell if their relationship went south. It wasn't that Darcy was against his friend's happiness, he told himself for the hundredth time; it was just that this was a national tour. It was more important than an infatuation.

His thoughts were broken by a shout. Darcy turned and watched Charles run from him, his face stricken. He turned back to the monitors and his breath caught at what he saw. Elizabeth was kneeling on the ground, Jane unconscious before her. "Rebecca!" he yelled, turning toward the stage.

She was there, firing orders into her headset, blocking Darcy's path to the stage with her body. "Wait, Darcy! I think it was a bottle, but I don't know yet. Don't go out there!"

A moment later, Charles came back, carrying Jane, her arms swaying like a rag doll; Elizabeth, clothes bloodied, and Charlotte followed, both looking very frightened.

"Did you see what happened?" Rebecca barked.

Elizabeth shook her head. "No, I was playing and she just went down and there was blood." She craned her head to see what was happening to Jane. Alex led a team of EMTs out of nowhere and they took Jane from Charles.

The roar of the crowd and Caroline's voice coming over the loudspeakers suddenly brought Darcy back to himself. "Rebecca, I need to know what it was, now!"

Rebecca nodded, her attention divided between Darcy and her headset. "It was a bottle. We found it, and my people have the assailant."

Darcy nodded, satisfied. "The police?"

"They're coming."

Darcy pushed between Charles and Elizabeth to look at Jane. "Is she going to be okay?" he asked the technicians working over her. Jane had regained consciousness and was crying softly. Darcy could now see the deep gash on her forehead that traveled up to her hairline.

"Yes, it looks like a concussion. We'll transport her, but I think she'll be all right."

Darcy sighed. "Good." He turned to his friend. "Charles, go get cleaned up. Caroline!"

"Right here, Darcy."

"Get the stage cleaned up and our set out there ASAP!"

Caroline nodded and started speaking into her microphone. Charles stared at him stunned. "We're going on?" he asked, astounded.

"We're going on," Darcy said firmly. "Go get ready." Charles remained where he was, frozen. "Do it!" Darcy snapped. "She'll be okay!"

Charles moved woodenly toward his dressing room while Richard came running up to the huddle of people Darcy was circling around like a shark. "What's going on?"

"We are, as soon as possible. Get yourself ready."

Elizabeth watched Darcy from the floor, where she knelt beside Jane, her eyes large and uncomprehending. Finally he turned back to her and gently pulled her to her feet. "Go with her, Elizabeth, make sure she sees a plastic surgeon." Darcy looked at Jane's prone form, then back to Elizabeth. "I'll take care of all the costs, but I don't want her to have a scar. Do you understand?"

Elizabeth searched Darcy's eyes, trying to understand what he was saying. She nodded dully.

"We'll come to the hospital when the show is over, but right now we have to make sure the crowd doesn't tear the house apart." He stopped and tilted his head. "Elizabeth, do you understand?"

Elizabeth's eyelids flickered and she seemed to come back to herself. "I understand," she replied softly.

Darcy stared at her a moment, then nodded. "Good. We will come right after the show. Take care of her."

They separated, one group moving toward the stage, the other moving toward the door; both focused on their tasks and forgot about the other.

❧

Elizabeth was staring at the floor of the private waiting room they had been given. She objected to being there. She objected to the bright lights, to the random droning of the TV that no one was watching, to the voices, some fearful, some calm. She objected to the waiting and worrying. Her eyes played over the brown, tan, and white pattern of the tile floor again and again as she waited.

Alex and Charlotte sat beside her on the vinyl couch; Charlotte flipped through a dog-eared magazine while Alex rubbed her back absently. The time for panic had long since passed and Elizabeth was left feeling tired and slightly nauseated.

She heard a bustle of footsteps and Darcy and Charles rushed into the room, with Richard following behind. "How is she?" Charles asked, his face stricken.

Elizabeth stood and walked calmly to him. She noticed he was still wearing his concert outfit, and she wondered in passing what Mrs. Wong, the wardrobe mistress, would think. "She's okay," Elizabeth told him, seeing his shoulders drop in visible relief. "She's currently having a CT scan, then we can go back to her."

"Why are they only doing the CT scan now?" Darcy asked impatiently.

Elizabeth took a deep breath. "Because her vitals were good, and the plastic surgeon insisted on working on her first." She didn't try to hide the weariness in her voice.

Darcy's face softened. "It's a concussion, then?" Elizabeth nodded. "What's the prognosis?"

"If the CT scan comes back like they expect it will, she should be free to go in a few hours. She's going to have to see a plastic surgeon again in a week, but it doesn't have to be the same one she saw tonight. If we know what city we will be in, the doctor here will give her a referral."

Darcy nodded and pulled his cell out of his pocket, while Charles took her hand. "Are you okay, Lizzy?"

The caring in his face was too much and Elizabeth's eyes stung with tears. Without a word, Charles took her into his arms, holding her in a protective hug. Elizabeth took advantage of his strength for a moment, then forced her emotions down and pulled away, nodding her thanks to Charles as she did. She was helped by the distraction of Darcy's voice speaking into the phone.

"Caro, she's going to be okay... It's a concussion... We're staying here tonight. Cancel tomorrow night... Okay, thanks." With a snap he hung up.

Elizabeth stared at him, stunned. "You're stopping the tour?"

Darcy nodded once. "We stick together. I'm not leaving you behind."

Elizabeth considered his words. They surprised her, since she half-expected that he would leap at the chance to leave LBS behind.

"The limo is waiting downstairs. Who'd like to go to the hotel with me?" Richard asked. "There doesn't seem to be much point in waiting here," he shrugged. "Might as well be comfortable."

Charlotte was on her feet before he finished speaking. Alex rose as well and looked at Lizzy expectantly. "I'm staying here," Elizabeth volunteered. Alex nodded and looked to the other two men. Charles stated emphatically that he was staying, and Darcy nodded in agreement.

"Is it okay if I go, Lizzy? Will you be all right?" Alex's eyes searched hers.

"You go," Elizabeth said as she waved him away. "You'll probably have a ton of work to do back at the hotel."

Alex nodded and stepped close, grasping her shoulders and kissing her forehead. "I'll see you later," he said quietly into her ear before he left with the others.

Elizabeth gestured to the couch, and Charles sat down beside her. Darcy remained standing, leaning against the wall. The private waiting room they had been given was tiny, but at least they were alone.

"What happened?" Darcy asked softly.

Elizabeth shrugged. "I wish I knew. I didn't see it. I was playing along and suddenly she was down." She looked at the floor, her expression somber. "I had just realized that I had to get her off the stage when Charles was there, and I followed him."

"I saw it," Charles said in a low voice. He was staring straight ahead, as if replaying a memory in his head. "I saw the bottle. It passed in front of Lizzy, and I could see it against her shirt a moment before it hit Jane."

Elizabeth nodded in comprehension. "I didn't know what it was. I thought that maybe she had been shot, but I didn't hear anything. I didn't know what to think." She sighed. "How did the concert go?"

Charles's expression hardened and he looked away.

"It was fine," Darcy answered quickly. "We played an extra set and it was fine." Charles refused to look at him, and Elizabeth could feel the tension coming off in waves between the two men. "Charles, do you remember the Montreal concert back in '92? Metallica and Guns N' Roses? The riot?" His voice was pitched low and deep. "I know you're angry with me, and I know you wanted to go with Jane, but if we had left, there very well might have been a riot." His eyes flashed. "And for what? So that we could sit here and wait?" He shook his head. "No way, Charles. I'm sorry if you are mad at me, but it wasn't worth damaging our reputation and possibly someone getting injured. Jane's going to be fine and you'll see her in a moment."

Charles turned to Darcy, his expression angry, when a nurse appeared in the doorway. "Miss Bennet?"

"Yes," Elizabeth said as the three faces turned toward the nurse.

"Jane is back in her room; you can see her now."

"Thank you," Elizabeth said, rising to her feet. "When will the report on the CT scan be in?"

"Not for a while. The doctor will speak to you when it's ready."

Elizabeth thanked the nurse and led the way to the room in which Jane rested on a bed. Her forehead was covered with a bandage that hid the sutures. She looked weary and her eyes were closed.

"Jane!" Charles cried out before Elizabeth could say anything by way of warning. Jane's eyes opened and a weak smile lit up her features.

"You came," she said, voicing her pleasure.

"Of course I did," Charles said softly as he took her hand. "How are you feeling?"

"Tired." She looked to her sister. "What did the doctor say?"

Elizabeth shook her head. "They haven't looked at the CT scan yet. It's gonna be awhile, so you might as well just rest."

Charles pulled up a chair and, without releasing Jane's hand, sat down beside her. His eyes were filled with sadness as he touched the hair around her bandage.

"How was the show?" Jane asked him softly.

Charles kissed her hand repeatedly. "Horrible. I hated it. I was so worried about you."

Jane's face softened with concern. "Oh Charles, I'm so sorry."

"No," he whispered. "No, sweetheart, shhhh. It's okay now." He smiled at her warmly and touched her cheek. "You're going to be all right, and that's all that matters."

Elizabeth watched their interaction with increasing discomfort. She looked away and caught Darcy's eye. He motioned with his head toward the waiting room, and Elizabeth followed him out.

She looked at him with an embarrassed grin and moved to sit on the couch. This time Darcy joined her.

"Have you called your parents?" he asked softly as they settled down.

Elizabeth shook her head. "I didn't want to worry them. I figured it's not worth calling until we have the test results, and by then they'll be asleep." She sighed resignedly. "I'll call them in the morning."

"You sound like you're not looking forward to it."

Elizabeth looked at him, annoyed. "Of course I'm not. It's going to be horrible." She shook her head, and her eyes flashed as she wondered at the stupid things he said.

"I'm sorry," he murmured. "I was just going to offer to call for you." He paused. "I thought it might be easier to have it come from me."

Elizabeth looked at him, her forehead crinkled in amazement. "Oh yeah, because it's so much easier to hear that your child has been injured from a total stranger."

"I am not a stranger!" he argued. "I'm her employer and she was injured on *my tour!*"

Elizabeth closed her eyes. *I forgot we were on the Control Freak Tour!* She fought to keep her emotions in, but it was too late. The dam had been broken, and tears began to leak out. She put her head in her hands. "I'm sorry," she said painfully. "I shouldn't have said that."

"No, no," Darcy disagreed, horrified, as he watched her collapsing in on herself.

"It's the stress," she explained, her voice muffled.

Darcy put his hand on her shoulder. "Lizzy?" he said softly. When he touched her, he felt it again; the spark of desire that tore through his body was like the crack of a whip. It disturbed him, the way he wanted her. In a split second he recognized this yearning as it ripped through him, and he was ashamed. He knew it was wrong in the way it overwhelmed his worry for her and for Jane. The guilt he felt for the attack, and even his long-held revulsion of hospitals, was submerged beneath the desire he felt for her at that moment. She looked up at him, tears running down her cheeks, and he was lost.

Elizabeth found herself in his arms, being held closely. She clung to him just as tightly as he apologized. His body and voice were tight with emotion. "It's my fault too, Elizabeth. I don't deal well with hospitals. I shouldn't have snapped at you."

"I just wish this had never happened. I wish—" she broke off raggedly.

"I'm sorry, Elizabeth." Darcy rested his cheek gently on the top of her head. He rocked her in his arms, calming her like a child, until she quieted. "It wasn't your fault, you know that, don't you?" he told her softly.

"Of course I do," Elizabeth snapped, and then she teared up again. "But I just keep asking myself, 'Why Jane?'" Her voice broke. "I mean, if you are going to hurt someone, why not hurt me, or Charlotte? Why Jane?"

Without thought, Darcy pulled her closer. He ignored the blood on her clothes and the scent of fear on her skin as he tried to comfort her sobs. "I'm sorry, Lizzy, I'm very sorry. It shouldn't have happened."

❧

When they reached the hotel, Caroline was waiting in the lobby. Charlotte and Alex gave her a full report, the news being mostly good, but Caroline realized right away that this would have a major effect on the tour. She handed the room keys to Richard and Charlotte and then took Alex to her room for a planning session.

Charlotte looked at Richard, shrugged, and moved toward the elevator bays. Once they were inside, he asked her softly, "Are you okay?"

Charlotte stared straight ahead and quietly answered, "Nope."

Richard took a deep breath. "Would you like some company?"

Slowly Charlotte turned to him, her eyes full of questions and disbelief. "Are you... hitting on me?"

"If you want me to, yes, otherwise I'm just offering a friendly ear," he said with easy frankness.

Charlotte looked away, considering the offer. When the elevator stopped and the doors opened, she said calmly, "Let's go to your room."

❧

"Do you remember anything?" Charles asked softly, his hands gently caressing her hair.

Jane shook her head sadly. "I don't even remember going out onstage. They told me that short-term memory loss is normal." She looked at him. "Tell me what happened."

Charles spoke slowly. "You started like you always do." He smiled briefly. "You were halfway through the set when someone threw a big

Jack Daniel's bottle and caught you in the head. I saw it on the monitor and ran out to you."

"Charles!" Jane was dismayed.

"Oh, Rebecca was pissed," he flashed a grin. "But I didn't care. I picked you up and carried you back." He looked intently into her eyes. "There was so much blood, Jane, I was terrified."

Jane squeezed his hand tightly.

"Alex and Lizzy took you to the hospital, and Will made us perform." He frowned guiltily. "I was horrible onstage, I was so worried about you, but Will was concerned that if we didn't go on there might be a riot."

"He was right," she said, her voice clear. "Don't feel bad; you did the right thing."

Charles looked up and saw the absolution in her eyes. He closed his eyes tightly and drew her hand up to his lips again. Whispering against the back of it, he confessed, "I hated being away from you, Jane, I hated it!"

"I know," she whispered back reassuringly, "I know."

⤬

Elizabeth pulled back from his embrace and shook her head, "Oh no, Fitzwilliam Darcy. If I can't take the blame for this, you don't get to either. It's no more your fault than it is mine."

"It's my tour," Darcy objected softly.

"So what?" Elizabeth shrugged. "We wanted to be there. You didn't hold a gun to our heads and make us go on the stage. We knew the risks," her voice slipped on the last word.

Darcy regarded her skeptically. "You've never had anything thrown at you, Elizabeth, have you?"

Elizabeth shook her head, aware that she had been caught. Then she shrugged once. "Flowers."

Darcy lifted up one side of his mouth. "This is a little different than flowers."

Elizabeth had to agree with him. "You're used to this?"

Darcy did fully smile this time. Elizabeth was distracted by the way it changed his face. "We started out playing clubs in New York that had fencing between the audience and the stage." He laughed once at the memories. "We became accustomed to all sorts of things being thrown at us. Bottles just meant the crowd was enjoying the show."

Elizabeth smiled for the first time all night. "Wow, we've never played any place like that."

"Until tonight," he challenged.

"Until tonight," she agreed, nodding to herself. "My guitars!" she exclaimed, suddenly recalling them.

"I had Ronnie take care of them. They were cleaned and should be in your hotel room by now."

Elizabeth looked at him gratefully, realizing he understood how important they were to her. "Thanks," she said softly before slipping into silence.

"Are you regretting being here, Lizzy? On tour?"

"No," she whispered. "I'm sorry that Jane got hurt, but this is what I always wanted. I wouldn't give it up for anything."

Darcy pulled her close to him, and she rested her head on his shoulder. "What about you?" she asked softly, her voice disconnected and distant. "Is this what you wanted?"

Darcy shook his head thoughtfully. "No, I wanted to be a musician. I love my music. But I never wanted this—the fans, the photo sessions, the interviews." He sounded weary. "If I could, I would walk away from it all."

"Why don't you?"

"Because at some point it became more than just me. It became this huge juggernaut, with a hundred people being my responsibility. I can't just walk away from it. I wish I could."

Elizabeth wondered silently at his words. She couldn't imagine the man she had known as Fitzwilliam Darcy trapped in a role he didn't want, but on the other hand, it certainly appeared to her that he was unhappy. She wondered how this had happened to him. When had he lost control of his life? Was this why he seemed to struggle so hard to regain it?

✥

Charlotte took four steps into the room and stopped. She listened as Richard closed the door and moved quietly behind her. She felt his hands come to rest lightly on her shoulders. "Char?" he asked.

She turned around and slid her arms around his waist. She pressed herself against his warmth and felt his arms enclose her tightly to him. "Char," he began again. "I just want you to be clear. You set the rules here. Anything you want, and nothing you don't, 'kay?"

She slowly raised her head and looked pleadingly into his eyes. "I want to forget about this night. Make me forget, please."

Richard nodded once as his mouth closed on hers. He kissed her firmly, forcing her lips to part against his and teasing her with his tongue. When at last he pulled back, he whispered, "Like that?"

"Yes," she sighed. He kissed her again as he propelled her farther into the room. A quick search found what he was looking for. He brought her into the bathroom, turned the shower on, and began stripping off her clothes in between kisses.

Moaning softly, she asked, "Won't I just get dirty again?"

Richard grinned wickedly. "Oh yes, you are going to be very dirty and sweaty. But first you need to get the smell of blood and hospital off of you." He kissed her fiercely, pulling in her bottom lip and grazing it with his teeth as he released it. "I promise you will enjoy it."

He led her into the luxurious shower stall and positioned her under the stream. Charlotte was never this docile with a man before in her life, but it was clear that Richard was an expert, and she had a unique trust in him.

She leaned back into the hot stream and realized he had been correct. She did need a shower, and a lazy smile came to her face. She opened her eyes to see Richard staring at her, his eyes dark and his appreciation obvious.

"Turn around," he growled.

Charlotte grinned cheekily and couldn't help the tiniest of wiggles. A light slap on her ass made it clear he had noticed and approved. Charlotte wondered what was next when she felt his hands massage her shoulders. "Christ, Char! You're tight," he said as he worked her muscles.

She put her hands up to brace herself against the wall. At that moment she didn't care if she got laid or not. What he did to her body felt so good she worried she couldn't remain standing. He massaged her shoulders under the hot water until they started to loosen, then he moved down her back, finding knots of tension and working them out. Charlotte was moaning softly before he was done. "See," he breathed into her ear, "I told you that you would like it."

Charlotte grinned and nodded as he quickly soaped her body. She shampooed her hair, suddenly eager to be out of there and on to the next step. Richard was very businesslike and in a few short minutes, they were wrapped in large bath sheets and moving to the bedroom.

"Are you hungry?" he asked her politely.

Charlotte shook her head and licked her lips. "Not for food," she replied naughtily.

Richard led her to the bedroom without another word. There he turned on a low light beside the bed and kissed her again, gently removing the towel. Charlotte blushed slightly, but the way Richard's eyes appreciably examined her body removed any feelings of embarrassment she might have. His eyes darkened with desire and she felt aroused just by his presence. He moved close to her again and touched her face, tracing her cheek and jaw, tilting her lips up to his. "Charlotte," he whispered before he kissed her.

She wrapped her arms around his neck, her senses saturated by the feeling of his lips on hers, his chest again hers, his erection pinned against her stomach, his hands cupping her ass. He broke away from her mouth to kiss the side of her neck as he lightly picked her up. "Bedtime, Charlotte," he murmured as he placed her on the king-size bed and lay down beside her.

As soon as his hands were free of the burden of carrying her, they began exploring. Caressing her smooth skin, from her face to the tops of her shoulders to her soft breasts to her stomach and legs. His mouth was kissing her in ways she had never imagined possible. With his kiss, he told her she was beautiful and sexy and that he wanted her very, very much. Charlotte could not find it in herself to disagree with such a persuasive argument.

His mouth left hers, but his hand was stimulating her breast so skillfully she couldn't draw a breath to complain. When she felt his lips at her hardened nipple, first wetting it with his tongue and then smoothly drawing it into his mouth, she moaned with the exquisiteness of it.

"Have you forgotten, Charlotte?" he asked softly as his lips trailed across her chest to her other nipple.

"Forgotten what?" she moaned, her mind blank except for what his mouth was doing and the way his hand was trailing down her stomach and between her thighs. With a contented sigh, he settled against her, her tit in his mouth and his fingers exploring her sex. She was impressed with his talent. His explorations were not the clumsy fumbling of an amateur hoping to stumble across a mythical location. No, this was the hand of a professional on a fact-finding mission. He quickly determined where she liked to be touched and, more importantly, *how*.

Charlotte was so caught up in the pleasure his fingers were bringing her that she didn't notice at first that he had abandoned her nipple. "Oh!" she gasped as she sensed him moving against her. "What are you doing?"

He smiled in a predatory way. "I want to taste you, Charlotte." He drew his face across the slight mound of her belly and gently parted her thighs.

"But," she objected, "I can't come that way!"

Richard looked up to her, his expression distinctly pleased. "Yes, you can."

"No, I've tried."

He laughed softly. "Just lie back and trust me, Charlotte. I think you might be in for a surprise."

Although dubious, she had to concede that everything else he had done to her so far had been flawless. She lay back and tried to relax, then she felt the first brush of his tongue and suddenly relaxation was the furthest thing from her mind. She had no idea what he was doing to her, but as long as he didn't stop, she didn't care at all. She found her fingers threading themselves in his long, soft hair, desperate to keep him from stopping. She cried out involuntarily as she felt his fingers penetrate her. Her hips began twisting in rhythm with his mouth and soon no force on earth could hold her back.

She came in an intense orgasm like she had never experienced before. She lay panting, her mouth still open from the shock as he discreetly wiped his face on a towel and lay down beside her.

"You can't come that way, can you?" he grinned.

"Oh my God!"

He laughed outright.

"Thank you," she sighed as she regained her breath.

"No, thank you," he purred in her ear, "you were delicious."

"Richard," she moaned, "fuck me."

"As you wish," he grinned and turned aside for a moment to prepare. Her body was starting to ache with need for him as she heard the rattle of a wrapper being opened. She felt the cool air on her body and then he gently mounted her. Quickly he filled the emptiness that was paining her and she responded like a fine violin in the hands of a master. He moved with her, drawing out her pleasure then roughly quickening the pace and stealing her breath from her. She wailed as he drove another shattering orgasm from her body, then in the daze that followed she felt him reach his own peak and collapse beside her.

Her eyes shut, she reached for him like a blind kitten and drew him close. Pressed tightly together, they rested until their breathing grew regular again. Only then did she try to express the gratitude in her heart.

"Oh my God, Richard!" she grinned. "You *are* a god. It's never been like that for me."

He smiled contentedly. "I aim to please, ma'am."

"Thank you!" she exclaimed and kissed him again. Taking a deep breath, she began to draw herself out of the bed, but his arms caught her before she could move.

"What are you doing?" he asked, puzzled.

"I was going to go back to my room," she said softly, confused.

"Stay with me," he told her, but it was clearly a request.

"Why?"

"I'm afraid of the dark."

She laughed once. "You could leave the light on," she suggested coyly.

He looked at her, and she saw a profound need in his eyes that she had never seen before in him. It made her throat tighten, as he softly pleaded, "Stay."

With a sad smile and a nod, she lay back down and snuggled beside him. His long arm switched off the light then draped over the curve of her hip. Softly his lips fluttered against her ear the words, "Good night, Charlotte."

CHAPTER 6

Elizabeth was quiet as she rode to the hotel in the back of the limousine. She had been awake for too many hours and had been through too much. The movement of the car had tranquilized her into a numb state, and she let everything go. She had no idea what time it was but knew it was after three and before sunrise. All she wanted was a shower and bed, in that order.

"Damn!" Darcy swore beside her, drawing her out of her fog.

She looked out the tinted windows at the hotel. "What?"

"The media has arrived," he told her, using the voice she had heard back at the concert. He then told the driver to circle around the block.

Charles's expression was adamant as he held Jane protectively in his arms. "No way. She's not going to be subjected to that."

Darcy nodded in agreement. "Here's what we're going to do. Lizzy, there are photographers at the hotel. Can you pretend to be Jane?"

"Me?"

"They don't know one Bennet from another," he explained. "They just know a pretty singer was hurt. Can you do this?"

"Of course," she answered without hesitation. She didn't quite know what she was agreeing to, but she realized with a shock that she trusted him.

"Good, grab one of the extra bandages the hospital packed for Jane. Charles, call Alex, have him meet you at the garage entrance."

Quickly, plans were made. Jane and Charles were moved to the corner of the limo farthest from the doors, and Darcy put his sunglasses on.

"It's the middle of the night," Elizabeth said, a confused frown on her face.

"I'm actually more recognizable wearing these," Darcy shrugged. "And we want to be seen. We will have to move slowly, to give Charles enough time. Are you ready?"

Elizabeth nodded. A moment later the limo stopped. Darcy climbed out, extending his hand to Elizabeth. Pressing the bandage to her forehead, she grabbed on to him and slowly exited, swaying on what appeared to be unsteady legs.

Darcy put his arm around her and whispered into her ear, "Lean on me."

Elizabeth leaned against him, feeling the strength of his body, faking the injury, but not the tiredness she felt. As soon as they passed into the lobby, she saw the flashes from a half-dozen cameras as photographers took their picture. Darcy conspicuously shielded her body as they slowly walked on. Halfway across the floor, Elizabeth gave a convincing stumble, and Darcy pulled her up, holding her tightly to him, pausing for a moment, and asking in a concerned voice if she was all right.

Elizabeth winked at him and he nodded solemnly, then whispered "well done" in her ear, as he tenderly kissed her hair, all producing another wave of clicks and flashes from the photographers. Moving slowly again, they made their way to Caroline, who was holding the elevator for them. She gave a nod of understanding as she stepped out to handle the press while they stepped in. Darcy took Elizabeth close in his arms, caressing her hair for the cameras until the doors shut.

Then they were suddenly alone. Darcy found himself very aware of the silence, broken only by the Muzak playing in the elevator. He gently released her and backed himself up against the wall.

Elizabeth also took a step back and smiled a little nervously. "Well, I hope we put on a good show for them."

Darcy nodded. "You realize, of course, that someday those pictures are going to show up on the front page of the *Enquirer*, with some stupid headline concerning a love child or some such nonsense."

She nodded easily and grinned. "I know." She shrugged. "It doesn't bother me. It's a small price to pay to keep Jane out of that."

Elizabeth watched his face as they rode upward. She couldn't tell where his eyes were with the sunglasses on, but she suspected that they were closed. She could either believe that or the discomforting thought that he was staring at her. Desire flashed through her like lightning at the possibility. She tried to keep from remembering how it had felt to be in his arms, his strong hands against her back, his lips in her hair, his voice in her ear. It'd been a long time since a man had held her like that, and she wanted him. She couldn't even begin to deny it; he was the sexiest man she had ever seen.

She knew it was stupid. She couldn't even have a two-minute conversation without getting angry with him. He was the most arrogant, controlling, condescending man she had ever met, and the only way she could ever stand to fuck him would be to cover his mouth with duct tape so he couldn't speak!

Uncomfortable with her feelings of desire and where they might and might not lead, she latched on to something she could control: anger.

She was angry that she let herself be dragged around by her libido, and she was angry with Darcy for being such a hot object of desire. She knew that Fitzwilliam Darcy could have any woman in the world, and he certainly had never thought of Elizabeth Bennet in that way. She reminded herself again of his words, hearing his voice once again in her mind: "Once they taste that different world, they'll try to do anything to hang on to it. And that would definitely include us."

She set her jaw as his warning cut her once again. *Not if you begged, Fitzwilliam Darcy! I don't care how hot you are, you'll never get me!*

It was a relief when the elevator doors opened at their floor. Elizabeth stepped out into the empty hallway, realizing with a pang that she was stuck without a key or even a room number. Luckily, a moment later the other elevator arrived with Charles, Jane, and Alex. Elizabeth was never so happy to see another person before in her life.

Alex handed Darcy his key, and with a nod he quickly walked off. The remaining foursome moved off in the opposite direction to the large suite at the end of the hall. Alex opened the door and let Charles help Jane in. Elizabeth thanked him for his help.

Alex gave her a big hug, pressing her head against his, asking once again if she would be all right. Elizabeth nodded, telling him she was fine, and with a light kiss, Alex moved off. Neither of them noticed that Darcy had watched then from the darkness of his open doorway, waiting until he had seen Alex leave.

⤕

Charlotte moved closer to the delicious warmth she sensed nearby. She was not awake yet, just merely aware. As she burrowed closer, she caught the scent that would be forever linked in her brain with astounding pleasure.

Her lips curled into a smile as his arm wrapped around her and pulled her close, and she buried her face into his chest with a contented sigh.

She awoke a few minutes later to the feel of light fingers tracing the tattoo on her arm. She was very proud of it: a crescent moon entwined with vines of ivy that trailed along the lines of her muscles up to her shoulder and down to her elbow.

"Morning," she said contentedly as she pointed her toes and stretched her legs out against him. Richard's lips caught hers in a tender kiss that set her nerve endings buzzing.

"Morning," he replied roughly. She could feel his erection against her stomach and she smiled wantonly. "Oh, Mr. Fitzwilliam, happy to see me?"

Richard smiled roguishly. "Why, Ms. Lucas, I'm always happy to see a beautiful woman in my bed." He drew the sheet down to look at her, his eyes admiring her nakedness.

Charlotte lay still, satisfied to be examined by him. She had never felt so beautiful before. She watched him watching her until instinctively she reached up to his hair and gently pulled him to her for a long kiss.

He pulled back a little later, his eyes asking, hers answering, then they met again and again for more kisses, each hotter than the last. Richard's arms locked around her slim body and pulled her with him as he rolled to his back.

Communicating only with their eyes, Charlotte knew nothing more was needed. They had both awakened filled with hunger, and both were ready to be sated. She quickly retrieved a condom from the package at the bedside table and applied it slowly, taking the time to admire him in the same manner in which he had just admired her.

Charlotte knew he was beautiful, but as she traced the well-shaped muscles under his perfect skin, Charlotte felt a lump form in her throat. Never had she touched such beauty or possessed it inside of her body. No matter how fleeting this was, she knew a part of his beauty would remain with her forever, a permanent mark, just like their tattoos. Her eyes wide with the sight of him, he pulled her close and kissed her again and again, telling her she was all he wanted.

With a grin, she nuzzled his neck, then rose up and, never breaking eye contact, impaled herself on his length. A long, low sigh escaped as he filled her. He watched her, his eyes devouring the expressions of pleasure on her face, his nose taking in the smell of her need, his body rejoicing in the sensations of being surrounded by her.

His hands reached up and cupped her soft breasts, massaging her nipples until they hardened to sharp points and squeezing them until Charlotte whimpered with pleasure. His body curled slightly into hers and moved to meet her every thrust. Charlotte lost control of herself in the intensity of the sensations she was feeling. Her hands coiled around his shoulders as she angled herself on him, her breaths coming in quick gasps.

With a force that moved the bed, she ground herself wildly into him, feeling the pressure build in her blood. Lost to everything but sensation, she came with a passion that left her breathless and shaking. Richard grasped her hips, using her to reach his release only a minute later.

Afterward, he rolled them onto their sides and pulled her body close, her arms draping limply over him. He kissed her sweaty forehead, murmuring, "Thank you, Charlotte."

The warmth that had filled her heart retreated as Charlotte pulled back her emotions, reminding herself that this was only a mercy fuck between friends. "What time is it?" she asked a few minutes later, her voice something like normal.

Richard stopped caressing her cheek, knowing the moment was over, and looked at the clock. "It's almost ten."

"I've got to get going," Charlotte said, her voice deliberately casual. "I hope everything is all right with Jane."

Richard lay back on the bed, stretching. "They would have called if there was a problem," he assured her. "I'm sure they're all still asleep."

"Let's hope so," Charlotte grinned as she dressed. She slowed as she realized she was getting to the good-bye part. She always hated this part, and her usual method of handling it had always been slipping out before her partner awoke. But somehow she didn't want to miss this. She knew she was playing with fire, but she wanted to see his reaction; if he had any regrets, if he would miss her as much as— She broke off her train of thought as Richard rose from the bed and once again she was stunned by his beauty.

"I'll see you at breakfast?" he asked her as he closed the distance between them. Charlotte nodded in response. "Thank you, Charlotte," he said softly, and she believed him. She believed he was grateful for what they had shared. She believed his eyes, which told her she had touched him.

He kissed her a last time, achingly sweet, and she left, finding herself in the hotel hallway with her key in her hand, not even sure how she had gotten there.

❦

Elizabeth woke to the sound of her cell phone ringing beside her. Seeing that it was Alex calling, she flipped it open. "What?"

"Good morning to you too, sunshine."

Elizabeth resisted the urge to throw the phone across the room.

"It's time to wake up." Alex continued, knowing exactly what the expression on Elizabeth's face was. "We need to have a meeting to decide what we're going to do, and we're having it in your suite in thirty minutes."

"Do you have any idea how much sleep I've had?" she whined.

"Slightly more than I've had, sweetheart. But we've got trouble, so get everyone up and I'll see you at ten thirty."

Elizabeth did throw the phone at that point. Then, resigned to her fate, she stretched, pushed the bedding off her, and went to wake the others.

She tapped on Charlotte's door, and getting no response, she knocked louder and louder until the door across the room opened and Charles stuck his head out.

"What's up?" he whispered.

"Alex and Caro are having a meeting here to make plans at ten thirty. How's Jane?"

"She's still sleeping. Thanks." He disappeared back into the room and the door shut.

Frustrated, Elizabeth opened the door to Charlotte's room and was surprised to find it empty. With an indifferent "hmm," she closed it and started the tiny coffee maker in the suite.

Elizabeth looked up from watching it fill slowly with the precious fluid when the door opened and Charlotte entered. She ignored Charlotte until the smell washing off her hit Elizabeth like a hammer between her eyes. If she were blind, her nose would have told her what Charlotte had been up to. As it was, the satisfied smile on her face only served as confirmation.

That smile faltered when Charlotte saw Lizzy. "What are you doing up?" she asked, surprised.

"Making coffee," Elizabeth yawned. "Caroline wants a meeting with us and Slurry here before the breakfast meeting."

"Oh."

"Where were you?"

"Out," Charlotte answered as innocently as possible.

It was the wrong answer. It was the worst possible answer. Charlotte had never been shy about her sex life, and Elizabeth knew if she was hiding something, it was bad. "Oh no! Please tell me you were with one of Rebecca's staff, or even a roadie. Please, please tell me you weren't *out* with Richard."

The look on Charlotte's face answered for her. "Jesus Christ, Charlotte!" Elizabeth snapped. "How stupid are you?"

Charlotte was completely baffled by Elizabeth's reaction. "It was just a friendly fuck, Lizzy," she defended herself. "He saw I was upset and offered me some company. That's all," she snapped. "What the hell is your problem?"

"My problem!?!" Elizabeth's voice came out in a screech. "My problem is that I spent the whole night at the friggin' hospital, worried about Jane and covered in filth, then I had to run through a gauntlet of reporters to get into the hotel, while you had your legs up in the air getting banged by Richard! So forgive me if I'm not in the best of moods right now!"

"Just drink your fucking coffee, Lizzy. I'm taking a shower," Charlotte replied sullenly as she walked to her room and shut the door.

"Good!" Elizabeth exclaimed, and then muttered darkly about "washing the smell of your whoring off." She poured her coffee and looked into it, searching it like a scrying bowl, seeking answers. But there were none there.

She lifted up her head, took a sip, and stared at the recently closed door for a long time. Then her eyes drifted to Jane's door, still shut, where she and Charles were sleeping. She wasn't thinking just then, or even feeling. She was just observing. She did some simple mathematical calculations in her head, and nodding at the result, she walked alone to her empty room and shut the door.

❧

Charles lay down and stared out into the semidarkness. He was surprised to feel Jane snuggle up close to him. "I thought you were still asleep," he said softly.

"I missed you," she sighed. "And I thought I heard voices in the other room. Is everything all right?"

Charles grinned slightly. "Oh, you know how Lizzy is until she gets her coffee. We're going to have a planning meeting in a little bit. That's all." He turned his head to look at her, gently smoothing her hair away from her face. "How are you feeling?" he asked.

"Better," she smiled. "My headache has gone away, and I feel much better."

"That's great!" he said softly, pulling her shoulders close in a tight hug. He could see in her eyes she wasn't quite as good as she was making herself out to be, but the fact that she was well enough to lie for his comfort was a sign of improvement. He hesitated a moment, knowing he had to ask what he didn't want to. "Do you want me to go now?" he asked with a deliberate ease.

"No!" she cried, then she looked away, embarrassed. "I mean, if you want to stay, that would be fine, but you don't have to."

Charles smiled at their clumsiness. "I don't want to go anywhere," he told her, his eyes filled with emotions that seemed beyond words, and then his eyes clouded as he struggled with his feelings. "Jane, I tried to leave you before, when we first got into the hotel. But I kept having flashbacks of you passed out on the stage, and I couldn't leave. I had to be here, to touch you, and to know that you're okay." He looked down, looking at his hand holding hers. "It sounds like I'm being some kind of hero, staying with you to help out, but in fact I'm being very selfish." He looked at her and tilted his head. "I'm afraid you're stuck with me, Jane."

She smiled as only Jane could, a smile of pure joy. "That's okay. I'm glad you stayed, Charles. Thank you," she said in a low voice that carried so much more than gratitude. "I'm very happy to be stuck with you."

They looked at each other for a long time, simply smiling and pleased with what they had shared. "So," Charles continued, after a suitable time, "do you want to go back to sleep, or do you want to get up?"

"I'll get up now," Jane answered pleasantly, yet not showing any inclination to move from her spot cuddled up against him.

"Good. Maybe after breakfast we could go outside." He looked at her caringly, gently touching her face. "You could use a little sun, sunshine."

Jane smiled back, then her face fell and her hand grazed the bandage on her forehead. "I, I don't want to go out, Charles," she said hesitatingly.

"I was just thinking we could sit by the hotel pool. I know you can't—"

"No!" she snapped. "I don't want to go out!" she said violently. She looked away from him and Charles could feel her trembling. "I don't want anyone to see me like this."

"Jane? What's wrong?" he asked cautiously.

"It's just," she hesitated, emotions flying across her face. "I was always the pretty one," she said brokenly. "Everyone always said, 'Look at that pretty girl.' And my parents and everyone always loved me because I was beautiful," her voice was thick with anguish. "I know it sounds stupid and conceited, but that's who I was. That was the way I stood out from my sisters. And now I feel like I'm ruined, Charles. I'm not beautiful anymore. I'm afraid to go out there. I know that everyone is going to look at me like I'm a freak and say, 'Oh, hey, there's that girl who fell down at a concert. Look, she's got a scar just like Harry Potter!'" She began weeping softly.

Charles pulled her close, partially to comfort her and partially to hide the grin he couldn't repress. When the tide of Jane's tears subsided, he knew what he needed to say.

"Jane, look at me." He loosened his embrace only enough so that she could see his face. "Jane, you are the most beautiful woman I have ever met. Without question, *the most beautiful*," he added for emphasis. "And it's not because of your eyes or your face or your body or any other part. It's because of your heart." He paused a moment, waiting to be sure that she heard him, and then he continued solemnly. "Jane, you could have a hundred scars on your face, and that wouldn't make you any less beautiful or change how I feel about you.

"I've been thinking about this since I met you, and what happened last night just made it clear to me. I know what I feel for you isn't going to change in a week or a day or a year. Jane, I love you." He paused and grinned shyly. "I have since the day we met, the day I asked you to sing with me."

Jane's eyes brimmed with tears again, and she smiled with heartbreaking happiness. "Charles?" she sobbed as she retreated back into the warmth of his arms. He held her close, relishing the feel of her soft body against his and the scent of her hair. Tilting her chin up with his hand, Charles kissed her with a slow passion. She responded with everything she had, trying to give to him the words she couldn't yet say.

He broke off, and Jane sighed in pleasure. Charles looked at the white piece of gauze taped to her head, considering. His fingers gently traced the edge of it as he told her softly, "I know this is scary, Jane. But I'm going to be here with you, and it's going to be okay. We are going to get through this together."

"You will be with me, as long as I need you?"

"Sunshine, I will be with you as long as I need you, and that will be a very, very long time."

She smiled again, and Charles wished he could freeze the moment; her joy was so beautiful and perfect. He was able to rein in the desire he felt easily, knowing it wasn't time yet. He wanted her, but he wanted her whole, in both her body and her spirit; he wanted her to be able to give herself to him. Waiting was not a problem at all. Reluctantly, he released her and stood.

"I'm going to throw some clean clothes on before the meeting." He looked at the clock. "I've got ten minutes. Think I can make it?"

Jane laughed. "No."

He smiled back before kissing her soundly. "Love you," he told her and he was away.

Jane looked at the door he had just closed and sighed happily.

◦◦◦

When Elizabeth came out of her room, Darcy was sitting on the couch. The shower had helped her calm down, and she walked easily to the coffee machine to refill her cup. "How's Jane doing?" he asked in his low voice.

Elizabeth smiled politely. "She's sleeping, last I heard."

Darcy nodded. Caroline, Alex, Richard, and Rachel entered the room from the hall in quick succession, relieving them from the burden of trying to make conversation. "Where's Char?" Alex asked.

Involuntarily, Elizabeth looked at Richard before answering. "I think she's still in her room."

Alex sighed and banged on her door, calling her name. Darcy stared at Richard, an uncomfortable suspicion growing in his gut.

A minute later, Charlotte emerged from her room and, with a friendly smile, sat down next to Richard on the sofa. Elizabeth looked at Darcy watching the pair, and she saw his expression turn stony.

"Okay, I think we can begin," Caroline said. Before she could say another word, Jane opened the door of her room, and dressed in shorts and a fresh T-shirt, she joined the group.

"Good morning," she smiled to everyone.

"How are you feeling, Jane?" Caroline asked.

"Better, thanks."

"You look better," Alex said, and the group agreed.

Jane took a seat next to Elizabeth. "Charles isn't here yet?"

Caroline smiled and shook her head. "He'll be late to his own funeral. Let's continue; the show for tonight is cancelled, but we're performing tomorrow." Caroline reviewed the next week's schedule while Elizabeth studied her sister. Jane was still plainly injured, but Elizabeth could see a change in her eyes. Jane was glowing, and Elizabeth was filled with a curiosity to know exactly what had happened.

"Jane's doctor has said that she is not to perform for a week. So the question is: What are we going to do for the warm-up act?"

Elizabeth spoke up. "I can do the show."

Caroline looked doubtful. "Are you sure, Elizabeth?" While she was talking, Charles quietly entered the room and sat down next to Jane, taking her hand. "We all know you can play, but can you get a set together in a day?"

Elizabeth considered. "It's only three more songs. I have that many on the CD. I'll need time to rehearse, but yes, I think I can do it."

"She can do it," Alex said confidently.

"What about bass?" Darcy asked. "You'll need someone to play with you."

Elizabeth nodded, conceding his point but not having a ready answer.

"What about one of the guitar techs? I think Simon can play bass," Caroline said.

"I can play," Charles volunteered.

"Are you sure?" Caroline asked in a tone that was much more appropriate for a sibling than a manager.

"I don't like it," Darcy said darkly. "Playing the warm-up set and then our show. I think that'll be too much."

Charles looked at Jane, who squeezed his hand, then turned to the others. "It's not too much. It's just for one set and it's only for a week."

"I don't know, Charles," Caroline frowned. "Maybe we should find someone else."

"We don't have time," Charles insisted. "I can do it. I know half the songs already."

"Excuse me," Rachel spoke up loudly. "That was Anne," she announced, as she closed her phone. "She's on her way with Collins."

A mass of groans and rolled eyes accompanied this statement. "Did you tell her not to come?" Darcy asked impatiently.

"I didn't get a chance. Her plane just landed."

Darcy swore softly.

"Let me play for Lizzy," Charles insisted. "If it turns out to be too much, we can try something else."

"Maybe in a few days, Jane could start to transition back in by just playing and not singing," Elizabeth suggested. Jane nodded in agreement.

"Jane is not going back on until the doctor says she is ready," Darcy said firmly. "Charles, if you really think you can do it, then go ahead. I'm not going to fight with you on this."

"It'll be fine, Will," Charles said easily.

Richard, as usual, had nothing to add. "When are we going to have time to rehearse?" Charlotte asked.

Lizzy shrugged and looked at Alex and Caroline. "That will depend on our travel schedule," Alex said.

"I'm going to work that out, and I will have some answers at breakfast, if that is all right with everyone," Caroline told them.

The meeting broke up to regroup ten minutes later in the dining room. Elizabeth found herself alone with Darcy as the room emptied out.

She noticed the hard set of his jaw. "You're not happy with this, are you?"

He shook his head.

"What would you have done?" she asked, wanting to know if there was an option she didn't know about.

"When we had a problem before, I stopped the tour," he told her flatly.

"Yes, well, that was fine for the *Slurry* tour. But being that this is not the *LBS* tour, I don't think that's the answer."

He looked away. An idea sprung up in Elizabeth's head that she knew could not be right. "You would have stopped the tour for us?" she asked incredulously.

"I did, didn't I?"

"But that was just for one night. You can't stop the whole tour for a week, not for us; that's crazy."

"I know," he said simply. "That is why we are going on. But I don't like it."

Elizabeth studied him openly. "Can I ask you something?" Her curiosity was risking more trouble, but she had to know.

Darcy's head moved down and up once, slowly in response as his eyes held hers.

"What is your problem with Charles and Jane?" she asked calmly. "I understand being concerned," she explained. "I know I am, but you seem so virulently opposed to them. I just want to know why."

Darcy's eyes expressed his surprise and interest in her question. "You're concerned?"

"Certainly," Elizabeth affirmed. She paused for the right words. "Jane only sees the best in people. She doesn't have a healthy sense of doubt. And she and Charles seem to be going really, really fast. I don't want to see her getting hurt." She looked up to Darcy challengingly. "But I don't glare at them every time they are sitting together. Jane is an adult, and unless she asks for my advice, I'm keeping my opinions to myself."

"Are you suggesting that I am not?"

Elizabeth buried the spark of anger that flashed at his words and replied politely, "I'm not suggesting anything. I'm asking why you seem to object to their relationship so strongly." Her eyes held on to his, not giving an inch.

Darcy looked away, staring at a distant point while he answered thoughtfully. "Charles is… impulsive when it comes to his relationships with women. He falls in love quickly and he falls hard. It's no secret that some of his relationships have ended quite badly."

"And you think Jane is playing him?" she asked softly.

"No," he answered quickly. "But I do worry that this might not last and that we have a very long tour ahead of us. Frankly, Lizzy, I don't want to lose another opening band."

Elizabeth thought carefully. "So you don't object to Jane herself?"

"I don't know Jane," Darcy answered honestly. "I only met her a month ago. Jane seems like a good person. She's a pretty girl with a nice voice. But in this business, girls like that are a dime a dozen, and many of them are ambitious enough to do something more to get ahead."

His candor surprised Elizabeth. "Is that how you see her? A pretty girl with a nice voice?"

"At this point, yes," Darcy answered easily. "The important thing is that even if Jane isn't in this to advance her career, if she gives off the appearance that she is it could be damaging to both of them."

Elizabeth was silent for a long moment. She realized that an answer was required, but she really didn't want to continue the conversation. "Thank you," she said, "for answering my question. It's… thank you."

"Do you want to go down for breakfast?" Darcy asked, not understanding her reaction.

"No," Elizabeth shook her head. "I'll wait for Charlotte and Jane," she said with a weak smile. "Thanks."

Darcy looked at her again, his dark eyes searching hers, then he turned and left the room without a word.

Elizabeth sank to the couch, drew up her knees, and put her head down. She felt like crying, and she had no idea why. She had asked Darcy the question and he had answered her honestly. He was worried about the tour. What more did she expect? He thought of them as "pretty girls with nice voices." When had she ever believed there might be something more? She was simply a performer, an employee. It was important for him to maintain a good working relationship, but nothing more. When had she ever wanted it to be something more? She detested him, didn't she?

It didn't matter. She hated to admit it, but Darcy was right. They had a long tour in front of them, and a friendly, respectful, and distant relationship was best for everyone. And frankly, she realized as she recalled his interactions with his staff, she was lucky to be getting that, rather than the arrogant way he treated most of the people on the tour.

❧

Richard smiled attentively at his companion. Charlotte had frequently found herself sitting beside him. The rest of the tour members were quite willing to leave the drummers alone so that they could eat without the table rattling from Charlotte's and Richard's never-ending rhythms.

This morning was no different from the others, with the exception of a knowing look being exchanged. As Richard ate, Charlotte reported on the morning's events.

Richard looked from his plate to the subject of their conversation.

"Poor Lizzy," he commented. "Well, it makes sense she would be a little cranky this morning. After all, she was probably more upset than Jane about the accident."

Charlotte nodded. "Plus, now she has the solo show to worry about."

"Yeah," Richard agreed. "She needs to get laid."

Charlotte almost spit out her coffee in shock at what she heard. She looked at him and she started laughing, covering her mouth with her hand.

"I've heard it's very good for relieving stress," Richard continued, his voice casual.

Charlotte had to bury her head against his shoulder, she was laughing so hard. When she finally calmed down enough that she could look at him, she said in a forcibly subdued voice, "I've heard that."

He nodded.

"Are you volunteering?" she asked saucily.

"Do you think I should?"

Charlotte shrugged. "Might help."

"If the situation gets desperate, I will. But frankly, I think she would prefer someone else."

As one, Richard and Charlotte looked at Darcy, who was ignoring Rachel, who was sitting beside him and talking, and was instead staring at Elizabeth.

Charlotte nodded in agreement. "And the sad thing is, I don't think that either of them knows."

Richard lifted a single eyebrow. "Oh d'uh! Of course they don't know." He paused for a sip of coffee. "And, my dear Charlotte, they would be deeply offended if anyone tried to tell them."

"It's sad, isn't it? How some people will let feelings get in the way of a good fuck?"

He looked at her long and hard. "Yeah." Then he smiled. "That's what I like about you, dear Charlotte. You know exactly what you want."

"Thank you," she said, pleased.

"Anytime," he replied.

❧

The breakfast meeting had gone well. Caroline had shown her skill and efficiency as she explained the plans and gave out directions. The tour would be moving out in two hours, and Elizabeth needed to get herself and Jane packed to go.

Elizabeth was exiting Jane's room when the suite door rattled with the force of someone knocking on it. She could hear loud voices from the hall as she crossed to the door and opened it. Standing there was a quartet of angry-looking people.

"*You!* You don't look hurt!" Mr. Collins snapped at her as he barged into the room, forcing her out of the way.

"Jane was the one who was injured," Elizabeth answered, too shocked to be angry.

"It was your picture I saw!" Collins challenged her. "With him," he jerked his thumb back at a glowering Darcy. Alex and Caroline followed them in and shut the door.

"Bill, I told you. Jane was injured and Lizzy will be filling in for her," Alex said through clenched teeth.

"And just who are you to be making those decisions?" Collins turned on him. "Did you even consult Ms. de Bourgh? I'll have you know she is very upset by this."

Collins turned back to Elizabeth. "I'm very disappointed in you." He looked at her disgustedly. "I thought we had an understanding that you would do whatever it took to get ahead." He glared meaningfully.

Elizabeth's mouth dropped open. She looked first to Alex, who was already beginning her defense, and then to Darcy, whose mouth was drawn into a thin line.

"Damn it," Alex swore. "Lizzy is doing everything she can. She is saving the show. What more do you want, Collins?"

"What's wrong?" Jane asked sleepily, coming out of her room, still clad in her T-shirt and shorts.

"*You!*" Collins rounded on her. "You're the clumsy fool who got us into this mess. What have you to say for yourself? Have you no shame? Couldn't you have ducked?"

Jane looked completely at a loss by Collins's attack. Collins was drawing breath for the next round when Charles joined Jane. Collins observed that Charles, who had just emerged from Jane's bedroom, took her hand and kissed it, and he stopped short.

"Of course she couldn't have ducked," Charles said lightly. "What? You think she wanted a concussion?"

"Oh! Oh! Of course not!" Collins smiled hastily. "You are correct. Of course, poor Jane." He transferred the smile to her, and then back to The Star who had his arm around her. "I just want to be sure Jane is all right and back onstage as soon as she is able."

Elizabeth felt bile rising in her throat. She was revolted and humiliated by what she was witnessing. Her shame was made complete by the fact that Caroline and Darcy were there, seeing it all. No wonder Darcy thought Jane was using Charles. Why shouldn't he, when clearly their own record executive did?

Elizabeth couldn't look up. She heard Collins saying, "I've spoken with Ms. de Bourgh, and we agree that it would be best for you girls that I stay with the tour to lend a hand and help get you girls on your feet," and she couldn't take any more. Muttering a soft excuse, she went to her room and finished packing.

❧

Sooner than expected, it was time to leave. Charles insisted that he was riding with Jane and Elizabeth volunteered to ride on Slurry's bus.

A few minutes later found their baggage being stored on the bus while Jane, flanked by Alex, Elizabeth, and Charlotte, faced a dozen cameramen and reporters. Jane read a brief statement and then answered ten minutes' worth of questions, which actually dragged out to fifteen. It was uncomfortable, but no one was rude in their questions and when it was over, Jane flashed a beautiful smile and they were off.

When Elizabeth climbed onto the Slurry bus, guitar case in hand, she was surprised by Caroline's presence. "Don't mind me," she said as she flipped through a fashion magazine. She was sitting on a sofa, her legs stretched out in front of her. "I'm currently having an important meeting with Darcy."

Darcy was across the length of the bus, sitting at the table, tapping on his laptop. As Elizabeth passed by, Richard could be heard snoring from his bunk.

"Oh," she said questioningly.

Darcy met her eyes. "You won't wake him up."

"What about your meeting?"

Darcy looked at Caroline, the corner of his mouth turning up. "She is just telling everyone that to avoid Anne. You can play. Don't worry about it."

Elizabeth nodded her thanks and settled down on the couch. Within minutes the bus was under way and Elizabeth had her guitar in her lap.

Darcy watched her, silently, his face half-hidden behind the computer, as she played softly. It wasn't necessary for him to hide, he soon realized. She wouldn't see or hear him where she was. He watched as her fingers moved lightly over the strings, deftly plucking and pinning them against the neck.

He recognized something he had only seen in himself. She wasn't rehearsing. She was healing, taking solace in her instrument and her music. He saw that she was working through the grief of the last day and making peace with herself. Suddenly she was different in his eyes. Someone who was much closer to himself now replaced the talented girl he had known. She was a peer. He had rarely found one before.

He realized he was being a voyeur, watching an intimate act. She was making love to her instrument. He knew he should look away, but he couldn't. His eyes were locked on the way her hands caressed the strings and pulled the wooden body closer to herself. When she started singing softly, he was lost.

Her voice was rough and smoky with fatigue and stress, yet to Darcy it only added to the beauty of her song. He let her words move through him as she sang to herself.

She knew, he told himself. She knew about pain. He heard it in her voice, in her music. He knew with dead certainty that this was no innocent string of words. She was singing about something that had happened in her life, about rejection and loss.

He wondered briefly if she was singing to him but dismissed the thought. This was clearly a song she had written before, about something in her past. He wondered: Who? Who hadn't she been good enough for? Who had failed her? The name Alex drifted into his mind, even as he pushed it away. He didn't want to think about that, about him, about the way he touched her and kissed her and held her trust. He felt again that irrational stab of jealousy he had felt before.

He wasn't troubled that she'd had other lovers; it was that they had not valued her. Not the way she deserved. Not the way he would.

He froze, abruptly appalled at what he had been thinking, and a wave of self-anger washed over him. He was being a fool! Admiring this woman who clearly hated him. It hurt him to admit that, but there was no denying it. The way she had looked at him in her room. The way she had reverted to her "polite" behavior. He didn't know what he had done, but obviously there could be nothing between them, and that was the way *she* wanted it. *Besides, it's not like I feel anything for her!*

That was a lie. He knew it, but it was not the only one he told himself as he wrenched his attention back to his work. At least no one else knows, he thought, to relieve his smarting pride.

Caroline Bingley watched him watching Elizabeth. She knew. She probably knew better than he did. She watched him and saw that he was hurting, while inside, her heart felt like it was being crushed. And just as Darcy did not have to worry about Elizabeth seeing him watching her, so Caroline knew she didn't have to worry about Darcy seeing her. It simply wouldn't happen; he would never see her.

CHAPTER 7

Voices in the bus awakened Elizabeth. She thought she had closed her eyes for only a moment, but it was clear she had been asleep for a while. It was dark outside the bus and an overhead lamp softly illuminated the table where Darcy and Caroline sat. She could still hear Richard snoring in his bunk.

"What are you doing?" Caroline asked conversationally.

"Writing to my sister," Darcy answered distractedly. Elizabeth heard him typing on a keyboard. His back to her, she watched him stop and look up to Caroline for a moment before returning to work.

Elizabeth suspected he must have smiled, because Caroline was grinning brightly at him. "Dear Georgie," she said sincerely. "I miss her. You must be so proud, her finishing school and starting college. Is she excited?"

"Oh yes," Darcy replied.

"I'm sure. How much longer until she graduates?"

"Two months."

Caroline laughed. "I remember my senior year of high school. I think I skipped math for a whole month."

"She better not be skipping classes," he growled.

"Oh, Georgie is a good girl; she would never do that," Caroline assured him.

Again he stopped typing, but Elizabeth saw that he didn't look up this time. His shoulders dropped, and a moment later he resumed typing.

"Tell her when she goes out to Stanford I'm going to take a few days off and show her around."

"You know, you can email her yourself."

"I don't have the time." She laughed. "I email for business, not for pleasure, I'm afraid." Her eyes flicked over to the couch and she noticed Elizabeth. "Oh, you're awake. Did you have a good nap?"

Elizabeth sat up and rubbed her face, nodding in response. She stood up, stretched, and stiffly walked to the table, where Caroline moved to make room for her. "How much longer to the hotel?" she asked.

Caroline looked at her watch. "Few minutes."

"Oh!" Elizabeth's eyes flared. "I'm sorry. I didn't realize I had slept so long."

"It's okay; you needed it after last night," Caroline told her.

"I did," she agreed, "but you were up just as late, if not later, Caroline, and I didn't see you taking a nap."

She smiled, touched by her thoughtfulness. "Yes, but I'm not performing, and it wasn't my sister at the ER." She shrugged. "I'm one of those people who just doesn't need a lot of sleep. But I guarantee you, I'll sleep tonight."

Elizabeth smiled and nodded in agreement. "Do you have any sisters?" Elizabeth asked.

"No," Caroline shook her head, "it's just Charles and me." She looked at Elizabeth, carefully weighing her. "It must've been nice growing up in a big family like yours. Like *The Waltons* on TV."

Elizabeth smiled politely. She had heard this before. "It wasn't like TV, but it was nice. There was always someone to do things with, so we never felt bored or lonely. But it wasn't perfect; there was a lot of fighting too."

"Oh, with five girls I'm sure there must've been."

Elizabeth grinned. "Yes, we were always arguing over clothes or makeup or books." Her eyes flicked to Darcy's again, and she noticed him watching her with that deep stare of his. She could see he wasn't enjoying her stories of her family, and she thought again about how cold he could be.

Luckily, at that point the bus pulled up to the hotel. A few minutes later found all of them in the hotel dining room. Elizabeth took a seat next to Charlotte, who was joined by Richard, and then by Darcy.

"How was your ride?" Elizabeth asked Charlotte after they ordered their meals.

"Good," Charlotte answered. "I slept."

"Me too," Elizabeth admitted. "But I got some practice in first. How's Jane? Did she sleep too?"

"No," Charlotte rolled her eyes in annoyance. "Charles and her spent the whole ride playing and singing together."

"What?"

"Yeah," Charlotte muttered. "You know what a perfectionist Jane is, and she wanted Charles to know the songs for your set, so they started playing your songs, then they started on her songs, then they were playing their favorite songs."

"Eighties music?" Richard interrupted her.

Charlotte nodded, her eyes bugging out in mock annoyance. "I swear they were doing Prince when the bus finally pulled up."

Everyone smiled. "That's Charles," Richard confirmed.

"Oh my God! I was ready to gnaw off my arm and beat them both over the head with it."

Richard laughed. "A one-armed drummer? Now who's living in the eighties?"

"Shut up!" Charlotte laughed and threw her napkin at him.

Richard retaliated with a dinner roll and before it could turn into a full-fledged food fight, Elizabeth yelled, laughing, "Stop! Stop! Talk about something else!"

"What?"

"I don't care! Anything else!" She grinned and looked to Darcy for help. "Will! Tell me about your tattoos," she chuckled.

Richard wiggled his shoulders and leered. "Oh yeah, Will, tell her about the lyre."

Elizabeth and Charlotte laughed, and even Darcy smiled as he slowly unbuttoned the top three buttons of his shirt and pulled it aside. "This?" he said confidently.

Elizabeth and Charlotte giggled and clapped. Charlotte asked, "Did they spike our drinks?"

"We're just punchy from the bus," Elizabeth replied playfully. She looked back to Darcy. "So why a lyre?"

"It's the lyre of Orpheus," Darcy explained.

"Orpheus is Darcy's personal myth," Richard added in an affected voice.

Darcy's eyes flicked to Richard and fixed him with an annoyed look before he turned back to the girls. "Orpheus was the son of Apollo, the sun god, and Calliope, the Muse of epic poetry," he explained. "His father gave him a lyre, and his music was magical in its power. It could move trees and rocks, as well as affect people. He traveled with the Argonauts—"

"That would be us," Richard interjected.

"To retrieve the Golden Fleece, and he overcame the sirens—"

"Oh, that's us!" Charlotte added, holding up her hand.

"With his playing," Darcy finished, grinning with a look of amused disbelief at Charlotte and Richard.

Elizabeth smiled. "It's a lovely tattoo, and it's a pretty unusual story behind it."

"Why is it unusual?" he asked.

"I just don't expect a rock guitar god to be familiar with classical mythology."

"When I studied literature, I never expected to be a rock guitar god," he said, dropping his voice to a more personal level.

"What did you expect to do?" she asked, intrigued.

"Work with my father, run Darcy Technologies."

"Why would you need literature for that?"

"I didn't study it for my career; I studied it for my soul."

Elizabeth paused, surprised at his admission. His contradiction puzzled her. He was so stony at times, so serious and businesslike. But then, he would say something like this, reminding her that he was a musician, an artist like her. She had found it was easier to think of him as a businessman, even though he usually behaved like an ass in that mode. When he behaved like a musician, she found him too approachable, too much like her. She found the differences between the two personalities too disquieting.

Realizing he was still looking at her, she smiled politely and turned her attention to her food.

༄

It was dark as Charlotte leaned against the wall of the hotel, watching the luggage as it was unloaded from the buses. She smiled to herself as she heard the familiar footsteps and took another drag off her cigarette.

"I was wondering," Richard said casually as he took his usual place beside her, pulled out a cigarette and lit his, "if you had any plans for tonight."

"Again?" Charlotte asked in a mockingly aggrieved tone.

"Well, you do know that I'm scared of the dark."

"I think you just don't like to sleep alone."

He smirked. "It's pretty obvious, isn't it?"

"I should get you a teddy bear," she said.

"So?" he dragged the word out.

"I think I could clear my busy schedule, somehow," she grinned.

"That's my girl." He smiled and kissed her once, while he pressed his keycard into her hand.

Charlotte smiled, grinding out her cigarette with her shoe. "I'll see you later," she purred and went back inside, sauntering for his benefit.

Richard laughed at her performance and took a long drag.

❧

Elizabeth heard the mistake, sighing just a second before Darcy's voice rang out across the stage of the empty theater. The rehearsal was not going well. Charles was a competent musician, but she was asking him to learn a lot of music under a hell of a deadline.

Nor was Darcy helping. Prowling about the stage since they began, he was all over Charles, erupting at every mistake. Elizabeth watched him as he stormed across the stage to confront Charles, and she stepped forward to block his path. "Will, please stop," she said clearly.

Darcy halted, surprised by the challenge. "He's doing it wrong."

"You think I don't know this?" Elizabeth said, a smile softening her words. "I wrote the song. I just think that yelling is not going to help."

"This isn't working," Darcy snapped.

Elizabeth could see he was concerned about the performance. "It'll work if you just step back and let me handle it."

"What are you going to do if he's not ready?" he asked, his voice low.

"He'll be ready."

Their eyes locked, Darcy's demanding assurance and Elizabeth's calmly waiting for him to yield. They stood locked in that pose until Darcy turned away and strode off the stage.

"Charles," Elizabeth said pleasantly, "come over here." They walked to Charlotte. "Let's go through just the changes again; it's always down by a fifth, okay?"

Charlotte lightly tapped out a rhythm while Elizabeth and Charles went through the chord changes of the song. Elizabeth didn't sing but instead called out the notes to Charles. They made it through once perfectly, and Elizabeth immediately insisted they repeat it. After three repetitions, Elizabeth declared they would try it with the words and they resumed their places onstage.

This time the song was successful. When they were done, Alex and Richard clapped for them, but Charles turned to Elizabeth with a look of dissatisfaction.

"It doesn't sound like the way Jane plays it."

Elizabeth frowned. "Oh, that's because she does a hammer-on to add a little trill." She put her guitar on the stand and held out her hands. "Here."

Charles passed over his Stratocaster bass and she demonstrated the technique. "See?" Charles nodded. "It's not that important to the song. Jane just added it 'cause she was bored," Elizabeth explained jokingly, and then looked up to find the dark face of Darcy staring down at her.

"You play bass?" he said coldly.

"Yes," Elizabeth answered, puzzled but not intimidated.

"Why didn't you tell me?"

"Why should I?"

"Because if I had known, I could have played guitar for you and we wouldn't be in this situation."

Elizabeth closed her eyes for a long time. "Yes, you make a good point," she conceded slowly. "But we'd be in a similar situation, the difference being that you would be learning the songs and I would be playing an instrument that I am less comfortable with." She sighed and shrugged. "I think this is a better solution, frankly."

Darcy studied her. Something had clicked when she said "less comfortable," not "less familiar" or "less proficient." He realized then that she was also nervous about tonight and immediately backed down. "Sorry, Lizzy. You're right," he apologized as he began to walk away.

"Will," she called out to his back. He turned to see her smiling to him. "Thanks for the offer."

He nodded once and moved off the stage. Elizabeth nodded at Charles and Charlotte and they began the song once again. When they finished, Elizabeth was disturbed to find Mr. Collins approaching her.

"I want a word with you, now," he glared at her. Elizabeth looked to Alex with a look that said, "What now?" Alex held up his hands and shook his head.

Elizabeth put her guitar down and followed Collins off the stage. "I am dismayed by your behavior, Lizzy. Who do you think you are, talking to Mr. Darcy like that? May I remind you exactly *who* is the star here? He could have you off the tour like that." He snapped his fingers. "I very much doubt he appreciated being spoken to in such a manner!"

Elizabeth pushed images of bodily harm being inflicted on Collins away. "Mr. Collins, what I think he doesn't appreciate is you taking my time away from a very important rehearsal," she told him coolly. She looked to see the subject of their discussion watching them, his lips drawn into a thin line, and embarrassed, she turned and walked back to the stage.

As she knew they would, by five o'clock Elizabeth, Charlotte, and Charles had the set together. Elizabeth went to take a well-earned break and to find something to eat while Faust ran the sound check for Slurry.

Grabbing a plate from the hospitality table, Elizabeth found a quiet corner in the green room and sat down. Her lips curled into a smile as familiar hands began rubbing the tension out of her shoulders. "Hey," she said softly.

Alex hushed her. "Don't talk, don't think, just relax."

Elizabeth nodded and followed his directions, letting him work out the knots in her muscles. After a while, she felt limp and relaxed. Alex stopped and sat down next to her, eating the food off her plate.

"Stop that," she muttered, slapping his hand away. "Get your own food." She looked at Alex, recognizing the pathetic look he gave her, and passed over her plate with a sigh. "You better get me more."

"I will," he mumbled, his mouth full.

Elizabeth stretched out her arms and rolled her shoulders. "So, how are we doing?" she asked.

Alex tilted his head, considering. He was easily recognizable as Charlotte's brother. They shared a similar build, though he was six inches taller. They had similar nondescript features and coloring, and like Charlotte, it was Alex's personality that made him truly unique. He had a wonderful head for business and a love of music that had kept him alive in a tough industry. "Well, the good news is that 'Everything You Are' is in the top ten, and it looks like the video will make *Top 20* sometime next week."

"But the bad news is that Jane is injured, so she can't perform our big hit," Elizabeth finished for him.

"That's about the size of it," he said as Elizabeth sighed. "Don't worry,

Lizzy; it's simply bad timing. It's not even a serious setback, really. In a week everything will be fine, and in fact, I think we've got much more name recognition because of the injury."

Elizabeth turned her head to look at him squarely in amazement and laughed. "Only you! Only you could take Jane's concussion and find something good in it."

"I'm the eternal optimist, aren't I?"

Elizabeth nodded. "Yes, you are." She paused to take a sip of water. "About Mr. Collins," she began.

"Lizzy, don't worry about him. We have to tolerate him, but I think you put him in his place today."

Elizabeth frowned, her eyes thoughtful. "But what if he is right? What if Will was offended by what I said?"

"Lizzy! Since when have you cared about other people's opinions?"

Elizabeth looked at him and frowned. "I guess since it meant possibly losing our tour."

"Lizzy, remember, they need LBS as much as you need them. And frankly, I think you are right. Darcy is much more concerned about the show being okay than about you mouthing off to him, especially when he deserved it." He put his arm around her shoulder and pulled her tight. "Don't worry, it'll be fine," he told her as he kissed her hair.

She looked at him and smiled gratefully. "You're right. Thanks."

Alex nodded. "It's my job, handling you temperamental divas. Now finish eating, then get cleaned up and dressed."

❧

As Elizabeth walked to her place for the meet-and-greet, she could tell something was different. It wasn't just the obvious lack of Jane, as they had decided Jane would stay out of public view until she was stronger.

But there was more. The number of people who wanted to talk to LBS had been steadily increasing, but overnight it had multiplied. The quantity of people who knew her name and asked about Jane's condition staggered Elizabeth. She signed more autographs and posed for more pictures than ever before.

At one point a tall man with blue eyes approached her carrying a large bouquet of yellow roses. "Oh, are these for Jane?" she asked, slightly surprised.

"No, they're for you," the man said smilingly. "I'm a huge fan of yours, Lizzy."

"Thank you!" Elizabeth said, delighted. She stopped to smell the beautiful blooms before putting them down. "It's a pleasure to meet you," she said, offering her hand.

"I'm Lewis," the man said, shaking her hand.

"Lewis?" Elizabeth repeated the name thoughtfully. "Have I emailed you?"

"You remembered?" He laughed. "I'm very flattered."

"I don't get as much email as you might think," Elizabeth deferred charmingly.

"You know, I'm really impressed that you actually take the time to answer your fans."

Elizabeth laughed. "I'm just so delighted when anyone likes our music enough to take the time to write us."

As she talked to the attractive man, Elizabeth was entirely unaware that she was being watched. Darcy was staring at her, watching her every smile and laugh with increasing unease.

Finally Elizabeth offered her hand again, signaling the end of the conversation, and standing on her toes, offered Lewis a kiss, which he gladly accepted.

Smiling shyly, Lewis reached into his pocket. "I've never done this before, but you're even more beautiful in person." He pulled out a key-card to the hotel. "Can I give you this?" he asked politely.

Elizabeth could feel her face turning red. "Oh, thank you," she ducked her head, embarrassed, "I've never received this kind of offer. Um, I'm flattered, but we are leaving tonight, right after the show." She laughed nervously. "I can't."

"Take it anyway, as a memento. You know, your first groupie," Lewis grinned good-naturedly.

Elizabeth smiled back and accepted the card. "Maybe next time?" she said as she gave him another kiss.

❧

Darcy was aware of pain in his arm. The pain flared again and he realized that Richard was hitting him, hard. "Hello? Earth to Darcy?"

"Stop," he snapped.

"Nice of you to join us," Richard quipped. "What is your problem?"

"Nothing," Darcy growled as he watched the man move away from Elizabeth. He was shocked at the jealousy he felt. He thought he was going to bolt across the room when he saw that stranger pull out his keycard. The only thing that stopped him was the question: "And do what?" He had no right to interfere with Elizabeth's relationships with anybody. Spitefully, he wondered if she regularly slept with her fans. He didn't know.

Taking a deep breath, he admitted to himself that she didn't sleep around. He had watched her closely enough to know that, at least. But he was deeply disturbed, not so much by what he saw but by his own reaction to it.

Darcy had never been so glad to see the end of a meet-and-greet. The fans were being led away and he was entering the green room when he saw Alex stop Elizabeth. "Make sure you are extra pretty tonight, Lizzy; the press is here."

Elizabeth's eyebrows disappeared into her hair. "Oh!" she exclaimed. "Okay, no problem." And she moved off to her dressing room.

Darcy stopped Alex by blocking his exit with his body, anger coming off him in waves. "Don't do that to her," he said in his lowest voice.

"Do what?"

"She's nervous and you're making it worse."

"She's not nervous; she's fine," he snarled defiantly as he pushed past the taller man. "And, Darcy, don't *you* do that to her either."

Darcy scowled at him, retreating to his personal hideout: the instrument area. He was not surprised to find Elizabeth there as well. He watched her walk back and forth, her guitar cradled tightly in her arms, talking softly to herself. Darcy observed her long enough to realize she was talking herself through the set.

She wore her concert outfit, the sleeveless green shirt with the low cowl neckline and black jeans. Her face was pale, and her eyes were wide and troubled. Why was he the only one to see she was clearly in a panic? Not that he was surprised. It was completely natural; she had fans out there, the press was there, she was performing a new set she had barely rehearsed, and she was going on without Jane. Darcy was impressed that she had held it together as well as she had so far.

He was tempted to talk to her to try to reassure her, but then he thought about what he knew of her personality, and he had a better plan.

"Are you ready?" he said abruptly.

Elizabeth's head jerked up. She hadn't noticed him watching her. "Yes," she said distantly as she visibly pulled herself together. "I'm ready."

"I hope so. I wasn't sure if you could play without Jane," he said coldly. "After all, she is the pretty one, and that's what your fans care about, right?"

Darcy could see he had hit the target as her mouth dropped open. He casually turned away and muttered, "At least I know that Charles will get a rise from them."

"How dare you?" she sputtered. Darcy smiled to himself before changing his expression to a scowl as he turned to face her. "Who the hell do you think you are?" she ranted.

Oh yeah, get a real good mad on for me. He closed the distance between them and got into her personal space, their noses almost touching. "I am Fitzwilliam Darcy. I'm the man every single one of those people came to see, and don't you forget it, Lizzy."

"You arrogant fuck!" she seethed.

"Jealousy doesn't become you, Lizzy. If you want to get ahead, you might want to try Jane's method," he sneered.

Darcy watched as her eyes got even larger. Before she could reply, Alex called her to the stage.

Elizabeth was too angry to say anything further to Darcy. She stormed onto the stage and directly into her first number, playing with a passion that bordered on violence.

She got through the set perfectly and was even able to cover up Charles's occasional stumbles. With a bright smile and a wave, she left the cheering of her fans and went directly to the instrument area.

"There you are," she announced as she closed in on him. "What the fuck was that about?" she snapped.

Darcy grinned guiltily. "You've got a hell of temper, Lizzy; I just helped you use it."

Realization dawned on her. "What? You said those things *on purpose!* Why?" she demanded.

"I knew you were nervous, performing solo for the first time," he said softly. "I also knew if I got you mad at me, you would charge right out there and be okay."

"*You* are the most arrogant man I have ever—"

"It worked, didn't it?" he asked as he put on his sunglasses.

"Bastard," she huffed as she turned away.

"Don't I get a kiss before going on?" he asked her retreating back.

The finger was her response. He laughed to himself as he moved in the opposite direction toward the stage.

~

Elizabeth went about her usual routine: cleaning and securing her guitars, showering and dressing, all the while a fierce dialogue was running in her head. When she ran out of things to do, she found herself with Jane before the banks of monitors.

Someone had brought Jane a chair, and she was smiling as she watched Charles. It was a private smile, as though she held a deep secret within. Elizabeth could make some guesses as to what that secret was, but she decided not to force Jane's confidence. Instead she stood behind her and watched the show.

While Jane seemed peacefully content, Elizabeth was anything but. She watched Darcy playing his music confidently, with what appeared to be complete indifference, and she returned to her boil. *How dare that man do that to me!* She fumed. *What gives him the right? I was nervous, yes, but I was fine! He had no business interfering! Arrogant fuck! Control freak who thinks he has the right to bully everyone on the stupid tour!*

By the time the set was over, she was ready for him. She moved with cold deliberateness to the place she knew she would find him. The instrument area was dark, and she waited there like a viper.

She didn't surprise him. He came in, a towel draped over his shoulder, his body pumped and hard. He saw her there, her eyes glittering in the darkness. "Lizzy?" he acknowledged.

"My friends call me that," she said coldly.

"Still pissed," he observed as he knelt down and carefully put his Paul Reid Smith back in its case. The shining black of the guitar body flashed in the low light against his body.

"Oh, I am way beyond pissed, thank you," she told him, her voice quivering with rage.

He looked at her a long moment, his eyes unshielded for once, but his expression closed. Carefully he turned back to his custom Martin and stored that away too. Then he rose to his feet before her.

"I did what I thought was best, Elizabeth," he said in his low, deep voice.

Elizabeth could smell the sweat coming off him. She was reminded again, up close, just how tall he really was, but she didn't care. "What you thought best," she sneered. "Well, thank God for that!" she added sarcastically. "Thank God we have the great and perfect Fitzwilliam Darcy, who always knows what is best for everyone!"

Darcy took a step closer and then froze as the sounds of the people around them interrupted him. "Perhaps we could continue this discussion in a more private place," he said coldly.

Elizabeth took a step back and gestured with her hands toward the dressing rooms. Wordlessly Darcy indicated her to go first and he followed her body, which was tight with anger, through the backstage labyrinth to the dressing area.

Elizabeth was through with polite smiles. She was going to tell him what she thought of him once and for all, and she was going to wipe that self-satisfied smirk off his face if it was the last thing she did! She opened the first door she came to and flung it back. She turned to enter the room and stopped short, gasping.

She heard Darcy's astonished "Shit!" above her as he saw what she was gawking at. Before her were Richard and Charlotte, both completely naked and joined in a most intimate embrace. Her butt was resting on the counter, her legs locked around his hips, which were pounding into her, as their mouths were joined in a hungry kiss.

Elizabeth leapt forward, grabbed and closed the door tightly, her chest heaving as if she had just run a mile. With wide eyes she stared at Darcy before she dropped her gaze and silently rushed out into the hot southern night and the safety of her tour bus.

❧

"Jane?" Charles called. She sat in his dressing room and turned with a bright smile. He had changed out of his concert outfit and was wearing instead shorts and a T-shirt. His hair was still damp from his shower.

She held out her arms to him and let herself be wrapped up tight to him. "I was waiting for you," she said softly in his ear. "You were wonderful tonight, Charles."

Gently, he placed his forehead against hers, their noses rubbing. "I missed you, sunshine," he told her softly.

"I missed you too," she sighed. "I hate being sidelined like this. I can't wait until I'm better."

His hand slid down from where it was resting at the small of her back to lightly caress the curve of her ass. "Neither can I."

She giggled softly and Charles regarded her, his face enchanted and curious. "What's making you laugh, darling?" he asked her.

"I was just thinking about how special you are. How different you are from any other man I've been with."

"I like the sound of that," he grinned. "How so?"

Jane ducked her head. "Well, you're the first man who ever told me he loved me before he slept with me."

"The first?" he asked disbelievingly.

Jane nodded. "And when they would say it, they always used it to get something from me," she frowned prettily, "like more sex."

He looked at her, his blue eyes sober as he realized what she was saying. He took her hands in his, waiting until she looked up at him. "Those men never loved you, Jane, not like I do."

"How do you know?" she asked, her voice tiny.

"Because if they did, they never would've let you go."

Jane's eyes watered at the certainty of his words. He pulled her close to him again, locking her safe in his embrace, nuzzling his cheek against her hair. "When the time is right, dearest, I'll show you what love is."

Jane smiled and kissed him. "Dearest love?" Charles said softly.

"Hmm?" Jane replied, her head resting on his shoulder, her lips tingling from his kisses.

"Could we please not talk about your others until after, uh, we, um, you know?" Jane looked up to see his face unhappy and embarrassed at the same time. "I'm not trying to criticize you or anything, I just, um, I just can't take it yet."

Jane reached up her hand to caress his face reassuringly. "There were no others, Charles," she said solemnly. "You were right. No one has ever loved me, or been loved by me, before you."

His eyes closed as his face softened to an expression of gratitude and he pressed her to his body. "My Jane, my beautiful Jane," he whispered over and over to her. He was again surprised at the intensity of the love he felt for her, and his heart felt like it would bust out of his chest as he realized she returned his love. He promised himself he would protect his delicate beauty, that she would never be alone, or hurt, again.

CHAPTER 8

Elizabeth stood in the crowded dining room, waiting in line for breakfast, watching Jane and Charles. They sat together, as they always seemed to lately. Although Elizabeth knew she could join them, she didn't see the point. Jane's attention was completely captured by the man she sat next to. Elizabeth felt a jab of envy at how Jane had become utterly enraptured with Charles, and he with her. Elizabeth couldn't help but wish that she too could fall so deeply in love. Elizabeth knew, however, that it wasn't going to happen. Oh, she believed in love, and at times she wished she had a relationship, but past experience had taught her that love and career didn't mix.

Elizabeth saw that she was not the only one observing Jane and Charles. Caroline stood in the next aisle, watching the couple with a similar expression.

She waited until Caroline's eyes met hers, and she shared a small half grin of commiseration. Caroline, for her part, looked surprised and then gave a nod of thoughtful gratitude, and the two women each found their own seats.

Elizabeth was purposefully avoiding Darcy that morning. She found she couldn't look at him. She wasn't angry with him anymore; rather she was ashamed of herself. Each time she saw Darcy now, all she could think of was how she had felt at that moment the night before, when they had found Charlotte and Richard in the dressing room. She was appalled by her own urges; she had wanted desperately to be fucked, and fucked by Darcy, right then and there. *She* wanted to be the one having a post-show quickie in that dressing room. Elizabeth was mortified at the idea that he might have guessed her thoughts. She resolved that the only way to get through the day was to speak to him as little as possible.

Later that day during sound check, a beautiful woman entered the room and walked onstage as Elizabeth sat offstage, warming up on her guitar. She was Elizabeth's height but willow thin, with shining black hair tumbling down her back and tiny, delicate features, enhanced by her pale ivory skin. She wore an expensive-looking red suit that complemented her figure and coloring and made Elizabeth feel grungy in her shorts and T-shirt.

Elizabeth watched, fascinated, as the woman walked straight to Darcy, who took her into his arms in a tight embrace. "Amy!" he said, his voice surprisingly happy. "Good to see you. Come on." Smiling, he led the woman offstage and toward his dressing room.

"Well, we won't see him for a while," Richard commented idly.

"Who was that?" Charlotte asked.

"Oh, that's Amy. She and Will go back a long, long way." He shrugged and turned. "Ronnie," he called out, "can you take Will's place for the sound check?"

Elizabeth looked down at her instrument until her features were under control. She was bewildered by the power of the emotions assaulting her. She felt hurt, betrayed, and disappointed. At the same time, she was disgusted at her own stupidity. Did she really think that Darcy was some kind of monk? Elizabeth had noticed that Darcy never bothered with groupies, and it had been a source of comfort to her, but did she really think the man had no sex life?

Elizabeth swallowed her disappointment and locked her hurt away. There was nothing more to be done. Any secret hopes or fantasies she might have harbored in her breast were banished. She had the dubious comfort of being certain where she stood in his regard. She was right where he had told her she was: a pretty girl with a nice voice, who was very talented.

She was surprised at the bitter hurt that she felt. When had she even thought about Darcy romantically? Elizabeth told herself that it was best this way. She was focused on her career, and getting involved with Darcy would only complicate achieving her goals. She walked to the green room and lost herself in playing her guitar.

❧

The next evening, Jane appeared at dinner, hand in hand with Charles. Elizabeth noticed that for the first time she was wearing her concert outfit and instead of the white bandage Elizabeth had grown used to, there was a smaller flesh-toned one on her forehead.

"Jane! You look great!" Elizabeth said sincerely. Jane smiled shyly and let Elizabeth hug her.

"Jane said she wanted to do the meet-and-greet tonight," Charles explained softly.

"Really?" Charlotte exclaimed, hugging Jane.

"That's wonderful," Elizabeth grinned. "Are you sure you are up for it?"

Jane smiled. "Yeah, I'm ready." Elizabeth noted the way she squeezed Charles's hand but said nothing. "You've been telling me about how everyone has been asking for me and, besides, I'm getting really bored with hiding out in the dressing rooms."

"You look great, Jane," Richard added warmly, and Jane smiled with real pleasure.

"Thanks, you have all been so good to me."

The meet-and-greet was set up differently that night. Instead of the two tables set on opposite sides of the room, the Slurry and LBS tables were put at a right angle to each other and Charles and Jane were careful to be positioned next to each other at the apex.

LBS had long ago adopted Slurry's practice of standing in front of the tables to greet their fans, rather than hiding behind them. It was a small thing, but it made it much easier for the fans to feel as though they connected with the stars when they could touch them.

When the fans entered, Slurry had the unusual experience of being practically ignored, as everyone wanted first to meet Jane. Elizabeth watched Jane carefully with a sense of worry. Jane had grown very quiet as they got ready, but once people started talking to her, shaking her hand, and telling her how they admired her bravery, the smiling, gracious Jane was back and Elizabeth relaxed.

Her eyes traveled to where Darcy was standing and she watched him observing Jane as well. She watched as he seemed to reach a similar conclusion about Jane and then his eyes met hers. They were both satisfied that Jane was okay. Elizabeth had time to raise one eyebrow in acknowledgment, which he returned with a slow nod, before they were both distracted by admirers seeking their attention.

A few days later, Elizabeth was in the green room practicing alone when she heard Mr. Collins's high-pitched nasal voice call her: "Lizzy!"

Elizabeth sighed. It had been five days since Collins had joined the tour, and he had made a point of speaking to her every single day. Elizabeth was sick of it.

At first he had criticized her. He was disappointed that Elizabeth wouldn't play "Everything You Are," even though it was Jane's song, and he was embarrassed by the way Elizabeth had spoken to Darcy. Then, after Elizabeth had proven herself onstage, he fawned over her, offering "helpful little suggestions," which made her want to heave.

"Lizzy," he said again, "I'd like to have a word with you."

Carefully arranging her face into a polite smile, she said, "Yes?"

Collins smiled, showing a row of disturbingly perfect teeth. "I wanted to take a moment to tell you how proud I am of your work this week," he told her, his voice oozing with flattery. He placed a hand on her upper arm and Elizabeth tried not to flinch. "You've really saved the day, and you should know that Ms. de Bourgh has noticed as well." He winked. "If you play your cards right, Lizzy, this could lead to a solo career."

Elizabeth struggled to keep her smile as she discreetly moved her arm away from his grip. "Thank you, Mr. Collins, but I'm really not interested in a solo career," Elizabeth told him for the eighth time that week. Collins couldn't get it into his head that someone might actually want to be in a band.

"Please, call me Bill." He smiled again. "Now I have to be honest with you, I've been watching you, Lizzy, for a long time. I'm sure you've noticed, haven't you? A smart girl like you."

Elizabeth's smile faded and she lifted an eyebrow in puzzlement. "Oh?"

"You know I have always admired your musical talent, Lizzy, but I can't deny that lately I have been feeling something more for you."

Elizabeth's eyebrow dropped. "Oh."

"You don't need to act surprised, Lizzy. I won't hold it against you. I know you are a good girl, and you would never pursue me for the benefits I could bring to your career. You're an artist, and I respect that," he said conceitedly.

"Mr. Collins," Elizabeth began.

"Bill! Bill, Lizzy, please, call me Bill," he said with forced sincerity.

"Bill," Elizabeth said the word awkwardly, "I'm afraid you misunder-stand, or I misunderstand—"

"All right, Lizzy," he said with a patronizing smile, "I'll spell it out for you." He took her hand and leaned closer. "I've been watch-ing you for a long time, and I've become completely smitten with you. You are a very beautiful girl, Lizzy; you've stolen my heart." He smiled at her sickeningly.

Elizabeth eyes grew huge as she forced herself to accept his meaning. "What? Mr. Collins! I–I'm shocked!"

"Really, Lizzy? Did you really not know?" he asked mischievously.

"Not at all!" She was horrified. "I'm sorry, but I really, I mean, this is so unexpected and, and, what about our professional relationship?"

"Lizzy, you sweet thing, I see I have overwhelmed you with the power of my passion," he tut-tutted her. "Don't worry, my dear, I'll make sure this doesn't get out. Actually, this can only help your ca-reer," he added thoughtfully. "After all, I have so many connections, and I am on very close terms with Lady Catherine herself," he added confidentially. "I know that you want to make the most of your career. I'll make sure that you get only the best: song rotations, video shoots, TV appearances."

He looked at her with a smug confidence that disgusted and appalled her. She was dumbfounded. "Why me?" she asked both the man in front of her and God.

"Well, isn't it obvious, Lizzy? The road is a very lonely place and I've become entranced by your talent. Not to mention the fact that Jane is already with someone else—"

"Excuse me!" Elizabeth exclaimed quickly, ignoring his protests. "Mr. Collins, I have to stop you. I'm sorry, but I do not want a relation-ship with you, I never have."

"Lizzy, it's all right. I can see what the problem is. I know you don't want to damage your reputation, but don't worry. I assure you, no one will think less of you for our love."

"Mr. Collins, you are not listening. I do not want a relationship with you. Not now, not ever!" Forcing her mouth shut to keep from saying any more, she stormed away from him and locked herself in her dressing room.

She sat down in a chair and didn't move for a full five minutes, outraged. She was shocked that he could have said such things. As she recalled their conversation, her astonishment grew. To think that she would fall for such an obvious line! And the fact that he didn't even have the decency to pretend that she wasn't his second choice after Jane!

The more she thought about it, the angrier she became. How dare he think he could bribe her with offers of song rotations and video shoots! Did she honestly come across as that easy? What did she have to do to be taken seriously as a musician?

Her anger grew, not only at Collins but also at Darcy and any other man who thought that she would pawn herself out for her career. She had not been lying that first night of the tour. She would do what she had to do to succeed; she would play whatever skanky club or travel as long as she must, but she'd be damned before she tried to sleep her way to the top. She was going to make it on her music or not at all.

When the time to perform came, she squared her shoulders and walked out of her dressing room. Claiming her guitar, she took the stage, where she proved to herself and everyone there that she was talented in her own right and that she would never be anyone's whore.

❧

Darcy watched the monitors, transfixed by what he saw. Elizabeth had impressed him all week as she had performed her solo show, but tonight was significantly different. Tonight she was on fire. There was a passionate energy about her that was so bright, it was almost painful to watch. He had no idea what inspired her, where her fire came from, but he wanted it, he wanted her. He wanted to capture her energy and pull it deep inside. She had never been beautiful or more desirable than right now.

When she came off the stage, he was in the instrument area, preparing. She came in with the energy of the show still around her, flashing in the darkness like light glinting off the blade of a knife.

"Elizabeth?" He had not used "Lizzy" since their fight.

"Darcy," she answered coolly.

"You were outstanding tonight," he told her, feeling suddenly embarrassed in her cold gaze. "I just wanted to tell you."

Elizabeth watched him, her calm exterior revealing nothing of the turmoil she felt inside. Her heart leapt at the words of praise that were so uncommon from him, yet her head told her he was just like the others, seeing her as someone who would sell out at the first decent offer. "Thanks," she said quietly as she turned her attention to her instrument. Her guitars, as least, had never disrespected her. "By the way, Darcy…" she said in a very remote voice.

"Yes?" he responded, trying to disguise the surge of hope he felt.

"Next time you are speaking to your *good* friend Lady Catherine de Bourgh, you might want to mention to her that Bill Collins is trying to trade professional favors for sex," she said, somehow managing to make it sound as if she were insulting him.

He stood there in shock, wanting to reach out to her, to say something, anything, but she clearly wasn't interested. "I… I'll do that, Elizabeth," he said, his low voice even softer than usual.

It was as if she did not even hear him. She closed the case and stood, walking away without even a glance at him.

Darcy watched her silently, his emotions churning. He swore to himself that something would be done. He'd be damned if he let Collins do something like that on *his* tour, especially to her.

He frowned as he thought of Elizabeth. It was as though she hadn't heard him speak when she left him. Darcy felt as if they were no longer on the same planet. All the warming between them he had tried to build up during the tour was destroyed. He felt that Elizabeth was farther from him than she had ever been.

It didn't matter, he told himself, she'd never really cared for him. She had made that clear from the start of the tour, and he was a fool to think he could ever change her mind. In a dark mood, he took the stage to play that night, and later both the audience and Elizabeth were impressed with the expressiveness of his performance.

❧

Jane looked up and laughed. Charles stood before her, wearing jeans and a T-shirt with JANE emblazoned across the front in large letters.

Charles smiled back brilliantly. "You approve?"

"I do," Jane said. "But I think you are missing an apostrophe S at the end."

Charles made a show of looking at the shirt. "Oh, so I am. Silly me." He looked back at her, taking her into his arms. "I'll have to change that tomorrow."

Jane nodded. They both knew that tomorrow she would see the

doctor and most probably would be allowed to return to work. She had no feelings about it though. The whole topic left her completely numb.

"What are you thinking about, sunshine?" Charles asked, his voice warm in her ear.

"Tomorrow," Jane said simply.

"You know you don't have to go back if you aren't ready."

"I know," Jane nodded, her eyes finally meeting his. "But I'm not sure how I feel, really." She frowned thoughtfully. "I know I'm sick of doing nothing, and I hate missing out on all the excitement when my song is doing so well." Charles nuzzled her hair as she spoke, absently. "Did you know 'Everything You Are' was on *Top 20* today?"

"No," he grinned, his voice pleased.

Jane nodded. "It didn't rank, but they named it as being close and showed a clip."

"That means you'll rank next week," Charles told her authoritatively. "Maybe we can fly up to New York on our day off and you can do a spot on the show."

"Really?"

Charles nodded. "It'd be a good time for that. Give the song a boost. I'm sure Alex and Collins are working on it."

"What happened to Mr. Collins, anyway?" she asked, puzzled. "Why did he leave so suddenly?"

Charles shrugged. "Will said he had some business in the New York office." He smiled and rubbed his face against hers. "Where you will be going soon, and I would be honored to fly with you, my lady."

Jane smiled back luminously and kissed him slowly, her mouth delighting in the taste of him. They kissed until Jane could feel him becoming erect against her, then she stopped and pulled back, resting her head on his shoulder. "Sorry," she muttered.

Charles shook his head. "No worries, angel. You can't help the fact that you are the sexiest thing I've ever seen."

Jane smiled and blushed. "You know, Charles, I am feeling better."

He drew in a deep breath and blew it out. "I can see that," he told her, his hand slipping down to lightly pinch her bottom, prompting a giggle. "But you are still not all better until the doctor says so and—" he raised his voice a level, cutting off her protest. "We are kind of lacking in suitable locations, my dear."

Jane's expression fell and she nodded, conceding his point.

Charles placed a hand on her cheek and lifted her face to his. "Tomorrow," he kissed her forehead, "you see the doctor," he kissed her left eyelid, "and," right eyelid, "we," right cheek, "will be," chin, "staying," left cheek, "in a hotel." He paused and kissed her lips lightly. "Then, my love, we will be able to see exactly how much better you are feeling."

Jane grinned and squeezed him tightly. "I'm looking forward to that, Charles."

"Me too, sunshine." He let her go and picked up his bass. "But now, I've gotta go be you. Will you watch me?"

Jane nodded and walked with him to the monitors, where Alex was giving Elizabeth and Charlotte their ritual pre-concert kiss. Alex shrugged and gave Charles a loud smacking kiss on the lips as well, prompting laughter from everyone on the floor.

Jane waved as the people she loved the most left for the stage, and she knew that she was ready to join them.

❧

The next evening the tension backstage was so thick even the techs were noticing it. Jane clutched her bass to her body, her face nearly as white as the instrument, as she walked back and forth. Charles hovered around her protectively until she finally became flustered with him, and Elizabeth had to send him off on errands to give Jane some space. The visit to the doctor had gone well. Jane's sutures were removed and she had received the all-clear to go back on stage.

It was decided it would be best for Jane to start by just playing for Elizabeth the first few nights, before LBS went back to their old set.

The rehearsal went flawlessly. Jane had played with her usual precision and, truth be told, Elizabeth felt better than she had all week having her sister back with her. Charles was a good replacement, but he wasn't Jane.

Now Elizabeth watched Jane pacing nervously in the green room, and she frowned. Her eyes wandered to Darcy's and she saw her concern mirrored in his eyes.

His eyes focused on hers, silently questioning her about Jane. Elizabeth thought for a moment, then put her plate of food down and rose, taking Jane by the arm and leading her away to their dressing room.

"What's wrong?" Elizabeth asked her, immediately cutting to the heart of the matter.

Jane could see that Elizabeth wasn't going to tolerate any attempts at denial, so she came right out with it. "I can't wear makeup."

"What?"

"The doctor said I'm not to wear my stage makeup, because of the incision."

Elizabeth's initial response was to dismiss the problem as frivolous, but she knew that would be unfair to Jane. She grinned slightly, "I thought you were worried about your playing or something."

Jane grinned back. "I know, it sounds kinda lame, but I have this routine I do before performing, you know that, Lizzy. And my makeup is part of it." Jane frowned and touched her bandage.

Elizabeth frowned in sympathy, although a piece of her wished her problems were as simple as a cut on her face. "Let's go talk to Sarah."

Sarah was Slurry's hairdresser. He was a six-foot-tall man with a goatee, heavily lined eyes, and lacquered fingernails that Elizabeth would kill for. Once Elizabeth had asked Richard about his name and she only received an indifferent shrug in reply.

Although he technically belonged to Slurry, Sarah had volunteered to help Charlotte maintain her turquoise blue hair color, then Jane's platinum blonde, and soon he was working on both bands.

Elizabeth had asked him once why he was working for a rock band when he could have his own salon, and he looked at her, cocking his head to the side. "Are you kidding me? Come on, sister. I get to run my hands all over the hair of three gorgeous men every night and get *paid* for it!"

Elizabeth liked Sarah and he had quickly become one of the "girls" with LBS, giggling with them over gossip. He was also responsible for the neatly trimmed goatee Darcy was growing, which Elizabeth thought improved his appearance even more, if possible.

When Elizabeth brought Jane to Sarah he clucked and cooed over her like a mother hen. Fifteen minutes later Jane stood up from the chair, and Elizabeth could see her confidence had returned. Elizabeth couldn't see a huge difference in Jane's looks—after all, gorgeous is gorgeous—but it was clear Jane could.

When they entered the meet-and-greet, Charles's eyes lit up when he saw his Jane looking at him with the self-assurance he had missed in her all week. He took the time to give her a long hungry look up and down her whole body, letting her know he appreciated the change. Jane looked back, her eyes returning his desire, measure for measure.

⚜

As the guests of the meet-and-greet moved away, Charlotte noticed a busty redhead of medium height remaining behind in the backstage area.

Playing a hunch, she wandered over to Richard and quietly asked, "Who's that?"

Richard looked up at the redhead, "That's," Charlotte smirked as she saw him pause for a moment, struggling to remember, "Amber," he answered finally.

Charlotte nodded her head knowingly as she carefully examined the subject of their discussion. "She's sure something. Are those real?" she asked, indicating Amber's ample bosom.

"I don't know," Richard leered appreciatively, "but I'm going to find out."

Charlotte bit down on the stab she felt inside. "You let me know, 'kay?" she said lightly.

Richard stopped and turned to her, his eyes concerned. "She's just a flavor," he said dismissively. "Why don't you find someone for tonight?"

Charlotte laughed. "I'm afraid that the guys who come back here want either Lizzy or Jane."

"So?" Richard asked. "Don't you think that most of the flavors that come back here are gunning for Darcy?" He shrugged. "But in the end, they see he is not buying, and they're happy just to bed a rock star."

Charlotte looked at him thoughtfully for a long time. "Eh, we'll see," she tilted her head and lifted an eyebrow. "I really haven't seen anything to catch my eye," she told him finally. "But you have a good time," she told him as his expression became even more worried.

He looked at her inquiringly, wondering if she was sincere. Charlotte nodded reassuringly and moved off to get wired for sound, careful to keep her face from him.

It wouldn't do to have him see the pain in her eyes caused by the lump in her throat.

⚜

Elizabeth had grown used to the roar of the crowd when she began her set. For the past week, it came when the audience recognized Charles playing on bass. But tonight, it was for Jane. Elizabeth smiled at her sister but she couldn't repress the tiny piece of her that was glad they were playing her own set tonight.

Elizabeth had always stood in the shadow of Jane's beauty. Beauty was Jane's domain, her identity. But Elizabeth had never allowed jealousy to stunt her. Jane was simply too loving and kind for Elizabeth to feel resentment toward her. And Elizabeth was intelligent enough to see that beauty came with its own price. Instead, she focused on her own gifts: her wit and her music. She trusted that she would be recognized for her own abilities and talents.

Jane understood this, both when they were growing up and tonight, as she sang and played supportively for Elizabeth, never once attempting to steal the spotlight from her.

When the set was over, Elizabeth hugged Jane tightly. The crowd was cheering for them, and then a chant began in the front left and quickly spread across the hall floor "Ev-ery-thing! Ev-ery-thing!"

Elizabeth laughed and looked at Jane, who blushed for a moment, then nodded. "Long intro, Lizzy," she whispered.

Elizabeth took her acoustic and began the introduction to the song and the crowd went nuts, screaming. It was this song they had been waiting for. "Everything You Are" was a hit nationwide and now they were going to get to hear it live.

Standing in front of the monitor, Charles Bingley jumped three feet into the air when Elizabeth began her introduction.

Jane smiled and stepped up to the microphone, "Are you listening, Charles?" she asked coyly, knowing he was watching her where she could not see him.

When he heard Jane's question Charles beamed brightly at Darcy and Caroline, and ran to the side of the stage to watch her.

Jane stood at center stage, singing to the man who loved her. She smiled glowingly as the crowd sang along with her, knowing every word. Elizabeth motioned with her head, and Jane looked to see Charles standing just offstage, his face radiant. She finished her song, looking from him to the crowd and back.

The crowd cheered in appreciation, and Elizabeth smiled with simple joy. She was so proud of Jane and so proud of LBS as a group. She looked back to see Charlotte coming from around her kit and the three women hugged and bowed, waving good-bye to the crowd as they left the stage.

When they reached backstage, a smaller but more devoted audience was waiting for them. "You did it!" shouted Alex as he picked up Jane and swung her in a circle.

"You girls were great!" Richard told them.

"Well done, Jane," Darcy said quietly.

"You were fantastic," Caroline said quickly, interrupting the scene. "Now, guys, you have to be onstage in ten minutes. Go! Go! Go!"

Darcy and Richard disappeared, while Charles stopped and took Jane tightly into his arms. "You are the most incredible woman I have ever known," he told her with unadorned honesty. "I love you." He kissed her again and left, leaving a glowing Jane behind.

❦

When the elevator stopped, Elizabeth, Charlotte, Jane, and Charles got off to find Richard, Amber, Alex, Darcy, and Caroline exiting a second one directly behind them. Elizabeth was surprised to see Richard wrapped around Amber, and she looked at Charlotte with a question in her eyes. Charlotte gave no sign but walked indifferently to her suite.

Elizabeth moved to follow when Darcy's voice stopped her. "Elizabeth?" he asked tentatively.

Elizabeth turned back to him, her expression pleasantly neutral.

"I was wondering if you would like to swim tonight?" he asked casually.

The focus of Elizabeth's eye slipped from Darcy to Caroline, who was standing just behind him. She saw a look of pain pass quickly over her face, which was replaced by a polite smile so quickly, Elizabeth questioned if she had actually seen it.

"Yeah, actually, I was planning on a swim, thanks," Elizabeth replied.

"I'll see you later then." Darcy walked to his door, leaving a confused and annoyed Elizabeth. Entering her room, she knew what was going on. He was just trying to be friendly, maintain a good working relationship. Probably trying to make up for what had happened with Collins. She grinned to herself as she remembered how she had torn him a new one that night. But why had he made a point of asking her to swim in front of everyone?

The sight of Charlotte sitting on the couch halted her thoughts. She was staring at the TV, but Elizabeth could see her eyes weren't on it. She immediately remembered Richard's guest.

"Who was that girl, Char?" Elizabeth asked.

Charlotte shrugged. "Her name's Amber; she's tonight's flavor." Her words sounded as defensive to her ears as they had when Richard had said them.

"Char," Elizabeth said slowly, dismayed, "I'm so sorry."

"Why?" Charlotte snapped, "I told you it was just a friendly fuck. There is nothing more between us, Lizzy. I don't have any claim on Richard and he certainly doesn't owe me anything."

Elizabeth grew very quiet in the face of Charlotte's outburst. "I guess I misunderstood the situation," she said after a beat. "I'm going to go swim."

Charlotte shrugged. "Suit yourself," she said as she turned back to the TV.

❧

Jane smiled brightly as she took Charles's hand and walked with him to his suite. He led her into the living area after closing the door and looked into her eyes for a long time.

Jane stared back at him with a beautiful expression, one of trust and love. Not needing anything more between them, she rose up and kissed him, long and lush, her mouth caressing his as he wrapped his arms around her slim waist and pulled her closer.

When at last they stopped, he was breathless. "Take me to bed, Charles," she murmured, her lips brushing against his throat.

"Are you sure, Jane?" he asked tenderly.

"Yes," she nodded at Charles's questioning expression. Without a word, he took her into his bedroom and shut the door. Jane eagerly flowed into his embrace. Long kisses followed as they undressed each other, becoming more impatient as they removed each garment.

Finally they were both completely bare. Jane stepped back with a wicked smile and posed provocatively as she eyed Charles.

"What are you doing?" he asked, amused.

"Taking a good look," she answered, her grin anything but innocent. "I thought you might like one, too."

"Thank you," he replied, his eyes darkening, "but I prefer to examine things close up." He moved close to her and captured Jane in the circle of his arms, his body burning wherever he made contact with hers. "See?" he asked as he kissed the line of her shoulder.

Jane nodded slowly, as her eyes closed slowly and her head tilted away giving him better access to her.

"You must be getting cold," he said softly, "better come to bed."

"I don't feel cold," Jane sighed as she crawled into the bed with him. It was a strange sensation. She had slept with him before. Being in bed with him was familiar, yet it was at the same time excitingly different and new.

Charles wasted no time. He was fully aware that Jane was finally in his bed and he had the green light to go. All the desires he had been holding back broke free with a rush. He plundered her mouth with his own and she trembled at his determination. Out of habit, her hands reached for his cock. Charles felt her grasp him and only allowed himself to enjoy it for a moment before he gently moved her hands away. At her questioning look, he told her, "Oh, no, not yet. You're too distracting."

Jane nodded and her hands slid up his body, taking the time to explore his chest and back.

Charles was working on his own exploration. His hand had started with caressing her stomach in slow smooth circles as he kissed her. Gradually, he worked his hand up to the lower edge of her breast, caressing more of it with each rotation. Jane moaned softly, which Charles took as a positive sign, and he slipped his hand farther up until he encircled the whole breast. "Perfect," he sighed against her throat as her body pressed into his.

Her nipple was already hard when his fingers reached it. With agonizing slowness, he dragged his lips to it, prompting even more moans from Jane. He kissed it once, lightly, as he looked at her with hungry eyes, then he went back, drawing it into his mouth and sucking on it gently, while his hand began circling the other breast.

"Charles," she cried.

"So beautiful," he breathed as he changed his attention to her other nipple. Jane's fingers buried themselves in his hair and held on tightly. His attention left her hardened nipples and traveled south, letting his lips and nose brush along her satin skin as he slowly surveyed her soft body until he reached the tiny golden triangle of fur over her sex. He kissed her there once, reverently, then pulled back to look at her, his eyes dark. "Are you ready, Jane?" he asked, his voice rough and sexy.

Jane opened her eyes, looking at him, not understanding his words, but willing to follow wherever he led. She nodded, her eyes never leaving his.

He moved back up to her, his face rubbing against her, his voice buzzing in her ear. "I want to make you feel very good, Jane, like you've never felt before." He lay on top of her then, but before Jane could open her legs to him, he rolled them both over, so she was on top.

"Oh!" she cried, and Charles smiled back to her then.

"Slide on, love," he gently directed her. And she did, impaling herself on his delicious cock, her eyes closing as she pushed herself all the way onto him. She reveled in the experience of him filling her, when she felt his hands on her shoulders. Startled, her eyes opened. "Trust me," he told her, his voice thick, "I'm going to teach you how to come."

Jane was confused but in no position to argue. Charles gently pushed her shoulders back until she was upright on top of him, his impressive length still buried deep inside of her. She looked down and smiled at the image of their blonde hairs mingled as one. "Now, rest your hands on my legs."

Jane did as she was bid, leaning even farther back, placing her hands behind her and balancing herself there. He placed his hands on her hips and encouraged her to move back and forth slightly. She didn't understand the purpose, and then her eyes popped open in astonishment before they locked tight again. Her movements against Charles had stimulated her and Jane could feel the stirrings of an orgasm already beginning.

He saw her reaction and smiled in a feline way. "I told you I was going to teach you how to come."

"How? What?" she mumbled incoherently.

"Shhhh, keep going. I want to watch you." He moved his hands to her breasts as he spoke and began caressing them in light circles again. Jane arched against him and soon found the sensations building to a miraculous wave.

"Oh my God!" she cried out as the pleasure overpowered her and she was racked with a powerful orgasm that left her shuddering. Charles locked his hands on her shoulders to keep her upright. She grasped his wrists with her hands as she looked at him in shocked surprise.

"That was beautiful, Jane," he told her as his eyes feasted on her. Gently he brought her forward and let her rest her head on his shoulder. Soon her panting faded and Charles tested her with an upward thrust.

Jane's breath caught. "Are you ready for more, love?" he asked, his hands stroking her bare back.

"Oh, yes," she moaned, lifting her head to look at him, her dazed look fading as she spoke. He stroked her lips with his thumb and she kissed him, her mouth hungrily working against his.

"Take me," he told her in a tight whisper.

Jane understood. She pushed herself up on her arms and began moving back and forth on his long length, producing feelings that were so different from the others, yet equally pleasurable. She watched him this time, watched his eyes close when the sensations became too strong, watched him offer himself to her.

Her body started to buck against his as the pleasure grew. Charles, his jaw clenched tightly, moved against her thrusts as their rhythm grew faster and more desperate. "Jaaaaaane," he moaned in a rising tone as he grew harder inside of her, and Jane knew he was hers. She tightened her muscles around him, prompting a gasp and strangled cry as he came. Unexpectedly, the action produced a similar effect on her, and she followed him immediately into bliss. Their bodies rocked as one until they collapsed into an exhausted heap and lay motionless for a long time.

Jane smiled dopily as she realized she was drooling onto Charles's shoulder and she didn't care. Awareness slowly returned and stiffly she rolled off him. Charles quickly turned onto his side and bundled her close to him. She started giggling as a full, unashamed burst of pure joy flowed out of her body. Charles smiled and kissed her forehead as he held her tightly.

"Did you enjoy that?" he asked, his eyes shining.

"Charles!" she exclaimed. "Oh my God! I've never... You... Wow!"

He laughed with her, delighted. Jane took a deep breath and looked at him, trying again to express her feelings. "Charles I never, ever—"

"I know," he hushed her with a kiss. "And to tell the truth, love, neither have I."

She looked at him puzzled and he sighed. "Jane, I've been with many women before. But never like that." He kissed her lovingly. "You're so special to me." He looked at her, feeling suddenly shy, realizing he had revealed so much.

Jane reached out to him, taking his face between her hands and kissed him slowly. When she pulled back to look into his eyes, she let hers fill with all the passion and love she felt for him. He smiled then, relieved and content. Jane, taking her cue, snuggled up tightly to him and rested her head on his shoulder. "Tell me," she said, tracing designs on the skin of his chest over his heart, "how did you know how to do that?"

Charles shrugged. "The women I dated before I met you. They, well, they were nothing like you." He grinned uneasily. "Anyway, while I can't say too many good things about them, I can credit them giving me an excellent education on how to please a woman."

He took in her guarded look and kissed her tenderly. "I never loved them, any of them. I thought I did, but I didn't. I loved the sex, but not them, not like I love you."

Jane smiled then, relieved. Charles looked at her, seeing the fatigue around her eyes, and he sighed, reflecting on what a long day it had been for both of them. "Come and sleep with me now, Jane," he said as he gently pulled her to a spooning position in front of him. "I'm really look-ing forward to waking up next to you."

The light clicked off, and Jane took his hand and squeezed it in the darkness. "I love you, Charles," she said softly.

"I know," he whispered back as he kissed her head good night.

CHAPTER 9

CHARLES BINGLEY ROLLED OVER. Without opening his eyes, he reached for the blonde goddess he fell asleep with the night before. She was gone. Furious patting of the bed failed to find any feel of her, and reluctantly he was forced to open his eyes.

Nothing. He was in bed alone. "Jane!" he called out, pushing the blankets away and sitting up.

"What?" Jane asked, her head appearing in the bathroom doorway, a toothbrush sticking out of her mouth.

Charles sank back down relieved. "I thought you had left," he explained.

Jane smiled consolingly. "Of course I didn't leave," she said. "I'm just getting cleaned up."

"Jane, do you remember what I told you last night?"

Jane returned to the mirror. "Uh-hum," she answered vaguely. Her eyes widened at the sight of Charles's naked body in her mirror.

He took the toothbrush out of her hand and put it down on the counter. "Spit," he ordered, and she did, into the sink. He removed the hotel bathrobe she was wearing, pleased to see her still naked underneath. "Come back to bed, Jane," he said in a voice that left no room for discussion.

"But—"

Charles calmly took her hand and led her back to the bedroom, ignoring her squeal of giggles. "I told you," he said as he gently pushed her down onto the bed, "I wanted to wake up *with* you," he continued as he crawled in beside her. "Now I'm just going to have to educate you as to why."

Before she could do more than draw breath to protest, he had his mouth firmly over hers and her body in his arms. Jane forgot what she was going to say and gleefully enjoyed her education instead.

❧

At breakfast that morning, Elizabeth was careful to sit next to Charlotte. She felt protective of her best friend, but at the same time, didn't know what more she could do. Alex took the seat on the opposite side of Charlotte, and Elizabeth observed with approval that he seemed to have the same idea.

"Morning," Darcy said easily as he sat down at their table.

The corners of Elizabeth's mouth couldn't help but curl up at the sight of him as she remembered their swim the night before. She arrived at the pool just as Darcy was undressing. Elizabeth watched him silently, observing once again that Fitzwilliam Darcy was one hell of a gorgeous man. She was able to rationalize her frank ogling by figuring that he was safe. She knew she had no chance with him, so she might as well enjoy the show.

When he caught her looking at him, Elizabeth merely lifted an eyebrow in approval. Darcy seemed taken aback to see her, but that soon changed as they both realized she was still wearing her clothes. He raised an eyebrow, signaling that it was her turn to get undressed.

Elizabeth took off her T-shirt, revealing the vivid red racer suit she wore underneath, neither rushing nor taking her time. She told herself she was merely going for a swim, as she had hundreds of times before. Darcy was nothing more than a pool buddy.

She was surprised by the splash she heard as she removed her sweatpants. Apparently Darcy wasn't as interested in watching her show as she was in his. A bit disappointed, she walked to the edge, dove in, and began her laps.

❧

Darcy was shocked when he saw Elizabeth standing there, her eyes examining his body intently. He had not heard her come in and thought he was alone. He was more than a little surprised by the look of appreciation on her face.

Although Darcy was used to women viewing him as a sex object, it was something he never had been really comfortable with. His way of dealing with it was by deliberately not thinking about it too much. However, this was completely different. If Elizabeth wanted to stare at his body, he had no problem with it.

He grinned inwardly as he realized that his generosity was about to be repaid measure for measure as Elizabeth started pulling off her T-shirt.

His eyes burned and he knew he would be replaying this scene over and over in his mind later that night. He watched as she twisted her long, thick hair with her hand and clipped it to the top of her head. He found himself swallowing hard as she bent down to remove her shoes, his eyes caressing every curve of her body.

As she sat down to remove her pants, Darcy discovered he had a problem. He had enjoyed Elizabeth's show too much, and the swim trunks he was wearing did nothing to hide that fact. He quickly walked to the pool, realizing that cold water and exertion were his only salvation.

❧

"Good morning," Elizabeth replied warmly. *See? This wasn't too hard. I can be friendly with Darcy.*

His eyes actually smiled slightly at her before he began eating. Elizabeth was snapped out of watching him when she became aware of the change in Charlotte's posture.

As Elizabeth looked to her, she heard Richard's voice ask, "Alex, could you move down one?"

Elizabeth looked from Charlotte to Alex and back. Charlotte gave her brother a silent sign and he moved, making room for Richard but looking unhappy about it.

Richard sat and poured himself a cup of coffee from the carafe on the table. "How is everyone this morning?" he asked pleasantly before taking a long sip. When he lifted his head, his eyes sought out Charlotte's.

"Just fine," Charlotte answered lightly.

"Good," Richard nodded, "good." He acted casual, but it was clear to Elizabeth that he was aware of the hostile glances he was receiving.

"So, were they real?" Charlotte asked quietly.

Richard gasped and choked on his coffee, which left him sputtering for a good thirty seconds.

Charlotte allowed herself one small smile at his expense. When Richard finally regained control, he looked back up at her. "Hum?" she prompted.

"Yes, they were, as a matter of fact," he answered glibly. "She had a tattoo, as well," he told her, placing his hand over his right breast to indicate the location. "But it wasn't as nicely done as yours," he shrugged.

Charlotte replied with an indifferent sound. "So," Richard continued, "has the honeymoon couple come down yet?"

Charlotte kicked him hard in the shin under the table, her eyes indicating Darcy. Richard mouthed "ow!" at her.

"You don't have to pretend I don't know," Darcy told them softly, his manner commanding even in this casual setting.

Elizabeth shared a look with Charlotte. "You don't have a problem with it?" Elizabeth asked, her light tone of voice softening the directness of her question.

"I didn't say that," he replied easily, taking a sip of his tea, "but I'm pragmatic. I know I have about as much of a chance of stopping Charles and Jane from being together as I do of stopping a tour bus with my bare hands."

"You didn't seem too pleased last night," Elizabeth observed.

"That was because I don't want this becoming public," he told her, looking over at Jane and Charles as they entered the dining room. "I don't think any of us want to see them on the cover of *People*, right?"

Elizabeth had to concede he was correct in that. She nodded in agreement, pleasantly surprised at how well they were getting along.

The meal progressed smoothly. Elizabeth was confused to see Charlotte behaving in her usual fashion toward Richard. They were gossiping and joking as if last night had never happened. Elizabeth didn't understand their relationship, and she worried for her friend. But it was clear that Charlotte wanted to continue the status quo, at least in public.

❧

The following Tuesday brought the last night of a long string of performances. They had been traveling and playing for nine consecutive nights, and everyone was looking forward to a break. They were relieved to know they would then have two nights to crash before starting up again. Elizabeth was simply looking forward to getting to sleep in a hotel again. It was funny, she mused, how something as simple as a private room and a real bed could come to mean so much to her, but right now, it was the height of luxury and exactly what she desired.

She mused on these thoughts as she watched Charles and the dancer for the tour practice. The exotic-looking girl wound herself around Charles in a fashion displaying her extreme flexibility. Jane had never been jealous of the girl, as it was clear that Charles had no interest in her. During their weekly hair touch-up session, Sarah had informed them that

Richard had bedded Lizbeth for a week or so during the first leg of the tour, which surprised no one.

"She was too obsessed with her own body," Charlotte had explained cryptically, when asked by Elizabeth why it hadn't lasted.

Elizabeth had been somewhat surprised to learn the name of the beautiful woman. She felt as exotic as white bread compared to the dancer in the skintight leather catsuit with whom she shared a name.

"So, tell me something," Elizabeth asked Richard and Darcy, who were standing beside her offstage clearly enjoying the show even if they had no deeper interest in the girl.

Darcy turned his attention to her immediately. Elizabeth indicated the music playing and asked, "Did Charles write that?"

Darcy and Richard looked at each other and broke out in huge grins, which showed their family resemblance. The song blaring on the playback was "Bound," a well-written, if somewhat shocking, song about sexual domination. The memorable chorus ran:

I wanna feel you smack my ass.

Elizabeth waited expectantly to be let in on the joke.

"No, actually," Darcy finally replied. "Richard wrote the lyrics, I helped with the melody."

Richard put his hand on his chest and bowed.

"Somehow I'm not surprised," Elizabeth said mockingly. "Do I dare ask why?" she grinned.

At this Richard and Darcy broke out laughing.

"What?" Elizabeth insisted.

Darcy pulled himself together. "We'll tell you, but it's a secret, okay?" He motioned her closer and placing a hand on her shoulder, said in a low tone, "The truth is we wrote it as a joke."

Elizabeth looked at him, confused.

"We wanted to see if we could get Charles to say 'Smack my ass' a half-dozen times a night," Richard chortled.

Elizabeth looked in disbelief. "I can't believe you did that," she deadpanned.

"Well, it's not all bad. After all, he gets Lizbeth writhing around him each night," Richard said, somewhat defensively.

"Yeah, except you were the one who did her," Darcy replied, chuckling.

Elizabeth was amazed. She had rarely seen Darcy so open and, well, playful. And she didn't believe for a moment that the only reason Richard wrote that song was to pick on poor Charles. Still she had to admit the image was very amusing.

"Oh, come on!" Elizabeth said with mock scorn. "This is *Slurry* after all, I thought all three of you would do her together."

Darcy made an "eww" face that Richard noticed and laughed at.

"You should know by now, Elizabeth, not to believe all the rumors," Darcy said, his tone still light, but she could see his eyes had turned serious.

Elizabeth nodded in agreement, realizing he was correct. But somehow his answer only raised more questions in her mind. She wondered where those rumors had come from. And where was the wild bad-boy party band everyone claimed they were? So far, with the exception of Richard's flavors, these guys had been the soul of respectability and professionalism.

❦

Charlotte rolled her shoulders back, talking a long drag on her cigarette. She knew that Lizzy hated her smoking in their suite, but at this point she didn't care. She stretched out on the couch, her head and fingers moving to their usual never-ending beat.

She heard a knock on the door and rolled her eyes, figuring Elizabeth had returned from her swim and had forgotten her room card again. *Honestly, hasn't the woman ever heard of pockets?*

She walked to the door, her feet continuing the rhythm that was playing on in her head. She opened the door and was turning away when she froze. The person at the door wasn't Elizabeth but Richard. Her mouth fell open for a moment as the rhythm died, and then she shut it with a snap. "What are you doing here?" she asked coolly when she regained her composure.

Richard shrugged and answered, "Muhammad, mountain, you know." He waited a moment in her silence, and then asked, "Can I come in? I'd like to talk to you."

Charlotte stepped back mechanically and pointed to the couch. Richard casually strolled over and sat down and waited for her to join him. He didn't say anything when she sat down on the chair nearby, but his eyes registered that she had not sat beside him. He gazed at her as she lit another cigarette and looked at him expectantly.

Richard took a breath, believing it would be best to be direct as possible. "I was hoping I could spend the night with you," he said with deliberate simplicity.

Charlotte felt a flash of anger with his words that ripped her control away from her. "What's the problem? Couldn't land a flavor?" she asked scornfully.

Her words hit him like a blow, but he didn't flinch. "I don't want a flavor, Charlotte. I want you," he told her sincerely. "I want to be with someone I know, someone who likes me, who isn't just sleeping with me to say that she scored a rock star. I want you, Charlotte," he repeated, his eyes beseeching hers.

Charlotte was stunned as she realized what he was asking of her. She was deeply touched but wasn't sure if she was able to accept him and what came with it. She looked away, thinking. "I don't know. This is kinda surprising."

"Char?" he asked softly, his eyes troubled.

Charlotte frowned as she tried to make sense of her feelings. "I just don't know if it would be smart. I don't know what to think, or what I am to you." She fixed him with a look, and with a voice deep with earnestness said, "I would hate to think I was just a convenient lay."

Richard's eyes flared. "No! Charlotte! You of all people should know that!" He grabbed her hand and held it tightly. "You know as well as anyone that I can get sex anywhere, but I came here because I want to be with *you*."

"But what am I to you?" she asked, her eyes demanding the truth. "Tell me, what am I? Where do I stand?"

He took the question with a seriousness that was atypical for him. "You are my friend, Charlotte. You are someone I enjoy being with. You laugh at my jokes, you tolerate my constant drumming, and you are someone I enjoy having sex with." He paused, thinking. "I'm not trying to hurt you, Charlotte, and I see that I have. If I misunderstood or misled you, I'm sorry."

"No," she said quickly. "No, you have always been," she took a deep breath, "very direct. It's me."

"Do you want to tell me what's going on?" he asked cautiously.

Charlotte looked down again. "No, it's nothing, I was just trying to make more of something than it is."

"Charlotte," he said, his voice unguarded, "don't put our relationship down. You are very special to me. You are one of the closest friends I have, and I really love being with you."

Charlotte looked at him carefully, studying his open face, fully admitting all his strengths and limitations.

"I hurt you, didn't I?" he asked softly.

Charlotte wasn't able to keep eye contact. "No, I hurt myself."

"I'm sorry, really I am. But I can't be what I'm not. It would be worse for both of us if I tried."

She grinned sadly and nodded. "I know."

Richard looked uncomfortable and started to move. "I better go then."

"Wait," she said in a firm, quiet voice. "Wait a moment. You don't have to leave."

He frowned. "Are you sure?"

She frowned thoughtfully. "I'm sure. Look, Richard, I know I can't have you for myself. Hell," she shrugged, "I'm not sure I would want you all to myself." She looked at him and smiled briefly. "But I do know that I like it when I'm with you. I like the way I feel when I'm with you, and I would rather have some time with you than not at all."

Richard looked at her silently for a long time, assessing what she had said, his face expressionless as he tried to cope with feelings that were both surprising and disturbing. He didn't understand why he felt so needy or threatened.

After a minute Charlotte smiled gently at him. "Would you still like some company for the night?"

Richard nodded slowly. "Yes, very much so," he said in a low whisper. He realized that perversely he was seeking comfort in the place that was troubling him the most, and he was amused at the irony of it.

"Come on," said Charlotte, rising, "I think we should go to your suite. I don't think Lizzy would like hearing us in the middle of the night."

Richard grinned wickedly, his good spirits returning. "Oh, I have a way of keeping you quiet."

Charlotte grinned back, recognizing the sexy tone of his voice. "And what might that be?" she asked provocatively.

"Why, by putting something in your mouth, of course."

"Oh," Charlotte sighed, her voice deep and breathy, "I think I like that idea."

❧

Long Borne Suffering and Alex left early the next morning, long before the regular morning meeting. They were flying to NYC, where they would do *Top 20*, and then they would return that evening. Charles and Caroline had been the only ones to see them off; everyone else on the tour was still in bed.

Charles turned from waving at the departing limo and faced Caroline. "No point in going back to bed. Would you like to get some coffee?"

Caroline smiled. Time alone with Charles was always a rare commodity on tour and lately it had become nonexistent, due to all the time he was spending with Jane. Together they walked to the empty dining room, filled their cups, and sat down.

"It will be weird having the morning meeting without them. I'm amazed at how quickly they've become part of the group," Caroline said easily.

"Yeah," Charles smiled his Jane smile. "They're pretty special."

Caroline looked at him, understanding everything he said and didn't say. "You seem happy."

"I am," he answered thoughtfully. "Happier than I've ever been before." He smiled at his sister. "And I have you to thank for finding her."

Caroline smiled, but it never reached her eyes. "Oh, I wanted to tell you before I forgot. I heard from Dad's lawyer. They have set a date for his hearing."

Charles face became serious immediately as he nodded.

"We're lucky. It's right after Georgie's graduation, so we'll be off that week. We can help him move back home and get settled in. I talked to Darcy and it's all set."

"Do you think he's going to get parole?"

Caroline nodded confidently. "I spoke to his lawyer and he assured me he would. It's pretty standard in cases like his."

Charles released a long sigh. "Good."

"Charles," Caroline said, her tone uneasy, "don't tell anyone."

He stared into her eyes, "You mean Jane?"

Caroline looked down and nodded. "Darcy said it's too soon, and

I agree with him. We have worked too hard to keep this quiet and I don't want this hitting the press right now, not when Dad's about to be released."

Charles frowned and nodded. "You're right," he agreed unhappily. He studied his sister. "How are you doing?"

Caroline smiled with false brightness. "I'm good. The tour is doing well, and I'm good."

Charles's face told her he didn't believe her at all. "It's hard, isn't it?"

Caroline nodded her head, her lips pressed tightly together. She was slightly surprised that Charles had noticed. She thought nothing penetrated the Jane fog, but this was Charles, the person who knew her better than anyone else. "It's hard," she admitted. "I mean, I," she paused, "I knew he didn't care for me like that, that he never would, but at least I had the consolation of there being no one else." She took a sip of coffee. "Now I have to watch him be completely obsessed with her, and it's hard."

"You know he doesn't mean to hurt you."

"I know. That makes it all the worse. He's completely oblivious to it, to me." She grinned mirthlessly. "And the sad thing is, I can't even hate her. I tried, but she's too nice. *Stupid*, but nice."

Charles shared her quick smile. "What do you think is holding them back?" he asked conversationally.

"She is," Caroline shrugged. "He is completely gonzo over her, but she doesn't seem to be aware of it. Hell, half the time she seems downright hostile toward him."

"When she's not staring at him."

"Right," Caroline agreed with a grin.

"Do you think it could be denial?"

"Maybe," Caroline replied tentatively. "I think a part of her is afraid to admit that she has feelings for him, because she doesn't know where it might lead."

Charles mulled over this. "It's scary to fall in love, sometimes. You have to give yourself over to someone, and that takes a lot of trust."

Caroline observed him, knowing he wasn't talking strictly about Lizzy and Darcy.

"But what about you?" he asked, bringing the conversation around. "Are you going to be okay?"

Caroline reached out and touched his hand. "I'm fine," she told him sincerely. "Who knows, maybe this is the best thing. Maybe now I'll be able to get over this unrequited shit and find a man who actually knows I exist."

Charles put his arm around her and pulled her close. He knew she was exaggerating; Darcy knew she existed, and that made it all the more painful that he couldn't love her.

⤴

Elizabeth hadn't seen Collins since his "proposition," and she wondered how he would act when he saw her again. She didn't know exactly what happened when he left the tour the week before. She never asked Darcy for the details and he didn't volunteer them. She worried that Collins would be hostile toward her, or worse, but she didn't have a choice, so she just hoped for the best and went ahead.

At the studio offices they were met by Nancy, the stylist who had designed their look for the tour. While Alex met with people from the marketing department, the women spent the next two hours trying on new clothes, hairstyles, and makeup.

When they emerged shortly after noon, Alex announced that he had a surprise for them. He took them to the top floor of the building and into a beautiful dining room with a breathtaking view of the city. The room was elegantly furnished, with a certain overblown quality that made Elizabeth think of the phrase "gilding the lily."

There they saw an older woman sitting with Anne de Bourgh in a large, heavy chair at a huge, dark cherry table. Bill Collins stood nearby, as if waiting on the tiny woman, and was talking in an obsequious tone when he noticed them.

"Oh, there they are!" he smiled patronizingly. He came behind the girls and escorted them to the old woman, who observed them with silent majesty.

"This is Lizzy, Jane, and Charlotte, and of course, Alex Lucas, their manager," Collins said grandly. "Ladies, may I have the exquisite pleasure of introducing you to Lady Catherine de Bourgh."

Elizabeth's face revealed none of the surprise she felt. This tiny, shriveled creature, with her carefully styled silver hair and conservative suit, this was the Gorgon that terrorized an entire industry?

She nodded to them once, then said in a crisp tone, "Elizabeth, I'd like you to sit beside me." Her voice was surprisingly strong and lightly accented. Elizabeth began to get a hint of the power she wielded.

Elizabeth took the offered seat, which Collins had nearly fallen over himself to get to and pull out for her, and smiled politely to the woman. "It's nice to meet you, Lady Catherine."

She was intrigued by the careful treatment she was receiving. Lady de Bourgh was always spoken of with awe and, sometimes, flat-out fear, and yet despite Catherine's obviously expensive tastes and imposing manner, Elizabeth had seen nothing frightening about her. Jane and Charlotte sat farther down the table, maintaining a cowed silence.

The men were seated and an elegant lunch was served. Although the tone of the conversation was deliberately kept light, Lady Catherine grilled the women about their backgrounds and their experiences on the tour, demanding to know the slightest details about their history. During this time, Collins maintained a running commentary, complimenting Lady Catherine on everything she said. His blatant sucking up disgusted Elizabeth, but Lady Catherine seemed to enjoy it, for all the marginal attention she paid to him.

When lunch was finished, Lady Catherine affected a subtle change in manner that caught Elizabeth's attention. "Elizabeth, would you please come with me." She rose from the table and moved slowly yet smoothly to the other side of the room and stood in front of the large window.

Elizabeth shared a look with Alex and joined her. "I have heard a great deal about you," Catherine said directly. "You should know that I follow what is happening with the tour very closely. Not only is Slurry my most profitable act but I am also quite fond of the band." Elizabeth was distracted for a moment with the impossible image of Richard hanging out with Lady Catherine behind the tour bus, sharing a cigarette.

"I was deeply concerned when your sister was injured." Catherine's eyes flicked to Jane and then back to Elizabeth. "But I was highly impressed by the way you were able to step in and take control of the set. That shows a professionalism and competency that is all too rare in this business." She stopped and waited imperially for Elizabeth's reaction.

"Thank you, Lady Catherine," Elizabeth answered politely. She was pleased to be receiving this attention from the head of the studio, but she wasn't going to fawn over the woman. "I believe there are many individuals who are merely in need of an opportunity to demonstrate their talents. I was happy for the chance to perform, but I have no doubt that Jane would have done just as well, had the situation been reversed." She smiled politely to the old woman.

"Indeed," Catherine observed. This was clearly not the response she was expecting. "Nevertheless, you did a great service, as the 'hero' of the day. Perhaps you've given some thought to a solo career?"

"You can't expect me to say such a thing in front of my band mates," Elizabeth replied, observing the similarities between Lady Catherine's and Collins's thoughts. "And in any case, I really don't want a solo career. I enjoy playing with my band. They are my closest friends and my greatest source of support. Beyond that, I believe that cooperatively we are able to create more interesting and enjoyable music than I ever could by myself."

Catherine's faded blue eyes stared at Elizabeth's, measuring her. "You seem quite confident, Elizabeth. That is also very rare in a young woman such as yourself."

Elizabeth wasn't at all certain that she had received a compliment; she looked pointedly at where Jane and Charlotte were talking to Anne and said, "Not in this room, Lady Catherine."

Lady Catherine walked back to her chair as she studied Elizabeth, ignoring the drone of praise that was coming from Collins. It seemed that she was resolving an issue in her head. Satisfied, she said, "Well, it's been delightful to meet you all. I hope you have a pleasant afternoon and I'm certain we'll have an opportunity to meet again." And with that they were dismissed.

Mr. Collins showed them to the elevator but did not get on with them; instead he returned to Lady Catherine's side. As the doors closed, Elizabeth could see Catherine speaking into his ear, while they were both staring at her.

❧

Waiting in the *Top 20* green room, Elizabeth was bored to tears. Jane was chatting politely with a production assistant, and Charlotte was flipping through a magazine. Elizabeth reflected that while she loved touring and the performing it brought, she had never done so much waiting in her life as she had in the last month. She thought about Slurry and how they had spent the better part of the last four years touring and wondered how they managed to stay sane.

She was pleased when the door opened and Alex came in, but that pleasure was short lived as Bill Collins followed him. Relief flowed through her when Collins ignored her and sat next to Charlotte.

"I have good news," Alex told her as he took the empty seat beside her, his hazel eyes dancing.

"What?"

"Guess who is shooting a video next month?"

Elizabeth's eyes flared open. "Us?"

Alex smiled and nodded. "Collins just told me." He leaned closer and said in a low voice, "It's for 'Can't Stop Me,' Lizzy. Your song."

Elizabeth gasped in surprise. After her meeting with Catherine, she suspected she was out of favor with the studio. "Oh my God!" she cried. "I can't believe it!"

"Believe it, Lizzy," Alex told her happily. "I've just signed the contract for a two-video deal. The tour has the three-day break next month and we'll shoot the first one then."

Elizabeth smiled brilliantly and hugged Alex then excitedly discussed the details until it was time for them to go on.

⌒✿⌒

Saturday night found them in Chicago for the first of two dates. The bands had settled into an easy routine; Jane and Charles lived days of peaceful bliss, Richard and Charlotte continued their friendly banter and occasional sexual encounters, and Elizabeth and Darcy maintained a pleasant relationship by reminding themselves constantly that they had no hope with the other.

Charlotte stood in her usual spot at the meet-and-greet. She had found to her pleasure that the only people who wanted to talk to her were other musicians, and due to this, she had enjoyed a number of interesting conversations.

But tonight did not seem to hold out any hope for her. She had already scoped out all the guests and none of them were musicians. She had also noticed Richard talking up a pretty girl who looked to be of college age, and she knew he would be busy for the night. She had been tempted to card the girl to make sure she was over eighteen but figured that with a rack like that she had to be. She sighed, frankly bored, as she signed the occasional CD case that was passed to her.

Eventually a pretty woman standing before her arrested her attention. "Charlotte?" the woman said nervously.

Charlotte smiled and nodded. "That's right."

The woman beamed. "It's so incredible to meet you!" she gushed. "My name is Dawn." She offered her hand.

Charlotte shook Dawn's hand and said, "It's nice to meet you too, Dawn."

Dawn looked as though she would melt. "I'm such a fan of yours, Charlotte. I love to watch you play; you're so strong." She looked down and blushed. "I was kinda worried it was all an image, but I see now that you are real."

Charlotte laughed. "Oh, I'm real! Sometimes a little too real for people," she shrugged, "but what can you do."

Dawn stared at her, then caught herself and smiled embarrassedly. "Charlotte, you are very pretty," she said softly.

Charlotte smiled knowingly, her suspicions confirmed. *What the hell?* "Can I kiss you, Dawn?" she asked softly.

Dawn's eyes got very huge and she nodded. Charlotte put her hand on the woman's face and gently pulled her close, letting Dawn decide how deep to make the kiss.

Darcy was signing a CD case when Richard hit him. "Wha?" he said looking up, but the word died in his throat. He hit Charles, who had a similar reaction. All three men stared across the room where Charlotte was intently kissing another woman.

Elizabeth and Jane were also just noticing. Jane opened her mouth to say something when Elizabeth stopped her with a hand on her arm and pointed to the guys staring with wide eyes and slack jaws across the room.

Jane instead looked at Elizabeth and struggled not to laugh.

Charlotte let the kiss end and, smiling, said, "Thank you, Dawn."

Dawn was blushing wildly and mumbled something before wandering away.

It didn't surprise Charlotte in the least when Richard appeared as if by magic at her elbow. "Who was that?" he asked, slightly dazed.

Charlotte grinned, fully enjoying herself. "That was Dawn. She's a fan of mine."

"She, um, she seems to really like you," he stammered. "Are you going to see her later?" he asked, trying to look innocent and failing utterly.

"If I were, I wouldn't invite you, sugar. Some things are not for sharing."

Richard didn't try to deny his interest, and she respected him for that at least, even if he was practically drooling on her shoes. "Besides," she said, "you have that pretty young thing over there. What's her name?"

"Becky."

Charlotte suppressed a snort. "Well, I'm sure that you and *Becky* will have a good time." She patted his arm in sympathy.

❦

Charlotte was already set to go, so she waited by the stage door, having a cigarette. Soon Richard took his regular place at her side and lit up.

"Where is *Becky*?" Charlotte asked mockingly.

"She doesn't smoke, so she's waiting inside."

Charlotte nodded and continued, "Did you enjoy the show?"

"Which one?" Richard asked flatly. "It seems to be the night for shows."

Charlotte's eyes widened a moment. "Ohhh, good one."

Richard acknowledged his conversational victory and said in a low voice, "I enjoyed the show *very* much. I wouldn't mind seeing a repeat of it."

"I'm sorry, Richard, but I think you'll be too busy tonight for any more shows." She ground out her cigarette with her shoe and walked back inside.

As she passed by the gates that separated backstage from the rest of the theater, she heard someone calling her name and stopped.

Pressed up among all the girls that were seeking to get backstage to meet Slurry was a man who was calling to her.

Her mouth twisted into a half smile and she approached the gate.

"Do I know you?" she asked the man. He was tall with reddish-brown curly hair. There was something about his voice that intrigued her.

"No, my name's Phil. I'm a big fan of yours, Charlotte," he said in a soft Australian accent.

Charlotte studied him for a moment and then gave Tommy, who was guarding the gate, the nod, and Phil was let through. Charlotte led him away from the screaming girls but kept in view of Tommy and the gates.

"Tell me about yourself, Phil," Charlotte said.

"I'd rather talk about you." He ran his hand lightly up her arm. "I think you are really beautiful and I love your music." He looked at her questioningly.

Charlotte saw Richard approaching from the stage door and lifted her mouth to Phil. He kissed her softly, and then opened his mouth to slip his tongue into hers. After a few moments, Charlotte pulled back. "You kiss very nicely, Phil, are you busy tonight?"

He kissed her again in response.

❧

Breakfast the next morning was carried out with an uncomfortable forced easiness. Charlotte and Richard sat next to each other, pointedly making loud jokes and laughing at everything, determined to prove they were okay.

Darcy observed this and for the first time, he was concerned for his cousin. He knew that Charlotte and Richard were having an affair, having been an eyewitness. But he had always trusted that Richard knew what he was doing and would keep from getting too close. Now as he watched them, he wondered if Richard had made a mistake.

His eyes found Elizabeth's and he saw that she shared his concern and uncertainty. Charles and Jane were the ones who had been prone to getting hurt in the past, the ones who had needed protection. Charlotte and Richard had always been tough, never letting themselves be touched by what was going on around them.

Yet now it was Jane and Charles who seemed strong and Richard and Charlotte who seemed almost brittle.

Darcy was distracted from his silent communication by a touch on his shoulder. He looked up to see Rachel standing over him. "Sorry, Darcy," she said with an apologetic grin. "Georgie needs to talk to you." She held up the cell phone. Darcy placed it to his ear, listening. A moment later, he rose and left the room.

Richard took a sip from his coffee, wincing at its bitterness. "So, who was that guy last night?" he asked casually.

"Oh," Charlotte replied with equal casualness, "that was Phil."

"Phil, huh?" Richard said, nodding. "What was he like?"

Charlotte looked at him a moment, then shrugged. "He was *nice*. He's a pilot." She took a bite of her breakfast. "How was *Becky*?" she asked.

Richard snorted. "You hate that name, don't you?" he asked with genuine warmth.

Charlotte had her first real smile of the morning. "Yeah, I do."

"Rebecca was very nice, and very young," he replied indifferently.

Charlotte turned to him with an expression of mock surprise. "Perhaps too young for the great Richard 'I'm a sex god' Fitzwilliam?" she teased.

"Perhaps," he shrugged.

Charlotte frowned thoughtfully. "I was never that young," she observed.

Richard regarded her carefully before answering, "I know," in a low voice. He cleared his throat, and then said in a lighter tone, "I'm glad you had a good night with Phil."

Charlotte's expression slipped. "It wasn't that good. I mean, don't get me wrong, he was nice and all, but," she looked away and ran a hand through her hair, "I've had better."

The conversation was forced to end as Caroline began her morning update. Both Richard and Charlotte were glad to move away from the increasingly uncomfortable topic, but as the meeting went on, Richard's jaw became more and more set.

"That's all for today. Make sure you have all your things out of your room before you leave for the stadium; we're back on the road tonight. I'll see you this afternoon," Caroline concluded, dismissing the tour personnel for a rare morning off.

Charlotte rose and quickly made her escape alone to the elevator. She stepped in, but before the doors closed, Richard slipped in with her. Charlotte attempted to speak, but one look at Richard's intense gaze and words failed her completely. She stared at his face, at his eyes devouring hers, and tipped her lips up instinctively to his. If time had slowed before he kissed her, it seemed to speed up as soon as they made contact. Suddenly her arms were around his neck, and his were around her waist and his mouth was everywhere, kissing, licking, and teasing.

"What's the matter?" she gasped as he pulled her shirt aside, revealing her shoulder, which he then covered with kisses and light nips. "Couldn't stand me being with someone else?" she moaned.

"Don't be," he panted as she nibbled on the skin under his ear, "ridiculous. I just—oh!" he cried as her hands slid under his shirt and found his nipples. "I just hate to see you left unsatisfied."

The elevator doors opened. Charlotte pulled down her shirt, which had somehow slid up, exposing her breasts, as Richard dragged her to his door. He fumbled with the keycard as her hand stroked his ass. Finally, with an emphatic swear he got the door open and they tumbled in, their mouths once again tightly pressed together.

"No," Charlotte broke away to gasp, "not the bed." She shook her head and licked her lip. "I don't want to—not there."

Richard looked puzzled, then picked her up and took her to the large luxurious bathroom. There he put her down and turned on the shower while Charlotte quickly undressed.

Richard left the room, coming back a half minute later with a condom in his hand. He stopped when he saw her, naked and aroused before him. "Oh God, Char," he groaned and quickly stripped off his clothes.

She stepped into the shower and adjusted the temperature, when he joined her. Once again he took her into his arms and kissed her, hard yet tender, over and over again. She made a whimpering noise in her throat as his hand slid down to cup her breast, and he could feel her push herself against him.

He broke off and, his eyes never leaving hers, sank to his knees. She took a ragged breath as he took her breasts in his hands and closing his eyes, rubbed his face against them. She wove her fingers through his hair as he sucked her swollen tit into his mouth and drank the hot water that was pouring like a stream down her breast to its apex.

His one hand rested on her hip, holding her steady, while the other slowly traveled up her thigh to her sex. Charlotte began a low moan in her chest as his fingers delicately stroked her, using the water washing down her body to heighten the slipperiness between their skins.

"Charlotte," Richard sighed, "you taste so good!" He gently moved her back so she was against the wall of the shower, still under the hot spray. Then he pushed her legs apart and knelt between them, lifting his face to her sex. Charlotte thrust her hands against the side walls, bracing herself as Richard's hands curled around her slim thighs and his mouth began pleasing her.

She wondered what his power was. How he alone could move her so much, pleasure her so completely. Then she stopped thinking altogether as the pressure built. Her hand found his head, and she held him close as she ground herself into him. He was so good, so strong, and so perfect. She felt sexy, and wanton, and wicked, and then she exploded, her passion and pleasure released in a scream that filled the tiny space they shared.

She slumped back against the wall, her chest heaving with each breath. Richard released the hold he had on her hips and she slowly slid down onto his lap and his embrace. She rested her head on his shoulder while he rubbed her back and murmured soft words to her, listening to her shuddering breaths.

After a minute she became aware of what he was saying: "Thank you, Charlotte. My beautiful, beautiful Charlotte." She lifted her head, and looked at his face, her eyes full of wonder and doubt. Tenderly, he touched her cheek, and then softly kissed her lips. "You are so beautiful, Charlotte," he whispered, his lips lightly brushing hers as he spoke. "Thank you."

Charlotte kissed him once more, then waited as he rose back into the spray of the hot water. He offered his hand to help her up, but she ignored it, instead rising to her knees, her face level with his impressive erection. "Char?" he asked, his voice shaky.

Charlotte smiled in a feline way. "Turnabout is fair play, Richard." She opened her mouth and slowly licked the head of his cock, pleased with the sound of his gasps. Holding him at the base with her hand, she slowly slid his length into her mouth then drew it back. She repeated the movement with agonizing slowness, enjoying his cries of pleasure. Gradually she sped up her strokes, as he placed his hands on her head. She let him set the rhythm for a few minutes, learning what he liked, and then she took him as deep as she could and held him there. "Jesus Christ, Char!" he groaned. She lightly raked him with her teeth when she slowly slid her mouth up him at last, delighting at the sounds he was making, as he begged her not to stop.

Again she returned to the rhythm he preferred, relishing the power she had over him. For once he was the one screaming and she was doing the pleasuring. She could hear his gasps becoming more frequent as she felt him growing even harder in her mouth. "Oh God! Don't stop! Please don't stop!" he cried and a moment later his body jerked as hot come filled her mouth. Dutifully she swallowed it all and gently licked him clean as he leaned against the shower wall, limp and breathless.

Only then did she rise and slide into his arms, where he held her close and kissed her. "Thank you," he said in a soft breathless whisper.

"Thank you," she sighed contentedly, pressing her head against his chest and letting the hot water wash over them as one.

CHAPTER 10

Elizabeth sighed tiredly as the elevator doors closed on her, and the small car spirited Darcy, Caroline, Alex, and her up to their floor. Weary after a long day and night of performing, Elizabeth had avoided the other elevator car, seeing that it contained Jane and Charles, Richard with his latest flavor (she heard the name Maria), and Charlotte with some man she picked up. No way was Elizabeth going to get anywhere near that situation.

Darcy's mouth curled in the half smile she now recognized as signaling his amusement with something she did. "What?" she asked.

Darcy's expression changed to a full smile at her. "It's funny. We live the lives that people dream about having: traveling, making millions of dollars, being adored by thousands of people every night, and at the end of the day, what's the one thing you want the most?"

Elizabeth chuckled. "A bed," she answered knowingly.

Darcy nodded. "Something most people don't even think about."

Elizabeth grinned. Somehow they had maintained their easy truce. While Jane and Charles were romancing each other, and Richard and Charlotte were banging everyone else, they found a comfortable niche with each other.

"How did the photo session go today?" he asked.

"Oh," Elizabeth groaned, as the unpleasant memories she'd been trying to forget came back. "It was fine, except for Collins."

Darcy's expression turned cold. "Did he harass you?"

"No," she said tiredly, "he barely even spoke to me, which is a good thing, but now he is making a big show of ignoring me. He spends all his time talking up Charlotte." She pulled her hair back from her face. "I find photo sessions to be so boring. The first time it was exciting, but after that, it's just dull. And I'm not sure I like how they are marketing me. The studio always puts me in these sexy poses. I'm not really comfortable with that."

"I know," he nodded. "On one level you are a product being marketed, and you know that, but you are still an artist, and you wonder where the line is between people listening to your music because they like it and people listening to it because they think you're sexy."

"Exactly. And I've put too much into myself and my work to be turned into a sex object."

"But you are sexy, Lizzy," Alex objected. "You are vital and confident and strong, and that's very sexy. It comes across in your performance, so you might as well use it."

Elizabeth smiled politely to hide her disagreement and looked away from Alex. She wasn't at all pleased with his observation. Her eyes moved to Darcy, who remained silent, but she saw his eyes travel up and down her body with a look that made her feel very warm.

Was it possible? she asked herself. Could it be that the super-hot Fitzwilliam Darcy found her desirable? She tried to dismiss the thought as being ridiculous, but a part of her burned with the idea. She definitely desired him. He was one of the sexiest men she had ever known, and she couldn't deny her attraction to him.

And then what? she asked herself. Spend the rest of the tour with him? She couldn't see herself in the type of relationship Jane had with Charles, all hearts and flowers, and she definitely didn't want to be in Charlotte's position. Not that she even knew what Charlotte's position was. At the last three stops, Richard had taken a different flavor to his room each night, seeming more and more subdued around Charlotte. Elizabeth had thought their affair was over, until she caught them in an intimate position in a tour bus bathroom yesterday.

Elizabeth also knew that if she slept with Darcy, she would prove all those websites correct. LBS were just Slurry's Bitches: their playthings for this tour.

She felt a flare of anger at the idea, but when she looked into Darcy's eyes, she knew it didn't matter; if he really cared about her, and if she really cared about him, all the rumors and innuendo would be of no consequence. A part of her knew she could love him. She didn't, but when she heard him play and when they had these easy conversations, she knew she could, and a part of her longed for it.

And then what? Elizabeth's personal history with romance read like the title of a book: *The Greatest Disasters of Modern Times: The Titanic, the*

Hindenburg, Elizabeth's Love Life. Past history had taught her it was much easier to fall in love than to stay in love. It would be much easier to have a casual affair with Darcy than to try to have a relationship. It would be much less painful when it ended, she realized with a frown. But somehow she couldn't do that. She couldn't treat him like an easy fuck. He was already more than that to her. So she was back where she started.

No, Darcy was a yummy-looking treat, and he might or might not be a good person inside. But Elizabeth didn't have time for it. She didn't have the time, or the emotional energy. She smiled sadly to herself as she realized that she would take a pass on him.

❧

Elizabeth sat in the private corner backstage, working on a new song, unaware she was being observed. She sang along with her strumming, testing out chord progressions and the flow of her lyrics.

> *Took so long, just to get enough.*
> *Took so long to get here.*
> *You're showing a path ahead,*
> *Spinning me around.*
> *You take me up, you take me down.*
> *I don't know where I'm going.*
> *And every time I look at you,*
> *It's like a new face is showing.*
> *Do you want me?*
> *Do I want you?*
> *Do you want me?*
> *Do I want you?*
> *Yeah, I think I do.*

He smiled to himself. How could he not? He felt instinctively that she was singing about him. It was the first solid sign of her affection for him and it made him grin with deep satisfaction.

"Careful," a voice said from behind him. "You'll burn your eyes out like that."

Darcy turned to see Alex staring at him coldly. "And I suppose you know this for a fact?" he replied, his voice coated with ice.

"Everyone knows you can't stare at the sun for too long. Didn't your mother teach you that?" He pushed past Darcy and walked to Elizabeth, calling her name to draw her attention, as Darcy watched.

"I've got great news, Lizzy."

Elizabeth stopped and tilted her head expectantly. "Well?" she smiled.

"Collins just called. He's bringing the video commissioner down tomorrow and we're going to have a meeting to plan your video!"

Elizabeth smiled brightly. "I still can't believe it," she said, then she laughed with delight. "That's great, Alex. Thanks for telling me."

"I'm going to go tell the others," he told her as he moved off.

Elizabeth nodded and returned to her guitar. As Darcy watched, she smiled again and then looked away thoughtfully.

He was puzzled. Elizabeth was not prone to sadness, and yet for the last few days, she seemed almost depressed. He walked up to her quietly, as she sat absently strumming and staring into space.

"Hey," he said easily.

"Oh!" she started. "Hey," she replied.

"I heard you got good news."

She nodded her head, looking very pleased. "I'm very excited. This is something I've been dreaming about for so long. I just hope I don't screw up too much. I've never done this before and I'm certainly not an actress."

No, you're not, he thought. "Elizabeth, is something wrong? You seem down lately."

She looked for a moment as if she was going to push him away, and then her face changed and she spoke. "My mom called today," she began. "She told me that a good friend of mine from college is pregnant." Elizabeth smiled in embarrassment. "And it's kinda bothering me. This girl is my age, and she's going to have a baby. Be a mom. All that responsibility for someone else." Her eyes widened at the idea. "I can't imagine being in that place. I'm just so not ready for anything like that." She looked at Darcy. "Does that make any sense?"

He nodded. "It makes a lot of sense." More sense than he could tell her.

Elizabeth nodded. "I've been putting all my energy and my attention into my music and my career; it's almost impossible for me to think about a family or settling down. I guess I'm worried I'm missing something."

"You are committed to your career, Elizabeth. There's nothing wrong with it. It's where you should be. Children can come later, if you want that. Right now you are creating music that touches millions of people, and that's no less valid than being a mom. You should be proud of what you've done."

Elizabeth looked into his eyes and smiled gratefully. "Thanks, Darcy, that helps."

He smiled softly. "Anytime." He was painfully aware of the distance between them. She was deeply committed to her career, and he respected that in her. But it didn't stop him from wanting her. He wanted to help her, to ease her way. He could. He could make it so easy for her, if she would only let him.

But she wouldn't. She would tease and play, but she would never let him close. She was so guarded and focused. He smiled mirthlessly as he recognized himself in her. The difference was that he had a career already and was willing to make room in his life for her.

He had no idea how to close the distance between them, or even if he should; would she welcome him, if he did? Yes, they had both shown an awareness of each other, but could they move beyond it?

He was almost to the point of despair when she went back to her song. Still, listening to her words again, he knew there was hope. It would take time and effort, but he had hope.

❧

Richard smiled lustfully at the woman before him. She was a tall, leggy blonde with beautiful blue eyes and a charming, quiet manner. He met her earlier at the meet-and-greet and was delighted at her ability to make him believe that he was her first choice, as opposed to being a poor replacement for Darcy. Gently he lifted her chin and kissed her, tasting her sweetness. *Oh yeah, this is going to be good.* He kissed her again, long and hard. She responded vigorously, yet no matter how deeply he probed her, he couldn't find what he was searching for. No woman, no matter how beautiful or sexy, had touched him the way *she* had. He didn't like that thought, and he pulled the girl closer, determined to banish it.

"Richard?" a soft voice spoke to him from behind.

He stopped, puzzled by what he heard. It was like his thoughts had invoked her presence and for a second, he doubted if he had really heard her. The reaction of the woman in his arms, however, made it clear that Charlotte was really there. He frowned at her in confusion. "Char?"

"Um," she appeared to shrink before him. "I was wondering if I could talk to you, but I see you're busy."

Richard looked from her small face to the blonde and back. "Oh, Char, this is Suzanne. Suzanne, Charlotte Lucas, of Long Borne Suffering."

Charlotte nodded and smiled politely to the blonde, who smiled coldly back.

Richard looked confused. "Is it important, Char?" he said uncomfortably. They were backstage, and Richard had only a short time before the buses would be leaving. He really wanted to be with the hot blonde, but he was concerned about Charlotte. He had never seen her looking this worried before.

"No," she shook her head. "It's nothing," she said as she turned away.

"Char?" His voice stopped her. "Is something wrong?" he questioned her, clearly torn.

She shook her head, not looking back. "It's nothing, Richard. I'll see you at breakfast."

∽

Elizabeth felt like she was walking on air. Winnie, the video commissioner from De Bourgh, had just spent the last two hours discussing plans for the video. It was going to be a challenge; she had never done anything so complicated or expensive before. The "Everything You Are" video had simply filmed them during their rehearsal. The money involved in the new video had definitely given her a moment of uneasiness, but Alex assured her that they had made enough from the tour to cover it, even if CD sales fell flat, which was highly unlikely. "First Impressions" was still in the top forty, and all the predictions were that it would be moving up rather than down.

In less than a week, they would fly to a race car track in Ohio, the setting for the video. They would meet the director and spend two days shooting. Elizabeth's excitement had reached a new high, and she was ready to celebrate with her friends.

She invited Alex and Winnie to join her in going out for dinner, but they declined, being too busy crunching numbers. She then found Jane with Charles in his suite, the door left open as it usually was. They were working on a song together. Elizabeth smiled with genuine happiness for them. It really seemed like they were made for each other.

"Congratulations, Lizzy!" Charles said when he noticed her there. He stood and gave her a friendly hug. "Jane told me all about the video. I'm really happy for you!"

"Thanks, Charles," she grinned. "Do you two want to come out for dinner?" It was a rare night off, and Elizabeth wanted to have fun.

The smiling pair agreed and Elizabeth walked across the hall to Darcy's door. She knocked determinedly. He wasn't going to beg off this time.

He was in a robe and holding his guitar when he opened the door. Elizabeth raised an eyebrow in confusion. "Why are you in your bathrobe?"

"I was playing," he answered in his soft voice.

"What? You play in the nude?" she asked teasingly.

"Yes," he answered her with complete seriousness.

Elizabeth's lips formed an O and her cheeks warmed slightly, but she maintained her nerve. "Well, get dressed. We're all going out," she announced.

"Out?"

"Yes, out to dinner to celebrate the newest Long Borne Suffering video, starring me." She smiled happily.

Darcy smiled back, enchanted by her infectious happiness. "Give me a moment."

"Okay, you can meet us at our suite. I've gotta find Char," she answered as she walked off. Darcy watched her move away, admiring the view, then shut the door.

❧

Elizabeth opened the door to her suite, a wordless tune of joy on her lips. She walked to Charlotte's room, where she heard noises. The door was open and she looked inside. The tune died.

She stared, her eyes not able to understand what she was seeing, her mind unwilling to process the image. Before her was Charlotte, pulling her shirt down, and sitting on her bed, far too close to her, was Bill Collins.

Shock and confusion froze her into place. "Char?" she whispered, completely unable to believe what her eyes were telling her.

Charlotte looked up, her face reddening. "What?" she snapped.

"What are you...? What are you doing?"

"Excuse me," Collins huffed as he stood up and pushed past her.

Elizabeth heard him leave; the sound of the door slamming broke her out of the trance. "Charlotte! What have you done?" she asked, horrified, as she rushed to her friend's side. She heard the door of the suite open and close again, but she ignored it. "Oh my God! He didn't force you, did he?"

"Nothing happened, Lizzy!" Charlotte snarled.

"Char, why?" Elizabeth's voice was trembling. "What the fuck were you thinking?"

"*Nothing happened!* Now, let it go, Lizzy." She moved to the window, lit a cigarette, and took a long drag.

Elizabeth looked at her in confusion, not noticing the two men observing from the doorway. "Charlotte, I find you with that, that... *thing* all over you and you tell me nothing happened?" Elizabeth was aghast. "How can you say that?"

"Because it's the truth, Lizzy," she retorted. "Nothing happened, and even if it did what business is it of yours?"

"I'm your friend, that's what makes it my business. Why didn't you tell me? I just can't understand why—"

"I know you can't understand! I'm not asking you to understand. I'm asking you to let it go!" Charlotte cut her off and then sighed and turned away. "I'm not like you, Lizzy," she said in a calmer voice. "I'm not idealistic, and I'm not romantic like Jane. I never was." She paused. "You want to know what happened? Fine. I'll tell you! Bill wanted me, and I didn't say no. That's all," she spat. "I *know* you would never do something like that, but I'm not you, and don't you dare look down on me for it!"

Elizabeth was stunned. She couldn't understand why Charlotte would have ever done such a thing.

"Lizzy," Elizabeth whirled around, surprised to find Richard standing in the room, his face pale and his eyes grave. "Could you excuse us please?"

Charlotte turned a sullen face to him then moved back to the window as Elizabeth left the room.

⤖

Richard closed the door slowly and turned back to Charlotte. Even with her back turned to him, he knew what she was feeling. He knew she was expecting him to blast her, so she could blast him back and avoid really talking about what happened. He could see it in the lines of her shoulders and the tension in her arms.

Instead he moved silently to her side and lightly put his hand on her shoulder. Charlotte flinched at the gentle touch but otherwise remained where she was. Richard felt it as she took a deep breath, and he felt the tension slowly draining out of her. When he thought she was ready, he turned her with his hands and took her into his arms, letting her rest her head against his chest.

"You are not supposed to be doing this," she said finally, her voice weak. "You are supposed to be disgusted and yelling at me."

"I know," he said, his voice quiet. "But you're talking to a recovering alcoholic. I'm afraid righteous anger looks pretty stupid on me."

Charlotte chuckled once and let him lead her to the bed. They sat there, side by side, as Richard held her hand, unwilling to let her go. "Want to tell me what happened?" he asked.

Charlotte looked at him. His question was an offer for her to explain. He was not judging her in any way. She sighed tiredly. "Collins has been hitting on me for the last few weeks," she admitted dully.

"Since Will threw him off the tour for hitting on Lizzy?"

Charlotte looked at him, her eyes wide. "What?"

Richard's eyes grew sadder. "I thought you knew," he explained. "Will threw Collins off the tour because he was hitting on Lizzy. That's why he left so suddenly and never came back except for meetings."

"Oh," Charlotte said, her lips pressed tightly together. Clearly this was news to her.

"So, Collins was hitting on you?" Richard prompted, trying to get back to the issue of Charlotte.

Charlotte nodded. "He never forced or threatened me or anything. He just clearly thought LBS owed him a fuck for all the 'wonderful' assistance he's given us. And he offered to help our CD along, so that didn't hurt."

Richard reached out and pulled her close to him, stroking her back comfortingly. "Why did you do it?" he asked.

"Why not?" she squeaked. "He was easy. I could kiss Collins and it was nothing to me. I could be in control with him. It would be a simple business transaction. He would help the band and I knew I would feel nothing for him, that he could never hurt me." She closed her eyes and bit her lip hard, struggling to keep control. "It was just a business deal."

Richard stayed calm, stroking her back, careful to remain open to her, but inside his heart was breaking in two. He was devastated to know that his Charlotte, his beautiful, beautiful Charlotte, could think she was worth so little. "Char, why didn't you tell anyone?" he asked, again not judging, only seeking to understand.

"I tried," she whispered.

Richard grew very still, his eyes not focusing on anything. Then slowly he licked his lips and attempted to speak words that were almost too difficult to say. "What do you mean?" he whispered hoarsely.

"I tried to tell you last night when Alex told me Collins was coming. I knew he would be expecting something from me today."

With her words, Richard's flesh turned to stone. He felt all the color, all the life draining out of his body, leaving only a worthless shell. He struggled to breathe as two facts became completely inescapable to him: he loved her, and just as surely, he was destroying her. He had a moment of breathtaking clarity and he knew what he needed to do. He had to save her, even if it meant losing himself. Gently he returned to stroking her back. "You should have told me, Char. I would have helped."

Charlotte looked at him and he could see the anger in her eyes. "When?" she seethed. "When you were screwing that blonde?" She snorted. "It was easier on my pride just to do Collins." She pulled away and walked across the room, crossing her arms in front of herself and pressing her hands to her chest.

"I'm sorry, Char; you're right," he said with a voice awash in sadness. He walked to her and rested his hands on her upper arms, her head fitting neatly under his chin, and they stood there, each lost in their own pain. "I'm very sorry, Charlotte. For what it's worth, he won't bother you anymore. Darcy will get rid of him and you'll never have to see him again."

Charlotte snorted derisively. "I told you, Collins was the least of my worries."

He turned her around, her body not resisting him. She looked into his eyes, and for the first time, she found a wall there, a barrier. "I know. I'm going to try to fix that." He kissed her once, softly. "Charlotte, you were wrong. You're too good for the likes of him. You're too good for the likes of me."

"What?" Charlotte asked, confused and suddenly deeply worried.

For a moment he couldn't answer her. "I just meant you sold yourself far too cheaply. You are very special, and I really hope that someday you know it."

Charlotte's chin began quivering and she shut her eyes tightly. "Please don't say that."

Richard took her close into his arms and nodded, his lips making soft soothing sounds in her ear. He could feel her fighting against her tears. He wished he could give her what she needed, so she could trust herself enough to cry in front of him. It was curious; she gave him every part of her body, but her soul she held far away from him. He smiled bitterly as he realized that this was for the best. He knew he could only bring her pain, and he loved her just enough to turn away from her.

He watched her pull herself together and put on a brave face for him. He smiled encouragingly at her. Yes, he told himself, this was best. He looked at her beautiful face, one he would always hold dear, and sincerely hoped that she would find someone who deserved her, someone better than himself.

✐

As Elizabeth entered the living room of the suite, she was surprised to see Darcy there. Then she remembered she had invited him for dinner. He was speaking into his cell phone as waves of anger washed off him. His voice was low and dangerous.

"I want to be explicitly clear. I will *not* work for a company that allows its executives to sexually harass its artists. Now you have five minutes to make this right or I will pull our contract and I don't care how much it costs me." There was a pause, and then he growled, "Well then, perhaps you should put your mother on the phone, Anne."

Elizabeth shivered at the cold rage she heard in his voice. She turned to see Charles, Jane, and Caroline all looking worried and puzzled.

"What happened, Lizzy?"

Elizabeth sighed disgustedly. "I don't know, really, I came in to tell Charlotte about dinner and I found her in the bedroom making out with Collins."

"What?"

"Oh my God!"

"Richard is talking to her now," Elizabeth reported in resignation.

"Where is Mr. Collins?" Jane asked.

Elizabeth shrugged.

"I saw him leave when I came in," Darcy said in a soft voice as he put away his phone. "Elizabeth, may I speak to you?"

Elizabeth nodded. A feeling of numbness had come over her. She walked into her bedroom, knowing he would follow.

Darcy closed the door firmly behind them. He turned to see Elizabeth pacing the room, her arms wrapped tightly around herself.

"Lizzy?" he said in a gentle tone.

Elizabeth's eyes closed and her face crumpled into a mask of pain as she put a hand to her forehead. "It's all my fault!" she said shakily, her breathing labored and quick. "I knew! I knew exactly what he was, and I didn't tell anyone."

"You told me," he said, standing as still as a statue.

"But I should've told them! I should've told her!" she cried. "Damn it! I was glad he was paying attention to Charlotte because it meant he would leave me alone!" She broke down into sobs and suddenly he was there, his arms wrapped around her as she cried out her guilt.

Her tears soon slowed and stopped. Elizabeth pulled out of his arms to turn to the window, her face hidden in her long hair.

"Elizabeth?" he said, his voice hardly a whisper. "It wasn't your fault."

Elizabeth was filled with shame and embarrassment. That he of all people should know of her failing. She couldn't look at him. She found herself conflicted, wanting both to flee and to go to him, to let him protect and hold her.

"Elizabeth, listen to me." He moved so that she was in front of him, her eyes staring up at his face, her expression one of loss and pain. "It wasn't your fault." For a moment, Elizabeth couldn't understand his words, because she was distracted by the fullness of his lips. They looked so soft she wanted very much to kiss them.

She stared at him with eyes wide and dark, and without thinking, he kissed her. It was the light, gentle kiss of one angel to another. He pulled his mouth away, and she made the softest sound of protest and he fell back to her.

Elizabeth opened her mouth to him, knowing nothing more than how good it felt. Darcy kissed her with a passion that burned her soul.

He explored her mouth, skillfully teasing her into entering his. She tasted him, lost in the feeling of pleasure that only made her want more.

Kissing Darcy was everything she had wanted it to be, and much more. She sighed as she felt his strong hands on her back, pulling her body tightly to his. She could offer no resistance, nor did she want to. Her hands grasped his shoulders as she struggled to maintain her equilibrium. Yet somehow she knew that if she fell, he would catch her and hold her up.

She opened her mouth wide, offering more of herself to him while she tried to possess as much of him as she could. Back and forth the hungry tide went: tasting, teasing, probing, then submitting to the sweet bliss of the other's penetration.

Elizabeth felt a need growing large within her. Stirrings of desire that made any lust she had felt before seem like a passing caprice. Unknowingly, she cried out as his lips left hers to travel to her throat, as he kissed the line between her ear and shoulder, murmuring her name over and over. She shifted herself closer to him and was relieved rather than shocked when she felt his hand cup her full breast. Her body pushed itself into him, without any awareness on her part, seeking what it needed so badly.

Any thoughts or questions in her mind were drowned away by the strong masculine scent of him that washed over her as she pressed her face into his neck. She licked him, trying to capture the delicious taste of his skin. Desire she dared not acknowledge before drove her on as she felt him bury his fingers in her long hair and move her head back so he could once again plunder her mouth.

Moans of impatient pleasure were the only sounds in the room, until a knock on the door thundered in their ears. Elizabeth froze then hurriedly stepped back as Caroline's voice came to them: "Darcy, Lizzy, we need you."

With a rush that almost knocked her off her feet, everything came back to Elizabeth: Charlotte, Collins, everything. She paled then flamed as she remembered her situation, even as her fingertips were tracing over her swollen lips.

Darcy looked at her, his dark eyes a one-way mirror, which she could not see through to his feelings. "Are you okay?" he asked with obvious concern.

Elizabeth nodded, not yet having found her voice.

"We better go back," his voice was soft.

Elizabeth closed her eyes and nodded in agreement as her hand unconsciously soothed her hair back into place. He watched her, his eyes drinking in the sight of her, then turned forcefully away and walked out of the room.

Elizabeth, still in a daze, followed him to the living room, where Caroline, Alex, Jane, and Charles were waiting for them. She sat down next to Jane with a weak smile, which Jane returned. "Where's Charlotte?" she asked softly.

"Charlotte needs some time alone," Alex answered quietly, his face one of shock and barely controlled anger.

"Did Richard leave?"

Alex nodded once.

"Now that everyone is here, I think it's clear we need to do something," Caroline said in her authority voice. "It's obvious that Collins is a problem."

Darcy interrupted her. "I've taken care of that." He cleared his throat and continued. "Bill Collins is no longer LBS's A and R. Anne de Bourgh will now be handling both bands."

Elizabeth came out of her daze with his words. She questioned for a moment if she heard them correctly, but Caroline was already speaking.

"Good. That takes care of a huge worry. Thank you, Darcy." She turned to the rest of the group. "Okay, why don't we go and get dinner. I think we all need to get out of this hotel room for a little bit, and food will help."

"I'll stay with Charlotte," Alex told the room. Caroline nodded.

Elizabeth stood up with the others and gathered her bag. She was silent, but inside her mind was reeling. She wanted to stay with Charlotte, but when she thought back to their last meeting, she feared she would not be welcomed.

Then she brushed against Darcy as they entered the elevator, and a new wave of questions overcame her. What had she just done? She glanced out of the corner of her eye at Darcy, but he was looking straight ahead. She wished she knew what he was thinking. Her lips were still tingling as the group traveled to the pair of limos that were waiting for them in the front of the hotel. She forced her hands to keep from touching them.

There was small talk in the cars, but Elizabeth didn't hear any of it.

Her thoughts were too full. She kissed Darcy, oh God! She struggled to make any sense of it. She knew she desired him, almost since their first meeting. She never tried to deny it. At first she thought he was completely uninterested in her. Clearly that presumption was incorrect. She shivered as she remembered the feel of his mouth working against hers.

But what did it mean? If he was attracted to her, why did he pick this time—when she was feeling horrible for her friend—to show it? A cold, still feeling overcame her as a dark part of her mind whispered, "Because he knew you were vulnerable." Her eyes tentatively glanced at him again. He was wearing his sunglasses, but his head was turned in her direction, and she could feel his gaze upon her. She could feel her pulse quicken.

Had he taken advantage of her distress? She was so upset when he came to her that she would have turned to anyone for comfort at that moment. And he did call her into her bedroom. She wondered if she had made a grave miscalculation in trusting him.

Yet, at the same time, she didn't really believe it. It was hard to believe that he could be interested in her, but when she remembered the kindness he had shown her, offering advice on the tour and comfort when Jane was injured, she couldn't believe he was that deceptive. Besides, she reasoned, he was Fitzwilliam Darcy; he received a dozen letters each day from women who would be happy to be used by him.

No, she couldn't believe he was just taking advantage of the moment. Besides, she admitted, she was hardly an unwilling victim. Her mind replayed once again the memory of kissing him. Maybe it was possible that he was attracted to her, just as she was to him, and in a moment of weakness, those barriers broke down?

She didn't know what to think. The idea that he was taking advantage of her seemed cruel, unfair, and wrong, yet the idea that he, Fitzwilliam Darcy, could be attracted to her seemed the height of vanity and foolishness.

The limo stopped and they exited. Elizabeth stopped to look up at the restaurant and was so struck by the absurdity of the situation that she laughed out loud.

"Don't you like Japanese?" Darcy asked, his voice so low that only she heard it.

"No, actually, I love it. It just seems like a weird place to be after," she shrugged, "everything."

Darcy took a casual look at the street and then his eyes met Rebecca's. He shared a nod with his security expert then said to Elizabeth, "Come on," guiding her into the restaurant.

The Osho was crowded, with a long, narrow dining room. The sushi bar was at the front, before a large bay of windows looking out on to the street. Long rows of tables lined the walls of the restaurant toward the back.

Elizabeth drifted away from the group to look appraisingly at the sushi counter, where rows of brightly colored fresh fish sat under glass.

"I hope you are not planning on eating that bait again, Will." Charles's voice rang out in her ears.

"Maybe if you tried it," his soft voice answered enticingly.

"Oh no, I like my food cooked," Charles laughed in reply.

"Do you like sushi?" Darcy's voice was suddenly much closer. Elizabeth looked up to find him staring over her shoulder at the selection of fish.

"Yes, I do," she answered. "But I usually don't order it. It bothers Jane."

Darcy removed his sunglasses and his eyes flicked over a small empty table in the window nearby. "We could sit here and have some together."

Elizabeth was torn. She still didn't quite trust him, yet at the same time, she wanted to give him the benefit of the doubt. It was the sushi in the end that won her over. She had not had it in so long, and she found it just too appealing to pass up. With a nod she agreed.

Darcy turned and put a word in Caroline's ear, and a minute later, the two of them were seated together at the lone table. "What do you like?" he asked her as they examined the menus before them.

Elizabeth's eyebrow arched. Here was where she would be able to tell if this was a sincere offer of fish or just a ploy to get her alone. "I usually prefer nigiri-zushi to maki," she said, deliberately using the Japanese words.

Darcy didn't react at all. "Do you like hako-zushi?" he asked, his eyes not leaving the menu.

Elizabeth remained indifferent and returned his serve. "I love hako-zushi unagi. It's one of my favorites." She waited to see if he would react to her preference for grilled eel.

He didn't. "I always order unagi at a new place. I find it's one way to judge the restaurant's quality." It was his ball and a tiny curl of his mouth told her that he knew it. "So, we'll have some unagi—how do you feel about tuna, salmon, yellowtail, mackerel?"

Elizabeth nodded to all of this. "Oh, do they have toro?"

Darcy's eyebrows shot up. "I'll check," he answered in a pleased voice. Then both sides of his mouth curled and Elizabeth knew he was leveling a big gun at her. "How do you feel about uni?"

Elizabeth grinned lightly. Truthfully, the ground raw sea urchin had never been something she could tolerate, but her honor was at stake. "I only like it if it's exceptionally fresh," she bluffed convincingly.

Darcy nodded once, satisfied. "Do you mind if I order for both of us and we can share?"

Elizabeth smiled, pleased in spite of herself. Whatever else he knew, Darcy at least knew sushi, and she was looking forward to it. "That would be nice," she answered.

The waitress came and Darcy ordered what seemed to Elizabeth to be a vast quantity, but she knew she could eat a disgustingly large amount of sushi, given the chance, so she didn't care.

The waitress came back a moment later with green tea for both of them. Elizabeth picked up the thick, handleless mug and blew across the hot brew. Her feelings were still jangled from before, but the tea helped her to relax. Darcy watched her silently and then asked, "Are you okay?"

Elizabeth smiled bitterly and shook her head no.

Darcy frowned, looking down at his teacup, then back at her. "I'm sorry, Elizabeth."

She wondered what exactly he was apologizing for.

"I should have dealt with Collins back when you told me."

Elizabeth ignored the uncomfortable sensations of relief that he hadn't apologized for kissing her and focused on his words.

"I had thought a warning and taking him off the tour would be enough. Apparently not, and I'm very sorry."

Elizabeth was touched by the sincere contrition in his words. "It wasn't your fault," she said, unable to meet his eyes. "It wasn't even your problem."

"If it happens on my tour, it's my problem," he said simply.

"No, it's not," she objected. "Look, he was our A and R executive. We should have been the ones to deal with him." She sounded angry, even to her ears.

"How?" he asked bluntly.

Elizabeth opened her mouth to respond, then closed it with a snap and a hard look at Darcy.

"The fact of the matter is there was nothing you could do, Elizabeth. You have no power over De Bourgh, and unless you wanted to take this public…" He lifted an eyebrow suggestively.

Elizabeth frowned at that idea.

"Exactly. So there was nothing you could do." He sighed. "I understand. You want to make it by yourself. You don't want to be helped. I know. I've been there." He paused as a small wooden boat covered with a beautiful arrangement of sushi was brought to their table.

Elizabeth smiled at the display then looked back to him, her expression serious as she willed him to continue.

"The fact of the matter is this had to be stopped and stopped now." He paused a moment to eat a piece of tuna. "I know it's difficult to accept help, but it's better than the alternative, and in the end, I simply couldn't let this go on. Five years from now, I don't want to be reading headlines about a 'Slurry sexual harassment' case."

Elizabeth admitted to herself that he made a valid point. It didn't make the truth any easier to swallow, but he was right and now she needed to admit it. "Sorry I jumped on you like that," she apologized.

Darcy nodded. "I know the person you are really mad at is fat, greasy, stands about this tall, and answers to the name of Collins."

Elizabeth smiled and felt a huge burden lift from her shoulders.

"You better hurry up," Darcy motioned with his chopsticks. "I don't know how long I can keep from eating all the toro."

She dug in, and as she ate, she was surprised again at how easy it was to be with him. She realized that he was carefully keeping the conversation to light topics, but even so, she was pleased at how similar their views were.

The combination of tea, fish, rice, and conversation was doing a great deal to improve her condition. "You look like you are feeling better," Darcy observed.

"I am," she confirmed. "Thank you." She smiled inwardly and then asked, "How do you manage it all without going nuts? This week I've been up and down so much emotionally, I don't know where I am anymore."

Darcy studied her face then carefully reached out and offered her his free hand.

She stared at it a moment, then took it with a squeeze. "A part of me wants to go away from all this. To go home and just be me again and stay in one place for a week."

Darcy's eyes turned sad. "You can never go back, Elizabeth. I thought you knew that."

Elizabeth nodded. "I know. I feel like I'm on a ship crossing the ocean. I can't go backward, and I can't get off, I can only go where the ship takes me."

"Do you regret your trip?" Darcy asked, his eyes searching hers.

"No," she said with a surprising certainty. "No, this is what I wanted. It's not always pretty, it's not always easy, but it is what I want."

Darcy seemed impressed with her answer. He squeezed her hand again and then released it to continue eating.

"Can I ask you something?" she asked as the waitress refilled their tea.

Darcy shrugged.

"I notice I've never seen you drink alcohol," she observed.

Darcy finished the bite in his mouth. "Simple reason, I don't."

"Not at all?"

"Not usually," Darcy shook his head. "I don't like to be under the influence of anything."

She smiled and arched her eyebrow. "Oh, the famous Darcy control."

He stilled and took a long look at her, his eyes sweeping down and up her body. Elizabeth swallowed hard as she knew they were both remembering their earlier moments together.

She licked her lips nervously and tried to continue the conversation. "I mean, um, you seem so different from your public, bad-boy image," she stammered.

Darcy visibly refocused himself. "That's because it is just that, a public image. It's useful to let people believe you are something you are not. It gives you some distance from the fans," he answered, not without some difficulty.

Elizabeth made herself look away from his lips. "I, um, I was just surprised." She smiled weakly. "You hear all these rumors of decadence and depravity, and you have all been practically monks."

Darcy looked at her in amused disbelief. Elizabeth laughed at herself and amended her statement. "Okay, well, Richard is certainly not a monk."

Darcy shook his head no, his mouth curled into a grin.

"All right!" Elizabeth said with mock surrender. "Okay, I take it back. I'm the only one living a monk life. Everyone else is getting plenty of action. Happy?"

Darcy's forehead crinkled. "You think so?"

"Well, Richard and Charlotte have been busy, we both know that." Darcy nodded. "And I suspect Jane and Charles are doing something more than just writing songs. And you have that Amy woman," she tried to say lightly, but failed utterly.

Darcy smiled to himself. "Amy is my head attorney with Darcy Technologies. Our relationship is strictly professional."

Elizabeth looked at him with frank disbelief.

"All right," Darcy sighed. "Years ago, Amy and I had a relationship."

"What happened?"

He lifted an indifferent shoulder. "She graduated from law school and got a position with a firm, and Slurry got big and started touring constantly. We soon figured out that we wanted different things."

Elizabeth nodded understandingly. "I know that story."

Darcy looked at her curiously and then continued. "She got married two years ago. We're still good friends, but that's all."

Elizabeth felt stupid for making him explain this to her. Then it dawned on her that he had been just as celibate as her.

"So, what is your story?" he asked. Despite the lightness of his tone, Elizabeth knew he wasn't asking just to be polite.

"Not much story to tell. Currently, my only emotional relationship is with my guitars."

He grinned and waited.

She grinned back, seeing she was not getting out of answering the question. "I suspect you know this one already. I haven't been able to find a man with whom I could make a long-term relationship work, and the one-night stand thing just isn't my style."

He sipped his tea thoughtfully. "But you've tried."

"Oh, I've tried. Don't get me wrong. It's just, well, you know, you're a musician. Most people don't understand that you have to work every Friday and Saturday night."

"And that you are going to be on the road as much as possible," Darcy added.

"Exactly," she replied, her words gaining speed, "and that you don't just have time to lie around all day playing house with them. That you actually do have to spend your time composing and rehearsing." She stopped short and blushed. "I'm sorry; I don't mean to rant."

He shook his head. "No, I understand completely." He took another sip of tea and continued. "Have you tried dating other musicians?" he asked with an upturned eyebrow.

"No, I, ah, dated someone once in the business, but it didn't work out. And besides, I'm so busy with my career I really don't have the time. I'm just putting romance on the back burner. You know?"

He nodded.

"So, this bad-boy thing that you do, it's all just an act?" she said, trying to bring the conversation back to him.

"Not all of it," Darcy replied. "Have you ever seen a stage magician?" Elizabeth nodded. "Diversion is the name of the game." He held up his left hand and fanned his fingers. "Keep looking at this hand, so you don't see the other palming the quarter."

"Okay, I get that, but why? What are you hiding?"

Darcy pointed over at the other table, where the rest of the party was eating. "If you were a journalist, with no moral fiber, what would you see there?"

"Jane and Charles holding hands," she answered softly.

"And what would happen if the tabloids got hold of Jane and Charles?"

"They would be all over it, putting it on the covers of all the magazines." Elizabeth frowned. "They would portray it in the worst possible light. Make Jane out to be a gold digger or something."

"Exactly."

"And that would really hurt Charles and Jane; they both want people to think the best of them." She turned her eyes to Darcy. "Whereas you couldn't really care less if they post outrageous lies about you. You are protecting your friends by using yourself as a shield."

Darcy lifted his cup in admiration. "Perfect."

"Don't you have secrets you want to keep out of the news?" she asked.

Darcy grinned mirthlessly. "Everyone has secrets, Elizabeth, but the image protects me as much as anyone else. They are so busy looking for the outrageous stuff that they miss the things that really matter."

She looked at him in a new light. She realized he was willing to sacrifice his own comfort for his friends, but she couldn't help but note that this was another way for him to control what was going on around him.

∽∾

Caroline Bingley sat alone in the dim light as she sipped her drink. From her table at the hotel bar, she could see the main entrance. There was no concert tonight, the bands were all safely in the hotel, and she had made sure that Collins was off the premises. Now her face reflected the exhaustion she felt as she took another sip of her drink, the whisky biting her throat as she swallowed.

She tried to erase the images that she kept seeing again and again in her mind, those of Elizabeth and Darcy: sitting together, sharing an intimate conversation, him holding her hand, and then later, the shy way he had put his arm around her as he led her to the hotel elevators. That was when Caroline decided she needed a drink.

She slumped back in her chair. She knew it had only been a matter of time. If she had been in Elizabeth's shoes, she would have been all over Darcy right away, like white on rice. That they finally managed to hook up was no surprise to her. She took another sip and closed her eyes to hide the stinging.

When she opened them again, she saw a pair of blue eyes sitting across from her, watching her patiently. "Do you mind?" a voice with a soft London twang asked.

Caroline shook her head. "Make yourself comfortable."

"Thanks," he said slowly. "You look pretty beat."

Caroline rolled her eyes and sighed tiredly. "You heard what happened?"

He nodded. Caroline had long ago learned that Faust had a remarkable information network. She was impressed by his ability to always know what was going on while remaining unseen. Except when she needed him, then he would be right where she wanted him. He had also shown a discretion that had bordered on saintly, which had earned her trust.

Caroline sighed. "Collins is gone, I have no idea what is going on with Richard, and Darcy…" she trailed off.

"I know," he said softly, his voice carrying a note of sympathy.

Caroline rubbed her forehead. "I keep asking myself why? Why her? Why not—" She broke off with a bitter grimace. "Sorry."

Faust shook his head. "Go on," he commanded in a gentle voice.

"What more is there to say? I love him. He doesn't love me. And now he loves her. Old story really." She took a sip of her drink and sighed. "I'm tired. I'm tired of killing myself for this job, and I'm tired of hurting."

"Caro, you need to understand something." He spoke in a way that demanded her attention, his voice vital and earnest. "You are an intelligent, competent, beautiful woman. Darcy may not see that, but that doesn't mean that others don't."

Caroline's blue eyes searched his. Her blond hair was still in the tight knot she usually wore it in, but at this point, a few tendrils had escaped and were framing the sides of her slender face. "Thank you, Faust," she whispered.

He reached across the table and lightly brushed her cheek with the back of his hand. Caroline closed her eyes, her breath slowing as she felt the effect of the simple human contact that she denied herself so long.

"Come on," he said softly. Together they rose and left the bar.

❧

Elizabeth smiled to herself when Darcy slipped his arm discreetly around her waist. It was flattering. She now had undeniable proof that he found her attractive.

Together they waited for a private elevator, both craving some time apart from the others. The door closed on them and he kissed her once again, but this time it was different; this time they both knew what they were doing; both were fully aware of their actions.

"Lizzy," he whispered between kisses, as he wrapped his arms around her. "I'm afraid I have to disagree with your ideas about romance and career not mixing. I think we could mix *very* well, Lizzy," he said as he kissed her again.

His lips were so soft on hers and he drew out of her an intense longing, even as her mind was warning her to slow down. She wanted to believe him. She wanted just to be with him. She wanted to give herself to him and damn the consequences.

The shrill ringing of his cell phone broke into their awareness. He kissed her again, and she sighed softly as he moved back and answered the phone.

"Hello?" he said somewhat distractedly. In a heartbeat his face changed. She watched as confusion, then worry, raced across it, then it shut down entirely, something Elizabeth found inexplicably disturbing. "Are you certain?" he asked. "I'm on my way," he replied, ending the conversation and giving Elizabeth a quick apologetic glance as he hit another button on the phone.

"Tommy, I need Rebecca now," he barked. A moment later he continued. "Georgie is missing," he told the woman on the other end of the phone, and suddenly Elizabeth understood. She knew that Georgie was Darcy's much younger sister. "I have to go to Choate. You're coming along."

Darcy hung up the phone and turned to her, his eyes filled with a distant regret. "I'm sorry. I have to go away."

Elizabeth nodded, understanding that whatever moment they shared was suddenly gone.

When the elevator doors opened, Rebecca was there waiting, an unhappy expression on her face. "Did you call Rachel?" she asked Darcy, who was speeding down the hall.

"Not yet," she heard Darcy answer as they disappeared into his room. Elizabeth sighed to herself and went to her room, feeling confused, lost, and empty. She attempted to tell herself again that romance and career didn't mix and that this was just further proof, but she didn't have the energy to believe that lie anymore. Exhausted, she went to bed, her sleep disturbed by uneasy dreams of Darcy both kissing and leaving her.

※

Caroline lifted her face, letting Faust cover her mouth with his. She sighed as she let herself relax for the first time in longer than she could remember. His hands were gently running up and down her sides, touching her softly, as he pleasured her mouth.

Caroline felt years of frustration falling away from her. She would have felt awkward with another man. She had actually been with far fewer men than her jaded exterior suggested, but she trusted Faust completely.

The ringing of her phone broke the mood. "Don't," he breathed in her ear.

With an apologetic frown she answered it. "Yes?" Faust moved behind her and began lightly running his fingers along her spine and placing featherlight kisses on the base of her neck. "What's wrong?" Caroline said into the phone. They both knew who it was. "Oh, Darcy, it's only ten thirty there. Is it possible she's just out with her girlfriends?"

"It doesn't matter," he snapped. "Either she is just out, as you say, and she's breaking the rules, and I have to be there, or it's something worse, and I have to be there."

Caroline sighed. She felt bad for Darcy, but she really felt he was overreacting. At least she was not expected to go with him; they both knew her place was with the tour. "Well, call me when you know anything." She hung up and put the phone on her night table.

Faust looked at her, expectantly. "Georgiana Darcy has gone missing," Caroline explained. "Poor girl is all of a half hour late and she has Darcy tearing up to Connecticut to check on her."

"He seems very protective of her."

She nodded. "He is. She's the only family he has left, and he's crazy about protecting her. I think maybe something bad happened to her before I joined the tour." She frowned. "Has to be something that would make him race out there in the middle of the night."

Faust stared at her for a moment. If he knew anything, he wasn't sharing it. Instead he walked back to Caroline and kissed her firmly. "That is all I want to hear of *him* tonight." He kissed her again with an intensity that left her trembling. "You are mine for the evening, not his, and I intend to make sure you know it."

CHAPTER 11

I N A DARKENED HOTEL room, two lovers slept. Completely relaxed, their bodies intertwined with each other as if, even in sleep, their skin sought contact with the other.

The phone rang, jarring the silence and forcing them to wake. A long arm reached out blindly and answered it. "Um?"

"Mr. Bingley, this is your wake-up call. It's six o'clock."

"Thanks," he groaned, and then hung up the phone. Turning to the woman lying with him, he said, "Jane, come on, baby, time to wake up."

Jane's face wrinkled like a kitten as she shook her head and moved closer to Charles, snuggling up against his shoulder.

Charles smiled. Even like this, her hair messed and her face puffy from sleep, she was precious to him. "Come on, you have to catch your flight." A low moan and frown was his only response.

Charles laughed. "Do you remember only a month ago you were the one getting up early and I had to drag you back to bed?"

Jane smiled and finally opened her eyes. "That was because I didn't know any better. You have since educated me on why being in bed with you is the best place to be." She kissed him softly on the lips, but when she sought to deepen the kiss, he slid away from her and got out of the bed.

"Up, Jane! You gotta go make a video."

"No," she pouted. "You come back."

"No time, angel."

Jane threw the blankets down and posed seductively. "Charles Bingley! Come back here and love me!"

Charles looked over his shoulder and smiled appreciatively. "I do love you, Jane Bingley, but I'm taking a shower."

Jane's face frowned in confusion. "What did you say?" she asked, rising out of the bed.

"I'm taking a shower," he yelled out to her from the bathroom.

"No, before that! What did you call me?" she asked as she entered the bathroom.

"What? Jane Bennet."

"No you didn't, you said Jane Bingley!"

"Did I?"

"Yes!"

"Oh," he chuckled. "Got you out of bed, didn't I?"

Jane's eyes grew huge and a look of mock fury overcame her. "You jerk!" she shouted, struggling to keep her laughter from ruining the indignation she tried to project. Charles's laughter prompted an additional, "You bastard!"

Charles took her into his arms, and their laughter bubbled and mingled together. In the shower, Charles took the time to wash her, committing to memory every part of her beautiful, beloved body. She would only be gone for two nights, but somehow, even that short absence seemed overwhelmingly painful to him.

❦

Two hours later found Jane holding her sister's hand tightly as their plane took off. The plane leveled off, and Jane relaxed her grip. "Thanks, Lizzy," she said softly.

Elizabeth smiled. "I know I'm not Charles, but I'll do in a pinch."

Jane's face lit up with her "Charles smile." Elizabeth could feel the happiness radiating from her sister. "So how is it going with tall, blond, and handsome?"

"Lizzy," Jane breathed, "I love him so much!" She looked as if she would burst. "It's like every fairy tale dream I ever had has come true. He's so perfect. He loves me so much." She looked at Elizabeth, at a loss for words. "I'm happy," she said simply.

Elizabeth smiled back, genuinely pleased for Jane's happiness. "I'm glad," she said, putting her arm around Jane and squeezing her tight, "You deserve it, more than anyone else I know."

Elizabeth sat back and listened to Jane bubble on about Charles and the things they had done together. Her own thoughts began to drift. She couldn't help but compare Charles to Darcy, and Jane's happiness to her own feeling of unease. She now had proof that Darcy found her attractive, and she had exposed her own desire for him. But so what?

Elizabeth was so tired of not knowing where she stood with that man. She was sick of feeling helpless and stupid about it. Everything had seemed clear that Thursday, five days ago. Kissing Darcy had been the sexiest experience of her life, and she was no blushing virgin. Her breathing grew shallow as she remembered his lips on hers, the way he held her and whispered her name. And their dinner together! She smiled inwardly at the memory of his admission that he was as celibate as she. It was a delicious little secret all her own. She had felt very close to him then; they shared so much, almost as if they were made for each other.

She wanted to wring Georgiana's little neck for that phone call. Rationally, she tried to convince herself that the call had been a good thing. It gave them both a chance to reflect on their actions and where they were going, but truthfully, Elizabeth wanted her rationality to stuff it! No, she didn't know very much about Darcy. She didn't understand much about him or even if she could trust him. She really hadn't cared at that moment. All she knew, and wanted to know, was that he was a handsome, sexy man who was a hell of a guitarist and she just wanted him to fuck her! Was that too much to ask?

Apparently it was. Darcy returned to the tour, but the warmth they shared was gone. He was the one now pulling back in this stupid game they were playing, and Elizabeth was left out in the cold, fully exposed. She felt very vulnerable and she didn't like it one bit. She wondered if he'd reconsidered his behavior in the restaurant and had changed his mind. It seemed the most likely explanation. She found herself remembering again his words about LBS's willingness to do anything to hang on to fame. She wondered if he had remembered those words too.

Damn it! She hated being so hung up on one stupid remark! She knew Jane would tell her she was ridiculous, and a part of her agreed. She wished she had never heard him that night. Instead, she wanted to believe what he had told her in the elevator: "They could mix very well." She wished, and she wanted, but it didn't help. In the end, she could judge him only by his actions, and since his return, his behavior strongly favored the previous remark over the more recent one.

He rejoined the tour the following afternoon in a foul mood. In the days that followed, he seemed distant and distracted. Elizabeth suspected that in part it was due to worry about Richard, whose behavior had taken a sharp turn for the worse. Elizabeth was not one to judge another person's lifestyle, but even she was uncomfortable by what she had seen.

Still, Elizabeth had to admit that even if Darcy expressed an interest in sharing her affections, it's not like they had a chance lately. Since the incident with Collins, they had been traveling and sleeping on the buses every night. They couldn't be together then, not even Charles and Jane attempted that.

Their only chance for some privacy was the night before, and Elizabeth admitted that then she had been the one unavailable. After the show, she discovered Charlotte crying, something she had never in all their years of friendship seen before. Elizabeth didn't need to ask what had happened; she knew it must have been something to do with Richard. Charlotte needed her that night, and Elizabeth even begged off swimming to be with her friend.

Darcy looked at her then, his dark eyes unreadable, but she thought she sensed disappointment in them. In the bright light of the morning, she wondered if that was just the imaginings of a bruised ego.

Now she found herself uncertain again. Why was this so hard? She was not normally this stupid about relationships. She envied Jane and her certainty in Charles's affection and wished she had a similar certainty in Darcy. It would have helped her face her fears about the day. Elizabeth was careful not to show it, but privately, she was terrified of making a fool of herself at the video shoot. She knew she wasn't alone, and she took comfort in the presence of her sister and friend, but, and she hated admitting this, she wished she had Darcy's support. He had a unique ability to say the right thing when she was nervous or worried, and today she missed it.

Of course, this thought made her feel all the more vulnerable. That wouldn't do. No, she was glad he wasn't here, she decided, because she was going to do this shoot, and she was going to do it on her own. She didn't need him, and she was going to prove it, even if it was only to herself.

⁂

While the sisters talked, Charlotte sat silently in the seat in front them. Her own thoughts were in bleak contrast to Jane's blossoming. Richard had left her. She was certain of it now. For all his kindness and sympathy on that day when he found her with Collins, it was clear he wanted nothing more to do with her.

Oh, he had never been cruel. He always spoke to her kindly, but it wasn't the same. The easiness of their relationship was gone. He grew silent around her. Gone were the jokes and put-downs that she enjoyed so much. He no longer even joined her for cigarette breaks.

And then there were the flavors. Her heart contracted away from that painful thought. He had changed there as well. She watched him going through a catalog of women. There were so many, she had stopped counting. He didn't even bother with a hotel room now, doing them backstage instead. He was out of control. She realized his addiction was back in full force; only this time it was sex rather than drinking. Her eyes pricked with tears, for she knew that she was the one who had pushed him over the edge. He was okay before she screwed everything up with Collins.

Her mind replayed the scene from yesterday, reliving the pain, like a bruise she couldn't keep from touching. She went to him during rehearsal, early in the day. Since the incident, he had not so much as touched her, and a part of her knew it was over, but she had to try.

He had been standing apart from the others, just watching the scene around him. She noticed with a jolt that just like her, he had stopped his unconscious constant drumming. The rhythm they both lived with had disappeared.

"Richard?" She tried so hard to sound casual; she didn't know why she even bothered. It wasn't as if they could hide anything from each other. "I was wondering if you," she stopped and licked her lips nervously. "I was wondering if we could be together tonight."

Richard looked down uncomfortably and right then Charlotte knew she was in trouble. "I don't think so, Char," he had mumbled.

"'Kay," she had responded, trying to hold in the hurt and keep an appearance of cool indifference.

"Char," he said, his voice rising slightly. "I'm sorry." His eyes looked at hers with a sadness that she didn't understand.

Charlotte shrugged. "No big deal," she lied. "I was just looking for a fuck." She turned away and walked out for a cigarette.

She had four cigarettes before she was ready to return. When she did, she saw Richard already talking up a girl. Her rejection was complete. He had discarded her. Nicely, as gently and humanely as he could, but in the end, it was all the same. He had dumped her, and somewhere, somehow, he had come to mean more to her then she had ever realized.

And the horrible thing was, despite the pain she felt, despite the fact that she knew it was over, despite the fact she could see he was sick and damaged, she still loved him. She wished she didn't. It would have made it so much simpler. He was giving her every chance to walk away, making it as easy for her as he could, and she couldn't. She loved him, and with that love, she knew she was damned.

❧

Winnie met the women and Alex at the airport. She smiled at them, leading them to a waiting limo. "So, how was your flight?" she asked brightly.

"It was fine," Jane smiled back.

"Great!" she replied. "When we get to the set, I'll introduce you to George and then we'll get you into makeup and wardrobe."

"George is the director?" Elizabeth asked.

"Yes, George Wickham," Winnie explained. "He's going to be directing this video, and the next one. He's very good. I think you will really like him."

"Great," Elizabeth said with an embarrassed laugh. "I'm a little nervous, I was worried he would be hard to work with."

Winnie smiled reassuringly. "Oh, no, Lizzy. George is very easy to work with. He's very patient. And he understands that you're a musician, not an actress. In fact, he used to sing himself."

"Really?" Elizabeth asked.

"Yes, didn't you know? He used to be in Slurry."

"No," Elizabeth looked at Jane and Charlotte to find similar expressions of surprise on their faces. "I had no idea."

Winnie grinned at their reaction. "I don't know all the details, but it's true. He left the band about three years ago and started directing music videos instead," she said with some indifference. "But the point is that he understands singers and you shouldn't worry."

Elizabeth smiled and looked forward with curiosity to meeting this man from Slurry's past.

❧

Darcy knocked on the door to Caroline's room for their morning meeting. The tour personnel were given two days' furlough to relax, but he was still working. He heard a soft giggle as the door opened.

Caroline stood there, looking content. She turned her head and Darcy saw with whom she was laughing; Faust was farther back in the room, clearly preparing to leave.

"Good morning, Darcy," Caroline said brightly. "You're right on time." She closed the door and walked over to Faust.

"Good morning," Darcy replied quietly. He was surprised, and more than a little uncomfortable, by what he saw. He realized with bitter irony that everyone on the tour was getting more action than he was. He tried to maintain a look of indifference.

Caroline laughed happily. "We were just saying I have to get back to the 'grind.'"

Faust touched her shoulder and said, "I'll see you later." He passed Darcy with a nod and left the room.

Darcy looked at Caroline with frank curiosity. "Do you want to tell me something?"

Caroline refused to let Darcy ruin her good mood. "Nope," she replied as she sat down at the table. "Shall we begin?"

Darcy's hard stare didn't change as he moved closer to the table.

Caroline grew annoyed. "Let's make a deal; I'll tell you everything about Faust and me, just as soon as you tell me *why* it is any of your business."

Darcy's expression broke and he looked away. "I'm sorry, Caro. I was out of line. I've just had a lot on my mind lately."

Caroline smiled and accepted his apology. "It's all right. I really didn't mean to rub it in your face like that. We're all a little fried from the tour. Luckily, we have a couple of days off, then two more weeks of tour, then a nice long break. I think that will do us all some good."

Darcy nodded; he was looking forward to the break. Looking forward to Georgie's graduation and getting to spend some time with her. To getting to forget about being Fitzwilliam Darcy, rock star, for four weeks and just be himself.

"So, what are you going to do today?" Caroline asked him pleasantly.

Darcy frowned. "I have a teleconference scheduled with Misty at two, but that's all. Maybe I'll do some composing."

"Charles told me he is going Jet Skiing on the lake. You might want to join him." She tilted her head. "It's been awhile since you two did anything together."

Darcy had to agree with that. Between Charles's whirlwind relationship with Jane, Darcy's concerns over Georgie, Richard's behavior, and the tour, he had barely even seen his best friend outside of their performances. He found that he missed spending time with Charles. "I've never been Jet Skiing," he said quietly.

"Oh, Charles can teach you," Caroline replied with a smile. "It's not that hard." She watched as he considered it. She might not be carrying a torch for Darcy anymore, but she still cared about him, as both a friend and an employer, and she knew he needed to stop brooding and get out and do something fun.

Darcy smiled briefly. "I'd like that." His expression became more serious. "Now, what have you got for me?"

Caroline nodded and slipped into work mode. She quickly updated him on their schedule and how the tour was doing. Then she took a deep breath. She knew that Darcy was aware of everything she was going to say, but it had to be said. "What are you going to do about Richard?"

"What about him?"

Caroline frowned, seeing he wasn't going to make this easy. "He's blown off rehearsal three times in the last week, and last night he held up the show by eight minutes."

"Eight minutes, Caro?" he said, lifting an eyebrow.

Caroline fixed him with a hard look. "He's losing control again."

Darcy looked away. "What's going on with him and Charlotte?"

Caroline pursed her lips. "As far as I know," she qualified, "it's over. They haven't been together since Thursday."

"But we've been on buses most of that time. What about last night?"

Caroline rubbed her forehead. "Richard hooked up with an old flame last night, someone named Ellen?" Darcy nodded in recognition of the name. "And besides, we all know full well that Richard and Charlotte have never needed a room." Her voice took on a tone of resignation. "No, it's over."

Darcy looked at her. "Maybe that's just it? Maybe he just needs time to get over it?"

"Darcy, stop doing this. He's losing it. We all know it. It's the same thing as last time, only now it's girls instead of bottles."

"He's not drinking again, is he?"

Caroline shook her head sadly. "He hasn't had the time, he's been too busy banging groupies."

Darcy sat still for a long moment, his expression grave. Caroline could read him like a book, she thought. She knew that Darcy was torn. He didn't want to accept the painful truth and how it would affect his tour. He was losing his carefully crafted control, and he was fighting it.

"Let's give him some time. We have the break coming up. If he is not better by then, I'll do something."

"Darcy!"

"No!" he snapped. "No, Caro, I cannot stop this tour again, not for him. If he has to go into treatment, that means three major tours we will not have finished! Our reputation will be completely shot! It will be the end of the band. I can't do that!"

"You don't have to stop the tour!"

"What are you suggesting? Get a replacement?"

"Yes, I am!" Caroline answered with equal fervor. "Look, I know he is a part of this group, and he's your family, but he is harming the band and the tour, as well as himself." She looked down. "It's not like it's you or Charles; we could replace him and keep going. I don't like this any more than you do, but we are not doing him any favors keeping him out here."

"I disagree! You think taking away his occupation, his identity, is going to help him? It's the last thing he has. I can't take that away from him and jeopardize the tour until I'm certain there is a problem." He sucked in a deep lungful of air and blew it out. "No, Caroline, he stays with us, at least a little bit longer. This could all just be a phase caused by him being upset over Charlotte! It's going to pass."

Caroline looked at him flatly. "When have you ever known Richard to be upset over a girl?"

"Are we done?" Darcy asked impatiently.

"Yes," she said quietly, with a tone of bitter resignation.

"Thank you," he said coldly, as he exited the room.

⁓⁂⁓

The limo pulled up and the occupants stepped out into the bright summer sunshine. In the months of touring, Elizabeth had lost track of the seasons. She was surprised as she realized that it was June. Summer was here.

The set was a race car track. Winnie led them past miles of electric cord and cables. A small army of people was moving around, looking very busy. Elizabeth was taken aback by all the equipment and activity. It was hard to believe that this was all for them!

Winnie finally stopped in the center of the hub and spoke into a man's ear. He turned around and Elizabeth caught her breath. He was gorgeous. Tall, with light brown hair that had been streaked blond by the sun, he wore silver-rimmed glasses that did nothing to hide his bright blue-green eyes. Elizabeth followed his deep tan down his chiseled jaw to his crisp white shirt and well-fitted jeans and sandals. He looked like he had just stepped out of a Ralph Lauren photo shoot.

"Ladies, this is George," Winnie announced. Elizabeth was at once delighted and intimidated. Then he smiled a smile of such friendliness, she immediately relaxed.

"George, this is Lizzy Bennet, our star," Winnie grinned.

"Lizzy, I'm so happy to meet you." George stepped forward and took Elizabeth's hand, shaking it cordially. He took off his glasses and looked at her appraisingly. "Have you done any video work before?"

Elizabeth shook her head. "No, this is my first time," she smiled.

"That's fine, Lizzy, I promise I'll be gentle," he grinned. "I saw your pictures, but they really don't do you justice. You have excellent features for video," he said warmly.

"Really?" Elizabeth asked.

"Yes, you do," he smiled sincerely at her.

"These are Jane and Charlotte, her band mates," Winnie continued.

George shook the girls' hands and then turned back to Elizabeth. Elizabeth was surprised that he barely made eye contact with Jane.

"Okay," George said professionally, "let's get started. Winnie, can you take Joan and Charlotte to makeup and get them ready? Lizzy, I want to talk to you a little bit."

The girls shared a look and smile over his slip, and Jane gently corrected him.

Winnie took Charlotte and Jane away and Elizabeth followed George to a small makeshift office. He pulled out a clipboard and reviewed it. "We are going to start with some concert shots, so you can get used to shooting, then I want to do some shots of you alone on the track. After dinner, we will do some night shots, and tomorrow, we will do the shots with the actual race cars. Will that be okay?" He looked at her for her approval.

Elizabeth was delighted by his suggestions. She had never been the center of attention like this before, even when she was soloing the show. "That will be fine."

George looked at her and smiled. "Don't worry, Lizzy. You'll be okay." His voice turned more personal. "I don't mind telling you, I was listening to your song and I developed an idea of an image I want to project in the video, and you are exactly what I had in mind. That doesn't happen too often in this business. Usually you have to fight to get the song and the singer and the video to all fit together. But I can see I'm not going to have that problem with you." He stopped and looked down, laughing. "I know, I get a little enthusiastic. Just tell me to shut up if I get to be too much."

Elizabeth laughed. "No, it's great. This is not at all what I expected."

He grinned dazzlingly at her confession. "We are going to have a great time doing this, trust me." He put his hand on her arm. "Why don't you go get ready, and then we'll start filming? Okay?"

Elizabeth smiled brightly. She felt so at ease with him, it was hard not to be affected by his excitement.

✎⟡

By the time a dinner break was called at six o'clock, Elizabeth was exhausted yet happy. The video went better than she could have imagined. George was a dream, so supportive, and funny. Elizabeth almost died from laughing when he took a turn with her guitar dancing and lip-synching on the racetrack.

She looked at him as they walked to the catering truck. He had worked harder than her and didn't have a team of makeup people working on him, and he still looked great. She wondered how he managed to keep his shirt so crisp after shooting all day in the sun.

He turned to her and smiled blindingly. "I'll tell you, Lizzy, I wish everyone I had to work with was as nice as you."

"Thanks," she replied, "I thought I was something of a pain. I mean, how many times did I miss my mark?"

George waved an indifferent hand. "That's nothing. I can work with missing a mark. It's the way you don't throw a tantrum and blame me for your screw-ups that makes you wonderful."

"Is that the way it usually goes?"

"In this business? Oh yeah." He handed her a plate and led her to a seat.

"Oh, Winnie was telling me something this morning," Elizabeth said, suddenly remembering. "Did you used to sing with Slurry?"

"Yes, I did," he replied, intrigued. "Why?"

"We're on tour with them now."

"Really?"

"Yup."

"Hmm," George said, with a thoughtful frown. "And how are they?"

"Oh, good," Elizabeth said vaguely, not really sure how to answer that question.

"Is Darcy still Darcy?"

"What do you mean?"

"Oh, hard-nosed, demanding, doing that tortured-soul bit?" he glowered in a startlingly accurate imitation of Darcy.

Elizabeth burst out laughing. "I'll take that as a yes," George grinned. "Have they been difficult to work with?" he asked when Elizabeth stopped laughing.

"No, not at all." She continued, "I mean, they have their bad-boy image, but actually they're very nice and professional."

George looked away doubtfully. "I heard Richard got cleaned up."

"Oh yeah, there's almost no drinking at all on the tour."

"That's good," George sounded relieved. "Richard was always such a player, you know? I worried about him."

Elizabeth rolled her eyes. "He's still a player, he just doesn't drink." She frowned. "He has a different girl almost every night. We call them his flavors."

He snorted. "That's nothing new. Frankly I'm surprised he's the only one sleeping around."

"Well, Charles has hooked up with Jane," Elizabeth indicated her sister, sitting with Charlotte nearby.

George nodded. "I've never met Charles, but I've heard he's very nice."

Elizabeth realized that Charles must have replaced George. "He's great. Everyone loves him."

"What about old Darcy? Who is he seeing?"

Elizabeth felt her cheeks turning red. "Um, I don't think he is seeing anyone right now."

"Oh," George said indifferently. "Is he a friend of yours?"

"No, not really," she said quickly. "I mean we are friendly on the tour and all, but it's not like we are close."

George studied her coldly for a moment and then nodded. "That's probably a good thing, you know, Lizzy?"

Elizabeth wasn't exactly sure what he meant but nodded along with him.

"Well, we have a couple of hours to kill until the sun goes down and we set up for the night shots. Why don't you and Charlotte and Jan go take a nice long break in your trailer? Debbie will walk you over." George nodded at the smiling production assistant, winked at Elizabeth, and left.

The women went to their trailer and enjoyed the wonders of air conditioning. While they were there, Elizabeth told the others about George's conversation.

"He sounds very nice," Jane said.

"He is. He's charming, actually," she grinned, "and he's so easygoing and real."

Charlotte and Jane shared a look. "Did you ask him why he left Slurry?" Jane asked.

"No, it's kind of uncomfortable, like asking a divorced couple why they broke up." She wrinkled her nose and then brightened. "But I like him, and I think he's doing a great job on the video."

"I thought you liked Darcy?" Charlotte asked impudently.

"I do," she said uncertainly. "But I can like two men, can't I? It's not like they're mutually exclusive."

They were interrupted by a knock at the door. "Can I come in?" George's voice called to them.

"Sure!" Lizzy yelled back.

George entered the trailer and smiled at the girls. "Lizzy, you're going to hate me," he said lightly. "I know I promised you a couple hours' break, but the sun is starting to set and it looks like we are going to have some great light for shooting. The DP wants to take advantage of the magic hour." He looked at her pleadingly. "I know it means we'll have to run like hell, but would you mind terribly if I dragged you back in front of the camera?"

Elizabeth grinned. "Of course not, George. What would you like me to do?"

"Marry me?" he joked. "Debbie is here to run you over to wardrobe. I want you to get into that leather outfit. You don't need a full makeup job, 'cause I just want to shoot some long shots, okay?"

Elizabeth agreed and followed him out of the trailer. "Thanks, Lizzy," he said, planting a kiss on her cheek, "you're beautiful."

Elizabeth spent a half hour in the pearly, shadowless light, dancing, playing, and strutting on the track. The warm light flattered her face and hair. Finally, George called it quits when the light had faded too much. He walked up to Lizzy and gave her a big hug. "You're so talented. Have I told you that?" he asked lightly.

Elizabeth smiled back. "Thanks. Have you done a lot of videos?"

George led them to a pair of chairs and sat down with her. A moment later a production assistant arrived with a pair of bottled waters. "Oh yeah, De Bourgh keeps me on their ready list, so I have as much work as I need."

"You don't work for De Bourgh?"

"No," he frowned, "I work for myself. I get a contract for each job. That's pretty standard." Elizabeth nodded. "Besides," he continued, "I wouldn't work for that Gorgon again."

Elizabeth had heard Lady Catherine called that enough times she wondered if it was on her business card. "So, you direct full time now?"

"Yep," he smiled his even white teeth at her. "It's not what I originally had in mind, but it pays the bills."

"Do directors make a lot?" George laughed, a warm, ringing sound. "I'm sorry," Elizabeth blushed, "I really just didn't know."

George looked at her. He had stopped laughing, but his eyes still twinkled with amusement. "I'm sorry. I shouldn't have laughed. No, I mean, don't get me wrong, I make enough, but not nearly as much as the artists I'm usually filming." He smiled. "I think that's where they get off acting like such babies."

"They forget you're an artist too," she said thoughtfully.

"I try to be, but this is sometimes not the easiest medium. I have to work quickly, with a lot of people, and that makes it hard to stay focused on creating something you are proud of."

"Do you miss singing?" she asked.

George gave a look of resigned indifference. "Well, that's a tough one. I mean I miss the fans. I miss getting to interact with my audience each night. But I don't miss the long hours on the tour bus and the constant waiting and the haughty attitudes. At least here, I get to call all the shots." He grinned wryly. "Something I never got to do with old Darcy." He looked at her warmly. "But let's not talk about him. We've got to set up for your night shoot."

The night shoot consisted first of Elizabeth singing in a tight close-up on her face. George had been careful to cast electric blue lights on her to pick up her lipstick and eye shadow. "Lizzy, you've got a wonderfully expressive face; now let me see it!" George cajoled.

Elizabeth had trouble getting into her performance. She felt awkward with the camera right in her face and the whole crew pressed up so closely to her. As George encouraged her to be more natural and easy, she instead felt more rigid and uncomfortable. Finally Charlotte walked over to her between takes and whispered in her ear, "Sing to Darcy."

Elizabeth looked at her puzzled, but before she could ask for a clarification, they called for another take. Having nothing better to do, she thought about him, not the kind man she had enjoyed dinner with, but the arrogant rock star she had first met. The man she was going to teach a few things to. She grinned as a sense of power came over her as she sang sexily into the camera. Oh yeah, Mr. Bad-boy wanted her, and as long as he did, she had the balls in this relationship.

With a cocky, coy smile she sang along with the playback while George howled his approval. "Perfect! Oh my God! Lizzy! You're making me crazy!" Elizabeth just lifted a knowing eyebrow at him. He was another man who wanted her. She relished the power she had over them.

After several takes of just Lizzy, George brought in the others and the band played together in the blue light. After what felt like hours, George called it a wrap for the night to everyone's relief.

Elizabeth was spent as she climbed into the limo for the ride to the hotel, but she was surprised to see George was still energetic. "You gotta know how to pace yourself," he told her with a laugh.

❦

Charles answered the cell phone resting on his chest on the first ring. "Jane?"

"Hi," the voice he loved the most smiled over the airwaves to him. "How are you doing?"

"Better now," he told her. "How was the shoot?"

"Truthfully? Very boring. The director spent most of the day shooting Lizzy. Char and I mostly sat around and waited, but my tan improved," she added lightly. "We just got to the hotel for the night."

"Long day," he murmured sympathetically.

"Yeah, we had to do a night shoot," Jane yawned.

"Sounds interesting."

"It wasn't," then she giggled, "except for Lizzy." She sighed then. "I love the sound of your voice."

Charles grinned widely. It was still rare for Jane to talk about her feelings and even rarer for her to say the "love" word. "I love all of you, baby. I'm missing you."

Jane nodded. "I'm missing you, too. Silly, isn't it?"

"I know, sweetheart. It's just for one more night, then I promise I'll make it all up to you, okay?"

"Okay, don't go yet," she said quickly, unwilling to end the call. "Tell me what you did today; let me listen to you."

Charles smiled and told her in great detail about spending the day with Darcy, Jet Skiing then having dinner.

"That sounds nice. I'm glad you had a good day off. Richard didn't join you?"

"No," he said, his voice expressing his unspoken concerns. "He spent all day with an old flame. I don't think they even left his room." He frowned. "Don't tell Charlotte that."

"Oh, I won't."

"How is she doing?"

"She's okay, not great. I think it's helping her to be away from... you know. It's been kinda nice, with Lizzy doing all the work and spending so much time with George, I've had a chance to spend some time with her."

"George?" he asked. "Does Will have some competition?"

Jane laughed, a melodic twinkle. "No, I very much doubt that. Lizzy is hooked; she just doesn't know it yet. George is our director, and while he's very interested in Lizzy, I don't think she shares it."

"Poor guy," Charles said teasingly. "As long as he's not looking at you, pretty Jane."

"You mean Joan, or Jan, or any other variants on my name he called me today," Jane laughed. "I don't think he even saw me, Charles."

"That's strange."

"It doesn't matter. I'm taken," she said, her voice warming slightly, "and it's nice for Lizzy to get the attention for once. I know she feels like an ugly duckling sometimes."

"Oh, that's crazy. She's not as beautiful as you, but she is a very attractive woman."

"Yeah, but you must know how she feels. You're always playing second fiddle to Will in the sex appeal department."

"Baby, the only woman whose opinion matters thinks I'm the sexiest man alive, so I don't really care," he said in a low growl.

"Oh, you are," she replied with a low and sexy purr, her sister and any other topic of conversation forgotten.

◦≪∞≫◦

Elizabeth walked down the hotel hallway back to her room, her dry towel over her shoulder. "Hey," a familiar voice called out to her, "what are you doing?"

"Oh," she turned and smiled at George, "I usually swim when we stay at hotels, but I forgot the pool wouldn't be open at this hour."

George checked his watch. It was 12:30 a.m. "This must be about the time you get in from your shows. How are the hotel pools open for you then?"

"Will has them stay open for us." She found herself blushing but didn't know why.

"Oh?" George said, lifting an eyebrow. "So you two are pool buddies?"

"Yeah," she said uneasily. "What are you doing up at this hour? I thought you would be bushed."

"I was just getting some ice." He held up the bucket. "Want to come to my room for a drink, since you didn't get your swim?"

"Sure," she answered easily. She followed him into his room and sat down. A moment later he presented her with a glass of white wine and joined her on the couch.

"I'm getting the feeling that you and my old friend are more than just tour mates," he said lightly.

Elizabeth took a sip and smiled. "Well, this is my first tour, so I can't say for sure if we are behaving in a manner that would be unusual for tour mates," she answered, smiling at her cleverness.

"Okay, good point." He grinned and took a sip from his own glass. "How would you describe your relationship?" he asked.

"I told you before, we're friendly. Why are you so curious?" she evaded answering the question.

"Oh, Darcy was an old, old friend of mine. Our fathers used to work together and we grew up together. It's just idle curiosity," he said, dismissing the question.

"You said *was* an old friend. I take it something happened?" she asked as she took another sip.

"Ah, well, yeah," he said slowly. "Darcy and I had a falling-out a few years back."

"Oh," Elizabeth said, wanting to know more but unwilling to be rude. George didn't say anything more, so she felt the burden of the conversation fall back on her. "I really don't know too much about him." She put her elbow on the back of the couch and rested her head in her hand. "I thought we were getting closer, but then something happened to his sister last week, and he's been kind of cold ever since."

George's eyes darkened. "Is Georgiana okay?" he asked with evident concern.

"Oh, of course you would know her," Elizabeth realized out loud. "Yes, she's fine. She just went missing for a couple of hours and Darcy panicked a bit, I guess you could say. But she was just out with some girlfriends."

George downed his glass, and then he silently got up and refilled it. Elizabeth watched him stare down at his drink for a long minute, until he looked up at her and grinned apologetically. "Sorry. Georgie was always very dear to me. Do you know anything more about her?"

"Not at all," she replied, sorry she couldn't tell him more. "Why don't you just call her?"

George smiled bitterly. "I don't think that would be a good idea," he replied as he sat back down beside Elizabeth. "Georgie was the reason Darcy and I had the falling-out."

"Oh!" Elizabeth said, her eyes wide. "What happened?" she asked before she could stop herself. She bit her lip and looked away. "I'm sorry. I didn't mean to—"

"No, it's okay." George said warmly, placing a hand over hers, which was sitting on her lap. "If you want, I'll tell you my sad story."

"Is it very sad?"

"Yeah, it is." He grinned bitterly. "But, Lizzy dear, if you are getting involved with Will Darcy, you ought to hear it."

"I'm not involved with him," she objected.

"Yet," he firmly added. "I know Darcy. He gets what he wants, and if he wants you, he will get you."

Elizabeth looked at him, an expression of unease over her face. "Just listen to the story; that's all I ask." He pulled her closer so he could place his arm around her shoulder. Elizabeth shrugged and settled beside him, letting his words wash over her. "Georgiana Darcy and I grew up together. She was always a pretty little girl, and I looked on her as a little sister, nothing more."

"Then I went away to college, and when I came back, the awkward teen I knew was gone, and in her place was a beautiful woman. I can still remember her at my graduation. It was like I was seeing her for the first time." His voice became distant and wistful. "She was gorgeous, and yet she was calling my name and laughing, and rushing into my arms, like the childhood friend she was. She didn't feel it at first, the change, but I did.

"I pined for her for six months before I let her know my feelings for her. It was right around Christmas and we had all gathered together as a family. I remember how surprised she was at first. I think she was flattered. She hadn't realized that she had become a beautiful woman, that she was capable of being loved by a man."

Elizabeth felt his hand playing with her hair, lightly, absently, as he told his story. He seemed very far away, lost in his memories. "It was New Year's Eve when we first kissed, at the stroke of midnight. It was supposed to just be a kiss for luck, but it turned into more." He grinned. "I admit it, I was completely in her thrall. We spent the rest of her vacation together, stealing moments together whenever we could. We were both so happy, discovering our feelings for each other. It was the happiest time in my life. All too soon, it was over; she went back to school, and I went back to work with Darcy.

"I didn't see her again until that summer. She had come home on vacation, and Will brought her touring with us. We couldn't wait to see each other. We had a great time, for a month, until one night when Will found us together."

"What happened? Is that why you left the band?"

"I didn't leave. I was thrown out," he answered her blackly.

"Why?" she asked, astonished.

"Because in the end, Georgiana Darcy is an heiress and I wasn't good enough for her," he said with a bitter sharpness. "Don't let that rock star exterior fool you; inside Darcy and Richard are still Fitzwilliams, old money that keeps to their own."

"But, I don't understand, how could he do that? Why?"

"Darcy couldn't deal with me having a relationship with Georgie, that was all. It turned ugly. He threw me off the tour and actually threatened my life if I ever tried to contact his sister again."

Elizabeth was shocked. "Why would he do that?"

"I think it's a control thing." His voice was calm and analytical. "I mean, there's the class issue and all that. Can't have Georgie sleeping with the help, after all. But really, I think Darcy just couldn't stand not being in control of what was going on with his band."

"Did you try to contact her?" Elizabeth asked sadly.

"No," he whispered sadly. "I wanted to. God knows I wanted to. It broke my heart to leave her, but I thought it would be best. She was in many ways still very young, and it was killing her to see the two people she loved the most fighting over her."

Elizabeth looked down into her glass. George's story was so sad, but she had no trouble believing it. He seemed so honest. She could see it happening all too easily, just the way he had told it. She knew the way Darcy had to control everyone around him, and his overprotectiveness of his sister.

George was somehow nuzzling his lips in her hair, kissing her ear and neck. She turned her face to him, not sure if she wanted him to stop or continue and found him kissing her lips. Surprised, she opened her mouth, and his tongue snaked in to touch hers. Elizabeth was startled by how fast it had happened, but it felt so good, she didn't resist.

Suddenly George pulled back. "I'm sorry, Lizzy. That was completely wrong of me."

Elizabeth's hand flew up to her lips. They were hot to her touch. She looked at his face, confused.

"You probably should go now," he said, getting up and going to the door.

Elizabeth left the room, saying a quick good night as she passed him and returned to her own room. There she stopped and sank down on her bed. What had just happened? Her emotions churned. How had she ended up kissing George? What was this new trend of hers to kiss random men? Was she that fickle? And how did she feel about Darcy now? She slipped out of her clothes and into bed, her conscious mind unable to make sense of the differences between the Darcy from George's story and the man she knew.

❧

George greeted her the next morning with a warm, intimate smile. Elizabeth immediately felt comforted. It was clear that *he* wasn't about to turn cold toward her. "Did you get a good night's sleep?" he asked kindly.

Elizabeth nodded and smiled. "Good." He took her hand. "Lizzy, I'm really sorry about last night. I probably shouldn't have told you all that."

Elizabeth shook her head. "No, I'm glad you told me. It's not pretty, but I'm glad I know. Darcy can be really controlling, I've seen that before, but I didn't realize how far he would go." She looked away uncomfortably, and George released her hand, but she grabbed it and squeezed it tightly. "It's nice to have someone looking out for me."

"Oh, anytime, Lizzy. I know how easy it is to get taken advantage of in this business." His expression lightened. "Now go get in costume; it's time to play with the race cars!"

Elizabeth grinned and went to the dressing area, where she was put in a white, formfitting racing suit. She spent the rest of the day driving, and when the sun started to set, George let her announce the end of filming. Feeling victorious, she shouted to the crew, "That's a wrap!"

Alex and Winnie took the band and George out to dinner. They were all happy, and laughter flowed with the wine. George toasted the ladies as being "the best band I've ever had the honor of working with."

When they returned to the hotel, Elizabeth was happy to see the pool would still be open for hours. She quickly changed into her suit and hurried to the empty pool. Shucking her clothes and towel, she dove in and began her laps.

A few minutes later, she heard a voice calling her name. She looked up to see George in swim trunks, standing beside the pool. "How's the water?" he asked.

"It's great!" she answered with a smile. She watched him dive in, mentally comparing him to Darcy. Angry with herself when she realized what she was doing, she compensated by telling herself that George had better abs and a nicer face, even if Darcy had a better dive.

George swam over to ask what she was doing.

"Laps, of course!" she replied. "Come on!" She started on her previous course, aware of George swimming beside her. Elizabeth soon hit her stride and relaxed in the exertion of her usual routine. She was turning into her tenth lap when she realized that George was no longer swimming beside her. She stopped and looked around, her old lifeguard training coming back to her, but quickly spotted him, resting in the corner of the pool.

"George!" she scolded.

"Oh, no!" he panted, holding up a hand. "I need a break."

Elizabeth grinned and swam over to him.

"You swim every night?"

"Every night I can," she answered. "It helps me keep in shape."

"And a very nice shape it is, Lizzy." He seemed to regain his breath. "Do you mind if those of us *not* training for the Olympics just hang out here in the kiddy end?" he grinned.

Elizabeth laughed. "I'm sorry. I'm just used to—" She stopped short and looked away.

"He's a great swimmer," George said, his tone conciliatory. "I hope I didn't upset you last night, Lizzy. I'm sorry again."

"No, don't apologize. I'm glad you told me."

"But if you had feelings for him…"

"I was very ambiguous in my feelings for him. What you told me simply helped me to understand what I feel for him and what I want. I'm grateful for that."

George looked at her and lifted an eyebrow. Elizabeth smiled and moved closer. He wrapped his arms around her and kissed her lightly. "Now that we are done working on the job, I can do this without feeling bad," he explained.

Elizabeth let herself be drawn into a deep kiss. He was very attractive, and she enjoyed the feeling of his body next to her, but she wasn't completely comfortable; after a little while she broke off and laid her head on his chest.

"Will you be okay, going back to the tour now?" he asked as he lightly stroked her back.

"Of course. I'm a professional. I can handle this."

George grinned. "You are that. You are one of the most professional artists I've ever worked with."

Elizabeth laughed. "Somehow this seems like a strange setting to be told that."

"Do you want me to stop?"

"No," she sighed and pulled closer. "It's nice to just be held sometimes. You know?"

"I know." His voice was warm and affectionate. "You miss it."

"Do you still miss her?" Elizabeth asked, her voice curious.

"Sometimes," he admitted. "I don't think I will ever be fully over her." He kissed her longingly. "I can't tell you how many times I wish I hadn't left, that I had stayed and fought for her."

"It took courage to walk away like that," she said, her eyes dark with admiration.

"Courage, or stupidity, I'm not sure which." He laughed softly. "I lost everything when I walked away from her and the band. I had to start over from scratch."

"Really? They didn't give you your share of the money?"

"No," he said uncomfortably.

"I can't believe they would do that. You were like family to them. Did you go to de Bourgh?"

"Oh yeah, I did." His face took on an expression of disgust. "She told me it was 'band business' and she wasn't going to be involved." He shrugged. "I could have sued, but that would have just brought the whole sad business out in the open, and I couldn't do that to Georgie. So I took my licks and started anew." He lifted his eyebrows at her. "And look at me now; I certainly can't complain about my current position." His mouth curled into a wicked leer and kissed Elizabeth deeply.

Elizabeth responded to his kisses, wrapping her arms about his waist. She felt her desire rising while in his arms; he was strong and handsome and wanted her. It was easy to be with him. She kissed him deeply until a wave of water splashed over them.

They broke apart, coughing and sputtering, to the sound of Jane and Charlotte's laughter. "Oh, did we disturb something, Lizzy?" Charlotte called out.

Elizabeth blushed as she realized her band mates and Alex were in the pool and she had never even heard them enter. She moved away from George and quickly found herself teamed with the other women in a volleyball game.

The group played and laughed for an hour, the women beating the men four games to two. Finally, Alex told them it was late and they had to get some rest. "We are back on the road tomorrow."

George climbed out of the pool with them but made no attempt to join Elizabeth. As they returned to their rooms, he said, "I want to thank you, Elizabeth. It's not very often I get to meet such a special person as you."

Elizabeth smiled in response. She wished the others would leave, but they seemed oblivious. "I hope I get to see you again."

"Oh, you will. I'm contracted to do the next video with you." Elizabeth beamed at this. "Lizzy? Can I call you?"

"I'd like that," she said, flushing slightly before wishing him good night and entering her room. Charlotte and Jane exchanged looks with Alex and said good-bye to George as well.

⚬

Richard's hand trailed over the flesh beside him. She was warm and so soft. He buried his face in her flat stomach, rubbing against her pliancy. He was almost there. He closed his eyes and the pain he felt was almost gone. He reached out his tongue to taste her, but stopped. The taste was wrong, and it was ruining the calm he was trying to find.

Gentle hands stroked his head, soothing him. "Who is she, Richard?" a soft voice asked. "Who is this Charlotte? Did she break your heart?"

He reared up, his eyes finding hers, stricken. "How?" he demanded.

Ellen smiled kindly. "I could take being called her name once, but after the fourth time, even I start to wonder, darling." She wasn't trying to hurt him, she knew he was already in so much pain, but she wondered what had happened. What memory was so horrible that he was trying so hard to forget it?

He leaned over her, his eyes wild. "Don't! Don't say that name again. She's not—Just don't!" He rolled away. Sitting on the edge of the bed, he lit a cigarette and took a deep drag until the shaking stopped.

"Richard, you know I love you, but this is no good. I've never seen you like this."

Richard slumped. She was right, but he couldn't face it. It was unacceptable. "I'm okay. I just need to get over this."

Ellen sat up, her blue eyes filled with concern for him. "Should I leave?"

He shook his head. "No, not yet." He lay back in the bed and drew her to him. "Stay with me till morning?" She nodded and rested her head against him. "I'm sorry, Ellen. I'm not myself."

She smiled bitterly. "This is supposed to be news?"

He chuckled and kissed her forehead. She settled down comfortably, her limbs easily tangling with his. "She must be very special."

He nodded. "She is."

"I never thought I would see you get caught, Richard. Did she dump you?"

"No," he whispered, "I left her."

Ellen pushed herself up on her elbow and studied his face. Her expression turned poignant. "Oh God, Richard," she said, her voice filled with sad wonder. "You really are screwed."

"I know," his voice was rough, "I know."

Ellen pulled him close, holding his head against her chest and let him pour out his agony into her.

⤡

Elizabeth smiled as again she held Jane's hand for the takeoff. "I never thought I would see you excited to be getting on a plane."

"If it means getting back to Charles, I'd brave a dozen planes," Jane said resolutely.

Elizabeth wished she could share Jane's sentiment. Right now she was dreading her return. Thank God she had met George and he had set her straight. She frowned at the thought of being trapped in a relationship with Darcy. And she knew that was exactly what would have happened. She would have been trapped.

She could see it all now. Her initial impressions of Darcy had been correct. He was arrogant, selfish, and controlling. Sure, there were two sides to every argument, and she knew that Darcy saw the breakup with George differently, but that didn't change the basic facts. Darcy had destroyed the happiness of George and Georgiana for money, for prestige, and for *control*. What the hell would he have done to her?

Deep inside of her, she mourned a lost opportunity. Darcy had come to mean so much to her. He was an artist like her, and his guidance had come to mean so much. While she'd never completely understood him, a part of her was excited at the possibility of a relationship with him. She knew now that was impossible.

Darcy had his good points. She couldn't deny that, but she could not let herself get wrapped up with a man who would try to control her like he would.

That thought opened up memories she closed off long ago. She looked at Alex sitting in the seat in front of her. She could see the top of his head, the hair she once ran her fingers through as he kissed her breathless. Alex had tried to control her too. Everything that had made him a great manager had made him an awful boyfriend, and when Elizabeth realized she had to end the relationship, it had not been pretty.

Darcy would be a thousand times worse. A man who did not shy away from hurting his oldest friend and sister would have had no qualms at all about devastating her, using her for as long as he wanted, then dumping her. Oh, she knew he might want her for a long time, but in the end it would be the same.

For the first time, Elizabeth was sincerely glad that they hadn't progressed any further in their relationship. She knew, from so many times before, that sleeping with a man put her on the fast road to heartbreak, and with Darcy, it might have been the end of her music career as well.

Fitzwilliam Darcy was simply too hot to handle. He had an intense flame that blazed within him that would burn her, consume her, and leave nothing behind. There was no more choice for Elizabeth. She had the certainty she was searching for. She and Darcy would simply not happen. They couldn't.

CHAPTER 12

DARCY WAS PLEASED THAT Richard had come to rehearsal. He finally emerged from his room that morning, joining them for breakfast. Darcy was beginning to hope he had been correct when he told Caroline that Richard just needed to get over Charlotte. In fact, he hadn't believed it when he said it; he was just stalling for time. But now, it looked like time just might have done the trick.

Although Richard seemed back to his usual self, Charles was now a mess, distracted and barely able to focus on their songs. Not that he needed to. The rehearsal was part of their routine, a ritual they did each performance day while on tour, but not strictly necessary.

If Darcy were completely honest, he would have to admit that he was off today as well. He wouldn't acknowledge it, but he had an itch on his consciousness, like a tiny part of his brain was unraveling, disrupting his ability to fully concentrate. He certainly wouldn't admit he was missing her, even if he knew he was.

Just when Darcy was about to snap at Charles for missing his entrance for the fourth time, he heard footsteps running toward them and saw Jane rush onstage. She didn't stop until she was in Charles's arms. He picked her up and swung her around, a scene worthy of any movie.

Darcy exchanged a look with Richard, clearly communicating that rehearsal was now essentially over, and then they both looked to see the return of Jane's band mates.

Elizabeth and Charlotte stood offstage, with Alex standing behind them like a mother hen. Both ladies looked distinctly uncomfortable. Darcy walked over to them. "Welcome back. We missed you."

"Thanks," Elizabeth answered lightly. She noticed that Charlotte just stared at Richard, whose gaze rested back on Charlotte. "Um, did you have a nice break?" Elizabeth asked, trying to save the uneasy reunion.

"Yes, we did," Darcy answered with the same intent. "We went Jet Skiing," he grinned.

"Oh," Elizabeth replied, a little surprised. "All of you?"

"No," Darcy answered carefully, "just Charles and I."

Elizabeth took his meaning, and her eyes rested on Richard before she quickly looked away again.

"How was the video shoot?" Darcy asked.

"It was good," Elizabeth said, nodding. "It was very... educational."

"Great," Darcy answered, and paused uncomfortably. He was quickly becoming frustrated with the situation. Talking with Elizabeth had never been this forced, and the staring match between Richard and Charlotte was simply ridiculous. "Well, we're just about done with our rehearsal. Do you want to take a break and then have your turn?"

Elizabeth looked at Charles and Jane, who were still tightly embraced, as soft, earnest words were shared, and nodded. "Yeah, I think that'd be best."

Darcy walked back onstage and began putting his instruments away while Elizabeth waited a moment for Charlotte. When she didn't seem inclined to move, Elizabeth left her and walked backstage.

❦

Charlotte was immobilized. She looked into Richard's eyes, reading them as if they were the most fascinating novel she had ever seen. She read in them a pain, which warmed her somehow; it helped her to know that she wasn't suffering alone. She didn't want to be alone. She wanted to be with him, but she saw by the sadness in his eyes that it would not be.

For his part, Richard was silently cursing himself. He tried for almost a week to disconnect from Charlotte, and here he was, as caught up as any fly in a spider's web. He saw her pain, her longing, and perhaps something more that he did not have the courage to face. She hadn't turned away from him, hadn't grown angry with him, and hadn't moved past him. She was in the same place he was, stuck in the same mire. He was tempted to chuck it all away, to quit his noble plan and pull her close, to bury himself in her sweetness and warm himself in her affection. But the vision of her, devastated and broken after the incident with Collins, stopped him. He was responsible for that; all the blame was his. He was poison to her, toxic to her spirit. He would not let himself destroy her. He loved her too much.

"Hey, Char," he said, discovering they were alone. "How're you doing?"

"Good," she replied, blinking as a similar awareness came to her. "How are you?"

"I'm good. It was nice having a break, you know?"

"Yeah."

"Course, you had to work; sorry 'bout that."

Charlotte shrugged. "It wasn't too much work. I mostly hung out in the trailer with Jane."

Richard shared a look of understanding. "I know. Sometimes you get the feeling they could replace you with a cardboard cutout."

Charlotte grinned at his perceptiveness. He knew her like no one else. Her heart was both swelling and breaking. Why? Why couldn't he see that they were perfectly matched for each other? She looked away, unable to face him. She wanted him so much, but she couldn't have him.

"Do you want to get a drink or something?" Richard asked. His eyes filled with sad comprehension of the moment.

"That'd be great," Charlotte agreed. They moved backstage and joined Elizabeth and Alex in the green room. Cold drinks were passed around, and they took refuge in the company of others.

Darcy and Caroline soon joined them. "Where are Jane and Charles?" Elizabeth asked.

Caroline smirked. "It could be awhile yet."

Elizabeth grinned in understanding. "You should've seen Jane on the plane. She was practically willing it to go faster."

Caroline laughed. "Charles poured orange juice on his Corn Flakes at breakfast this morning."

"The worst part is he didn't notice until the bowl was half-gone," Darcy added. This got a chuckle from everyone. "I don't know what they are going to do during the break."

Elizabeth's eyes grew quiet and sad. "I forgot that was coming up."

"Yup," Caroline said happily. "Nine days of work, then we are off for a month."

"We are off the tour for a month," Alex corrected. "You're not really off, Lizzy Bennet. You have some appearances scheduled, a video to shoot, *and* you have a performance," he added cryptically.

Elizabeth eyed him, puzzled. "Performance?"

He grinned like the cat that just caught the canary. "I just got a call from Anne. Long Borne Suffering will be performing 'Everything You Are' at the VMA pre-show in three weeks."

"That's great!" Caroline exclaimed, echoing the general sentiment of the room.

Elizabeth's jaw dropped. If he had told her she was winning a Nobel Prize she would not have been more surprised. The MTV Video Music Awards was one of the biggest shows in the business, and being asked to perform, even in the pre-show, was a huge mark of both their success and their potential.

"I guess we will see you there," Darcy grinned.

"Are you performing?" Elizabeth asked.

"Yes. We're the closing act."

Elizabeth was impressed despite herself. The closing slot was the most prestigious appearance of the night; in the past, acts like U2, Madonna, and Guns N' Roses had held it. Considering Slurry was basically unknown four years ago, it was quite a testament to their talent.

Elizabeth felt a surge of emotions for Darcy she didn't understand, and she struggled to control it. "So, we'll see you there," she said politely.

Darcy nodded.

⁓

Jane and Charles had left the planet and entered their own private world.

"I missed you so much, baby," he said between kisses. "It's so good to hold you."

"I know," she grinned, light-headed from the sensation. "I missed you, love."

"I think it's going to be a couple days before I can let go of you again." Charles sighed.

"That's okay," she giggled, "we'll just move Lizzy and Char to the Slurry bus."

Charles laughed. "Oh, that would work," he said sarcastically before returning to the sweetness of her lips. "I'm going to hate being away from you during the break, Jane."

His words cut her sharply. Irrationally, she felt betrayed. A dozen questions sprang up in her mind, but her natural restraint kept her from asking any of them. Instead, she merely looked at him, waiting for whatever explanation he could give.

"I have to go home for a week. I have… business I'm required to take care of there, but it's just for a week. Then I'll come back to New York." Charles was so unhappy. He wanted to tell her the truth. He wanted to explain everything, about his father getting out of prison, about setting up his house. He wanted to take Jane to California with him and show her the places where he grew up. But he knew he couldn't. "We can go to the VMAs together, and then we'll spend the rest of the vacation together, just us, I promise," he told her lamely.

Jane was mollified. She gave him a weak smile as she chose to think about the time they would have together, rather than the time apart. She kissed Charles longingly once more and then walked him back to the others.

❧

Elizabeth was complimenting Darcy when Jane and Charles entered the room, and the news about the pre-show performance was repeated. Charles's excitement over the news was overwhelming. "Jane!" he shouted triumphantly. "I'm so proud of you! Next year you will be on the main show with us!" He took her into a great hug, his face illuminated with love and pride.

The group spent a few more minutes chatting, updating everyone on the plans for the rest of the tour and the break. Darcy was aware of the uneasiness between Charlotte and Richard, which he understood, but the distance between himself and Elizabeth puzzled him. It seemed that each time he tried to reach out to her conversationally, she politely backed away. He knew they hadn't parted on the best of terms, but he didn't understand her reaction.

"Elizabeth," he called to her as she was about to leave for the stage. She turned and walked to him, her face neutral. "Anne is coming down tomorrow and she's bringing the web designer. They want to update the Slurry page. Would you come to the meeting? I really don't know anything about this and I could use your advice."

Elizabeth was careful to not react to him. "Sure, Darcy. Just let me know when."

"Thanks," he said, and smiled privately to her. He was disturbed to see that his smile was not returned. She gave him a slight nod and walked away.

⤬

Elizabeth sat at the table in the LBS bus, her coffee cup forgotten in her hands, her mind a thousand miles away. Jane exchanged a look with Charlotte, who moved off to the back, allowing Jane to join her sister alone.

"Lizzy?" Jane called softly. She touched her sister's arm.

Elizabeth visibly broke out of her trance and smiled with embarrassment at her sister.

"What's going on?" Jane asked softly.

Elizabeth's face fell, and she looked down at her plate. "I'm feeling a little confused, I guess." She looked into Jane's patient eyes and took advantage of the silent offer before her. Elizabeth knew she could tell everything to Jane and receive nothing except understanding and support. "When I was talking to George, he told me some stuff about Darcy." She paused. "It wasn't very nice."

Jane encouraged her to continue.

"I…" Elizabeth frowned and began again. "When I was with George, it was easy for me to be sure of my feelings. But now we're back, and Darcy has been… I don't know. He's been pleasant and warm, and I'm not sure what to think anymore," she concluded.

"Well, how do you feel about George?" Jane asked practically.

Elizabeth shrugged and then smiled. "I like George. He's very nice. He's very easy to be around." Her expression turned inward again. "But he's not Darcy. Will is much harder to be with, but when I'm with him, I feel…" she trailed off, unable and unwilling to describe the intensity of her feelings for Darcy.

Jane took her hand and smiled sympathetically.

"So, now I'm lost between the man who is easy and who likes me and the man who is hard and likes me." She grinned at the ridiculousness of it.

"Well, Lizzy, you have to make up your own mind, but personally, I've always preferred a hard man," Jane winked. Elizabeth laughed, grateful for Jane, who was always there when she needed her.

⤬

Darcy watched as the tour had breakfast the next morning. Elizabeth sat with Charlotte, her concern for her friend obvious. Charlotte was not eating and looked like a wreck. He was disappointed to find that Richard was sitting across the restaurant and was also not eating. Darcy knew the two incidences were related, and he suspected the cute blonde named Dorothy whom Richard had been with the night before had something to do with it.

Right now, he was focused on the attractive picture of Elizabeth. Since her return to the tour, she had been polite to him. He knew her well enough to know that was the kiss of death from her. She was only polite to people she disliked. The question was why. Did something happen at the shoot? She was warm enough to him before she left. He would ask Caroline, but he suspected this was beyond even her formidable intelligence capabilities.

He regretted that they would not be staying in any more hotels before the break. It cut down on the chances for private time to talk to Elizabeth, to try to work out what was going on.

As Caroline gave her morning briefing, Anne entered the room with another woman and took a seat at his table. Darcy nodded a cool greeting to Anne and turned to examine the woman more closely. She was tall and shapely, with dark hair and eyes.

When Caroline finished, Anne spoke up. "Can we begin? I've got things to do," she snapped.

Darcy slowly leaned back in his chair and deliberately took a slow sip of his tea, his gaze never leaving hers. "Of course, Anne. I *certainly* don't have anything else to do." He paused to take another sip and rose. "Excuse me," he told her, leaving the table before she could respond.

He walked to Elizabeth's table and bent low over it. "I need you for that meeting I was telling you about," he told her softly.

Elizabeth's eyes flashed. "Right now?"

"Yes," he answered, his eyes holding hers. "If you aren't finished yet, I can wait. It's no problem."

Elizabeth shared a look with Charlotte and rose. "No, it's no problem at all." She wasn't surprised that he would demand her with no notice like that. After all, he was Fitzwilliam Darcy. She took her coffee cup and the bag containing her laptop and followed him to the table where Rachel, Anne, and the woman waited.

"Anne," Darcy said formally, "Elizabeth will be joining us."

Anne looked like a cat that had been dropped in a bucket of cold water. She gave an equally hostile look to both Elizabeth and Darcy, saying, "Fine. This is Sylvie Duval. She's our web designer. Sylvie, this is Fitzwilliam Darcy of Slurry and Lizzy Bennet of Long Borne Suffering."

Sylvie smiled and extended her hand, first to Darcy then to Elizabeth. "It's a privilege to meet you both," she said with a light and charming Parisian accent.

"This is my personal assistant, Rachel Brown," Darcy said, introducing Rachel to Sylvie.

"Can we begin?" Anne said impatiently.

They all settled around the table. Sylvie opened her laptop and began. "I have reviewed your current website. It's been in need of an update for a while now, no? I contacted marketing and received some new material from them. This is what I have come up with so far."

She passed the laptop to Darcy, who reviewed it, his eyes quickly scanning the screen without expression. He then passed it to Elizabeth.

Elizabeth studied the site. It started with a pop-up presenting a montage of images of the band—taken mostly from their videos while "Control" was being played. After a minute, Elizabeth skipped the intro and went to the main page, clicking around to view all the features.

"It's good," she observed, clearly impressed. "I like the frame idea and the rock motif." She pursed her lips. "These pictures are pretty old, though." She showed Darcy. "Look, you still have long hair here."

Darcy nodded. "We had a photo shoot last month, Anne. Do you think Ms. Duval could have access to those pictures?" Darcy said with exaggerated politeness.

Anne stared coldly at him and nodded, while Rachel made a note in her Palm.

"You don't have any songs to download, or videos," Elizabeth observed while still focusing on the laptop.

"That is De Bourgh policy," Sylvie told them.

Elizabeth sensed that Sylvie disagreed with the policy, but unlike Darcy, she was not at liberty to openly criticize the management. Elizabeth immediately found herself liking the woman.

"Well, I have to say, I don't agree with it. Our video and audio bring a lot of traffic to our site, where fans can find information about the tour, buy tickets, or buy other merchandise right there," she said professionally. "The lucrative sales of our CD off our web page have been extremely impressive."

Anne's eyes narrowed. "You are providing downloads off your web page?" she asked incredulously. "That's against De Bourgh policy. We aren't giving these songs away."

"Well, De Bourgh never told me that, and since it's my web page, and not De Bourgh's, I don't think it's any concern of yours," Elizabeth said calmly. "The sales off the web page fully support my decision."

"I'd like to see that!" Anne snapped.

Elizabeth calmly produced a packet of papers from her case and passed them over to Anne. "For the purpose of comparison, I used the sales off Slurry's web page," she explained. "I think you will be favorably impressed."

Darcy quietly took out a pen and scribbled on his napkin a note he passed to Elizabeth. It read: "How did you get the sales report off the Slurry web page?"

Elizabeth didn't even look down as she wrote back one word: "Hacked."

His eyes grinned at hers and he crumpled the napkin and put it in his pocket.

Anne put down the report and she looked at Darcy. "Is that what you want, Darcy? Audio and video downloads?"

Darcy took another slow sip of tea. Elizabeth saw him grinning behind his mug as she could almost hear Anne's teeth grinding. "Yes, I do."

"Fine!" she snapped. Looking at Sylvie, she commanded, "Add it."

Sylvie nodded and looked pleased. "Now, about Long Borne Suffering," she began with a smile at Elizabeth. "Your website is very up to date, isn't it? But I do have some suggestions."

Elizabeth frowned in confusion. "No, I'm sorry. I think you are confused. I do my own page for the band."

"Oh?" Sylvie looked from Elizabeth to Caroline, who was staring at Darcy.

Darcy spoke up. "I asked if De Bourgh could take some of the load off you, Elizabeth, with the web page."

"What?"

Darcy looked at the three other women at the table then rose. "Could you excuse us a moment?"

Elizabeth followed Darcy away from the table with an air of

incredulousness. "What?" she asked him again, when they were alone in an alcove by the restrooms.

"It's just that your career is taking off now, and I want you to have more time to focus on it," Darcy said. "I'm not suggesting you give up the site; just let Sylvie help out a bit. When Anne told me she was coming down, I simply asked her to have your page reviewed. That's all."

"Where do you get the idea that I don't have enough time to manage my own website?"

Darcy frowned. "Well, you are always on that laptop, Elizabeth, and you told me yourself you answer all your fan email."

Elizabeth closed her eyes and sighed angrily. "Has it ever occurred to you that I might be doing something on my laptop other than the website?"

Elizabeth could see by his expression it hadn't. "For your information, I'm spending the time on my computer doing web pages for my customers."

Now it was Darcy's turn to be astonished. "What?"

"You know I have a degree in computer science. Before you 'discovered' us, I designed web pages and networks for small companies."

"Yes, but you don't need to do that now."

"I don't?" she questioned him sarcastically. "Look, I'm not taking on new customers, but I'm not dumping my old ones either."

"But you have your music career; you're a success at that."

Elizabeth laughed derisively, her eyes flashing. "You've never heard of a 'one-hit wonder'? Until my music career is a lot more stable, I'm keeping my other business," she explained. "And I'm keeping my own website, thank you very much."

Darcy's face was a blank. "I'm sorry, Elizabeth. I didn't know. I was only trying to do what was best."

"Of course you were," Elizabeth said, her voice scornful, "because you *always* know what's best." She found that any warming she had felt for Darcy had evaporated. Darcy was exactly the arrogant, controlling jerk George had told her he was. Her rational voice told her that he had only been thinking of her best interests, and she had to concede that, but would it have been so hard to ask her if she needed help?

No, she told herself, this is his way to try to control her, and she wasn't going for it.

Elizabeth left Darcy and returned to the table. She politely asked Sylvie about her suggestions, not willing to take Darcy's arrogance out on her, and found she was favorably impressed with some of Sylvie's ideas.

Darcy returned a moment later and had a low conversation on the other side of the table with Anne, then exited the restaurant, presumably to return to the bus.

"Sylvie," Anne said quietly, breaking up the women's conference, "I have to meet with Caroline. You can ride to the venue with me or with Lizzy here."

Elizabeth smiled and offered Sylvie a lift on the LBS bus. As the tour moved out of the restaurant and to the parking lot, Sylvie indicated Richard and quietly asked Elizabeth, "Who's that?"

Elizabeth smiled and informed her of Richard's identity, marveling all the while at the amazing Fitzwilliam magnetism.

"Is he single?" Sylvie asked, her eyes trailing over Richard's form.

"Oh, he's highly single. But don't expect any kind of commitment. He's a confirmed bachelor."

"So am I, so am I!" she answered thoughtfully. "But when I see an appetizing cake, I always try to get a slice."

Elizabeth grinned. "Help yourself! He's a whole buffet."

❧

Darcy sat on his bus with Rachel, listening to her voice with only half a mind. *Damn! I really screwed up with Elizabeth this time. I don't know what was bothering her before, but she sure has a reason to be angry with me now. Damn!*

"Georgiana called; she is going to have Lars Ulrich's love child," Rachel reported evenly.

Darcy nodded then looked up at her confused. "What?"

"You remember Lars, don't you? Drummer with a pushy attitude?"

Darcy's face darkened. "That's not funny."

"No, it's not," she replied flatly. "But I was getting tired of talking to myself. Now, do you have anything to say about the quarterly reports? Or should I just chuck them?"

"You know, I don't pay you to give me lip."

"No, but you don't pay me to put up with your crap either."

Darcy took a long, deep breath. She was right, and he knew it. "Sorry, Rachel."

"It's okay. We all need this break," she said softly. "I take it Lizzy was not a happy camper?"

Darcy shook his head. "Nope. I was trying to help her out, and I just succeeded in pissing her off." His expression turned from annoyed to depressed. "I don't know why I try."

"She's stubborn, just like you."

"She *is* just like me. She's so much like me it's scary. You would think I would understand her better."

"Yeah, you would think," Rachel replied with a hint of sarcasm. "Maybe you need to understand yourself better, then you can understand her."

Darcy regarded her for a long moment. "Let's get back to work," he said finally.

❧

Charles felt as if the tour were falling apart. In the day since the girls returned, Darcy and Elizabeth were as cold to each other as he had ever seen them; Charlotte was hiding out in a dressing room during dinner while Richard was talking to Sylvie; and even Caroline had snapped at Alex over something Anne de Bourgh had said.

He looked at Jane, who also had a worried expression on her lovely face, and took her into an empty dressing room. Once there, he drew her into his arms and relaxed.

At times like this, he felt the only place he could be happy was in her arms. When he was there, he felt nothing could harm him. He inhaled her sweet scent deeply and kissed her honeyed lips, feeling her firm body press close to his.

The tour had been brutal on them both. He missed sleeping beside her and waking up to her bright smile. He questioned the fate that brought this perfect woman to him and yet seemed to be constantly scheming to separate them. "Jane," he said softly as he broke away from her kiss and felt her lips traveling to his neck. "We need to do something about the bands."

If Jane heard him, she gave no sign of it. She instead steered him to the couch in the small room and sat down on it. Charles followed her, and soon they were lying on it, her beneath, him above. Charles's worries about the band left him. Jane clearly had more important concerns, which required his immediate attention.

He kissed her, his tongue delighting in the sensation of her mouth caressing his. Their hands were everywhere, quickly removing clothing, which was suddenly binding, hot, and uncomfortable. Once they were naked, they were able to slow down, their awareness focused on the sensation of flesh against flesh.

Jane stared up into his eyes, letting words fall away from them. She didn't need to speak to be understood. She loved the way his eyes would glow with hunger for her. He delighted in every touch and taste of her, and she could read the delight in his face. She loved the openness of his expression. The way he hid nothing from her. It was what made his secrecy over the upcoming break disturbing.

When he finally parted and entered her, she could see the satisfaction upon him. He relished the sensation, letting himself be lost in her. Jane's hands moved over him, encouraging him. She didn't want this to be slow or gentle. She wanted him fierce and hard, the way she knew he could be. She could easily picture him like this when he faced something greater than himself, either a wave or a mountain. Now he faced her desire, which was greater than her body, greater than her soul.

With infinite care, he rode her, watching her every reaction, measuring each response. Like testing each toehold or balancing on his board, this was an act of complete physical precision. Every motion had a purpose, yet at the same time, brought him satisfaction and joy.

Jane was lost. Charles Bingley might be smiling and easygoing to the rest of the world, but only Jane knew this side of him, the side of him that was a manic perfectionist. She surrendered her body to him, trusting him to bring her complete pleasure and release, then drive himself home. The softest sigh was the only sign of her final climax. Through gritted teeth, Charles told her, "Jane! Oh God! *Jane!*" and she squeezed him tightly within her as he exploded.

After a moment, their smiles returned. Charles kissed her sweaty brow and rolled them so they could rest on their sides. Jane's toes were still curled from the intense pleasure she had felt, and she cuddled close to him, fully content.

When they began to grow cool, they rose and took turns showering. Jane emerged first and dried her hair, then dried Charles's with the blow-dryer, enjoying the chance to pamper him. "I always feel selfish when you do that," she said quietly. "I feel like you're doing all the work."

Charles reached behind him and squeezed her tight. "Don't," he admonished. "You have no idea how it excites me to see you come like that. It's so sexy and really makes it good for me."

Jane smiled happily, then said, "Now, about what you were saying—"

"You can remember that?"

"Yes."

"I'll have to try harder. I must be losing my touch."

Jane lightly smacked the side of his head and continued. "I agree with you. And I was thinking we are musicians. Maybe we could all play something together. Something new, so that we would all have to learn and practice together."

Charles stood up and took her face in his hands, kissing her deeply. "You're brilliant, Jane. That's why I love you."

Jane giggled. "I know, and that's why I love you, because you are the only man who sees *me*, all of me." She kissed him again. "And because you are so hot you make my toes curl."

Moaning suddenly pierced the air. From next door, they heard Sylvie crying out as Richard made another conquest. They exchanged a look of understanding, knowing they were going to need something to hold the two bands together.

Charles waited until the meet-and-greet was over to make his proposal. He was worried that Richard wasn't going to be there, but halfway through the session he emerged from the dressing room with Sylvie, who was wearing a distinctly satisfied smile as she kissed him good-bye and rejoined Anne.

"Jane and I were thinking, we are almost halfway through the tour and we haven't done anything as a group. We thought that it would be nice for the bands to perform a song together before we leave for the break."

"What kind of song did you have in mind?" Darcy asked impassively.

"We could do an eighties cover," Charles suggested. "Maybe some Whitesnake!"

"We do not do covers, and we are certainly not doing Whitesnake!"

For once Elizabeth found herself in complete agreement with Darcy, as were the others.

"I've been writing a new song," Jane said pleasantly. "Maybe we could do that?"

"Is it ready yet, Jane?" Elizabeth asked.

"It's not totally finished, but if everyone would help, I could have it done in an afternoon."

"Well, I'm game," Richard said easily. "It sounds like fun. Char?"

Charlotte lifted up her shoulders. "Sure."

"I'll play, Jane," Elizabeth said warmly, her eyes daring Darcy's.

Darcy looked at Elizabeth, his eyes unreadable. "I'm willing to give it a try."

Elizabeth looked away and Darcy could not tell if she was pleased or disappointed. He realized that it was unusual for him to care about the disappointments and pleasures of others, but he discovered that for some unknown reason, he was disappointed not to know Elizabeth's reaction.

∝↜

It was after the rehearsal and sound checks when they were ready to start on the song. Jane had just begun when Alex's cell phone rang. He turned away to answer it, but Elizabeth was completely distracted by the call until Alex turned to her and shook his head.

"Has he called yet?" Jane asked sympathetically.

Elizabeth shook her head and shrugged.

"Who is she expecting to call?" Charles asked Jane, sotto voce.

"Oh, the director from the shoot, George Wickham. She kinda had a thing for him, and he said—"

"Wait! Did you say George *Wickham*?"

"Yes," Jane answered, confused.

"Will!" Charles turned to his friend, his face deeply concerned. "Jane just told me the director of their video was *George Wickham*."

Darcy turned on a surprised Elizabeth. "Is this true?" he snarled.

Elizabeth nodded slowly. "Yes, George was our director. What of it?" she said in a challenging tone. "He told us he used to sing with you. He's a very nice man."

"He's not, Lizzy," Richard hissed. "He's nothing but a lying bastard."

Darcy savagely kicked the nearest amplifier and wrenched out his cell phone and hit a button. "Get me Anne de Bourgh," he growled. "*Now!*"

"Oh, you're gonna get your boyfriend in trouble, Lizzy," Charlotte teased.

Darcy spun around, his face turning white. "What does *that* mean?" he asked coldly.

Elizabeth stuck out her chin. "It means that George is a friend of mine. What are you doing, calling Anne de Bourgh like that?"

"That bastard is *never* to have anything to do with my band, and she knows it!" White-hot rage was coming off his body.

"Luckily, he didn't have anything to do with *your* band," she observed frostily. "George was directing Long Bourne Suffering, not Slurry. I suggest you try to remember that." She closed the distance between them. "You might have been able to control him, but you will not control me."

"You have no idea what he is capable of."

"Maybe not, but I know what you're capable of, to even your oldest friend."

"Lizzy, whatever he told you, it's a lie."

"Is that why you're so scared?" Elizabeth asked.

Darcy clenched his jaw and turned away, walking to his dressing room and slamming the door.

"Fuck! Fuck!" He swore, over and over again, his rage searching for release. He wasn't surprised when Richard walked in a minute later. In truth, Darcy welcomed his company. Richard was the only other person there who knew the whole story.

Darcy flashed him a black look, but Richard knew to whom his anger was really directed.

"Well, that was exciting," Richard said mockingly.

Darcy snorted; a moment later his fury was back. "God damn that bastard!" he growled as he threw a glass against the wall, watching with satisfaction as it shattered. "How? How the fuck did that asshole know? How the hell did he get on that shoot?"

Richard shook his head. "Come on, Will. He's a lot of things, but he's never been stupid." He frowned and clenched his fists. "It's no secret we're on tour with them. He probably just kept his ear to the ground. You know how he is."

"I know. The lying snake!"

Richard waited a moment, watching Darcy prowl like a caged panther. "Are you going to tell her the truth?"

"You know I can't do that! What is going to make her believe me, anyway? Who knows what lies that bastard fed her?"

"Will! You can't leave her to him. She doesn't deserve that! No one does."

"I won't. You know I won't," his tone was rueful. "But I can't let her know that I'm trying to protect her, either. That will just make her angrier and push her to him."

"Or you could just tell her what he did."

Darcy just shook his head.

"What are you waiting for?" Richard asked. "You know you love her. Talk to her. Tell her."

"Oh! And you're one to talk?" Darcy replied angrily. The two men regarded each other, eyes locked.

"Leave me out of this," Richard said, biting off each word, and turning away.

"I just think it's ironic that you are here giving me advice about talking to Elizabeth when you sure as hell aren't talking to Charlotte!"

"It's a completely different situation."

"Yes, it is, because at least you know that Charlotte loves you!"

Richard looked at Darcy, quickly, his eyes questioning what he had heard.

"Oh come on!" Darcy said in disbelief. "Don't tell me you didn't know this! I don't know what the hell you are up to, putting her through hell like this, but at least you must know that."

Richard looked away. He put his face in his hands and rubbed it tiredly. "Are you certain?" he asked weakly.

"Yes, as much as anyone can be without hearing it from the other person."

Richard sighed out a deep breath. "Damn."

"What's the problem, Richard? Level with me. If you don't love her, it would be kinder to just—"

"I wish I didn't love her! That's what I've been trying to do! Forget her!" His voice was tight with tension. "But it's not working."

"So, why don't you try making it work with her? I don't understand the problem here."

"The problem, Will, is that I'm a bad man. I'm toxic. It was my fault she ended up with Collins. I'm no good for her."

"I think that you should let Charlotte decide that."

"Yeah, I'll do that. Right after you tell Lizzy about Georgie."

Darcy scowled and turned away, and Richard dropped tiredly onto the couch. "You were right, Will; we should have stayed away from them. Now look at us. All fucked up," he snorted in bitter amusement. "Except for Chas, of course."

"Charles is better than both of us," Darcy pronounced in his soft dark voice. "He deserves his happiness."

"I hope it lasts for him."

"So do I."

⸎

The next week was incredibly difficult. Tempers were short and everyone seemed to be snapping at each other. Elizabeth took every opportunity to bait Darcy for a fight, her usual good spirits having completely abandoned her.

Darcy found out through an angry phone call to Anne that Bill Collins hired Wickham to direct LBS's video. Of course, Bill had pleaded ignorance of Darcy's strict rules about Wickham never having any contact with Slurry, but Darcy knew it was all just a lie. George's being there had been a setup, a classic Wickham maneuver that had succeeded perfectly.

Richard's behavior with the flavors continued unabated, even as he pulled further away from Charlotte. Idly, Darcy kept a mental list of the women who had received Richard's "Golden Dick" treatment: Jodi (twice), Tracey, Deidre, Tara, Leah, Julie. All had received his special attention as he had tried to forget the woman he really wanted.

Charlotte, for her part, seemed to be growing colder and more distant by the day. At one point, Elizabeth had suggested that she enjoy a flavor of her own, but she had simply looked at Elizabeth sadly and said, "It didn't work." Elizabeth was deeply worried for her friend and was hoping that some distance between her and Richard would help.

The air of gloom had even touched Jane and Charles. They became prone to long periods of silence when they would just hold each other tightly, unable to talk about what was disturbing them, yet unable to find comfort anywhere else.

It was killing Charles that he couldn't tell Jane the truth. He needed her at that time, needed her understanding and comfort. His father's incarceration for insider trading twelve months ago had been a source of private torment. It caused him to question the legal system and meaning of morality. Charles knew in his heart that his father was a good person, yet he was a convicted criminal in jail. He had never been able to reconcile these two realities in his mind, and now that his father was facing release, he found they disturbed him again.

He wanted so much to share this with Jane, to share his worries about what his father would be like. He was certain that prison changed him. A part of him was afraid of what he would find when his dad was released, and he longed to unburden himself of all those fears in the woman who had come to mean everything to him. But he knew he couldn't. Darcy had been right. They had tried too hard to keep the secret. He couldn't risk it now.

For her part, Jane could not understand what was going on with Charles. At moments he would look at her and hold her with so much love, she felt she would burst, and at other times, his eyes were filled with a profound sadness that made her blood run cold. She found herself questioning everything: herself, Charles, their relationship, his feelings, and her feelings. Doubts were weighing her down, and the only times she felt comforted was in her music.

The new song had been completed. It had changed from a simple love song to one of yearning, expressing the feelings she could not put into spoken words. Yet it still maintained the basic upbeat spirit that was Jane's nature.

They would rehearse it every afternoon, and in a way, it served its purpose. The bands did spend time together, just the six of them, and they got to know different sides of each other. It would be true to say that exposure to the true musicianship of each person caused them all to fall deeper in love, but only Jane and Charles were free to admit it.

Each of them had brought something different to the song: Jane had provided the lyrics and melody, while Charles had provided the initial harmonies. Charlotte had provided a Latin beat, which had allowed Jane's voice to take on a slow and sultry air, and Richard had added a wealth of accent percussion, adding an energy and excitement to the song. Elizabeth had brought her formidable theory talents to bear and had written an elaborate orchestration for the song, making it thick with a brass section, as well as adding her voice and guitar.

But it was Darcy who totally changed the song. After three days of doing little more than observing, he came in on that Tuesday with a guitar solo that blew them all away.

Charles was grinning like a maniac as Darcy's electric guitar became another voice, singing a duet with Jane's. "I knew it!" he proclaimed to the group. Richard also grinned, glad Darcy was finally participating.

Shock would be the best way to describe LBS's reaction. "Guitar virtuoso" was a title that had been dropped around Darcy so many times it had become meaningless with repetition. Nevertheless, when faced with this demonstration of his talent, they were forced to acknowledge his legitimate skill.

Jane was delighted, eager to share her song with him and the excitement of creating something new. She threw herself into the song with even greater enthusiasm. Charlotte was pleased as well. Suddenly the song had become something exciting and completely different. It was no longer a product of LBS's with some backup help from Slurry; it was now a true collaboration.

Elizabeth was the only one not enraptured. She certainly couldn't deny Darcy's musicianship or that his addition had dramatically improved the song. But she was angered by where it left her. True, she had a very clear acoustic guitar line, and her vocal harmonies with Jane were crucial, but it infuriated her that Darcy had to step forward and grab the spotlight. It was so typical of what she knew of him. He couldn't be a part of the ensemble; he had to be the star.

She felt pushed aside by him, and it hurt her more than she could admit or understand that he wasn't willing to play with her. It was only in being denied what she wanted that she really understood what it was. She wished they could have played together: a real duet, between the two of them. But instead she was stuck playing backup while he played the star.

⚜

Charlotte took a deep breath and forced her feet to move. It was the last day of tour before the break and the last hour of free time before they faced the meet-and-greet and then performed.

She found him and was grateful he was alone. He was hanging out by the bathrooms, smoking. "You're not supposed to do that inside, you know," she said lightly.

Richard looked at his cigarette and shrugged. "It's too hot to smoke outside."

Charlotte lifted half of her mouth in a smile. "Good point. Do you mind?" she asked, pulling out her own pack.

Richard shook his head and made room for her. While it was a casual action he had done a hundred times, it was touched with melancholy. Even this straightforward act of sharing a cigarette break with Charlotte had become so dear to him he almost couldn't stand it. He stared at her as she lit her cigarette, her head turned down slightly, and he tried to understand it. When had her face become the most beautiful he had ever known? When had her voice, her eyes, her smile become a part of him? He struggled to maintain his calm, wanting to both run away and to throw himself at her.

"How are you doing?" he asked with forced casualness.

Charlotte smiled, a vain attempt to pretend. "Okay. You know."

Richard nodded. He knew.

"What are you going to do during the break?" she asked, playing the game with him.

"Oh, I've got my cousin's graduation on Sunday, then I'm probably just going to hang out at home."

"In the city?"

"No, my family has a summer place in Massachusetts."

Charlotte nodded. He was so easygoing with her; it was easy for her to forget how wealthy he was.

"What about you?"

"Oh, pretty much the same. Alex has some record signings for us, and the VMAs of course, but otherwise I'm just going to crash at home." She took another drag and looked straight ahead. "You know, Massachusetts isn't that far from me. Maybe we could get together during the break."

Richard grimaced. He hated this. He hated the way she was desperately throwing herself at him, he hated the way he wanted her so badly, he hated this stupid charade they were playing, trying to pretend this wasn't killing them inside. "No, Charlotte," he said angrily.

She looked at him then, and nothing could mask the hurt in her eyes.

"Don't you get it, Char? I'm no good for you! What do I have to do? I've tried over and over again to make you see. I've given you every excuse. Just walk away from me!"

"No," she said softly. "I can't."

Richard closed his eyes and drew a long breath. "Do you realize what you are doing? You can't turn away from something that's harming you. Do you know what that is Char? It's addiction."

"Really?" she said, pulling the last bit of her dignity together. "I thought it was compassion."

Richard flinched. When he spoke again his voice was softer, pleading. "Please, Charlotte, don't do this. Don't hurt yourself anymore. Turn away from me."

Her eyes were large and pouring into his. "Don't you think I've tried?"

Richard looked down and licked his bottom lip nervously. In a voice that was little more than a whisper, he asked, "Do you love me, Char?"

"Yes," she whispered back, not needing to think about it. "I wish I didn't, I know it's all wrong, but I do."

With great sadness, he took her into his arms and kissed the top of her head tenderly. "I'm sorry, Char. I'm so sorry."

Charlotte screwed up her eyes, forcing her tears back. She didn't need to ask what he meant. She had never had to. They had always understood each other. He didn't love her; he couldn't. She had to give him up. She embraced the bitter knowledge that of all the women in North America, she was the only one being denied what would mean the most to her, him. That pain helped her pull away. "Have a good break, Richard," she said as calmly as she could.

"You too, Char," he told her, unable to see her face but knowing what it contained. He felt a huge emptiness opening inside of him, which could only be filled in one way. The pain brought him up short, and the lies he told himself could no longer be believed. Turning away from her had been hard, but turning back to her would be even harder. But he had failed at forgetting her, so now he had no choice. If he was going to survive, he would have to change. He couldn't do it for his own sake, but he would try for hers.

❦

They ended the set with "Lost Myself," the way they always did. The room was alive, the energy of the crowd feeding the energy onstage in a symbolic cycle. Charles's voice, rough and gritty, had filled the hall, paired flawlessly with Darcy's guitar.

From her place offstage, Elizabeth watched alone, feeling once again that gnawing desire that she had come to despise as her own weakness. She hated that she wanted him, she lusted for him, and she burned for his touch. It was wrong. It was wrong in so many ways she couldn't even count them, but here, alone in the dark, she let her desire run wild. She let her eyes drink in his tall form; she pictured his long arms holding her tightly. She recalled the heady scent of his skin, alive with the fresh sweat of the show. For a moment she would have given anything to feel him on her, pressing her flat and invading her body. But it was impossible. He was the sweetest fruit and completely forbidden to her.

"Thank you!" Charles's voice cut off her yearning, and her attention snapped to the here and now. "We've got something special for you tonight!"

Elizabeth moved forward onto the stage with Charlotte and Jane, and the crowd began cheering. "You know how wonderful our opening act is," Charles paused for more cheering. "Well, we've been working together and we have something to share with you."

Charlotte walked to her usual space as Richard stood. "This is your chair," he told her, with an unusual expression of seriousness on his face. Charlotte took her place behind the drum kit.

Darcy turned to Elizabeth as she plugged in the hookup for her Gibson and set up her microphone. His eyes inquired if she was ready, hers answered that she was.

Jane walked fearlessly to the mic stand, which Charles yielded to her. Then everyone turned to Darcy and Elizabeth. They would be starting together on the same beat. Their eyes locked as Charlotte raised her hand to the cymbal.

Without an outward sign, they all moved simultaneously and they were off. Jane began singing with a voice full of longing.

Darcy's awareness was limited to a tiny area, encompassing only himself, his guitar, and Elizabeth. He didn't even hear Jane or the others. It was only he and she. He was playing to her. He hoped she could hear it, that every riff was for her, telling her of his feelings. He watched her play, skipping in and out of her rhythms, sometimes moving with her, sometimes dancing around her.

His eyes were focused on her, and his fingers required no additional guidance. He smiled his private smile for her, knowing this was one place she could not avoid him. It didn't even matter that she didn't return it; she understood. He moved with her, circling each other, her Gibson to his PRS, balanced perfectly together.

When she had to stop before the microphone to sing, he positioned himself beside her, close enough to touch her, as he played along with her voice. This was the time he had been waiting for, the time when she was his alone. There was no escape for either of them, no retreat. He played the oldest song known: a song of prowess, designed to prove himself worthy of her.

It didn't matter now that they were parting as soon as the song was over. It was only a temporary separation, but the marking he made on her was permanent. She would be his. He was playing for her, something he had never done for another woman, and he knew the power of his music. Like Orpheus, no one could resist it.

Playfully he finished the song, his spell complete, his point won. He bowed low to Elizabeth, his eyes never leaving hers, before they addressed the screaming fans. He held out his hand to her, and as he knew she would, she took it. Together they bowed to the audience, who had witnessed his performance.

They left the stage together and walked to the instrument area. Darcy put away his PRS, not needing to say anything to her, as she stored her Gibson. When she rose, he faced her. He saw the uncertainty in her eyes as he gently touched her cheek. "Good-bye, Elizabeth. Have a good break," he said, kissing her. Her lips welcomed his of their own volition.

They kissed for a long moment before he pulled back. The uncertainty was still there. He recognized that she wasn't even aware of what happened. He smiled kindly to her and walked away to the limo that would take him and Richard to their flight. His pride wished that Elizabeth recognized what had happened, that she had leapt into his arms and asked to come with him, but it didn't matter. She was his, and she would know it soon enough.

Chapter 13

Elizabeth heard the phone ring as she worked at her computer. She checked the time, ten thirty. He was calling early that night. In the past week, Charles consistently called around midnight. Her heart skipped a beat as she wondered if by chance the caller wasn't Charles, and instead the call was for her? But she could hear Jane's voice and knew from her tone it was Charles.

Not that she really expected a call from him. Still, it didn't mean she didn't think about it. It was a sweet fantasy she played within her mind. Darcy would call her, his voice rich and soft in her ear, and he would tell her... what? She had trouble there. The fantasy always broke down at the point. Would he tell her he loved her? And that he was on his way to carry her off to his palace? No, he was not Prince Charming, not even in her fantasies. Would he be shy and softly ask how she was? Would he be dirty and involve her in a hot game of phone sex? She tried all of these fantasies, and none of them really fit. The only one that worked, that really made her sweat, was when she imagined she would pick up the phone and his guitar, not his voice, would answer her. Yeah, she liked that. She could see herself grabbing her own Guild and answering him. Telling him, lick by lick, what she wanted and how she wanted it.

The fantasy continued, their playing becoming more intricate and exciting, until they were playing in unison, their music loud and powerful. Then the music would fade away, and he would be there, holding her, growling her name, as he pushed himself into her yielding body. She would take him then, take him into herself and he would fill her, answering that longing, the emptiness she knew for so long.

Elizabeth's eyes refocused on her computer screen. She licked her lips and fanned herself a little, telling herself that her discomfort was from the July weather, not her imaginings. Besides, he wasn't going to call. She told herself again and again, like a mantra. It was fun to daydream, but she needed to focus on the here and now.

Yet even as she thought this, she wondered what it would be like to see him again. She had been so angry when *that song* had started. Angry with him, and if she was being really honest, angry with herself. She was angry because she felt needy and ignored. Then the song started and suddenly she was *not* being ignored. Elizabeth didn't need to see his eyes. His music and his mouth were enough. She still trembled slightly at the memory. How had she managed to keep singing? How could she have stopped? Darcy played to her like no one had ever done before. It was as if he directed all the power of his playing at her. The song was just a framework for his message, which was solely her own.

What did he say to her? He wanted her. It was so pure and clear a message that it was almost overwhelming. She cried sometimes at the intense memory of his song. Yet she had never felt that it was too much when they had been together. Together, she could answer him, play with him, and stand with him. Only when she was alone did she feel weak.

She couldn't even take shelter in the denial that served her throughout the tour. Everything seemed so clear there on the stage. She didn't understand what happened afterward. The way he kissed her and walked away, as if he played passionate serenades to women every night.

It was his arrogance, she reasoned. He could just walk away because he had made his point. And he had, hadn't he? Here she was, dreaming about him. Wanting him like any panting fangirl. She hated to admit it, but she'd go to him in a minute if he called and told her "meet me in half an hour." She hated that he was right and that he knew it.

She remembered George's warning: "Once he finds something he wants, he gets it." She hated that Darcy messed with her head throughout their acquaintance. If only she didn't know the truth about him. If only she didn't know he could be so cruel. She longed to give herself to him, to trust in him, to let him take her, in every way.

She knew from the way he played, and the way he kissed, it would be explosive. Even now, as she muddled over it all, her nipples were hard. And it was so long since she had gotten laid! She wanted to just push aside all her frustrations and drive to Darcy's house and submit to him.

It was a good plan, except for two things: One, she didn't know where he lived, or even where he was; and two, it wasn't a joke. He had all kinds of power over her, and she didn't like that one bit.

If he reached out to her, called her, or even emailed her, just to talk to her and let her know he was similarly affected by what happened, she could happily surrender to him, even knowing what George told her. But she knew from his arrogance this was not to be. He might want her, but he didn't love her. And she had no desire to be his plaything.

❧

Jane answered the phone on the first ring. "Hello?" she said hopefully.

"Hey, beautiful," replied Charles. His California accent had grown stronger over the week.

"Hi." He could hear her smiling. "How are you doing?"

"Good. It's been nice being home, but it will be better to get back to New York."

"I know one person who will be happy to see you back."

"Tell me about your day, Jane."

"It was good. We had our record signing at Tower."

"Did you have a good turnout?"

"Yeah, we did! I think it was our best ever!"

Charles relaxed as he listened to her voice and walked along the beach. As Jane told him about meeting her fans, he could easily picture her face, and the pain he felt at missing her was briefly dulled.

He knew the pain was a message, his heart's way of telling him what he needed to do.

"Is that the ocean I hear?" Jane asked.

"It is," he smiled back to her. "I wanted to be alone when I called, so I walked to the shore."

"Oh," Jane said. "Is your house close to the water?"

"Yes, I have a house near Muir Beach."

"Where is that?" Jane asked, clearly delighted.

"It's near Sausalito. It's a nice little town. It's remote, but I love it here."

"It sounds nice," she said guardedly.

Charles made up his mind. Enough was enough. He was tired of this, of them pussyfooting around each other. He was going to tell her the truth when he got back to her and hope that she would accept it. "Jane," his voice reflected his determination. "I need to talk with you."

"Of course," Jane said. "Is something wrong?"

"I have to tell you something, Jane, in person. Not over the phone."

"Is it bad?" she whispered.

"Yes, it's bad," he said sadly.

"Charles, whatever it is, you can tell me."

"Jane, I will tell you, just not now. Not on the phone."

"So, you are coming back tomorrow?" she said bravely.

"Yeah, we're flying out of here around eight in the morning, we'll be getting into JFK at four thirty."

"Do you want me to meet you at the airport?" she offered.

"Oh, don't bother," he said tiredly. "We're going to have the limo take us right to the apartment."

"I could meet you there."

Charles sighed. He had been avoiding this. "You can't. I'll have to get cleaned up, and then we're expected at a De Bourgh party."

"We?"

"Slurry."

"Oh."

"I'm sorry, Jane. Believe me, I would take you if I could, but it's a media thing. We're going to be seen and photographed before the VMAs. All the big De Bourgh names will be there." He sighed, tired with the charade he was playing. "Jane, look, tomorrow is just not going to work, but I promise, we'll see each other on Tuesday, and we'll talk then."

"Charles, what's wrong? You sound so down. Tell me what's going on, please."

Charles let the ocean water wash over his feet. He could hear the frustration in her voice. "I know, Jane. I'm sorry. There's a lot of stuff going on here, and I promise as soon as I see you, I'll explain it all."

"Yeah, when it's convenient for you," she sulked.

"Jane, please try to understand."

"Charles, you haven't given me anything to understand."

Charles could see Caroline waving to him from the house. "I'm sorry, Jane. Just hang on two more days, and I'll explain it all."

"Okay," Jane said dully.

"I have to go; bye, Jane."

"Bye, Charles," she answered and hung up. He frowned at the dial tone coming from his phone and then hurried up the beach.

Darcy sighed as he entered his loft. He dragged his Pullman case into the bedroom and dropped onto his bed. It was still early in the day, just as it had been early when he left Paris eight hours earlier, but he was exhausted. Sleeping on the plane had not worked, so he tried to read, but mostly he found himself thinking about her. In his mind he kissed her a hundred times. She was receptive and eager. He held her close, and together they pleasured each other again and again. His favorite image was one in which he entered her room, to find her wearing only her Gibson and a smile.

Tomorrow, he told himself. Tomorrow he would see her again, then he would know how to act. So many times he had picked up the phone to call her, he even had an email draft ready to send. But he wasn't certain. Words with her were still hard. He didn't trust himself not to say the wrong thing.

Playing to her was a completely different story. Tomorrow he would play to her, and she would know what he felt, what he wanted.

Darcy heard the elevator stop at his floor. Georgiana was on her way to Pemberley, so this could only be one other person. He recognized Richard's footsteps as they entered the gallery.

"Will," he called out.

"In here," Darcy said, sitting up.

Richard entered Darcy's bedroom. "How was Paris?" he asked easily.

"Great," Darcy answered. "Georgie had a good time."

"Good, good."

"How was Hazelden?" Darcy asked, his tone a shade darker.

Richard shrugged. "Good," he replied simply.

Darcy respected Richard's privacy. After Georgiana's graduation the previous Saturday, Richard surprised them by telling the Darcys he would not be joining them on their river cruise of Paris. Instead he would return to the clinic where he was treated for alcoholism. Richard's decision greatly relieved Darcy; it meant that his cousin was facing his problems himself and was perhaps ready to do something about it.

"Will you be going back?" Darcy asked.

"That depends."

"On the VMAs?"

Richard nodded. "Before I can really work out why I'm… doing this,

I need to get things straight with her, but I can't do that to Charlotte until I've gotten myself together."

Darcy regarded Richard uneasily. "Sounds like a catch-22 situation."

Richard nodded. "One day at a time, that's all I can do."

Darcy nodded. "I'm going to try to sleep before tonight."

"What time is the party?"

"Eight o'clock."

"Okay, I'll wake you in time."

Richard closed the door, and Darcy stripped off his clothes, climbed into his cool bed, and enjoyed the vision of Elizabeth and her guitar.

❧

Elizabeth was worried. Jane looked like a wreck and moped in her room all day. Elizabeth had never seen her like this, and it was late in the day before Jane would talk about it.

"It's Charles."

Elizabeth guessed as much. That he was due back in New York today and Jane wasn't seeing him clearly signaled that something was wrong.

"He told me he needs to talk to me about something important when he gets back."

"Did he say what?"

"No, he wouldn't talk about it over the phone," Jane said sadly, looking at the floor. "I think he means to break up with me."

A week ago, Elizabeth would have said that was crazy, but the week had been long and hard on both of them, and Elizabeth had become cautious. Nevertheless, she did not want Jane to worry. "Jane, I really don't think he would do that, do you?"

"I don't know," Jane said softly. "He's been sounding so down and unlike himself over the phone, and he said it was something bad."

"Maybe it's not you. Maybe it's something totally different that's bad, and it's been getting to him."

"Then why wouldn't he tell me?" she asked, her eyes begging for hope.

"I don't know, Jane," Elizabeth said, putting her arm around her sister's shoulder. "But I do know there is no sense in worrying about it. There's nothing we can do but wait, right?"

Jane nodded. "I know," she smiled weakly at Elizabeth, "I'm trying."

Elizabeth tried to smile back but found it hard in the face of her sister's obvious pain. She squeezed Jane tight, then heard Lydia calling to her from downstairs. "Lizzy! Phone call!"

Elizabeth reached over and picked up Jane's extension. "Hello?"

"Hey, gorgeous," George Wickham's voice answered.

"George!" Elizabeth exclaimed. Jane smiled at her and lifted her eyebrows. "How are you?"

"I'm great! I just got into New York, and I wanted to make sure I would see you tomorrow at the VMAs."

"Yes!" Elizabeth grinned, surprised. "Are you going to be there?"

"Oh yeah. A couple of my videos are up for awards."

"Oh! That's wonderful!"

"So, I'll see you there?" George said coyly.

"You will! I'm looking forward to it," Elizabeth said pleasantly.

"Bye, Lizzy."

Elizabeth hung up and turned to an expectant Jane. "That was George."

"Who will be at the VMAs and is looking forward to seeing you," Jane continued.

Elizabeth laughed. "Yes, basically that's it."

"And are you looking forward to seeing him?"

Elizabeth inclined her head. "Of course I am. George is my friend."

"What about Will?"

Elizabeth frowned thoughtfully. "Yeah, what about him?" She sighed. "Well," she said, drawing the word out, "I guess we're both going to have to see what happens."

⚬‌⚬

As usual, Charles and Caroline were late. Darcy would have left without them if it weren't for the media exposure. That was the whole point of the party. It was after eight when they finally arrived. Darcy and Richard were in their "Slurry-wear," waiting in the kitchen.

Darcy was struck by the change in his friend right away. Physically Charles looked good; his skin was tanned, but his eyes were an emotional mess inside. "What the fuck?" Darcy asked him. "Didn't your father get parole?"

Charles waved the question away. "Oh, he did. I have him all settled in the apartment at my place."

"Then why do you look like your puppy got run over?"

"Jane," Charles said simply. Caroline said nothing, but the set of her mouth made it clear this was not a new topic.

"What happened?"

"I miss her. I hated being away from her. She sounded so sad, and I couldn't even tell her why we were apart." He pulled his hair back. "And now I can't even see her tonight."

"Charles, this is a business thing. It will be full of photographers and reporters. Why would Jane want to come to this?"

Charles looked at Darcy, his eyes haunted. "I know that. I told her that, but still she would have come, just to see me."

"Did you call her?"

"Her line was busy."

Darcy sighed. This was not going well. He had seen Charles get into trouble emotionally before and he knew the signs. "Look, Charles, tomorrow you will see her, and you two can work it all out."

Charles nodded dumbly.

"Now let's go."

❧

Elizabeth answered the phone. An angry voice said, "Finally."

"George?"

"Yeah, it's me. Damn, it's hard to get through to you!"

"Sorry, too many girls," Elizabeth explained lightly. "What's up?"

"I got some bad news, Lizzy."

"What?"

"I won't be seeing you tomorrow night."

"Why not?"

"It's that friggin', bastard."

"Who?"

"Darcy!" George growled. "I'm sorry. I shouldn't take it out on you, Lizzy." His tone softened. "It's just that the jerk must have found out I was going and he pulled some strings, so now I don't have an invitation to the show."

"What?" Elizabeth was shocked. "How could he do that?"

"Oh, he could do it. He's fucking Fitzwilliam Darcy. If he said jump, all of MTV would ask how friggin' high!"

"I can't believe he would do that!"

"Oh, believe it, Lizzy," George said with certainty. "Did you tell him about me?" he asked.

"Yes," she said, puzzled.

"Well, there you go. He doesn't want me anywhere near you."

"Oh God!" Elizabeth said in a low voice. "Oh my God!"

"I told you he gets what he wants, didn't I, Lizzy?"

"George, you were right," Elizabeth whispered.

"It's okay, Lizzy. I'm just pissed because I wanted to see my work win."

"That bastard," Lizzy whispered harshly, her anger building. "I can't believe him! That arrogant prick! It's bad enough he thinks he can fuck with me, but it's so wrong that he would mess with you."

"He's something, that arrogant jerk," George snorted.

"Well, what are you going to do?" Elizabeth asked tentatively.

George sounded sad. "Nothing I can do, Lizzy. He's got me."

Elizabeth remembered Darcy's anger as she told him about Wickham. "That's it! He's not getting away with this. Tomorrow I'm going to tell him off!"

"Lizzy, don't get yourself in trouble for me."

"It's not for you, George! It's because he's wrong! He's an arrogant bastard and I'm going to tell him just what I think of him!" She stomped her foot. "God! If I knew where he was, I would go there right now!"

"Oh, that's not hard," George said lightly. "He's no doubt at his big fancy loft. Hasn't he ever taken you there?"

"No," Elizabeth said, her tone soft and hurt.

"Figures," George muttered darkly. "It's on Broome Street in the Village."

A plan came to Elizabeth. "Could you tell me how to get there?"

❧

Darcy stretched and hit the lights. He was dead tired. The nap hadn't helped much, and the nervous energy that came from traveling was wearing off. He was happy to leave the party the first chance he could and go back home. Richard volunteered to stay and to look after Charles when Darcy announced he was leaving at ten thirty. Anne gave him an evil look, but he hadn't cared. He pressed the flesh and posed for pictures. His job was done. Darcy got himself a large glass of water. He hated affairs like that. The hypocrisy of it all disgusted him.

He was surprised when the phone rang ten minutes later. Even more surprising was the message. The doorman had an Elizabeth Bennet to see him. He ordered her sent up and went to the gallery to meet her, smiling. She had come! Just like he knew she would!

The elevator stopped and Elizabeth stepped out, her eyes flashing. She was surprised to find Darcy in a white shirt and his leather pants. Elizabeth bit down hard on her lust and snapped, "What? You wear those all the time?"

"I was just at an appearance," he explained.

"Do you know why I'm here?" she asked.

"I think so," he replied, lifting an eyebrow.

"You aren't even ashamed, are you?" she said, appalled.

"Why should I be?" he asked, suddenly uncertain.

"Oh! That just takes the cake! You ban your oldest friend from receiving awards he rightfully deserves and it doesn't bother you in the least!"

"Lizzy, what are you talking about?" Darcy asked, confusion plain on his face.

Elizabeth rolled her eyes. "So now you're playing stupid? Fine! I'll tell you. I'm talking about George Wickham, who just told me you had him banned from the VMAs," she snarled scornfully.

Darcy's expression hardened. "That's a lie, Elizabeth. No doubt one of many he's told you."

"Why would he lie to me?"

"Probably to get back at me, I suspect," he said calmly.

"George would never do that!" she said defiantly.

Darcy looked at her carefully. "Why do you believe him?"

Elizabeth paused, speechless. The question had caught her completely unawares. She pursed her lips and replied a moment later. "Because," she stammered, "he told me everything that happened between him and you and Georgiana."

Darcy smiled bitterly. "No, I'm sure he didn't tell you everything. Quite sure." He looked at her, his expression completely open. "Elizabeth, would you please sit down with me, and allow me to tell you my side of the story?"

Elizabeth nodded, surprised, her anger blunted by his reaction. This was not what she expected. He led her down a long hallway to a huge open space surrounded by shaded windows. Elizabeth sat on the couch and waited, still tense and hostile.

Darcy sighed deeply and began in a calm voice. "I trust that once you hear what happened you will know why I have to ask you to keep it a secret."

She watched as his face turned raw with anguish and he paused, visibly struggling to continue. Elizabeth felt confusion and pity for the pain he was attempting to master. Clearly whatever had happened had deeply affected Darcy as well. "Can I," she stopped when he looked at her, then she blurted out, "help?"

"Maybe it would be easier if you told me what Wickham told you," he said, somewhat gratefully.

Elizabeth spoke in a matter-of-fact way. "He told me about how he grew up with Georgiana, and they were childhood friends." Darcy nodded. "Then he went away to college, and when he returned, he saw her differently, as a beautiful woman." Elizabeth watched as Darcy's jaw tightened. She licked her lips and continued. "He told me how he fell in love with her, and she with him, until you found them out and forced them to break up." Her tone and her expression turned hard. "Now, tell me that was a lie."

Darcy had been pacing, listening carefully to her words. "It's not," he said shortly. "Nothing of it was a lie. I can see why you believed him."

Elizabeth was dumbstruck. "And you admit to this? To forcing them apart? To breaking their hearts?"

Darcy looked down for a long time. Then he lifted his eyes to her and said, "Excuse me, I need to get something." He disappeared into a side room and returned a moment later, sitting this time beside her on the couch. In his hand was a white folder with the words "Choate Rosemary Hall" printed in gold letters on it.

"It's all true what he told you, Elizabeth, but he left out one very important detail. From the way you tell the story, I do look like a monster. I can see that, but, well—" He sighed and turned to the folder. "Last Saturday, I was at Georgiana's graduation. Her *high school* graduation."

He opened the folder and passed it to her. In it was a large picture of a girl in cap and gown, standing next to Darcy, smiling with pride. The program in the folder was opened to the list of graduates, and the name Georgiana Helen Darcy was circled in black ink. Elizabeth noted absently that she had been an honor student. A cold, confused, surreal feeling came over Elizabeth as she looked at the words written there and the date, only a week prior.

Darcy spoke softly, his voice far away. "It started when George and

I were in college together. At first, I ignored it. It wasn't unusual for freshmen to be dating high school girls, but he never stopped, even as he got older. By the time he was a senior, I was aware there was something strange going on, but he was careful to hide it. He would never bring his dates to any place I might be.

"Then we started the band. At first, we only played for ourselves, but George really pushed us to perform in public and he even set up the first shows for us. It was summer, and it was hard to tell how old the girls he was hanging around with were. Truthfully, I was too busy working on our songs to even notice.

"Then that spring, he started to slip. Richard and I were starting to notice we had a surprising number of high-school-aged girls as fans, but we just figured it was the music. We caught George with these girls once or twice, but he always claimed he didn't know, or that they had told him they were in college."

His voice grew softer as Elizabeth looked at him, horror building on her features. "Then that tour came. I made the decision to take Georgie with us because I missed her, frankly. She was at school all spring and I wanted her around. I had no idea..." His voice faded, then with effort, he began again. "It was the Fourth of July, at the Ramsgate festival." Darcy looked up into Elizabeth's eyes, and she knew he had never told this to anyone before. "And I walked into George's dressing room and found him on top of my *fourteen*-year-old sister."

Elizabeth's hands were trembling as she moved them over her mouth. "Oh God," she cried so quietly no one could have heard. A memory slammed into her head, of her lying on the couch on Darcy's bus and listening to Caro discuss Georgie going to college.

She stood up, knowing she was going to be sick. Darcy looked at her, puzzled, until she squeaked out, "Bathroom?"

He took her arm and half-led/half-dragged her down the hall and through a door. Elizabeth fell to her knees and emptied the contents of her stomach into the toilet. Only when she finished did she realize that Darcy was still there. He silently filled a glass of water and knelt down to give it to her.

Elizabeth took it, her hand still shaking. She took a sip and spit it out, and then with Darcy's help, she gingerly stood. He helped her to the sink, where she washed her mouth out, and he gave her a damp washcloth.

"Did you sleep with him?" he asked finally.

"No," Elizabeth breathed, "no, thank God." Realization hit her; she was mortified by her actions and needed to escape. "I'm sorry. I'm so sorry," she said brokenly. "I'll leave now."

She turned to the door, but Darcy caught her. "Elizabeth, you can barely stand," he said with a gentle smile. "I'm not letting you leave yet."

He gently led her back out to the bar that looked into the kitchen. "Sit," he told her as he pulled out a stool.

Elizabeth put her elbows on the bar and her head in her hands. "How could I have been so stupid?" she whispered to herself.

Darcy was moving around the kitchen and served Elizabeth a glass of juice. "Drink that, slowly."

Elizabeth didn't want to drink anything, but she was so shaky she took a sip. Darcy came back around to her and lightly rubbed her back as he sat beside her. "Don't blame yourself, Elizabeth. George is a master of deception. I know. I've been the victim of it more times than I can count."

"I shouldn't have been so gullible," Elizabeth chastised herself. She looked at Darcy and remembered how she had come here to defend Wickham, and a fresh horror dawned on her. "Oh my God! You must hate me!"

Darcy shook his head, his eyes on hers. "I could never hate you, Lizzy, never. You have every right to be angry with me. I should've told you right away about Wickham."

"No," Elizabeth said, putting her hand on his arm, "I understand why you couldn't." She felt tears forming in her eyes. "No one else knows?"

Darcy shook his head. "Only Richard, my attorney, and Georgie's counselor."

"So what happened?"

Darcy shrugged as he took her now empty glass and walked around the bar to the kitchen. "I threw George off the tour and told him never to come near us again. He knew I wouldn't press charges. Not for his sake, but for Georgie's."

Elizabeth nodded. She cringed as she realized that without meaning to, her eyes had fixed themselves on the vision of his tight ass encased in his leather pants, an image that seemed totally out of place in this setting.

"He disappeared and I had to deal with Georgiana," he said as he returned to his seat beside her.

"Did she blame you?"

"Yes," his soft voice expressing his long-held grief. "It was only after George didn't come back and didn't even try to contact her for six months that she was willing to accept the fact that he had victimized her." Darcy looked at her, and again Elizabeth saw that bitter, self-mocking grin. "Then she hated both of us," he said with bitter humor.

"I can't imagine," Elizabeth said as she took his hand in her own and squeezed it. "That must have been so hard."

"It was," he said, his voice very soft. "I failed her. Georgie was my responsibility. I was the only one she had to care for her, to protect her"—he laughed, a harsh angry bark—"and I took her on tour with a fucking pedophile!" He stopped, overcome by guilt, his fist clenching. Turning to Elizabeth, he continued, his voice deep with irony and hurt. "So you can see how I can't really blame you for trusting George."

Elizabeth touched his cheek, gently. He was suffering so deeply, the hurt raw on his face. She didn't know what she was doing, but her instincts told her to help him, to heal him. She pulled his face closer and kissed him gently on the lips. "I'm sorry," she whispered, her voice thick with feeling. She kissed him again, and suddenly his arms flung around her, like a drowning man grabbing a life preserver.

He kissed her, hard, before he opened his mouth, to find hers eagerly waiting for him. He plundered her mouth, tasting her sweetness and moaning her name as he gasped for breath, "Lizzy, Lizzy…"

She whispered one thing only in reply: "Don't stop."

Her words unleashed a torrent of desire in him. His hands explored her, sliding under her shirt and stroking the smooth skin of her back until with a cry of frustration she grabbed his hand and placed it on her breast.

Darcy stared at her, his eyes searching hers as their chests rose and fell, then she squeezed his hand and sighed with pleasure. Darcy didn't need anything more. In a moment, her shirt and bra were reduced to tattered rags on the floor. He squeezed her full, round breasts, kissing her as her head tipped back from the pleasure. Soft cries rose from her throat as he bent down to suck a rosy-tipped nipple into his mouth.

Her hands moved desperately, one clasping his head to her, the other reaching down the back of his shirt to pull him closer. His suckling started gently, but soon became harder as her cries grew more frantic. Her nipple grew hard and swollen in his mouth and he was sure he had never tasted anything so luscious.

His feast was interrupted as she pulled his head away and looked at him with an expression of need. His shirt was quickly removed while she disposed of her shorts and panties. As he opened his pants, she stared at him, hard and sweating. Brazenly she put her hand on his, stopping him. "Don't," she commanded. "Leave them on."

Darcy's eyes widened with understanding. He opened his fly as wide as possible and Elizabeth was mesmerized with the sight of his large erection rising out from his tight leather sheath, his tight dark curls peeking out from his base. Breathing heavily, she sat back on the stool and spread her legs wide open for him.

Darcy grew harder at the searing vision of Elizabeth, aroused and naked, exposing herself to him. He took her into his arms, his one hand at the flat of her back, pressing her close to him, the other touching her sex. He kissed her again, his tongue demonstrating exactly what his cock would be doing. Positioning himself, he moved both hands to cup her ass and entered her with a series of long, hard strokes.

A strangled cry escaped Elizabeth's mouth as she kissed him again, her hands grasping his shoulders and her legs wrapping around his leather-clad hips. Their tongues dueled while he thrust into her, again and again until finally he penetrated her fully.

He paused for a moment, and Elizabeth relished in the feeling of him deep inside of her, until he rasped, "Hang on!" and fucked her with a fury she had not believed possible. Over and over, he banged into her, and Elizabeth welcomed every impact. She cried out as she felt him thickening and growing larger inside of her. The sweet pressure was building up in her, making her beg desperately for him to never stop. She tightened her legs around his leather-clad ass, locking him close as she exploded on him.

He gripped her ass tightly, hammering his last blows into her as he reached his peak and his seed burst out.

Panting, he gathered her close to him and sat down with her still mounted on him. "I'm sorry, Lizzy," he whispered as he kissed the top of her head. "I'm sorry, I didn't want it to be rough with you."

Elizabeth giggled as she struggled for breath and lifted a glowing face to him, her lips finding his. "Now who's being stupid?" she teased as she kissed him again. "What makes you think I wanted it any other way?"

He smiled rakishly back at her. "Naughty girl." He kissed her deeply and Elizabeth gasped as she felt him hardening inside of her. His eyes sought her approval, given as she clenched him tightly inside of her.

Grasping her thighs, he rose and managed only a few steps before he stopped and pressed her against the wall. "I don't think we're going to make it to the bed," he gasped.

"You have a bed?" she asked, the humor lost on them both as Darcy plunged himself into her slick wet opening at a fervent pace and Elizabeth's head fell back, her hands reaching up to cup her breasts. Darcy's eyes locked on the image of her fingers pinching her nipples and he slowly pulled himself out and slid down the wall with her to the floor.

Elizabeth looked at him questioningly as he gently laid her back on the thick hand-woven rug. Kneeling down beside her, he reached out to touch her chest, still heaving deeply with each breath. Slowly he traced his fingertips down her body, dipping into her navel and following the gentle curve of her belly, before he finally reached the soft dark fur crowning her sex.

Elizabeth watched his expression of wonder mixed with a powerful lust. His touch stirred her and left her needing more. She arched her hips up, allowing his fingers to drop just a little lower, into the place she craved.

"Oh God!" she sighed as his rough calluses finally touched her. He dipped his finger into her well, using his own come as a lubricant as he returned to her center.

Her hands were back at her breasts, and he found he needed to taste them again. He leaned forward, pivoting on his knees, and captured one in his mouth. A low moan of satisfaction arose from Elizabeth as the pleasure of his tongue and his touch combined in her.

Elizabeth's free hand reached out and found his long thigh at her side. It was still encased in the smooth leather, which did nothing to hide his hard muscles from her touch. She closed her eyes and let her hand explore his lower body, sliding out his leg and over the tight curves of his ass, squeezing it as she arched higher, her body seeking the release she needed. With a sudden cry, he tipped her over the edge and she came violently, her head involuntarily rocking against the floor with each wave of pleasure.

Then she stopped, her body curling into a tight ball as the waves of pleasure ebbed away. He collected her into his arms, his lips placing tender kisses on her face as she slowly returned to herself. Gradually her body relaxed and her legs stretched out again to feel the curious sensation of his leather-clad ones intertwining with hers.

He slowly laid her back and positioned himself above her. Taking his large cock in his hand, he lightly teased her center with its head until she sighed and parted her lips to him in supplication.

Their mutual wetness made it easy for him to slide into her. He marveled distantly at the difference from the last time, until she lifted her hips to him and drew her nails down his back, and then he didn't notice anything. She grabbed at him wildly as her legs wrapped around his waist and attempted to bring him deeper. Forcefully he rode her, unable to stop until he achieved the release he sought in her. Elizabeth's voice was in his ears but he could not understand what she said. Then he felt her body tightening, pulling on him, and he knew he was there. He held on tightly, as her screams were soon joined by his moans when he came inside her once again.

"Are you okay?" he asked when he could speak again.

Lizzy could only nod. Leaning on each other, they got up and made their way down the hall to the master bedroom. Darcy's bed was still unmade from his nap, and with Elizabeth's permission, he finally removed his pants and crawled in beside her.

Elizabeth rested her head on his chest, listening to the soothing sound of his heartbeat. One of his hands stroked her back while the other covered her hand as it rested on his chest.

They rested together silently for what felt like a long time, each of them reflecting silently, Darcy kissing the top of her head, Elizabeth kissing his chest. Darcy heard her giggle and looked down to see her fingers lightly fanning over his chest. "What are you doing?" he asked, his voice relaxed and amused.

Elizabeth looked up at him, her eyes dancing with mirth. "I'm playing your lyre," she replied with a wicked grin.

He lifted his eyebrows. "Are you now?"

"Hmm mmm," she replied, her fingers dancing lightly over the tiny ink strings on his chest. "I love this," she told him with artless honesty.

Darcy felt his heart swelling as a sweet sensation of rightness overcame him. Never in all his fantasies could he have imagined it would be like this, that making love to Elizabeth would be so intense, or that she would touch him so deeply. She pressed her face to his tattoo and tenderly kissed the spot directly over his heart. Darcy could feel his flesh and his very soul being branded by her lips. He squeezed her tightly and said, "Thank you."

"Thank you," she replied. "That was..." She smiled, not having words to express her experience. "I've never had it like that before."

"Neither have I," he told her sincerely as his fingers lightly brushed her hair from her face. "But I knew it would be special for us."

Elizabeth nodded as she found herself in agreement with him. "Me too," she giggled and rolled onto her back. "Oh!"

"What?" he asked as he followed her roll, to end up lying half on top of her.

"I think I'm going to have a problem when I go. My clothes," she grinned, "got kind of damaged."

"Oh, that's no problem," he smiled, his hand stroking the muscles of her arm with featherlight touches.

"No?" Elizabeth asked as she yielded to temptation and nibbled on his yummy dimple.

"Who said anything about you leaving?" he intoned with mock seriousness and wigging eyebrows.

Elizabeth laughed, drunk from the pleasure she had received and the closeness of him now. With a contented sigh, she rubbed her nose against his neck and let her head fill with his delicious scent.

"Seriously, Elizabeth," he said in a subdued tone. "I would like it if you stayed tonight," he told her, his expression curiously vulnerable.

Elizabeth reached up and rubbed the frown from between his eyebrows. She remembered the pain he had shared with her earlier and she felt her heart go out to him. "I'm not going anywhere," she told him softly.

She could see the relief on his face as he bent down to kiss her. She found it a delightful sensation. "Why didn't we do this before?" he asked, once again playful.

Elizabeth yawned. "I don't know."

He turned Elizabeth on her side and spooned snugly beside her. "Neither do I, but I don't think it matters now, does it?" he asked sleepily.

Elizabeth grinned and shook her head. She tried to go to sleep but something bothered her. "The lights are still on in the hall."

"So?"

Chuckling, she rose and shut them off, gathering their clothing in the process. She realized that he lived alone and this was probably unnecessary, but old habits died hard. Quickly she hurried back to the bedroom and his bed.

Darcy bundled her close to him and planted a kiss on her ear before dropping off. Elizabeth smiled in contentment and surrendered to her emotional and physical exhaustion.

❧

Elizabeth felt great as she awoke. She smiled cheerfully, stretched her legs, and snuggled closer to the warmth beside her. A hand rested on her cheek and she felt a kiss on her lips.

"Good morning," the owner of the delicious warmth said. "You seem happy."

Elizabeth's smile grew wider. "I am." She opened her eyes to find Darcy looking at her with amusement. "What?" she asked indignantly.

He laughed and kissed her lightly. "I've just never seen you so happy in the morning before."

Elizabeth kissed him back. "Well, I did have the most gorgeous sleep," she replied, sighing luxuriously. "Thank you."

Darcy grinned lustily. "Glad to have been of service." He reached out and kissed her, pulling her body close. "God, you feel good," he exclaimed as his hands traced her soft curves.

"Hmmmm, so do you." She reached down to stroke the erection that was pressing into her stomach. "Do you mind?" she asked as she gently indicated where she would like him to go.

"Not at all," he breathed as he mounted her. "I didn't want to bother you."

Elizabeth sighed as he slid home. "Oh, such a bother." She closed her eyes and delighted in the sensation that was him. She loved his smell, and the soft grunts he made when he thrust into her. However this time it was different. This wasn't the frantic hell-for-leather ride of last night. It was slow and exacting. As he grew larger and deeper within her, his movements became smaller and more precise. She grasped his shoulders as her excitement built inside of her. She remembered how many times she had longed for this, to feel his weight on top of her and his cock buried deep inside of her. He breathed her name in her ear and she was gone.

Darcy watched her come beneath him, her head tipped back, her body grasping his, and he gave up. The pleasure he had been holding back enflamed inside of him, she was so wet, so tight. He gave himself over to the sweet pleasure that was Elizabeth and rode her to his release.

When he caught his breath, he rolled with Elizabeth to their side. "You are amazing," he told her.

Elizabeth grinned, looking quite pleased. "I know."

He smiled at her contemplatively as he reached out and stroked her hair, locking this image of her into his memory. "What?" Elizabeth asked, puzzled by his "deep thoughts" look.

Darcy shook his head dismissively. "I'll tell you later." He sat up smoothly. "Do you want to start getting cleaned up? I have to do something." Elizabeth nodded and stretched her arms over her head as she openly stared at Darcy's perfect body as he left the room, still stark naked.

The massive bed was suddenly unappealing without Darcy in it, so Elizabeth rose and went to the large bathroom off the bedroom. It was bright and sunny, yet private, with a toilet, double vanity, sunken tub, and a separate shower enclosure. She relieved herself and was hunting around for a toothbrush when she heard Darcy's knock.

"Come in!" she replied.

He entered, still naked and looking exceptionally pleased with himself.

"Do you have a toothbrush I can use?" Elizabeth asked.

He pulled a purple one, still in its wrapper, out of a drawer. "For you."

"Thank you," Elizabeth grinned as she opened the package and started to use it. Darcy came up close behind her and wrapped his arms around her middle, staring at their reflection in the large mirror. Elizabeth's breasts were full and round, brushing his upper arm.

"You seem happy," she observed around her toothbrush.

"I am," he told her. "I've waited so long for this, to see you like this, to touch you." He smiled and hugged her tight. "It was amazing to wake up with you."

Elizabeth leaned forward as far as she could and spit out her toothpaste. She was a little embarrassed, but Darcy didn't seem to mind. She leaned back and kissed him over her shoulder, leaving a trace of toothpaste on his lips.

"Is that coffee I smell?" she asked as a familiar scent hit her. Darcy smiled and nodded slowly to her. "For me?"

"Well, I'm certainly not going to drink it."

Elizabeth smiled gratefully then looked down. "I didn't think you would have any in the house. I know you don't drink it."

"No, I don't," he said as he started brushing his teeth. "But my assistant does, and my cousin does, and," he stopped, spit out his toothpaste, and stared at her eyes in the mirror, "my lover does."

"Oh," she said, moved by the intensity in his eyes.

"You are the only one who is sharing my bed, Elizabeth. Don't worry."

Elizabeth's cheeks flamed. She hadn't realized she was that obvious and she was embarrassed.

Silently, Darcy walked around her and turned the shower on. "Is this hot enough?" he asked, moving aside for her.

Elizabeth was grateful he hadn't said anything more. He seemed to understand her uneasiness. Elizabeth tested the water and then stepped in. It was very hot, just the way she liked it. *Like Darcy*, she giggled to herself. She watched him step in with her, still not quite able to believe this beautiful man had made love to her. The shower had a half-dozen heads mounted at different angles. Elizabeth was glad Darcy was here, because she would never have figured out the knobs and switches by herself.

"It's not that complicated," Darcy told her, seeming to read her mind. "I usually just use one shower head, but this is a special occasion."

Elizabeth smiled uneasily. Darcy gently turned her away from him and started massaging her shoulders. "Talk to me," he told her gently. "What's bothering you?"

"I don't know," Elizabeth answered honestly.

"Is it me?"

"No," she replied. "You've been amazing. It's me, I guess. I just don't have a lot of experience with this whole morning-after thing." She felt herself blushing again. "I don't know what I should do or say or when I should leave or what."

Darcy moved her long mane of hair to the side and kissed the nape of her neck. "I love this spot on you. It's very sexy," he breathed as he dragged his lips slowly over it, and Elizabeth felt her pulse rising. "As for the rest of it," Darcy continued, "I think we don't need to worry about traditional roles, Elizabeth. You and I are different. We're artists and we make up our own roles. We don't live the everyday lives that other people do." He kissed her again, his lips lingering on her neck. "And besides, I don't have much practice at this morning-after thing either," he said in a rush.

Elizabeth laughed, her tension ebbing away. She turned, twined her arms around his neck, and kissed him happily. "Thank you," she grinned.

Darcy smiled back radiantly. "Any time. I want you to feel completely welcome here."

"You do?"

He nodded, his expression pleasantly earnest. "I like having you here. It's an experience I want to repeat."

Elizabeth smiled, pleased that he had seemingly effortlessly relieved a number of her questions: Was this a one-night stand? Did he want her to leave? And so on.

Darcy reached behind her and picked up a plain white bar of soap. His eyes asked permission, which she silently gave, and she relaxed as his hands moved over her body. Slowly he washed her, starting with her arms then moving to her chest and tummy. She opened her eyes when he tickled her slightly and she shyly asked what he was thinking.

"I was thinking about all those times we were swimming together and I wanted to do this, to touch you all over."

"You did?"

Darcy stopped and looked up at her, puzzled. "Of course, wasn't it obvious with the way I was staring at you?"

Elizabeth looked away. "I thought you, I don't know, I didn't realize."

Darcy stopped his careful bathing and stood up. "Lizzy, don't you know I've been crazy about you for months?"

Elizabeth met his gaze with difficulty. "I'm not sure. I thought that you might like me, but you were so... I wasn't sure." She frowned then. "And then when George talked to me—"

"Stop!" Darcy told her, "You will not think about him in my shower."

"But I was so wrong. I believed him, and I was so cruel to you."

Darcy took her face in his large hands and gently forced her to look at him. "Lizzy, I told you before, it's not your fault. George is a master at lying, and he knew that you would be the one I would care about. He knows me well enough to know that I would be attracted to you. That is why he targeted you." Darcy kissed her lightly. "But it doesn't matter now, does it?" He lifted an eyebrow to indicate their current setting and Elizabeth nodded.

She rose up on her toes and kissed him, opening to him the feelings that she couldn't talk about yet. Darcy released her face to wrap his long arms around her body and pull her closer. Elizabeth was heady from the sensation of his bare wet skin against hers. She moved back and smiled wickedly as he became erect against her belly.

It was Darcy's turn to be embarrassed. "I'm sorry, Lizzy. I don't know what you do to me," he told her. "If you want to go and—" The words died on his lips as Elizabeth, with large hungry eyes, sank to her knees and drew his hard cock into her mouth.

"Oh *my God!*" Darcy growled as she took her time, blissfully sucking and releasing, nipping his head and planting featherlight kisses on his balls. "Lizzy," he moaned between labored breaths. "Damn it, Lizzy!"

In a rush Lizzy felt movement and found herself being lifted. Darcy took her and placed her on his lap as he sat on the bench that ran along the rear wall of the shower. "Oh?" she gasped, then Darcy thrust upward and entered her, and Elizabeth found that she was beyond intelligent conversation. Darcy was pleased to find this position left her breasts at the perfect height and he helped himself to her hard nipples, sucking and teasing them with his teeth.

Elizabeth buried her fingers in his thick, wet hair and arched herself back, trying to improve her position. She enjoyed the feelings of Darcy inside of her, and his mouth was making her lose her mind. She raised her hands over her head, stretching herself against him, allowing herself to savor the full length of him. He suckled harder as she ground herself into him. She could hear him moaning softly as she felt herself getting closer. She felt sexy and wicked, enjoying the knowledge that literally the sexiest man she knew couldn't get enough of her. Finally she exploded in a fantastic rush. Darcy's hands clamped tightly to her hips as he pounded himself into her. Elizabeth relished the sinful feeling of his body slamming against her again and again until she felt him pause and then come in her with a ragged gasp.

They separated, Darcy sitting on the bench, and Elizabeth, panting, leaning heavily against the wall. When he could speak, Darcy said, "I'm sorry, Lizzy. I promise someday I'll make love to you properly."

Elizabeth looked at him disbelievingly. "What was wrong with that?"

He grinned shyly. "I want to taste you."

"Oh," Elizabeth smiled wantonly, "I'm sure we can arrange that."

Together they washed, deciding that washing themselves would be a safer course of action, and soon tumbled out of the shower in a wet, happy, steamy pile.

Darcy took great delight in drying her off, while Elizabeth took her own turn drying his back. When they entered the bedroom, Elizabeth was pleased to see Darcy had laid out her shorts and a Slurry T-shirt. As she dressed, she giggled. "I guess it's official. I'm a Slurry groupie now."

Darcy looked at her, his eyes lingering over her unbound breasts, which were plainly outlined by the T-shirt. "No, you are *the* Slurry groupie," he said lustfully.

"I hope that doesn't mean I have to do the whole band," she replied, deadpan.

"Oh no!" Darcy said playfully. "No sharing."

He led her to the kitchen area and let her fix her coffee while he operated the remote and opened the shades.

As the morning light flooded the room, Elizabeth looked around in surprise. In everything that had happened the night before, she had never really seen Darcy's home. "Will," she breathed, admiration apparent in her voice, "this is amazing. Look at the view!" She stepped to the far end of the living area where there were windows on three walls. "This is so beautiful," she told him.

He looked at her, his face an expression of pride and joy. "I've wanted to bring you here, to share this with you for so long, Elizabeth."

Elizabeth was touched and she hugged him close. "Tell me what I'm looking at."

Darcy took the time to point out all the landmarks from each window. Then he led her back to the bar, where they sat, discussing getting a plaque for "The Stool" when he said, "You know, it's silly for you to go back up to Meryton and then turn around and come back here."

"Yeah, I was thinking that. Would it be okay if I called home and asked Jane to bring my stuff?" she said. "I should probably tell them where I am anyway."

"You are home," he told her softly, his eyes cradling hers.

"What?"

"My home is yours, Elizabeth."

Elizabeth was very uncomfortable with what he said, so she tried to hide it in a joke. "Oh, that's all? No prenup, no wedding, just three or four quick ones and I get the house?" she grinned teasingly. "Your attorney must love that."

Darcy rolled his eyes. "You have no idea."

She grinned, glad the moment had passed, and reached for the phone.

❦

Richard nodded to the doorman and entered the elevator. When the doors stopped, Richard was immediately struck by something odd. The smell of coffee was there when it shouldn't be. He walked toward the voices coming from the living area.

He stopped and gaped when he saw Darcy wearing nothing but a pair of cotton drawstring pants and Elizabeth wearing shorts and a Slurry T-shirt. Their hair was damp, and if that wasn't enough, it was clear from their body language they had been "close."

Darcy was explaining to Elizabeth that Richard seemed to live in his fourth bedroom when Richard recovered the power of speech. "Lizzy! I didn't expect to see you so soon."

Elizabeth blushed slightly and smiled. "Hi, Richard."

"Good thing I got extra croissants this morning," he said lightly. "Have you eaten yet?"

"No," Elizabeth said with an embarrassed chuckle.

"Will," Richard said as he put a bag on the table, "could I have a word with you?"

Darcy followed his cousin into his office and waited. "That's great, Will, that's just fuckin' great," Richard observed. "You dumped me with Charles, who spent all night moping over Jane, getting drunk, and then barfing, while you're back here shagging her sister!"

"Richard, believe me, this wasn't planned," Darcy replied calmly.

"Damned amazing timing then."

"As a matter of fact, you can thank Wickham for that. He called her last night and got Lizzy so worked up, she drove down here to read me the riot act."

"Well, I can see that was one of his more successful plans," Richard commented dryly.

"Indeed," Darcy grinned, taking a sip of his tea.

From the table where Elizabeth was setting out the food, she could hear every word. She wondered why they had even shut the door.

"Fine, you enjoy your playmate, but I suggest you give Charles a call later. It's your fault he's in this mess." He opened the door and announced, "I'm going to bed," and walked to his room.

Elizabeth looked at Darcy with open curiosity. She figured it was his house, he must know the walls were as thin as tissue paper. "What did he mean about Charles?"

Darcy shrugged as he crossed over to her. "Truthfully, I don't know. Charles was depressed last night over Jane. He's been missing her terribly."

"Really?" Elizabeth asked. "Jane thinks he wants to break up with her."

Darcy looked confused as he walked with her to the table and sat down. "Why would she think that?"

"Charles has been distant from Jane lately, he's been keeping things from her," Elizabeth told him as she sat down. "And when they talked Sunday night, he said he needed to talk to her face-to-face and that it was something bad."

Darcy nodded knowingly. "He's not going to break up with her."

"Are you sure?"

"Yes," Darcy took her hand. "He is going to tell her about his father." Darcy took a sip of his tea and continued. "Charles's father was just released from jail, where he served twelve months for insider trading."

Elizabeth was shocked. "Why didn't I hear about this before?"

"Because we've been working like crazy to make sure that *nobody* heard about it. I told Charles not to tell Jane."

Elizabeth froze. "So, why did you tell me?"

Darcy looked at her warmly. "Elizabeth, you know about Georgiana, there can't be any secrets between us now."

"But why did you trust me when you didn't trust Jane?"

Darcy stopped, put his cup on the table, and turned to her, taking both her hands in his own. "Because I love you, Elizabeth. Don't you know that? I ardently love and admire you, with all my heart."

Elizabeth felt chilled. She pulled her hands back. "Wait," she told him. "Will, you're going too fast."

"Elizabeth," his voice was filled with wonder, "did you really not know?" He studied her eyes and found the truth of his words. "I'm sorry, Lizzy. I didn't mean to startle you, but it's true. I do love you. And I have for the longest time."

"No," Elizabeth breathed and got up. She moved away from the table and faced the window.

"Lizzy," he said gently as he placed his hands on her shoulders.

"Will, I told you, you have to slow down!" she told him, pulling away.

"Lizzy, I'm not trying to rush you. I just want you to know how I feel." He held up his hands in a nonthreatening way. "Besides," he grinned, "you can't tell me that after last night, you don't feel the same way."

"What?" Elizabeth exclaimed. "Will, how can I know if I love you? I feel like I barely even know you!"

"Elizabeth, you know me!" he snapped. He could sense they were getting into trouble again. He fell back on the one thing he could trust. "You may not know the stupid details of my life, but you know my music. You know what counts about me." He stepped closer. "You can't tell me that you would have touched me, have comforted me the way you did last night if you didn't love me. You wouldn't have done that for anyone else."

Elizabeth looked up at him, her expression confused and troubled. "Actually, I don't know that. What you shared was so horrible, and you were hurting so badly. I don't know if it was love or what. I just wanted to comfort you. So I don't know if I would have done the same for someone else. If it was someone I respected and liked, and I had no other reason not to, then maybe I might have slept with someone else if they had shared something that painful with me. I don't know."

"No, Elizabeth, I don't believe it."

"Will, it's true. Look, *please*, you've got to slow down. I like you, you're a good friend and a great lover, but I don't know if I love you, not yet." She looked saddened by the realization.

"You cannot make love the way we did and *not* be in love!" He shook his head in stunned disbelief. "I love you! Only you! Of all the women I have known, I want you! Can't you see that? You have seen all the women I could have. I could be worse than Richard, for Christ's sake, but I don't want anyone but you, Elizabeth," he said, his words vibrating with intensity. "Don't you understand? Didn't you hear it when I played for you?"

"You're not listening to me." Elizabeth stepped back slowly, her face shocked. "I'm sorry, Darcy. I'm very, very sorry. But... I need time." Then she turned away and quickly moved toward the elevator.

Darcy followed her. "Stay!" he told her as the doors began to close.

Elizabeth only shook her head, unable to look at him, tears forming in her eyes.

⤜⤛

Elizabeth found herself walking, not knowing what to think. Her truck was parked in the Village, but Elizabeth soon realized that she was heading north and figured she might as well keep going, rather than double back and have to find another parking space. In fact, she frankly didn't care if she ever saw her truck again. She felt like she could simply keep walking for the rest of her life.

What had happened? In twelve hours, her life had changed completely. Oh, she could deny it. She could pretend that it was just a meaningless fuck with no consequences, but nothing could be further from reality.

No, nothing was the same.

She slowed as Darcy's face appeared before her eyes. How could she have been so blind? No wonder he was stunned by her ignorance. He had been offering his affections to her for so long, she realized now. With the remarkable clarity of hindsight, she was able to see it all: the kindness he had shown her when performing, the way he comforted her when she was troubled, the solo he had played just for *her*. She shivered in the July heat as she saw his eyes again as he looked at her, as he fucked her, as he professed his love for her.

No, she told herself, quickening her step and trying to push the image away. *Don't think about that.* She laughed out loud like a madwoman. When else was she to think about it? Realizing the necessity of putting her thoughts in order, she found one of the ubiquitous coffee shops, got herself a triple vanilla latte, and sat down by herself to sort things out.

Okay, point one: He loved her, or at least he thought he did. Did she love him? All the orderliness of her thoughts fell away at that one question. Did she? She didn't think she did, but she remembered what he had said: "You cannot make love the way we did and *not* be in love!" Was he right? Her cynical side said, *Of course not. You had great sex, you did not make love.* But she wasn't so sure. She sipped absently on her drink as she lost herself in the fresh memories.

She certainly had never had sex like that. She caught a whiff of his scent trapped in her hair and her gut clenched. "Oh God," she whispered. What had she done?

She struggled to pull herself together. Even if he was right, even if they had made love, that didn't mean she loved him and even if she did, he was pushing her. Of that fact she could be sure, and she grasped on to it tightly. She had asked him, begged him to slow down, and he hadn't. He wouldn't back down, and in the end he had pushed her right out the door.

And now they were on opposite sides of the door, and neither was happy. She sighed heavily and rose. When she returned to the sidewalk, she paused for a full minute, not sure which way to turn her feet. In the end, her pragmatism turned her toward the north. She knew she would see Will at the rehearsal and they could speak there. It would be better that way, safer, because they couldn't get distracted or carried away.

Realizing she had found as much peace as she could, she put the question of "what comes next?" out of her mind and walked uptown. She still couldn't admit that she loved him, but she wasn't willing to rule that out of her future, and she did know she needed to know him better, and he needed to know more about her.

That thought triggered a flash of annoyance in her jaw. He hadn't seemed to care about her feelings. He was so certain of her, which in a way was flattering, but at the same time galling. Was she that predictable? And even if she was, where did he get off telling her what she felt? Okay, yes, she was very uncertain of her feelings, but still, she disliked the way he told her what she felt—once again, taking control of everything around her. Mr. Control Freak.

At least she understood now why he was so controlling. She still felt sorry for him for what happened to Georgiana, but at the same time, she needed to work out her own life, not be controlled by someone else, no matter how well meaning.

It was a relief when the hotel where she would meet Jane and the others finally came into view. She entered the restaurant, knowing she was an hour early. She wasn't hungry, but she knew she needed her strength for what was to come.

She ordered and ate her meal without tasting any of it. Her mind and indeed her spirit were miles away.

Darcy watched the elevator doors close with a feeling of helplessness. Without knowing what he did, he grabbed the first object he found and threw it, the crystal vase smashing into the closed doors and shattering to a million pieces.

"Nice job," Richard said quietly.

Darcy gave him a black look.

"I heard your discussion with Elizabeth," he continued, ignoring Darcy's expression. "That was good. I was impressed."

"Shut up!" Darcy growled violently.

"No, really, it was good. I especially liked the way she walked out on you."

Darcy spun on his cousin, finding his right fist pulled back by his ear and not knowing how it had gotten there. He froze. He had not punched Richard since he was fifteen. "Why? Why are you doing this?"

Richard shrugged. "Just wanted to share the misery."

"Fuck you!" Darcy swore emphatically as he walked to his bedroom.

"Why not? Everyone else has."

Darcy slammed the door and slid down against it. He couldn't go to his bed. It was too much. Too many memories lay there. "Lizzy," he breathed.

Why? Why had she walked away? He loved her, and she loved him. He was certain of it. He knew, from the way she had kissed him, last night, on the stool.

His mind was distracted by the memory of the stool, by the incredible feeling of entering her, of sinking himself into her, of their limbs being tightly intertwined and her cries of passion as he pleasured her again and again.

The ice-cold fact that she was gone broke in on his awareness, shattering the beautiful memory. She was gone! The vision of her face, sad and pitying as she told him she didn't love him, replaced the vision of her ecstasy, and he was desolate.

Why? He had offered her everything: his love, his home, his wealth, his very soul. He simply wanted to love her, to worship her with his complete being.

He snorted. Apparently that wasn't enough. Elizabeth Bennet didn't want that. Where she thought she would find better, he could not, in all honesty, imagine. No one would, or could, love her the way he did.

And her career! Didn't she see what he could do for her career? She thought she wanted to make it alone? Fine! She would see just how alone she could be.

With an ugly scowl, he dressed himself. He had a rehearsal to make, and he was going to teach Elizabeth a lesson.

⤝⤞

It was one of those days that Caroline Bingley was sure she was not paid enough. She was stuck at Radio City Music Hall with three of the crankiest men on the planet and a bitch producer from MTV, and to top it off, she hadn't seen her lover, or gotten laid, in over a week!

"TJ? How much longer?" she asked the friendly production assistant who had been assigned to Slurry. The rehearsal had been delayed, as she expected, but they were now well over an hour late and things were getting out of hand. A hip-hop medley of five different artists was the holdup, and it was with a sense of relief that Caroline saw they were finally finished.

"Ten minutes," TJ answered with a sympathetic smile.

Caroline nodded her thanks, grabbed the bottle of Advil that Charles was about to hurl away in frustration, and opened it for him.

"Thanks, Caro," he moaned as he popped four of them. Caroline asked TJ for another round of bottled water for the band as she stood and stretched her legs in the aisle. The band that had been troubled last week was a ragged mess today. Charles was clearly hung over, Richard was snarling from lack of sleep, and Darcy—she paused, Darcy looked worse than she had ever seen him. His expression was dark and bordering on flat-out mean. Caroline found herself in the unusual position of having no idea what had happened. He was fine when he had left the party the night before, but now, she wouldn't want to meet him in a dark alley.

The call came and Slurry finally moved onstage. The plan had been that they would play an acoustic version of "Bound," but the look in Darcy's eye told Caroline that was not going to happen.

⤝⤞

Darcy looked at the bitch producer from MTV who had insulted them all day to Anne de Bourgh, who looked at him with open disdain. He was fed up with women right now, convinced they were the source of all the misery in his life, but it was only when he saw Elizabeth and her band mates enter the theater and take a seat in the back that he knew what he was going to do.

He walked to Charles and put an arm over his shoulder. "Let's have some fun," he said, his voice darkly persuasive.

"What do you want to do?" Charles said foggily.

"Change the song," Darcy grinned wickedly. Charles matched his grin.

"I know what you're thinking," he agreed, delighted with the prospect of some harmless mischief. "Let's do it."

Darcy began a simple melody line to which Charles joined eight bars later.

It's like the stories, you always see,
In the movies or on the TV.
Girl meets boy, true love is found,
Till that Bitch turns it around.
It's all a joke!
It's all a joke.
Love, sex, all of the rest,
It's all a fucking joke.
I thought this was it.
I thought she was the one.
Turns out, she just wanted some fun.
Now I'm alone, it's easy to see,
All this time, the fucking joke was on me.

From her seat, Elizabeth felt her jaw drop as she recognized the introduction Darcy was playing. Shock overwhelmed her as she watched Darcy staring coldly at her, snarling and mouthing the chorus to her. The message was unmistakable, even for someone as blind as she had been.

CHAPTER 14

INSTINCT FOR SELF-PRESERVATION ALONE drove Elizabeth out of her seat and into the lobby. Charles's voice followed her, but at least she was away from Darcy's eyes. His eyes were so angry and hurtful. As she listened to the hurtful, mocking words, Elizabeth felt sick to her stomach.

A moment later Jane joined Elizabeth, looking at her in shocked confusion. "Why?" she stammered.

Elizabeth could only shake her head and hold up her hand, not ready to speak yet.

Charlotte and Alex burst through the doors. Charlotte took a look at the Bennets' expressions and said, "Okay, we're out of here. Let's go and get a drink."

❧

Darcy was pleased when he saw Elizabeth leave the theater. His temper was broken by her expression of surprise and hurt. But as his rage and vindictiveness were appeased, he found that he was left with little more than a cold emptiness inside. Intuitively he knew that he would regret his action at some point, but now he just felt numb.

"What the fuck!" the bitch producer screeched as she stormed the stage.

Caroline intercepted her and listened to her ranting for a minute as Charles and Darcy laughed together at her.

"What the fuck was that? They are not going to fucking sing that on my show! I can't broadcast that! Everyone told me they were professionals!"

Caroline stopped her there. "They are professionals, but they are also artists," she told her calmly. "You don't keep professionals cooling their heels for over two hours! Now, they are not going to sing that song tonight; they were merely blowing off steam."

"They better not!"

Anne de Bourgh appeared out of nowhere and spoke up imperially, "I promise you, Vicki, they won't."

Vicki glared at both the women and muttered, "They better not! Friggin' bastards!" before marching off in an angry huff.

Anne looked at Caroline, her eyebrows lifted.

"They won't," Caroline said in a much less certain tone.

"Perhaps you should have a word with them."

Caroline gave her a stiff nod while making a mental note to give herself an extremely large raise and went to speak to the band.

⌘

Richard walked slowly from around his drum kit to Darcy and Charles. "Well, that was fun," he observed, his voice dripping with sarcasm. "Do you feel better now?"

Darcy gave him a black look but otherwise ignored him.

Charles took a moment to study the audience while Caroline and Anne talked. "Do you guys see Jane?"

Richard fixed Darcy with a look and shook his head slowly. "Oh no, don't tell me he didn't know."

Darcy glared at Richard, then answered, "I saw her before, but I think she left. We'll see them later, I'm sure."

Charles frowned. "I really need to see her."

"Charles, we've all got rooms at the same hotel. We'll see them there, I'm sure."

Richard exhaled loudly. He could already feel the headache starting.

⌘

At the King Cole Bar in the St. Regis hotel, the two Bennets and the two Lucases found a table for an emergency meeting.

Jane was pale, her hand shaking as she sipped her drink. "Why? Why would Charles do that?" she asked no one in particular. "I mean, we sort of had a fight Sunday night, but nothing to warrant this."

Elizabeth sighed. She didn't want to talk about what happened, but she had no choice. "Jane, it wasn't you."

"What?" Jane asked, completely dumbfounded.

"Want to share, Lizzy?" Charlotte asked knowingly. Charlotte hadn't missed Darcy's vicious expression. When compared to Charles's "little boy acting out" expression, it told her everything she needed to know.

Elizabeth blew out a long breath. She fixed her eyes on the Maxfield Parrish mural dominating the room and told her story. "The song was directed at me. I went to Darcy's loft last night, and one thing led to another and I spent the night." As she spoke, she kept her voice as dry and emotionless as possible.

Elizabeth heard Charlotte snort, but she couldn't look at her. "This morning he told me that he loved me. I wasn't ready for that. I asked him to slow down, and he kept pushing, and in the end, he pushed me right out the door." She stared at her drink as she stirred it, and then took a long sip.

"Bastard!" Alex seethed.

Elizabeth realized that just the night before, George used the same word for Darcy and she felt the wrongness of it. Regret colored her voice as she said, "No, no, he's not. I hurt his feelings." She pushed her hair back from her face. "Well, maybe he is. That song was pretty shitty. I think he thinks I didn't believe that he was sincere. I didn't know," she shrugged at her own confusion.

Charlotte sat back, an expression of disgust on her face. "So let me see if I have this straight. He had amazing sex with you, then screwed you over, right?" She snorted. "Well, that's three for three for Slurry!" She raised her glass in a mocking salute.

"But the point is Charles isn't breaking up with you, Jane," Elizabeth finished.

"I wouldn't be so sure about that," Alex said, taking the newspaper that sat abandoned on the next table. It was a city daily open to a picture of Charles, smiling, his arm around the shoulder of a scantily clad actress. The caption informed them that the picture was from the De Bourgh party the night before.

Elizabeth looked from the picture to Jane. "I'm sure this doesn't mean anything, Jane."

"It doesn't really matter either way, Lizzy." Her voice was quiet and her gaze inward. "I knew Charles was breaking up with me. This picture doesn't make any difference."

"Jane, he's not," Elizabeth said quickly. "I'm sorry. I should have told you before. Darcy told me what's going on. Charles, um, it's not what you think." She frowned, frustrated. "Look, it's something bad about his father, and while I know what it is, I really think he should tell you, because it's personal. But I can say it's nothing about you and him."

Jane looked at her a long time. "He still should have told me. I'm tired of being told he loves me and to trust him, when all I'm getting shown is that he doesn't trust me. And frankly, I *don't* trust him anymore." She sighed and took a long sip of her drink. "Well, at least we know why Dead Man Walking left the tour," Jane said thoughtfully.

"Jane, I don't think they left because of romantic problems with the band," Elizabeth objected gently, while Charlotte's mouth twisted into a smile at the idea.

"No, but they probably left because they found out what we have: that Slurry is destructive, to themselves and to anyone around them."

"Jane?"

"Think about it. I know you were making a joke, Charlotte, but you were right. They have hurt all of us, badly. We aren't the same as we were before the tour. We used to be so strong. And now look at us. Richard has dragged you through the mud, Charlotte. Lizzy just got her heart handed to her on a plate, and even Charles," her voice broke here, and she stopped to pull herself together. "I can't sing 'Everything You Are' tonight," she announced finally. "It means too much to me."

Elizabeth felt Jane's words like a blow. "What?"

Alex snapped, "Jane!"

"No, I can't. These men, all of them, they have done nothing but hurt us. They are destroying us."

"What do you want to sing, Jane?" Charlotte asked quietly.

"'The Longest Good-bye.'"

Elizabeth took Jane's hand and squeezed it.

"You know if you do that, De Bourgh will have just cause for terminating your contract," Alex informed them. "Anne's been looking for a reason to get rid of you since the mess with Collins. You'll be giving her one on a silver platter."

The three women all shared a look of determination. "We know, Alex," Jane told him softly.

It was seven when their call came. Elizabeth, Jane, and Charlotte were dressed, warmed up, and ready. Nervously, they held their instrument cases in their hands as they descended in the hotel elevator.

The tension was palpable as they walked through the lobby, regal as queens, to the doors and their waiting limo. Once safely ensconced in the car, they shared a sigh of relief. They had all feared an encounter with Slurry, but the men were nowhere to be seen.

Fate was playing a bizarre game of chance, keeping the paths of the two groups from crossing until it was too late. LBS went to the theater and settled into the pre-show green room. Then Slurry left the hotel to enter the Music Hall in a flash of cameras.

Charles was on tenterhooks. He had not been able to reach or even see Jane all day. She would not answer her phone at the hotel, and he was beginning to wonder if something was wrong. He had even cast off his chronic lateness trying to reach his beloved Jane.

Slurry sat in their prestige seats, close to the stage in the large auditorium of the Music Hall. A large screen was lowered over the stage to allow the audience to watch the pre-show.

The men had given up talking to each other; Charles was too nervous over Jane, Darcy was sulking, and Richard was too annoyed with Darcy. Caroline and Anne, both looking elegant in evening gowns, sat with them, shepherding the men.

Slurry's attention locked on the screen when the last act of the preshow was announced. Their personal feelings were too intense to share with each other, but each was glued to a woman taking the stage.

LBS had changed their look for the VMAs. Richard's jaw dropped when he saw Charlotte. Gone was her short blue hair. She had let it grow out slightly and it was now dyed a soft black with a slight purple undertone. Her makeup was different too. It was softened and the overall effect was pretty, where before it was hard. She wore her trademark black, upgraded to a neat top and slim pants.

Elizabeth's long mane had been carefully dyed, so her rich brown now had a coppery sheen. She was wearing a white, textured vest and white jeans with brown sandals.

Jane was the least changed. Her platinum locks were shorter and arranged in beautiful curls that fell around her face. She wore a white leather mini-dress that showed off her flat stomach and long legs.

The spell that the women's appearance worked on the men was broken with the first notes Elizabeth played. Instead of the quick, light melody they were expecting, a slow, dark song began. Charles's smile was wiped away and he looked on in confused horror as Jane sang.

> *It seemed so good when it started.*
> *I gave my trust to you.*
> *I came to you open-hearted,*
> *Hoping it was true.*
> *Now I've gotten smart.*
> *Now I've learned some things.*
> *Now I know that what once was a start,*
> *Is just an ending.*
> *The longest good-bye*
> *I ever knew,*
> *The longest good-bye*
> *Was the day*
> *I said hello to you.*

Darcy closed his eyes against the vision before him, but it didn't block the song from reaching his ears. Their playing was perfect; he had never heard them better. He opened his eyes against his will, and again he saw the deep sadness in his Elizabeth's eyes.

He grew sick with the knowledge that he had done this. Only the harsh curse of Anne sitting nearby could reach him.

"Those bitches!" she spat. "I don't know what those whores think they are doing, but they just ended their career!" Her cell phone rang and she answered it. "Yes, Mother. I will, don't worry!"

"Anne, wait!" Darcy spoke suddenly. "Let me talk to Lady Catherine."

Anne glared at him, but reluctantly passed over the phone. Darcy took it and spoke quickly, "Lady Catherine?"

"Darcy?"

"Yes, it's me. Don't terminate them. It's my fault they are doing this. Don't blame them."

Catherine's voice was clearly surprised. "Darcy, I don't understand what is going on here, but the fact of the matter is those girls are not performing what they were told to do." She clicked her tongue. "I cannot tolerate that."

"Lady Catherine," Darcy said, his voice becoming desperate as Charles's horrified eyes focused on him. "Please don't terminate them. We need them for our tour. We cannot get another opening act; you know that."

Catherine mulled. "I don't like this, Darcy. Not at all."

"I know you don't, Lady Catherine. But I promise I'll make it right. If I have to, I'll guarantee De Bourgh's investment—out of my own pocket. You won't lose money on this."

"You will what?"

"I will buy Long Borne Suffering's contract myself. Don't terminate them."

Charles looked back to the horrific image on the screen while he listened to Darcy and everything clicked into place. "I'll buy half," he told him in a firm voice.

"Charles?"

"Oh no, Will. I have no idea what you did, but I don't want you owning anything of Jane's."

Richard watched and then quietly announced, "I'm in too."

Darcy looked at the men and then turned his attention to the phone. Catherine was listening carefully. "I heard that. And I will hold you to it."

"Put it in writing. We'll sign it," Darcy growled.

"Oh, you will. Trust me on that, Darcy," Catherine said in a clipped voice and hung up.

Jane's song was over, and the two-minute warning was given for the main show. Slurry was out of their seats, and from their position, they watched Long Borne Suffering enter the room and take their seats toward the back. The women looked at Slurry with resolve as they took their place, knowing this might be their last time there.

Charles tried to go back to Jane, but Caroline and Darcy stopped him. "Wait for the break," Caroline said.

Charles turned angrily on Darcy. "Tell me what happened, everything."

As the show opened and the host sang and made jokes, Darcy softly whispered the story of the previous night, of that morning, and of the song that triggered LBS's reaction.

Charles listened, his face expressing the betrayal he felt. "You told Elizabeth about my father? No wonder Jane—damn it!" His eyes narrowed with anger. "I should blame you for all of this, but I was the fool who trusted you!"

Darcy swallowed hard. "I'm sorry, Charles. It's my fault. I let my temper get control of me. I fucked up. I shouldn't have had us do that song."

Charles was struck by Darcy's apology and the genuine regret he heard in his friend's voice. "I just hope I can make things right with Jane."

Darcy nodded. "I'll do anything I can to help."

"You've done enough."

⤜✦⤏

At the break, Slurry lost no time following LBS out of the theater and into the crowded lobby. The girls stood together, posing for pictures. A pretty woman approached Alex as he stood nearby.

"Alex Lucas? I'm Kristin D'Andrea, MTV News. We would like to have Mark Cole interview LBS when the show is over."

Alex nodded. "That'd be fine."

Kristin smiled as she recognized Anne de Bourgh approaching them. "Anne, you must be happy."

Anne smiled and lied through her teeth. "We are so proud of all our artists, and LBS has certainly proven themselves tonight."

"I heard," Kristin said confidentially, "that management wants to work out a deal with De Bourgh to have the footage of the pre-show made into a video."

Anne smiled and winked, and then laughed as Kristin moved off. "You're damn lucky, Lucas," she breathed coldly under her breath.

"Don't I know it," Alex replied while he smiled to the crowd.

⤜✦⤏

"Elizabeth."

Elizabeth froze as she heard his voice. A chill raised goose bumps along her arms. She wished she could be angry with him, but she couldn't. At this point, she just felt sorrow about everything. She turned to Darcy and smiled politely.

Darcy's heart contracted painfully with her polite smile. "I wanted to compliment you," he told her. "Nice show."

"You too," she said coolly.

Darcy understood her perfectly. "We're not done yet."

"I am," she replied quietly and moved off.

❧

They watched each other as Richard slowly moved closer to her. Richard had an open smile on his face, revealing his clear admiration for her new look.

"Hey, Char," he said easily. "You look great."

Charlotte leaned forward and without thinking about it, lightly kissed him on the lips. "Thanks, Richard."

As the words left her mouth and she pulled back, they were both stunned as they became aware of their actions. Suddenly all the easiness between them was gone.

"How was your week off?" Richard asked nervously.

"Good," she answered automatically, then smiled quickly. "It hasn't really been much of a break. We've been doing appearances almost every day."

Richard nodded, suddenly very aware of his hands, which wanted to touch her again. He was so focused on controlling them he almost missed her question.

"How have you been?"

"I've been good," he replied. "I've been doing some thinking." He looked down at his feet, then back into her face, laying his emotions bare to her. "When we get back together for the tour, maybe you and I could talk." He paused and smiled uncertainly. "There are some things I need to tell you."

Charlotte looked at him, unable to accept the open affection in his face without breaking down. "*If* we go back on tour," she said lightly, trying to hide in humor.

"Oh, you'll be there. Your performance was a huge hit. You're now De Bourgh's latest discovery." His voice emphasized the last word.

"Oh," Charlotte said, her surprise evident.

"That is, if you want to come back to the tour. I…" he paused and shrugged. "We would all be very sorry to see you and the others leave."

Charlotte thought a moment, completely stunned by the change in their fortunes. "We'll have to see what happens, won't we?" she replied cryptically and walked away. As she returned to the theater, she found she couldn't erase the vision of Richard's face, of his open affection and admiration, from her mind.

◌✑◌

Charles came up to Jane and stood next her, handing her a drink. He tried to talk to her, but when he opened his mouth, he found himself speechless. He could only stare at Jane, his eyes overflowing with emotions.

"Not now," Jane said quietly, all the while maintaining a pleasant expression. "Not here, Charles."

"Jane," he choked out.

"No." Her eyes looked into his, and for a second the curtain lifted and Charles could see the ruined emotional landscape she was hiding from everyone. "No, Charles," she told him as the curtain fell and Jane returned to her bright and smiling mask.

Charles felt like his soul was being ripped from his body as he watched Jane and Elizabeth walk back into the auditorium.

He spoke to Darcy, who was standing next to him like a shadow. "We are singing 'Feel Me' tonight."

Darcy nodded in complete agreement. "Charles, I'm sorry."

"Don't talk to me, Will," Charles said, holding up a hand. "Just don't talk to me. In fact, after tonight, I don't want to see you again."

"Ever?" he asked softly.

Charles exhaled a long breath. "We'll see after the break is over."

◌✑◌

The introduction was made. The audience applauded and the lights came up. But it didn't matter that thousands of people were cheering for them; the three men played only for three other people in the house. With an expression of intense earnestness, Charles sang:

In a world full of lies,
I don't know what's my own.
Passions I can't understand and
Feelings I can't control.
When confusion buries me,
You reach out your hand.

And when I look at you,
The chaos fades away.
You alone, is what's real to me.
You show me the way.
Touch me.
Hold me.
Feel me.
Heal me.
Let me be with you.

As Jane watched them play, she felt her heart break. What was happening? She had started the day thinking that Charles was about to dump her, and now she was breaking off from him and he was begging her, in song, not to turn away.

As Darcy played, Elizabeth felt it again: his power, his strength. It was the third time he had played for her, and each time he moved her profoundly.

She couldn't look at him anymore, so instead she turned to Jane and watched as her sister's face crumbled. Elizabeth put her arms around her, and they held each other up, as Darcy's deep voice joined Charles's in the chorus, surprising Elizabeth even more than she already was.

All three women were stunned by the message they knew was for them. Slurry was not going to let them go without a fight. Their lovers were pleading with them to not leave, to come back.

It was a bizarre reversal of events, and all Elizabeth knew for certain, as she looked at Jane's shattered face, was that they needed to pull back, and get some distance, before they could move forward.

❧

Caroline stood alone watching the scene before her. Darcy and Richard had left as soon as the VMAs were over. Caroline would have been happy to escape with them, but Charles insisted on going to the De Bourgh party. She felt pity as she watched Charles hovering around Jane, who was ignoring him.

Caroline hadn't been able to hear their brief conversation, but Jane's body language made it clear. She was not willing to listen to anything Charles would tell her. She felt her twin's pain as he couldn't leave her yet couldn't be with her, doomed to circle her like a planet orbiting the sun. Jane was politely talking to a writer and an actor Anne had introduced to her, and together they were discussing the possibility of LBS's doing a theme song for an upcoming movie.

Caroline felt a certain boredom with it all. Slurry had done several soundtracks and the experience had only shown her that the movie industry was more shameless than the music industry. At moments like this, Caroline found she shared Darcy's disgust with the whole business.

Caroline turned away and her eyes fell on Elizabeth Bennet. Elizabeth was talking politely with the people standing next to her, but Caroline knew her well enough to know she was bored.

Caroline made excuses and took Elizabeth away from the group and to the refreshment table. "I hope you don't mind," she told Elizabeth.

Elizabeth chuckled once. "No, I'm quite in your debt. I have never met such boring or fake people in my life."

Caroline smiled in agreement. "Now you know why Darcy avoids these like the plague."

"Is that why he's not here?"

Caroline knew the curiosity in her voice was more than just idle conversation. "No, I don't think so, but why don't you tell me, Lizzy?"

Elizabeth's eyes met hers, and Caroline waited while Elizabeth considered the offer. Finally Elizabeth said, "Could we find a quiet place to sit?"

Caroline nodded and led her to a private corner, near the windows. Elizabeth looked out into the darkness and tried to find a starting point.

"He loves you, you know," Caroline said, relieving Elizabeth of the burden.

"I do now," Elizabeth replied softly. "I know you all must think I'm really stupid, but for the longest time, I didn't think he liked me at all." Elizabeth gave a bitter huff. "Change that: I also think I'm stupid."

"Lizzy," Caroline said gently, "why did you think he didn't like you?"

"Because he was so cold and abrupt when he spoke to me. And he said things that were very arrogant and hurtful."

"He can be hard, Lizzy. No one knows that better than me. But believe me, he never meant to hurt you."

"You mean before today."

Caroline nodded and sighed. "Yes. What happened today? I've never seen him like this."

Elizabeth shook her head. "I guess everyone is going to know now." She shrugged. "What the hell? It's not like I don't live in a damned fishbowl anyway."

"Did you sleep with him?" Caroline asked her calmly.

Elizabeth nodded. "And in the morning, he told me he loved me." She could hardly believe it had only been this morning.

"What happened?"

"I ran."

Caroline had to laugh at the irony of it. "If it's any comfort to you, Elizabeth, I think that you're both stupid right now."

"Thanks," Elizabeth said sarcastically. "You know what, I actually agree with you." She put her hand to her face and rubbed her forehead.

"So what comes next?" Caroline asked.

"I don't really know. We tried to get kicked off the tour, and I'm told we fucked that up good, so frankly, I just don't know."

Caroline smiled. "The one time you are trying to not advance your career and you end up giving yourself a huge boost, right?"

Elizabeth nodded and held up her hands. "I don't get it."

"I'm sorry, Lizzy. You need to work this out for yourself, but I can tell you one thing: Don't give up."

"On what? The career or Darcy?"

"Both, actually, but I meant Darcy." Caroline looked at Elizabeth, letting her true feelings rise. "He's a good man. He's one of the best men I know. He's very hard, I know that, but he does love you, and he only wants to make you happy."

"And this afternoon?"

"He was hurt, badly, and lashed out."

Elizabeth nodded. She knew that, but it validated her feelings to hear it from someone else.

"I know he comes on strong, but that is his way. He doesn't realize that other people can't read his mind. He thought it was clear to you that he loved you."

Elizabeth nodded, feeling very sad inside. "You love him, don't you?"

Caroline smiled. "Of course I do." To Elizabeth's unasked question, she said, "I love him enough to want to see him happy. And that's you, Lizzy."

"Caro, I don't think he will ever want to see me again after today."

Caroline reached out and rubbed Elizabeth's arm. "Of course he does. He loves you, and one little spat isn't going to change that. Couldn't you see it during 'Feel Me'?"

Elizabeth nodded, her lips tightly pressed together, and Caroline took her into her arms and hugged her. "It's okay, Lizzy. You go home, and take a couple of weeks to get your head together. Darcy will be waiting when you come back."

Elizabeth blinked back her tears. "I will."

Elizabeth walked to her sister, suddenly very tired. "Let's go," she told Jane. Jane nodded and found her eyes resting on Charles.

"Have Alex get the car, okay, Lizzy?" she told her as she stared at Charles.

Elizabeth nodded and stepped away, letting Jane have her needed privacy.

Jane signaled to Charles that he could come to her now. "Can I touch you?" he asked softly.

Jane shook her head no.

"What happened, Jane?"

Jane knew she owed him an explanation. "I realized some things this afternoon, that Slurry was hurting us all, and we needed to stop it. To pull away."

Charles's eyes revealed the pain he was feeling. "Why didn't you talk to me?"

"I tried," she said, her voice dropping to an intense whisper. "I tried to talk to you and all I got was 'wait.' And I waited, and what did I get? 'It's All a Joke'!" Jane stopped and visually struggled to regain her control.

"So you did hear that?"

Jane nodded, her eyes cast downward.

Charles pushed aside a surge of anger. "Jane, that was never about you. I don't know how you could ever even think it was."

"But I did!" she answered him, her voice full of wretchedness. "I did! I thought you were tired of me and I thought you wanted to break up with me. And frankly, now I don't know what to think."

Charles's expression sobered. "My God, Jane, I love you!"

Jane looked like she had been struck. "Please. Don't say that."

"Jane?"

Jane took a deep breath. "I have to go."

"But we need to talk."

Jane shook her head. "Charles, I don't trust you, so I don't know what we have to talk about." She turned and left the room, rushing so he wouldn't see her tears.

❧

The next morning, Jane took Elizabeth to the train station. Mechanically Elizabeth got a ticket and took the metro north to Grand Central Station. There she took a subway down to Greenwich Village.

As she rode, her mind traveled like a train on the same track. She remembered the events of yesterday, from waking up in Darcy's arms, all the way to her talk with Caroline. She traveled the same route again and again, without finding any answers.

She was so deeply lost in her thoughts that she was only slightly surprised to find herself not at the lot where she had left her truck a lifetime ago but at Darcy's building. She realized that her thoughts weren't going to give her any peace, so she entered the building and asked the doorman to announce her.

The doorman was a kind man who had been in the Darcys' employ since the late seventies. He recognized the young woman from her last visit. "I'm sorry, Miss Bennet. Mr. Darcy is away and won't be returning for a few weeks."

Elizabeth was shocked at the disappointment she felt. She thanked the man and left the building, feeling completely adrift. Numbly, she returned to her truck, paid the huge bill, and started her drive home.

Automatically, she turned her radio on. She smiled when she heard Jane's voice singing to her.

> Once I could believe
> Everything you promised.
> That pretty story you told me,
> I held it close and loved it.
> Now I've gotten smart.
> Now I've learned some things.
> Now I know that what once was a start
> Is just an ending.
> The longest good-bye
> I ever knew
> The longest good-bye

Was the day
I said hello to you.

With a deep breath, Elizabeth accepted that she was going down. She couldn't avoid it. She didn't know where he was and couldn't contact him for at least two weeks.

Oh, she knew in an emergency she could reach him, through Caroline or something, but this was hardly an emergency.

No, she had to face her worst demon now: herself. She had two weeks to do what Caroline told her to do: pull herself together and figure out what she wanted. She laughed to herself. She didn't need two weeks. All she needed was twenty minutes. She wanted him.

The song ended and the announcer came on. "That's Long Bourne Suffering, who really stole the show at the MTV awards last night. And you can see LBS. They are touring with Slurry now and they have dates coming up at Madison Square Garden at the end of this month. I've got tickets for that show for caller number twelve…"

The words died away but not the impression. It was a surprise to Elizabeth to realize that she had reached one of her goals. Her band was being talked about on a major radio station. Somewhere, during the tour, she had become a hit. Oh, they still had a long way to go, but they had made it.

Elizabeth found the knowledge puzzling. She had dreamed of this for so long and she had expected that when she made it, she would feel different, be different. She looked in her rearview mirror at her reflection.

The face she found there was basically the same, but as she stared, she found tiny differences. *Mileage*, the voice in her head told her. She wasn't the same Lizzy Bennet who had left on tour back in March. But she wasn't quite finished either.

The other thing that surprised her was how little her success meant to her. She was surprised and certainly happy. But she certainly wasn't fulfilled as she had always imagined she would be. Success had proven to be not a panacea but merely a job. She received satisfaction from her job well done, but that only went so far. She found that she still needed something. She needed Darcy.

He wasn't perfect, that was for sure, but she needed to talk to him. She needed to find out what she felt for him, to figure out if he was right.

With a deep breath she realized her train of thought had finally stopped. She had the answer she needed. And now she needed to wait.

CHAPTER 15

ON THURSDAY MRS. BENNET answered the phone at her home. "Oh hello, dear. No, I haven't asked them yet."

Elizabeth and Jane exchanged a look. They were enjoying a quiet dinner with their parents. Both of them could tell by their mother's tone that Lydia, her baby, was on the phone and probably asking for a favor. Kitty and Lydia were working for their aunt and uncle as nannies over the summer.

"You know, dear, they don't have much time off," Mrs. Bennet spoke into the phone. "All right, all right, I'll ask them."

"That was Lydia," Mrs. Bennet said, unnecessarily, as she hung up. "You know how they have been working so hard all summer, and their friends are going to the beach next week, and they wanted to know if one of you could fill in for them, so they could have a little vacation."

Elizabeth rolled her eyes. Mary was away at the Tanglewood Music Center for an eight-week fellowship, which left her and Jane to cover for Kitty and Lydia. It was pointless for Elizabeth to remind her mother that she and Jane had been working hard for the past four months. She sighed and looked at Jane.

Jane's expression surprised her. The deep sadness that had shadowed her since Tuesday lifted, and she smiled slightly. "Tell Lydia I'd be happy to go to Aunt Maddie's." Jane then looked to Elizabeth and winked.

Elizabeth considered her sister's hint. She had to admit the idea had merit. Getting away from Mom and spending a week with her aunt would actually be more relaxing. Watching her young cousins would give her something to do besides thinking about Darcy and how she had screwed up with him. "I'll come too," she volunteered suddenly.

"Hey," she said excitedly as a thought occurred to her, "we could go and stay with Aunt Maddie, and when Lydia and Kitty come back next weekend, we could go see Mary at Tanglewood."

"That is an excellent idea, Lizzy," Mr. Bennet pronounced. Elizabeth and Jane had been disappointed that they would be back on tour during Mary's big performance at the end of her fellowship, but at least this way they could share some of the experience with her. Mrs. Bennet called the Gardiner household back to finalize the plans. After dinner, Elizabeth found Jane staring at the two bouquets of flowers sitting in vases in the living room. Both were of pure white roses. One arrived Wednesday, and the second had arrived today. The first card said simply, "I'm sorry"; today's read, "Forgive me, please." Neither had been signed, but that was unnecessary. Jane knew exactly whom they were from, as did Lizzy.

"Are you going to call him to let him know where to send tomorrow's flowers?" Elizabeth teased gently.

Jane smiled slightly. The sadness was back on her face. "I don't think so," she answered vaguely.

"Jane," Elizabeth said, all her concerns expressed in that one syllable, "you have to do something. You are so miserable, and I know Charles is too. I saw him at the De Bourgh party. He looked like he was dying."

Jane looked up to her sister with gentle reproach in her eyes. "I don't think it's a good idea, Lizzy," she said softly.

"Couldn't you just talk to him?"

Jane shrugged. "And say what?" She looked away, shaking her head. "No, I made a mistake. I moved too fast, and I trusted him before I should have. Now I have to pay the price." She held up a hand to stop Elizabeth, who was already drawing breath to protest. "I know; you think I should talk to him and let him explain. But I don't trust him, Lizzy, and if I don't trust him, how is anything he says going to make a difference?"

"But you love him."

Jane closed her eyes for a long time, then she opened them slowly and said, "I thought I did. Maybe I do. I'm just not sure." With a sad look, she left the flowers and went to her room to pack.

❧

Elizabeth couldn't be sure whom she felt worse for: herself or Jane. It was a tough call. She sat alone in her room and felt a pang of intense loneliness. She lay down on her bed, arranging the pillows so that, just for a second, she could try to believe she was back in the loft, in his bed, her head resting on his shoulder. She closed her eyes and tried to remember his scent and the sound of his heartbeat, the rise and fall of his chest against her cheek.

The memory failed; the moment faded. She sat up, feeling even more alone. The now-familiar dull ache settled upon her heart and she wished for the millionth time she hadn't walked out on him, that he hadn't pushed her so. Was it only three nights ago that she had slept in his arms? It felt like a lifetime ago. She hadn't meant to hurt him. She really hadn't, but nothing could change the fact that she had.

She was filled with a deep longing to find him, to make it better. But did he even want to see her? It was so hard to know what to think. Caroline believed he did, but what if she was wrong? What if the time away brought him to his senses and he realized he wanted nothing to do with a moody bitch like her?

She drew her Gibson into her lap. A memory of his words returned to her, surprising her. "My home is yours," he had told her that morning. His words comforted her, even as she questioned them. Did he still feel that way? Could he understand that she had just needed time? Could she somehow make things right with him again?

As her fingers begin idly picking out a tune, she laughed softly to herself. What exactly was "right" for her and Darcy? The moments when they were together and happy seemed dwarfed by all the times they were fighting or angry. She wished they had shared more good times together, but with a surge of regret, she realized how much of it was her fault that they hadn't. He had said it; he had loved and admired her for months. How had she missed this? Why had she been so dead set on disliking him, so blind that she missed the warmth he offered her? It was mostly because she misunderstood him. And a moment of fairness made her admit that he was so very hard to understand. But she realized that the fact of the matter was that she had been prejudiced against him from the start.

She felt stupid now. Stupid and unworthy of anyone's love or admiration, and yet, even as she felt she didn't deserve it, she craved Darcy's love more than ever. She longed for the warmth in his eyes when he spoke to her, the dry jokes that made her burst out laughing, and his soft, deep voice saying her name again.

Her hurting and sorrow were too much, and she found herself

stringing words together into a song. It was rough and unfinished, but it expressed her feelings better than her heart could.

Tears ran onto the paper on which she wrote the words and chords. On a whim, she created a song file by recording it on her computer. She wasn't sure what she was doing, but she just needed Darcy to hear her song, to know that she was hurting too, and to maybe feel better. She agonized a moment, questioning her actions. Was she being a fool? The file sat on her desktop for a long time as she stared at it and thought. If she sent it, she would be committing herself. She would have to trust him.

That thought made her stomach turn over. Trusting others had never been her strong suit. She was much more comfortable trusting herself. But then she looked at her small, lonely, empty room and realized that she didn't want this and that if she were ever going to move beyond it, she would have to trust him. In a rush, she sent the file to Caroline, with a request for her to forward it to Darcy. She bit her lip, wishing she had Darcy's email address, but this was the best she could do.

Then she sat back on her bed and pulled her Gibson tight. It was done, and she hoped that he would understand.

⊱⊰

"Hey!"

Charlotte's heart lurched in her chest as she recognized the voice on the other end of the line. It was last person in the world she expected to hear from.

"Richard?"

He laughed, a warm, rich, touchable sound. "Don't sound so surprised, Char. I can dial a phone, you know."

Charlotte grinned. "I know. So how are you?" she asked, puzzled by his call.

Richard sighed. "I'm good. I'm kind of missing all the company of the tour. You get used to living in the middle of a hive of people, you know? It's hard to readjust to the quiet when you're home."

"Oh, so that's why you called? You're lonely for the tour?"

"Something like that, Char," he said, in a way that let her know that it had nothing to do with his call. "What have you been doing? Keeping busy?"

Charlotte struggled to steady her breathing as she answered him. "I've been hanging out mostly. Getting caught up with things at home and going to some of my old haunts."

"Going out with Lizzy?"

"No, she and Jane have gone off to stay with their cousins for a week."

"Oh, that explains it."

"What?"

"Jane," he explained. "Charles isn't speaking to Darcy right now, so instead he's been calling me to moon over Jane every night. He can't find her."

"Oh," Charlotte said, not sure how to take this information. "He's taking it badly?"

"He's crushed, Char." Richard's voice held sympathy for his friend. "I've never seen him like this."

"That's too bad," Charlotte replied. She felt an awkward pause in the conversation and asked, "So what else have you been doing?"

Richard chuckled. "You're not going to believe this."

"Tell me," Charlotte replied.

"I've written a song."

"Really?" Charlotte was surprised. "Can I hear it?"

"That depends on if you come back on tour or not," Richard said in a deceptively easy way.

"Ooooohh, I see a carrot dangling before me."

"Char," Richard's voice was relaxed and sincere, "the song is not worth you coming back for, but I do hope you come back. I miss you."

Charlotte's lip was trembling as she heard him speak. "You do?"

"I do. More than I can tell you. Please say you'll come back."

"Richard," she said, her voice ragged.

"I know," he hushed her soothingly. "It's not just your decision. I'm sorry; I didn't plan on calling you to ask you to come back. It just slipped out."

Charlotte nodded, even though he couldn't see her. She pulled herself together and tried to think of something safe to say. She opened her mouth, and her heart defeated all the rational plans her mind had made. "I miss you too," she whispered.

"Char," his voice was heavy with emotion. He wanted nothing more than to drop the phone and run to her.

"Richard?"

"I'm here," he said. He took a deep breath and blew it out. This was so hard, but every second convinced him it was right. "Can you just talk to me a little, Char?"

"All right," she said, oddly touched. It was so infrequent for him to ask her for anything. "I almost got into a fight Saturday night."

Richard listened to her dear voice as she talked about her adventure at the local bar. He smiled as he pictured her face, telling her story. He was breaking his promise to himself by calling her, but he had to. He had missed her too much, and he was terrified she and the others would not return to the tour.

He'd promised himself at Hazelden that he would remain celibate for three weeks. He figured that if he could do that, he could then go to Charlotte, tell her he loved her, and ask her, hell, beg her to forgive him. He wished he could offer her more. He was hardly a prize. She deserved so much more. But he had tried to let her go, to push her away, and still she loved him.

What else could he do? He had wanted so badly to tell her how he loved her that last day of the tour. But he couldn't then. First he had to prove to himself that he could love her, that he could stop sleeping around and be true to her.

But he was weak. Seeing her at the VMAs had been his undoing. She was so beautiful that night. All he wanted to do was hold her and kiss her again and again. Instead, he had been terrified by the idea that LBS might be leaving the tour.

In the end, it didn't matter. He still would go to her, even if she didn't come to him. But the fear had haunted him and he had, in a moment of loneliness, called her, to hear the sweetest voice he knew. And now he knew he was hooked. She had told him she missed him!

If his new addiction was phone calls to Charlotte, he could live with that. It was certainly less destructive than drinking or sleeping around, and if it helped him, helped them get back together, he was frankly all for it.

They spent the rest of the evening talking and laughing, until their eyes drooped and reluctantly they said good-bye, promising to talk again.

❧

"Jane, I just wanted to tell you that you got another dozen roses," Mrs. Bennet sounded delighted over the phone.

"Oh?"

"Yes, these are pale pink. I guess the florist ran out of white ones." She laughed at her own joke. "They're really pretty. Exactly the color your hair used to be."

Jane felt a tightness in her chest. "Could you read the card to me?"

"Certainly, dear; it says, 'Please call me,' and there's a phone number." Her mother recited the digits. "Hmmm, funny, no name again. Do you recognize the number, Jane?"

"Yes," she whispered. "Thanks, Mom."

"Are you okay, Janie?"

"Yes, I just have to go, Mom."

"You take care, Janie dear. Bye now."

"Bye, Mom," Jane replied automatically and clicked off the phone. The number was one she would never forget: Charles's cell phone. She bit her lip, fighting back tears. It was supposed to be getting easier, not harder. Yet every day she found herself missing him more and more. She seemed to be on the verge of tears all the time, and last night a nightmare, in which Charles rejected her, woke her up and left her in a panic. In truth, she hadn't been able to relax all day while she waited to see if this day's flowers would arrive.

Now she knew. The flowers had come, but with what? A request? A command? Jane knew the pink roses had been no accident. She knew Charles picked them deliberately to match her hair color from the night they first met. He was going back, trying to start over and make it right.

Without her knowing quite how it happened, the phone was at her ear again and it was ringing, although Jane could not remember dialing. "Jane?" a desperate voice answered.

"Charles?" she choked out.

"Jane! Oh God, Jane, oh my God! Did you get my flowers?" He was panting with relief.

"I got the message," Jane said with a weak watery smile. She couldn't believe how much she missed his voice, or how good it made her feel to hear it again. "You asked me to call?"

"Jane," Charles breathed. "Jane, could I please, please come and talk to you? *Please*. I need to try to explain what happened." He paused. "Jane, I need to see you."

There was a sharp pain in Jane's chest and tears were falling down her face unnoticed. "Okay," she whispered.

"I'll come right now!"

"No!" Jane exclaimed. "No, you can't. I'm at my aunt and uncle's, and now would not be a good time."

"Tell me when."

"Could you come tomorrow?" she asked softly.

"Yes, I'll come anytime, angel." She could hear the desperation in his voice. "Tell me where you are."

The Gardiners lived in Kent Cliffs, a small community about forty minutes from the Bennets. Jane gave him directions and listened as he read them back. "I'll be there, first thing tomorrow," Charles said soulfully. "How have you been?"

Jane bit back her response. She wanted to tell Charles that she had been horrible and let him comfort her, but she couldn't. Not yet.

Instead she ignored his question and just said, "I'll see you tomorrow," and hung up.

Elizabeth found her, crying helplessly on her bed. "Jane, what happened?"

Jane tearfully explained everything, from the flowers to the phone call. Elizabeth's heart went out to her sister. Jane was trapped in a world of hurt, surrounded by thorns on all sides with no clear path to get free. Elizabeth understood exactly how she felt. Her own way was blocked with pain too, so she focused instead on Jane.

"Jane, you have to give him a chance. Listen to him. Let him explain what happened." Elizabeth was adamant. She knew this was the result of a misunderstanding and it hurt her to see Jane in so much pain. "Please do it for me, sweetheart. You know he loves you. He screwed up, but he's very sorry."

Jane nodded, her faced closed off. "I'll try, Lizzy."

Elizabeth left Jane alone and went to the room she was using. She checked her email and was disappointed to find nothing from Darcy. She wasn't sure if this was a bad sign, or merely a glitch in the system. She lay down in the darkness and wondered where he was and what he was doing.

❧

Darcy sat with his mother's guitar in his lap. He ignored the sheet music on the stand before him; it was memorized a long time ago. His fingers flew lightly over the nylon strings, his thoughts focused on his task.

His concentration was not broken by the arrival of his sister. He nodded to Georgiana as he continued playing, until the movement was finished and he turned the CD player off with the remote sitting on the floor beside him.

Then he looked to her, waiting. The young woman asked, "Got a moment?"

"I'm playing."

"I know," she replied gently, biting her lip. "But I'm only asking for a few minutes."

Darcy frowned. He was caught and he knew it. He motioned to the nearby chair and waited. He had tried to hide his mood from Georgiana, but he had clearly been unsuccessful. So instead he had taken to dodging her for the past few days. Now that had failed as well.

"Will, what's going on?" Georgiana asked softly.

"What do you mean?"

Georgiana took a deep breath, screwed up her courage, and spoke. "I mean that I left you in New York a week ago today, as happy as a clam, and on Wednesday you drove up here a different person. You've been moody and sulking all week."

"I have not."

"Will, you're listening to U2!" she told him, gently contradicting him. "If I hear 'With or Without You' one more time, I'm going to snap the CD in half."

Darcy was forced to smile slightly. It was bizarre what his sister gauged to be a sign of his depression, but he couldn't deny it.

"Will, what happened on Tuesday? Did something happen at the awards? I watched them and you were great."

Darcy sighed. "Did you see the pre-show?"

Georgiana nodded, unwilling to interrupt her brother once he started talking.

"Did you see LBS?"

"Yes, they're the group on tour with you, right?"

Darcy nodded. "The guitarist, Elizabeth…"

Georgiana's eyes got large and round as she stared at him with dawning comprehension. "You? And her? You've been dating?"

Darcy nodded, his jaw tight. Then he forced himself to speak. "Not exactly. It's kind of hard to date on tour. But we have been together a lot."

Georgiana smiled, excited at the idea of her dear brother having a girlfriend, then she thought about his behavior for the last week and frowned. "Okay, so you and Elizabeth have been together and getting to know each other. So what happened?"

"The Monday that we came back from Europe, she came to the loft." Darcy's voice stumbled a moment as he did some quick mental editing. "The next morning, I told her I loved her and that I never wanted her to leave, and she left." He shrugged. "I guess she didn't feel for me what I felt for her."

Georgiana paled slightly as she realized what Darcy had left out. "Will, your problem is you are very black-and-white in your thinking, and you don't realize that other people aren't."

Darcy looked at her coolly. "And how would you know this?"

"*Years* of therapy, Will. You pick up stuff after a while."

Darcy sat back in his chair, his eyes reassessing the little girl who had become an adult before his eyes.

"Okay, let's look at it this way," Georgiana continued uncomfortably. "Let's say I was at school, and I met a guy. Say we were in the same dorm and had some classes together." She hesitated and licked her lips. "And let's pretend that after a few months I decided that I like the guy and I go to bed with him." She wasn't quite able to make eye contact with him, but her point was so important, she pressed on.

"And it's great. It's the best sex I will ever have in my life, okay?" she said quickly. "But then, the next morning, he tells me he loves me and he even wants me to move in with him, right away." She stopped, letting the idea work on him, and then asked Darcy in a soft voice, "Would you want me to move in with him? Even if he was a great guy?"

Darcy frowned and shook his head. "Of course not."

"Then how could you expect this of Elizabeth?"

Darcy looked away. "It's just that I was happy. I didn't want that happiness to end," he said softly.

Georgiana put her arm around Darcy's shoulder. "I know. And she probably didn't either, but that's really, really fast. She probably needed some time. Did you give it to her?"

Darcy snorted. "She walked out. How could I not give it to her?"

"So what happened next?" she asked gently.

"I got mad, and when she came in at rehearsal for the show, I tricked Charles into playing 'It's All a Joke.'"

Georgiana put her head in her hands for a moment then laughed and kissed her brother on the temple. "Only you, Will."

Darcy smiled at himself. "I might have overreacted just a little bit."

"Just a bit," Georgiana agreed. "So then what happened? Did you talk to her?"

"I tried to, but she wouldn't have it."

"I can't really blame her." Georgiana took a moment to add up everything that had happened. "So what did you do then?"

"We changed our song. We played 'Feel Me' for them."

Georgiana nodded. "I remember. Did it work? Did you talk to her after the show?"

Darcy shook his head. "No, I just left."

Georgiana lightly slapped the side of her brother's head.

"Ow!"

"Will!" she whined. "I can't believe you. You've got to give her a chance to talk to you. That poor girl probably doesn't know what to think."

"I thought that if she loved me, she wouldn't have walked out like that."

She frowned. "Did you ever think that maybe Elizabeth just needed some time to think, and she was going to come back to you? After all, you played this song for her. Don't you think you might want to see what she thought?"

"I thought she didn't want to see me again. She said she was done. They played that 'Good-bye' song." Darcy pushed away from his sister and stood up. Slowly he walked to the huge window overlooking the Berkshire Mountains and put his forehead against it.

"But that was before you played your song, right? Will, I really think you screwed up here."

"You're right, Georgie," he said in a defeated voice.

Georgiana put her hand on his shoulder. "Before you make yourself crazy hating yourself, you might want to instead think about what you are going to say to her when you see her again."

Darcy turned and pulled her into a close embrace. "I will," he said. "Thanks, you give good advice, you know that?"

Georgiana looked into her brother's eyes. "So do you," she smiled lovingly.

※

Elizabeth looked with sympathy at her sister. Jane had dark circles under her eyes and despite the kind and gentle way she was dealing with the three children, Elizabeth could tell she was deeply anxious.

Jane seemed to be functioning, albeit slowly, as she brushed and braided the hair of the little girl who sat in her lap. "Lizzy," she said softly.

"Yes?"

"I want you to stay with me when he comes."

Elizabeth nodded. "When do you expect him?"

"I don't know," Jane said, her eyes once again losing focus.

"What are you going to say to him?"

"I guess that depends on what he says to me."

"What do you want?"

"I want the hurting to stop, Lizzy. I just want to be happy."

It was at that moment that their cousin, a nine-year-old boy named Erik, came running into the kitchen. "Jane, come here, quickly!" he exclaimed.

Jane and Elizabeth followed the boy into the living room where the television was on. MTV was positioned between Cartoon Network and Nickelodeon, and the children found something that stopped their channel flipping. Jane was on the screen singing "Everything You Are."

"Jane," the eldest child said, "Erik said this was you on the TV, but I told him it couldn't be you."

"Actually, Steph, it is Jane," Elizabeth answered cheerfully. "Look, see? There's me and Aunt Charlotte."

Jane was watching the TV, a sad smile on her face.

"Oh," said Stephanie, "I just thought it couldn't be you. I forgot you are famous."

Jane smiled and pulled the girl close. "That's me," she said, "your famous babysitting cousin." They laughed and watched the TV some more.

"You look pretty there," Stephanie told Jane, with the typical honesty of a child.

"Thank you. I had a lot of people working on me to make me look pretty."

"You know, that's the third time this morning I've heard that song," a deep voice said. "I'm beginning to wonder if it's a sign."

Elizabeth and Jane turned around quickly. Behind them stood Charles, holding the hand of the seven-year-old girl.

"Jane," said Michaela, "I answered the door. This man was looking for you."

The color drained out of Jane's face. "Thank you, dear," she replied automatically.

"Why don't you all watch TV, and a little later I'll take you swimming," Elizabeth told the children.

The young cousins gave their general assent, and Elizabeth led the adults into the kitchen. Automatically, Elizabeth found herself pouring a cup of juice for Charles, knowing it was his morning preference. She smiled bitterly at the ironic situation they found themselves in, and brought the cup to him, sitting at the table with Jane.

Jane stared at her cup, unable to speak as Charles looked at her nervously. "How have you been, Charles?" Elizabeth asked conversationally.

"All right, I guess," he shrugged. "How are you? I was surprised to find you here."

Elizabeth smiled. "You know our glamorous life."

"We're giving Lydia and Kitty a week off," Jane explained.

Charles smiled warmly at Jane, carefully examining her with his eyes. "I'm not surprised. You're so generous and kind." Then he paused and looked away.

"How has everyone been?" Elizabeth asked, trying to keep the conversation going. "Caro, Richard, Will?" Her voice was a trifle unsteady on the last name.

"Oh, Caro is fine. Faust is coming back from London tomorrow, and she is going to spend the last week of the break with him. Richard's been hanging out at his family's place on the Cape."

"And Will?"

"I haven't spoken to him," Charles said simply. He turned to Jane. "Could I speak to you—alone?"

Jane looked from Charles to Elizabeth. Elizabeth's eyes told her she would do whatever Jane wanted.

"Please," Charles added softly.

Jane nodded and moved to the dining room. There they could speak softly without being overheard, but they were still close enough to Elizabeth. Elizabeth kept herself busy by washing the morning dishes, then by finding random chores to do. She wanted to keep her promise and stay with Jane, and the work helped her think. She wished Charles had some news about Will; she was starting to worry about him. Elizabeth set up her laptop on the kitchen table and was disappointed to find there was still nothing in her email box from either Will or Caroline.

∞

"You look tired," Charles said gently as he sat down at the table with Jane.

Jane's mouth curled up in what could have been a weak smile or a grimace. "I didn't sleep well last night."

Charles smiled gently. "I understand. I haven't slept well in over two weeks." His hands were restless. Instinctually, they kept reaching for Jane and he had to keep reminding himself not to touch her, not to hold her the way he wanted. "It's amazing, isn't it? How much can change in two weeks?"

Jane looked at him mutely and nodded.

"Did you mean it?" he asked. "When you sang 'The Longest Good-bye'? Did you mean it? Were… Are you really ready to give it all up? Just like that?" He couldn't mask the bitter hurt in his voice.

"What else could I do?" she asked, her voice low. "Did you expect me to just sit around? To let you and your friends keep messing with my friends and me? You hurt me. You hurt all of us, and I couldn't stay there and let it go on."

Charles looked down at the table and closed his eyes. Her words cut him deeply, and even more painful was the knowledge that she was right, and he deserved it. "Will you let me explain, please?"

"What difference will it make?" she asked wearily.

"It will make a difference because I love you and you love me." Jane shook her head but he would not be stopped. "No, Jane. I was wrong, completely wrong and I admit that. I didn't trust you with the truth and I should have. But I know you told me the truth when you told me you loved me. And you may not believe me, but I do love you. I have since the night we met and I will never stop." His words were fierce and intense. He carefully took one of her limp hands in his own and said, "Please, let me explain. You deserve to know."

Jane looked at him for a long time. His hair and body were the same, but his face had changed. He looked older, and his eyes were marked by a sadness she had never seen in him before. His perpetual cheerfulness was gone, and looking at him, Jane was hard pressed to remember it; his face was so stricken. Jane squeezed his hand and nodded to him to start.

Charles squeezed her hand back in gratitude and began. "Almost six years ago, my mom was diagnosed with breast cancer." He closed his eyes against the painful memory. "At first I thought it was nothing. Yes, it meant an operation, but I figured with all the different treatments, she would be okay." He paused and looked into her eyes. "I was wrong. She fought it, we all fought it together, for nineteen months, but in the end, there was nothing left. She died four years ago this month."

Jane's mouth fell open in involuntary sympathy. She reached out to take his hand in both of hers.

Charles continued, "When she finally died, I was devastated, but I was also exhausted. Caro and I had been pushing to finish our degrees, because that was what she wanted, while we were spending as much of our free time with her as possible. I got to the point where I knew the flight schedule between San Francisco and Providence as well as I knew my class schedule," he said with a quick grin, "but in the end, there was nothing we could do but grieve together, and we did."

"I'm sorry," Jane said compassionately.

"So am I. She would've loved you," he told her, his eyes gently holding hers. "Anyway, after she was buried, I found I needed to get away from California. Home had too many bad memories and I just needed a break, so I flew out to New York and spent some time with my best friend, Will." His voice was thick with memories. "Will was going through a hard time with his band, and somehow focusing on him and his problems made it easier to handle the pain from my own loss." He looked at her and shrugged. "Well, you know this part of the story. I joined the band, we were a huge success, I got Caro to come out and work with us.

"But I left my father behind," he said slowly. "I talked to him regularly, but I was busy, busy being a star, and busy working through my grief. I didn't realize that I had left Dad all alone or that he wouldn't be able to handle it." Charles frowned.

Jane could see he was blaming himself for something. "What happened?" she prompted him gently.

"You know, I still don't totally know," he said in bitter amusement. "I was doing great, top of the world, and one day I get a call, and Dad's been arrested." His face struggled with his emotions. "He was charged with insider trading." He looked at Jane, his face puzzled, as if she might have an answer. "Apparently he pissed off the wrong people. I don't know. All I know is that he was alone. Mom was gone and Caro and I were gone, and no one was there for him."

"Charles, it's not your fault," Jane told him, her hand on his arm.

Charles shrugged. "The worst part of it was I still couldn't be with him. Will was there when this all broke. He was great. He was the clear head we needed. Right away he saw what would happen if the tabloids got hold of the story, so he and Caro worked like crazy to make sure it didn't happen. That's where all those crazy rumors about the band came from. Darcy deliberately leaked them, so the press would chase him and ignore me."

He sighed. "But even still, I couldn't go to the trial. It was too chancy. Instead I stayed in New York, very publicly, while Caro slipped out to him." His voice was bitter and tired.

Jane couldn't believe what she was hearing. Elizabeth had told her it was something bad with Charles's father, but she had no idea. She was touched by the pain and guilt he felt, and as she held his hand, trying to help him deal with his feelings of guilt, Jane realized something. Charles hadn't kept the news of his father from her because he didn't trust her to keep the secret. He hadn't told her because he was ashamed. He felt guilty and ashamed for his father and for himself, and he was afraid she would be ashamed of him too. Her heart broke with this knowledge, and she knew then that she loved him, that she would always love him.

"He was convicted and sentenced to two years in prison." Charles's voice had taken on a strange, emotionless tone that was quite unlike him. "He served for a year, and during that time, I only visited him twice."

"You should have told me," Jane said gently, her hand stroking his. "You shouldn't have carried this all on your own."

Charles looked at her, his eyes filled with so much despair that it had completely defeated him. "I know. I know," he told her regretfully. "I still can't believe it. My dad, he took me on my first camping trip and taught me how to ride a bike and now he's an ex-convict. I just can't reconcile... Anyway, two weeks ago was his parole hearing. That's why I was in California. He was released and Caro and I spent the week getting him settled. When he was convicted, he had us sell his house. There were too many memories there and most of his money was gone with all the fines he was forced to pay. When I bought the place in Muir Beach, I made sure it had a separate apartment on the grounds, so he would have a place to live when he was released. I spent the last week helping him get readjusted to being free."

Jane's hand reached up and brushed his soft golden curls. "That was very kind of you. You're a good son."

He shook his head slowly. "Jane, if I were a good son, this never would have happened. I would have stayed closer to him and made sure he was okay, instead of running away."

Jane touched his face, stilling him and bringing his eyes up to meet hers. "Charles, it's not your fault. He made his own choices." She stopped and took a deep breath then committed to her course and revealed something she had never told anyone. "My parents, they have a lot of problems too. It's not obvious, but it's there. My mom overspends terribly and my dad is..." she sighed, "he's very hard on her. He hurts her feelings and puts her down all the time. And it's very hard. You want to help your parents, because you love them, but you can't. You have to break away and let them live their own lives, because you can't rescue them every time and you can't make them change. I've tried."

Charles looked at her eyes, which were open to him, and he saw the truth in her words. He opened his arms to her and she was there, holding him tight, and he wasn't certain who was comforting who, only that they had a moment of perfect understanding.

"I missed you so much, Jane," Charles whispered into her hair. "Every day I missed you and every night was a thousand times worse. I can't tell you how many times I picked up the phone and started dialing you, to tell you to fly out. I needed you."

"Why didn't you?" Jane asked.

"Because I'm a fool. Because I didn't think you would understand. I knew you had appearances and work, and I didn't... I couldn't tell you about Dad over the phone, and I didn't think you would just drop everything and fly out to California because I asked you."

Jane locked eyes with him. "If you had called and told me you needed me, I would have come. Nothing would have kept me away."

"I know," Charles said as he kissed her lightly and pressed his forehead against hers. "I'm a fool, Jane. I'm so sorry. I should have told you."

Jane found that once she had loosed her emotions, she couldn't hold them back. "What happened when you came back?"

Charles gave a bitter snort. "You mean when I sunk from fool to moron? I was miserable. I just needed to see you. I don't know why, but I went to the party and I got drunk. I hated myself and my life and I couldn't take it anymore, so I got blotto."

"What about the picture?"

"What picture?" he asked, genuinely confused.

"There was a picture of you in the paper with that girl," Jane explained, her voice carefully neutral.

"Really?" Charles asked. He shrugged. "I had no idea." Then he looked at her as a thought passed over him. "You didn't think that I...?"

Jane shook her head. "I didn't know what to think, Charles. From your phone calls, I thought you wanted to break up with me."

"No! Jane, never!" He sighed and dropped his head, "*Christ*, when I think about what I said over the phone. Oh, Jane, I can see where you would get that idea. I'm so sorry. I had no idea. I didn't know about the picture and I didn't know that you were in the theater when I sang 'It's All a Joke.' I was hung over and had sat around waiting for too long, and when Will suggested it, I thought it was just to piss off the MTV people. I had no idea, really."

Jane believed him. He was holding nothing back, either verbally or emotionally. She moved back, out of his arms, and tried to make sense of her thoughts and feelings. This new information did explain many things, but still, she had been hurt deeply by him. She still wasn't sure if she could trust in him.

Charles watched her pull away. He understood. "I don't blame you, Jane. I'm very sorry. I made the biggest mistake of my life, but please believe me when I tell you I do love you, and I'm sorry."

He stood up and moved to the doorway. "Thank you for letting me explain everything, Jane. I hope you will forgive me someday." He left then, with a nod to Elizabeth, let himself out the front door, and walked to his black Denali. His limbs felt shaky, like he had just run a mile.

He leaned against the SUV as he opened the door and let the July heat escape. He had done it. He had apologized to Jane, but he found that he completely agreed with her. He wasn't good enough for her and he didn't deserve her forgiveness.

Jane sat perfectly still, trying to understand what had happened, when an icy coldness hit her. Charles, who had brought warmth and love to her, was leaving, and all she had when he was gone was pain. She got up and ran.

He was swinging himself up into his seat when she burst out the door. "Wait!" she yelled as she ran barefoot to him. Charles was back on the ground when she reached him and flung herself into his arms. "Don't go," she cried, as she buried her face into his T-shirt. "Please don't go."

"Jane?" he asked, his heart in his throat.

"I know! I know, but when you held me, I felt better than I had in weeks." Her words tumbled out in a rush. "And then you went away, and all the hurt came back." She looked up to him, her eyes brimming with tears. "I need you, Charles," she admitted brokenly. "I need you and I don't know what to do."

Charles found himself comforting her, his emotions spun out of control. He rubbed his cheek against her soft blonde hair as her hands clenched in his shirt and she sobbed convulsively.

"Let's go back into the house," he said with far more confidence than he felt. Holding each other, they got through the door and as far as the entryway before they stopped and just held each other tightly, their bodies taking mute reassurance from the presence of the other.

Charles pulled himself together first. He gently eased Jane's face up to his and kissed her tear-stained cheeks. "It's going to be okay, Jane. We're going to be okay."

Jane listened for a second to Charles's heartbeat pounding against her own chest. It comforted her. Just the return of his scent to her nose eased some of the pain she carried. She opened her eyes and looked at him worriedly. "But there are so many things to work out," she sighed. "And what about the others? Char and Lizzy?"

Charles kissed her forehead gently. "I know," he said softly. "It's a lot."

"I just wish we could go away together for a while, just you and me."

Charles looked at her and smiled, his thoughts quickly falling into order. "Why can't we, angel?"

"But," Jane murmured, puzzled, her soft mouth left open in confusion.

"I'm sure Lizzy can handle things here, right, Lizzy?" Charles looked up to see Elizabeth exactly where he knew she would be, watching from the end of the hall. He smiled to her.

Elizabeth smiled back. "He's right, Jane. You go with Charles. I'll take care of things here."

Jane looked at Elizabeth and smiled gratefully. "Thank you, Lizzy." Turning to Charles, she said, "Okay, I'll go pack." She hurried up the stairs, leaving Charles alone.

He pulled out his cell phone and dialed his home number and waited for his sister to pick up. "It's me. I need you to find a place for Jane and me to be alone for a few days."

"I take it things worked out?" Caroline sounded pleased.

"Well, let's just say we are in the process of working things out." He looked down and grinned. "But things are looking good."

"Where do you want to be?" Caroline asked.

"I don't care, just someplace nice and close."

"Okay, I'll get you something."

Asking her to call him back, Charles hung up just as Jane was coming down the stairs.

"Will you be all right?" Elizabeth asked her, appearing again from the family room.

Jane felt an odd sensation of dreaminess. She had no idea what was going to happen, but she knew these next few hours were going to affect her for the rest of her life. She looked at Charles, who held her hand, and then back to Elizabeth. "I think so. Thank you." She hugged her sister, who hugged her back.

"Call me," Elizabeth said in farewell.

Jane nodded and walked out the door with Charles. He helped her into the passenger side of the SUV and stored her bag in the back before taking his place in the driver's seat. He put the keys in the ignition, then stopped and looked at her, as if he suddenly couldn't believe it was real.

Jane looked at him and took his hand. "I do love you, Charles," she said simply, her smile radiant.

Charles planted a quick, earnest kiss on her lips and started up the Denali. Jane didn't know where they were going or what was going to happen, but she had her trust back, and that was enough.

CHAPTER 16

ELIZABETH HEARD HER AUNT calling to her to pick up the phone. Glancing at the clock, she smiled in anticipation. "Hello?" she sang happily into the phone.

"Lizzy!"

It was not Jane as she expected. Quickly shifting mental gears, Elizabeth replied to her best friend.

"Char! How are you?"

"I'm good, how are you? Have those little monsters made you crazy yet?"

Elizabeth laughed and spent a few minutes talking about the Gardiners.

"So, I was wondering how's Jane doing? She seemed pretty upset last time I saw her."

Pleased to have good news for once, Elizabeth announced excitedly, "Oh Char! She made up with Charles!"

"She did?" Charlotte replied in a shocked voice. "Wow! I'm so happy for them. I thought it was over."

Elizabeth laughed. "I know. I did too." Elizabeth went on to tell a quick version of the story. "As a matter of fact, I thought that it was her when you called."

"Wow," Charlotte said, a bit thoughtfully. "I'm really happy for them."

"What's wrong, Char?"

"Nothing's wrong; it's just, well, Richard's been calling me."

"No."

"Yeah."

"Tell me what happened."

Charlotte giggled at the excitement in Elizabeth's voice. "Well, nothing really happened. He's just been calling me. We talk."

Elizabeth could hear Charlotte shrugging. "And what do you talk about?"

"Oh, just stuff. It's nice, you know?"

Elizabeth felt a pang, because she didn't know. "Yeah," she agreed. "So, are you two getting back together?"

"I'm not sure, really. It's not like we ever really had a clear definition of our relationship, so I don't think you can say we are getting 'back' together. But we talk, and it's good. You know, no pressure."

Elizabeth had the clear feeling that there was more to it. "How often does he call?" she asked simply, scouting around for details.

"Every night."

"What?"

"Yeah." She laughed.

"Char," Elizabeth's voice held a note of significance. "Is this serious?"

"Um, yeah. I think it might be," Charlotte answered, her confidence suddenly gone.

"How do you feel about it?"

"I'm not sure. We talk a lot, but we haven't talked about us. It's like he's purposefully avoiding that topic. So I'm not sure what to think." She paused. "Lizzy?"

"Yeah?"

"He really wants us to go back on the tour with them."

"Oh."

"But I don't want to do it if you and Jane aren't fully behind the idea," she added quickly. "It has to be all of us."

"Well," said Elizabeth pragmatically, "I don't think you have to worry about Jane."

"True, but what about you, Lizzy? I saw Darcy at the VMAs. What's going on with you two?"

"I don't know," Elizabeth said dumbly. "I haven't spoken to him at all. I even went to his loft, and the doorman told me he would be gone for a few weeks, so I'm stuck waiting."

"Do you even want to see him again after all that?" Charlotte was skeptical.

"I do," Elizabeth said softly. "I really do, Char. I can't explain it, but I want to talk to him at least."

"Okay, I get that." Charlotte understood better than anyone what it was like to have feelings for someone you couldn't rationally explain. "So, what are we going to do about the tour?"

"Well, I have to talk to Jane, but I say we go for it. It's only four more months, and if things don't work out with Darcy, I can just ignore him again." She was struck by how pathetic her own joke was.

"Are you sure, Lizzy?" Charlotte asked.

"I'm sure," Elizabeth said quickly and decisively. "So will I see you on Monday for the video shoot?"

"Yep. Have a good time at Tanglewood."

"Thanks, I will."

They both said good-bye and hung up. A minute later the phone rang again. This time it was Jane.

"Oh Lizzy! I have wonderful news!"

Elizabeth smiled at Jane's infectious joy. "Tell me."

"We're going to California tomorrow!"

"Really?"

"Charles wants me to see his house and meet his father," she said somewhat shyly.

"That's great! I'm so happy for you," Elizabeth cooed. "Oh! I just got off the phone with Charlotte and you'll never guess who she's been talking to!"

"Richard?"

"How did you guess?"

Jane laughed. "So how are they doing?"

"Charlotte says it's good. They have just been talking, friendly like, but she seems pretty happy about it. Jane?"

"What?"

"Char wants to go back on tour with them. She wanted to know what we think."

Jane smiled. "Oh Lizzy! That's great news. Yes, I want to go back on tour." She slowed down a bit. "Charles and I are very worried about this all. It's one thing for us to be back together as a couple, but it's not good if the two bands are still having trouble."

Once again, Elizabeth found herself in the uncomfortable situation of being the one without a relationship. "I think for now we should plan on going back."

"Are you going to be okay, Lizzy?" Jane asked, her concern apparent.

"I'm not sure, but I'm going to try. That's all I can do."

"It'll work out for you. I know it will."

Elizabeth smiled wanly. "Now, you are going to be back in time for Tuesday, right?"

"Yes, we're coming back Sunday night. Are you going to be okay working with George again?"

Elizabeth sighed. Again, she wasn't sure. Knowing what she knew now, the last thing she wanted to do was make that second video with him, but she couldn't suddenly refuse to do it. Not without revealing Georgiana's secret, something she could never do. And if she did back out, she would be liable for all that money. There was nothing to do but grit her teeth and make the video with him, hopefully as quickly as possible.

"I'll be okay, Jane," she told her sister.

"Oh, Charles is back. I got to go. Take care, Lizzy. Say hi to Mary for me."

Elizabeth said good-bye and hung up the phone. She sat down with a sigh on her bed. It had been six days since she sent the email, and still she had no response. After biting her lip and thinking for a long moment, she found herself looking a number up and dialing.

"Hello," a crisp male voice answered.

"Oh, um, Faust, hi, it's Lizzy Bennet." Elizabeth found herself blushing furiously.

"Hello, Lizzy, how are you? Are you enjoying your holiday?" Faust seemed perfectly relaxed, and his ease helped Elizabeth.

"I am, thank you. And you?"

"Very nice, thanks. Caro is," he paused, as if he was looking around himself, "um, not available right now. Can I take a message?"

Elizabeth heard Caroline's voice calling out from a distance, "Who is it?"

"Hang on," Faust told her. A half minute later, he returned to the phone. "Lizzy? Caro said that she did forward your email to Darcy. Is that what you called about?"

Elizabeth smiled. "Yes, it is. Thanks."

"Oh good. Glad to be of service, Lizzy. See you soon."

Elizabeth sighed. She had her answer now, but she wasn't at all sure if she liked it. Darcy had her song, but he hadn't replied to it. That meant either he had rejected it and her or… or what? She tried to come up with a reason, other than he wanted nothing to do with her, and failed utterly.

But despite the fairly damning evidence, Elizabeth still couldn't give up hope. Maybe it was the way he had looked at her when he sang "Feel Me," or maybe it was Caro's advice to not give up. Or maybe it was just plain stubbornness. But Elizabeth was not ready to quit yet. She had been too blind in this relationship before, and she had made too many wrong assumptions. She wasn't going to do that again. She was going to go back on tour, and she was going to tell him what she felt. At least she could do that much.

It was with a heavy heart she tucked herself into bed. She might tell Darcy she loved him, and he might laugh in her face. After what happened in the loft and at the rehearsal, it wouldn't be impossible.

She wished she could just see him. Every day of waiting just became longer and longer. She closed her eyes and again imagined herself back in his arms. It might be nothing more than a fantasy at this point, but it was the most comforting one she had.

⬥⬥

Elizabeth enjoyed the two-hour drive to Tanglewood. She loved looking out the window at the beautiful scenery. The Berkshire Mountains rose up tall and green on either side of the highway. The summer sunlight was fading, but Elizabeth was still struck by the natural wonder of the place.

She exited the Mass Pike at Lee and quickly made her way to the hotel. Elizabeth had hoped to stay someplace nicer, but at this late date, the Day's Inn was the only place with rooms available.

It didn't matter; it was close to Tanglewood and it was clean, Elizabeth told herself. She couldn't help but smile as she realized that the hotels they generally stayed in while on tour were nicer than this. From the tour, her mind made the short hop to Darcy, a subject her mind spent so much of its time on lately.

Elizabeth allowed herself a quick fantasy that she was actually checking in with Darcy, rather than by herself. She knew it was foolish. Darcy would never stay in such a humble establishment. But it amused her briefly and made her feel less uncomfortable about being alone.

⬥⬥

Tanglewood was the summer home of the Boston Symphony Orchestra. Nestled in the Berkshire Mountains of Western Massachusetts, the large campus hosted performances daily in the two concert halls, and provided educational experiences for young musicians.

As Fitzwilliam Darcy walked along the path with his sister on the warm July morning, he found himself imagining a third member of their party. She was there again, his Shadow Elizabeth, who went with him everywhere and with whom he shared his favorite moments. Darcy could see in his mind's eye her smile as she took in the beautiful campus. He knew it was a hopeless fantasy, but he found comfort in it, imagining what she might say and listening to her laugh.

He paused in his steps. For a second he could have sworn he had actually heard her laugh. He worried that he was spending too much time in his fantasy when he heard her voice.

"Darcy?" she called. "Will?"

Darcy spun around and found himself looking at the surprised face of his love.

"Elizabeth?"

He took three steps closer to her without knowing he did so. She was there. She was real. She was wearing a summer dress in a soft melon color and her hair was arranged in a graceful cascade.

A similar look of shocked surprise had graced Elizabeth's face. She moved closer to him, and it was only when she stopped that Darcy was able to control himself and stop himself from embracing her. His awareness of where he was returned with a flash, and with it came the memories of their last parting.

Darcy smiled nervously. "What are you doing here?"

Elizabeth smiled with equal trepidation. "Mary," she indicated her sister, "is here for the summer on a conducting fellowship."

Darcy's eyes flicked to the younger woman. "Mary, it's nice to see you again," he said warmly.

"It's nice to see you, Darcy," she said easily.

"Um, call me Will, please," he replied awkwardly as he took a quick look at Elizabeth and then shook Mary's hand.

Mary nodded politely in response, not quite able to keep an amused smile off her face.

"Elizabeth?" Darcy said, turning back to her. "This is my sister, Georgiana." He indicated the girl who was waiting quietly for her turn. Georgiana was a little taller than Elizabeth, with Darcy's dark coloring and features. But where those features were extremely attractive on Darcy, they were merely pleasant on Georgiana.

Elizabeth shook the girl's hand and smiled warmly. Georgiana looked extremely nervous and ducked her head as she was introduced to the party.

When the introductions were finished, Elizabeth found herself facing Darcy again. She looked into his dark eyes and paused, and then touching her tongue to her upper lip, she found her voice again. "So, what are you doing here?" she asked warmly.

"We have a long connection with Tanglewood from when my mother played as a guest artist. My summer home is nearby and we try to get here at least once every summer."

Darcy stared at her, smiling for a long moment. Then he caught himself. "We were just about to go to lunch. Would you like to join us?"

Elizabeth looked at her sister and then to Darcy. "Certainly," she smiled.

Darcy beamed as he directed the party along the path, falling into step with Elizabeth. He was no further than asking how Elizabeth's parents were when Mary asked in a loud voice, "Where are we going?"

Darcy pointed in the direction of what looked like a large older house. "The Manor House," he replied. "We're expected at a luncheon there."

Elizabeth's face grew troubled. "Wait a minute. What kind of luncheon is this?"

Darcy stopped. "It's a reception for supporters of the festival. We have an endowment, um," he drifted off uneasily.

Elizabeth smiled embarrassedly. "We can't go to that. It sounds very formal and we're not invited," she stammered.

"Lizzy," he said softly. "It's not a problem. They're expecting me to bring guests. I was actually a little nervous before because it was just Georgie and me." He smiled appealingly. "Please come."

"Are you sure you don't mind?" she asked.

Darcy shook his head, looking as stunned as she by the situation they found themselves in. "Not at all. Please, I would like to have you there," he said carefully.

She smiled and nodded. As they continued to walk, Darcy asked her about her health and that of her family and of the band. The warmth in her face astonished him. All his plans for what he was going to say to her when they saw each other again had completely fled from his mind. He was running on instinct now, but at least he had the comfort of knowing she was just as surprised. If nothing else, that put them on equal ground.

❧

Elizabeth found it hard to believe he was here. And even more amazing was that he was talking to her. He was making it clear that he wanted to be with her, something she was hardly expecting. She ached to ask what was going on and why he hadn't replied to her song, but at the same time, she knew this wasn't the place, and more importantly, she just wanted to be with him, without fighting, and see what happened.

As Elizabeth answered his questions, she studied him out of the corner of her eye. He looked good. He was wearing a white polo and stone-colored twill pants. He still had his goatee, and his hair had been brushed back.

"So you have an endowment?" Elizabeth asked when he had run out of family and friends to ask about.

He looked at her and nodded. "My mother used to play here pretty regularly when I was growing up. I even played a duet with her once," he grinned. "When she died, my father set up an endowment in her name." He looked down at her and smiled as if he was reminding himself that this was real. "I'm really glad that you are here. It's..." Words seemed to fail him.

Elizabeth seemed to understand and could see his apprehension. She recognized that he was hesitating because he feared her response, remembering their terrible fight. She smiled gently at him and reached out her hand to him.

Darcy looked at her hand then her face. Wordlessly, he grasped her hand in his, never breaking his stride but moving minutely closer to her.

Elizabeth looked up to him, her eyes full of emotions, and she said softly, "I'm very glad to be here too." She smiled shyly at him and was delighted by his response.

They reached the Manor House, where an elegant buffet was laid out. Mary led Elizabeth and the Darcys around, introducing them to the other musicians and staff.

Upon entering the room, Darcy had released Elizabeth's hand. However, he found himself drawn to her, like a magnet to iron. He lightly rested his hand on the small of her back as the waiters served them.

Elizabeth turned and looked at him, indicating her approval of his touch. When he had to remove his hand to shake hands with an acquaintance, the electric shock of Elizabeth's hand lightly resting on his arm distracted him. Her eyes caught his and the wicked look he saw there told him she knew exactly what she was doing to him.

They sat down together to eat on a pair of seats against the wall, still in plain sight of the rest of the room. As Darcy chatted politely with the conductor for the night's performance, he nonchalantly crossed his leg, pressing his foot against Elizabeth's. Elizabeth smiled, making the briefest eye contact, before she returned to her conversation with the concertmistress. The game continued, each one seeing how long they could maintain physical contact with the other. It was blatantly obvious to both of them, yet they didn't speak of it, only continued to play, coming up with more creative and interesting excuses to touch each other. Darcy's hand grazed Elizabeth's calf when he picked up the napkin she dropped; Elizabeth caressed the back of Darcy's neck while brushing away a piece of lint from his collar. After each of these contacts, their eyes would meet, and a silent communication encouraged them to go on.

In that hour, Elizabeth felt happier than she had in the past two weeks. She was beyond understanding how they had met; it was fate at her most generous. But she was not at all interested in questioning it. Instead, she delighted in each touch and in the glorious knowledge that he had not rejected her.

The luncheon was, in fact, simple for her. She had been to functions like this with her father all through her childhood. The familiarity of the setting helped her feel more at ease with Darcy. They were not yet at liberty to speak freely with each other, but perhaps that was for the best. Instead they allowed their eyes and hands to speak for them while they were in this safe environment. They knew that neither could speak harshly or hurtfully here, and that encouraged them to be closer than they would have otherwise.

They played their discreet game throughout the whole meal, believing themselves to be completely unnoticed, although Georgiana followed it easily. As soon as she saw her brother's reaction to Elizabeth, even before he had introduced them, she realized who Elizabeth was. Georgiana was as surprised by the chance meeting as anyone else, but she quickly took advantage of it to study the woman Darcy had chosen in her "natural state."

Georgiana liked what she found in Elizabeth Bennet. Elizabeth had clearly been just as nervous as her brother, and considering what she knew of their relationship, Georgiana could completely understand that. But it was also clear that they had a great interest in each other, and more than anything, she wanted her brother to be happy. So she was willing to play along and act completely oblivious to their little touching game, all the while smiling politely to the strangers she didn't dare speak to.

All too quickly the luncheon was over. Darcy frowned slightly as he walked with Elizabeth out of the Manor House and into the bright sunshine. She smiled for an instant as he put his sunglasses on.

"Lizzy," he said slowly. "I have to meet with someone from the foundation for an hour." He frowned again, clearly not wishing to leave.

Elizabeth understood his frown and found it matched her feelings perfectly. "I see," she said politely.

"Will?" Georgiana said softly. "I don't really feel like going to the class. Perhaps I could stay with Elizabeth and Mary?" She looked pointedly at the Bennet girls.

Darcy looked from his sister to Elizabeth. "That would be great. You don't mind?"

"Not at all," Elizabeth nodded agreeably. Georgiana had symbolically offered herself up as a hostage to ensure they would meet again. "I'll see you later?"

"Yes," he grinned. He planted a quick kiss on his sister's cheek and was off. Elizabeth watched him move away, smiling to herself as she admired the strength of his frame.

Elizabeth let Mary direct them to a cool spot to enjoy the beautiful afternoon, and then she turned to Georgiana. "So, I heard you just graduated from high school," Elizabeth said, trying to open up a conversation with the girl.

Georgiana nodded and mumbled, "Yes."

"Where are you going to college?"

Georgiana squeaked something that Elizabeth thought was "Stanford," but she couldn't be sure.

This was turning out to be more difficult than Elizabeth expected. With a final effort, she said, "Did I hear you were in Europe with Will recently?"

Georgiana finally made eye contact with Elizabeth and with a tiny smile she nodded.

"Could you tell me about it?"

Slowly Georgiana told her about being in Paris with her brother. Elizabeth soon found that she got the best response when her questions involved Darcy, so she kept to that. Soon the girl was speaking more freely and even told her a funny story about her brother and his passport.

Elizabeth smiled warmly. "He seems very fond of you," she observed.

Georgiana blushed. "He is very good to me. He was so young when our father died, and he has never complained about taking care of me."

"He sounds like the perfect big brother." She wrinkled her nose. "But he can't be all perfect. Tell me, what does he do when he's bad?"

"Plays U2," she said simply, with great solemnity.

Elizabeth laughed until she fell back on the grass. When her chuckles subsided, she asked, "Anything else? Does he tease you or something?"

"No, he would never do that."

"Wow," said Elizabeth. "He is perfect."

Elizabeth was impressed at how much she enjoyed talking to the younger woman. She was startled when Darcy rejoined them to find how quickly the time had passed.

"How did it go?" she asked.

"It was fine," he assured her. Then he added, with a playful glint, "When you're giving them money, they're generally very accommodating."

Elizabeth matched his smile. "I honestly wouldn't know, but I can see your point."

"Can we walk a bit?" Darcy asked.

The ladies stood, and Mary and Georgiana took the lead, giving their siblings some needed privacy.

"Elizabeth," he waited until her attractive eyes meet his. "I need to apologize. I'm very sorry about what happened before. I'm appalled at my own behavior, and I hope you can forgive me."

Elizabeth looked at him with undisguised surprise. Her mouth worked for a few seconds before she was able to speak. "I'm sorry," she whispered earnestly. "I'm so sorry, Will. I shouldn't have walked out like that."

Darcy focused on walking and remaining calm in this public setting, when all he wanted to do was snatch her up in his arms and cover her face with kisses.

"You were right, Elizabeth, I was pushing too hard and I wasn't thinking about your feelings."

"I don't think," she interrupted, "either of us can say we were thinking about the other's feelings that morning." Her hand slipped into his.

"You may be right, but you have to admit I really screwed things up at the VMAs." He looked away and his mouth puckered in disgust, "When I think about what I did, Elizabeth, I'm so ashamed."

"Don't think about that," she admonished gently. "I'd much rather you remembered the good things about me," she smiled very slightly, "and us."

He squeezed her hand tightly in a show of what he wanted to do in a less public setting. Elizabeth squeezed back and smiled. "You can call me Lizzy, you know," she said playfully.

Darcy's lips curled. "I think I like calling you Elizabeth. It's something no one else does."

Elizabeth nodded. "Except my mother, when she's mad."

Darcy lost the battle against his self-control and leaned over and kissed her smiling lips. "Perhaps you could call me Fitzwilliam, since no one else does," he said conversationally, the tone of his voice was greatly relaxed.

She replied in the same easy tone, "Not even your sister, when she's mad?"

Darcy shook his head. "No, she hits me when she's mad."

"That's because you're a moron," Georgiana grumbled from ahead of them.

Elizabeth laughed, her buoyant joy warming Darcy as he watched her, completely bewitched. He was delightfully surprised by Elizabeth's reaction to him and was forced to conclude that his sister had been correct. Elizabeth had only needed time, and he had been a fool to not talk to her again. He was grateful that he had been given another chance, especially in a setting such as this, which was so different from the tense, tight, rushed experience of touring.

Here, in this open and sunny place, there was no need to hurry. Darcy's time was not his own, and his chances of being alone with Elizabeth were null. He was resigned to this and in fact, he was somewhat glad of it. He felt safer moving slowly right now, building the comfortable rapport with her that had always eluded him in the past.

Mary was performing in the concert at six o'clock, so the group decided to have an early dinner. Mary had arranged for a large picnic dinner and wouldn't hear of the Darcys not joining them.

Darcy and Georgiana shared a look but happily agreed. The meal was a lively affair, with everyone taking turns telling family stories. Soon it became apparent that the Darcys and the Bennets had more in common than they thought.

Darcy told the group about his childhood and how he spent many summers there at Tanglewood. "It's like coming home, being back here."

"So you said you have a house nearby?" Elizabeth asked.

"My father had it built for my mother as a wedding present, and it was her retreat. We spent all our summers there. It's called Pemberley."

"That sounds lovely," Elizabeth said and laughed softly. "It must hold a lot of special memories for you."

Darcy was touched by her perceptiveness. "It does."

"We always spent our summers sweating at home while Dad traveled around doing his research," Mary interjected.

Elizabeth nodded. "Yeah, and at the community pool. No cottages for us."

"Would you like to see it?" Darcy offered. "I would love to have you come over after the concert. We could have a late supper." He was careful to include the whole party in his invitation, but his heart was directed at Elizabeth.

Mary declined, but Elizabeth was all too happy to accept.

⚜

They attended Mary's concert in the Ozawa Concert Hall. Elizabeth and Darcy sat next to each other but were prohibited from talking, so Elizabeth took the time to put her thoughts in order.

She questioned if this was all a dream. During their time apart, Elizabeth had contemplated Darcy and realized that she had misjudged him. But the reality she was finding in him now shook her to the core. Had he always been this wonderful? Had she really been that blind?

It didn't seem possible. She knew she was at fault for being harshly judgmental of him, but this was a different man than the one she left that night so long ago. She realized that she was a different woman as well.

Remembering the events of the day, Elizabeth was once again surprised by Darcy's openness. She had never seen him so warm or friendly. She couldn't help but wonder if this was for her. Could she possibly have affected him so?

She felt the need for comfort and instinctively reached out her hand to him. Without hesitation he took it, lifting it to his lips and kissing it lightly before setting it, still firmly grasped in his, on his lap.

Elizabeth forced herself to be calm. In this setting, she couldn't do more than what she was doing; she needed to accept that. She longed to talk to him though. She wanted to talk to him and tell him her feelings and hear his reply in kind.

She wanted to know why he hadn't responded to her email, her song. Despite all the obvious signs of his affection, she was still troubled by it. She struggled to find meaning for his behavior. He clearly wasn't rejecting her, and in that she found great comfort. She wondered if perhaps he had wanted to see her face-to-face before he reacted to it. But he still had said nothing about it. Maybe he was so startled by her sudden appearance that he didn't know how to respond to it. But when she looked at him, he didn't show any signs of hesitancy or questioning.

Elizabeth felt like a dog chasing its own tail. She didn't know what was going on, and she hated that, but clearly she wasn't going to divine the answer on her own.

She was surprised to find the concert was over. With amused embarrassment, she realized she hadn't heard any of the last half of it, she was so lost in her thoughts.

"Elizabeth?" he said as they rose from their seats. "Are you okay? You seem a little distracted."

Elizabeth blushed slightly. "Sorry," she mumbled. Together they went outside to wait for Mary. "Do you have tickets for the main concert?" Elizabeth struggled to find something to talk about when all she wanted was to be alone with him.

"Yes, do you?"

"Yes, Mary got us some."

Just then Georgiana's cell phone rang and she stepped away to talk, as Darcy and Elizabeth compared their tickets.

"How did Mary get you better seats than us?" Darcy asked, puzzled.

Elizabeth laughed. "You don't know Mary."

"Will," Georgiana said, her phone pressed to her chest. "Kimberley is here for just this weekend. Do you think we could skip the concert so I could visit her?"

Mary tilted her head, "You know, this evening is the all-Sibelius program. I would not mind missing it at all."

"Oh," Elizabeth looked to Darcy, surprised to find her wish so quickly granted. "Well, then I'm fine with going to your place."

Darcy nodded, his confusion quickly turning to pleasure.

Neither of the lovers noticed Mary and Georgiana exchanging a silent high-five.

≈

It was quickly decided that Georgiana would ride with Elizabeth to direct her to Pemberley. "I'm glad you and Will are such good friends," the girl said. "He gets so lonely, especially when he's on tour."

"He does?"

Georgiana nodded. "I know it seems strange, because he's with his best friends, but he puts himself under so much responsibility, he has trouble getting close to anyone, even his friends."

Elizabeth had seen that side of his personality. But Mr. Control Freak seemed like a completely different person from the man she had spent the day with. Elizabeth was so puzzled by this that she almost missed Georgiana's next comment.

"I almost wish music wasn't his profession," she said feelingly.

"Why is that?" Elizabeth asked, astonished.

"Because Will's music is the only place where he can fully express himself, and now his music is tied to his work." She sighed. "He is so afraid of making mistakes that he drives himself too hard. I worry about him."

Elizabeth smiled distractedly as her head swam. Knowing what she did about Georgiana's past, she understood now why Darcy was so careful to never screw up, but she could also see that his manic drive was powered by fear. He had lost so many people who were dear to him that he was terrified of making a mistake and losing another, as he almost had with Georgiana.

No wonder he's strung up tighter than a bank vault, Elizabeth thought as she drove. Suddenly everything about Darcy made much more sense. She cast her mind back to that morning in the loft and realized that he was simply trying to not lose her as well. If Georgiana was correct, and Darcy didn't open up to anyone easily, then she could suddenly understand his emphatic attempts to hold on to her. She had seen for herself that he never let anyone close to him on the tour.

But why her? She found herself pondering. What made her so special that Darcy, who could have almost any woman on the planet, should want her, who had been at best polite and at worst flat-out bitchy to him?

"Will told me he really admires you as a musician."

Elizabeth was slightly surprised that he would talk about her to Georgiana, not by her news. Darcy had told her before that she was talented, almost from the start. "Really?" she replied, somewhat indifferently.

"Yes, I was surprised because I almost never hear him say that, and especially not about another guitarist."

Elizabeth looked over with wonder then. She examined Georgiana's face but found nothing other than complete sincerity. "Really?" she said in a much different tone.

"It's true," Georgiana assured her. "I think he feels like you are a peer to him. Someone who isn't always looking up to him, but an equal."

"Oh," Elizabeth had breathed, before sinking into her thoughts. She never even noticed the tiny smile curling the corners of Georgiana's lips.

Suddenly Georgiana pointed. "Look."

Elizabeth looked and gasped. Before her was a beautiful building made of glass and stone. It was well lit and Elizabeth could see through the huge windows, which made up most of the front walls, to a great room that glowed with the softness of light-colored wood.

Elizabeth was stunned. She had expected it would be nice and rich, but nothing like this. This was a house out of her dreams. It was large and clean looking, with no wasted space or false ornamentation. The gardens around the front porch were lit and Elizabeth was struck by the beautiful display of flowers, which seemed perfectly balanced for the house. In her mind, Elizabeth could see the house in all the seasons, and she was pleased by how well suited it seemed for its surroundings.

As she parked, she saw Darcy waiting for her. He opened her door and offered his hand to help her out of the truck. "Welcome to Pemberley," he told her, his eyes full of warmth.

She turned to him and said with complete sincerity, "This is the most beautiful house I've ever seen."

Darcy smiled blindingly at her. "I'm very pleased you like it." He led her through the entrance and into the great room. The room lived up to its name in every way. It was large, with a vaulted ceiling and a massive stone fireplace along one wall. Fine art mixed liberally with photographs on the walls in a way that was both random and pleasing. A pair of leather sofas sat facing each other in one part of the room, but the rest of it was left mostly empty to enhance the feeling of open spaciousness.

"Will," Georgiana said softly, "I'm going to grab my stuff and go to Kimberley's. I'll see you tomorrow. Bye, Lizzy," she waved as she left the room.

Once they were alone, Darcy took her into his arms. She opened herself to his hungry kisses. The privacy of an empty room was something she had been longing for all day. Her fingers tangled in his hair as she felt his hands pulling her closer to his hard body.

His mouth broke away from her only long enough to plead, "Please stay here tonight," before he fell back down to hers. Elizabeth kissed him back, trying to get as close to him as she could.

"Yes," she gulped, in between kisses, as he lightly sucked her lower lip between his. "I missed you," she cried. "Missed you so much."

"Lizzy," he moaned as he buried his face in her soft hair. "Lizzy, I haven't been able to think of anything but you. I'm so sorry."

"No sorries," she insisted, "just kiss me again."

He took her softly parted lips and brushed them with his thumb, caressing them gently. "Lizzy, listen, please, I have to tell you." Her eyes drifted shut with an expression of exquisite pleasure. "Oh God," he cried distractedly before kissing her again.

The pained tone in his voice pulled Lizzy out of her haze. Gently she turned her face away and buried it in his shoulder, as he caressed her hair, their chests rising and falling together. Elizabeth felt the pressure of her desire fade slightly. "What did you want to say?" she asked.

Darcy led them out of the great room and up a short flight of stairs to a door. Behind it was a huge, lavish bedroom. As Elizabeth stared, Darcy wrapped his arms around her waist and started kissing her neck. "I hope you don't mind. It's just that last time, we had a little bit of trouble reaching the bedroom."

Elizabeth spun in his arms and determinedly kissed his self-satisfied grin away.

After a few moments, he pulled back and studied her face thoughtfully. "Can we talk now?"

Elizabeth bit her lip. "We can try."

He guided her to the bed and they lay down together. Elizabeth was burning for him, but she was afraid enough of a repeat of last time that she was willing to go slowly.

"I've been thinking a lot about what happened that morning," he began. Elizabeth snuggled close to him and rested her head against his. "And I realized something. I realized that it's not that I want you to be mine, Elizabeth; it's that I want to be yours."

Elizabeth heard the plaintive loneliness in his voice and she wrapped him up as close as she could. "You are mine," she assured him. "Didn't you hear that in the song?"

Darcy stared at her with a look of utter confusion. "What song?"

"The song I emailed you."

"What?"

"I sent you a song," Elizabeth exclaimed. Then she slowed down and tried to explain. "I've been thinking too, all the time," she smiled ruefully, "and I tried to reach you. I went to the loft the morning after the VMAs and you were gone, so I went home and I wrote a song."

Darcy's eyes got progressively larger as he listened to her story. "You came to the loft?" he asked, his expression incredulous.

Elizabeth nodded as she sat up. "I tried to send you the song, but I didn't have your email address, so I had Caro forward it to you."

"Oh my God," Darcy breathed as he sprang out of bed to the computer sitting on a desk beside the window. Elizabeth joined him. "When was it sent?" Darcy asked as he brought up his mail file. Elizabeth was shocked to find a dozen unread messages, all from Caroline.

"A week ago Thursday. That's it, the forward," she said, pointing. "Here, let me," she told him as she sat down and took the mouse from him.

"I never read emails from Caro," Darcy explained haltingly.

Elizabeth was stopped from asking why as she heard her song coming from the speakers. Her lips moved along with the words as she looked up nervously at him.

> *Sometimes the feelings are just too strong.*
> *They overwhelm our hearts, and make us weak.*

Sometimes, you need some distance to think.
And then, you can speak.
Let's talk about it.
When you touched me, you gave me a reason to hope.
You gave me more to think about than my fears.
When you left me, you took away the key
To the answers and left me with just my tears.
So now, I need to find my own truth,
To trust in what I believe,
To give you the courage of my faith,
And see where the future leads.
I believe you.
In your heart you know it's right.
I hear what you've been trying to say.
I've pushed out my pride and opened my eyes,
And I see us in a new way.

Slowly, he sat beside her, his eyes bright with wonder. He trembled with her song. "This is for me?" he whispered.

Elizabeth nodded, her arms reaching out to caress him. "You were right, Fitzwilliam, I couldn't make love like that without being in love."

The sound of his name on her voice tore through him and he grasped her close, covering her in kisses as he rubbed his face in her hair, letting her sweet fragrance wash over him.

Her lips quivered, her heart swelling with the love she needed to express to him. "You are so bright, so powerful, so sexy, and you terrified me because you were so sure of your feelings. But I know now, I knew within ten minutes of walking out of that loft, that I needed to go back to you. And that scared me too." Her voice shook with the deep emotion running through her.

Darcy was kissing her, his lips pressing against her neck and moving up to her jaw. "I love you," she cried before his lips found hers once more. They kissed hungrily, as all their yearnings were released.

"Lizzy," he moaned between kisses, "I love you, my dearest."

Elizabeth let out a sharp cry of relief. "I worried I would never hear you say that again," she whispered happily through her tears.

Darcy merely pressed her close, so their two hearts were beating against each other, and held her until Elizabeth recovered and started placing featherlight kisses along his neck. Then he released her and sat back on his heels, his eyes dark. "You're feeling better?"

Elizabeth nodded uncertainly.

Darcy's mouth curled into a wicked smile. "Good, because we have some unfinished business, my love." He returned to kissing her while slowly working her sundress up. When he stopped kissing her to pull it over her head, Elizabeth cooperated by extending her arms. She didn't know what he was up to, but she recognized that expression on his face and knew whatever it was, she would enjoy it.

Darcy tossed the dress aside and returned his gaze to Elizabeth. Slowly his eyes traveled up her form, observing every inch of her body. Elizabeth assisted by sitting up in the chair, pushing her breasts forward and spreading her legs. She felt very sexy as she watched him examine her with his eyes, still fully dressed.

She hoped he was excited by what he found: Elizabeth was wearing under the dress a strapless hot pink bra and matching satin panties. He reached out to touch the soft satin and compare it to the smoothness of her skin. "You're beautiful, Elizabeth," he murmured as he returned to her lips.

Elizabeth closed her eyes and let his mouth devour hers, delighting in the feel of his suit fabric against her bare skin. She sighed softly as Darcy's hands cupped her breasts, squeezing and massaging them until she whimpered with need, then she gasped in relief as his hand slipped into her bra to touch her skin. "Better?" he whispered, his warm breath in her ear.

Elizabeth nodded and reached behind her and quickly unfastened the bra, eager to be free of it. Darcy wasted no time in grasping both breasts in his hands, as he kissed her deeply.

"Lizzy, I've been wanting to touch you like this all day. Your breasts are so soft and full. You're so beautiful."

Elizabeth whimpered slightly.

"Stand up, Lizzy."

Elizabeth didn't want the pleasure to stop, but he repeated his request, so she stood, leaning a hand on his shoulder for support. As she stood, Darcy's hands slid down her sides to the full curve of her hips and he hooked the panties with his thumbs. Smoothly he drew them down until she was completely naked before him. He worshiped her with his eyes, overflowing with admiration and desire. Gently he eased her back into the chair and moved forward, placing himself between her legs.

"Dearest?" he asked. Elizabeth watched him, her eyes locked on his, like she was mesmerized. "Do you remember what I told you before?" Gently he placed his hands on her thighs and pushed her legs apart.

Elizabeth felt her breath coming in short gasps. She watched his eyes as he lowered his face to her core. When she felt his lips brush her, her eyes shut and her head slowly tipped back. Darcy's hand continued to push her legs apart and she was more than willing to cooperate, opening herself wide to him. She shuddered as his tongue lapped at her, tasting her sweetness.

"Lizzy," his deep voice called to her. Raggedly Elizabeth opened her eyes and looked up at him. "My love, you taste delicious." Her gut tightened at his words. "I want to watch you. Look at me."

Elizabeth watched him as he returned to her. She saw him watching her reaction to his every touch. She felt particularly excited by the experience and experimented by letting more of her enjoyment show in her actions and expressions. She was pleased to see him respond with greater excitement. On and on it went, with her giving and receiving more of his pleasure. She could feel the tension building and knew she was getting close. Her hand slipped down and her fingers tangled in his hair as she held him tightly against her and let her pleasure show in her eyes. Then she was in the white place, as her excitement crested and it happened, waves of pleasure rocked her body as her hips bucked against him.

Her nails bit into her palms as she struggled against her screams. Then the waves faded away and she slumped in the chair.

"Are you okay?" he asked, his voice rough, as he rose to his feet.

Elizabeth nodded, not having breath enough to speak.

He smiled hungrily, bent down, and scooped her up into his arms. Her head lolled like a rag doll as he carried her the few steps to his bed. "Rest now," he told her as he laid her down on her bed.

Elizabeth watched through her lashes as he quickly stripped off his clothes. She was fascinated as the refined philanthropist was ripped away and the earthy rock god emerged. Standing before her, she gasped at his pure beauty, his pale skin glowing in the soft moonlight.

"Do you like what you see?" he asked, his voice a deep growl.

Elizabeth smiled guiltily. "Very much so," she whispered lustfully.

"What would you like?"

"I want you on top of me, inside of me. I want to feel you."

Moving with catlike grace, he crawled onto the bed until he was directly over her. Elizabeth reached out and touched his flesh, firm and warm beneath her fingertips.

"Lie on me, love. Let me feel you."

His lips brushed hers as he lowered himself on top of her.

"Oh yes, yes," she cried happily. "You feel so good." Elizabeth relished the feeling of his weight pressing her down. She had longed for this feeling for so long. She opened herself to him, and with agonizing slowness he entered her.

"Lizzy, I don't know how long—"

"Yes, yes, don't stop."

He kissed her, his mouth sealing hers as he thrust deeper into her. She crooned low in her throat as every thrust brought him deeper inside, increasing her pleasure. Once fully inside, he reached down, cupping her ass in his hands. Elizabeth's eyes popped open with the astonishing feelings, and her cries increased in pitch and volume. Over and over he pulled her to him as he buried himself as deep as he could go.

Elizabeth was helpless, going along with the ride as he drove himself to his release, and it was the wildest ride she could imagine. She reveled in the sensations of him, surrounding, filling, dominating her. She was his, body and soul. Soon cries she couldn't control were pouring from her lips and her body was wracked by the pleasure that engulfed her.

Somewhere in her awareness, she felt him growing larger inside of her and she knew his climax was near. She squeezed him as tightly as she could and with the next thrust the orgasm that had been building inside of her exploded. Darcy's own climax added to her pleasure and their frantic movements gradually slowed and stopped. Darcy wrapped his long arm around her shoulders and gently rolled them to their sides as Elizabeth snuggled her head against him and caught her breath.

Once again, their hearts were beating against each other, and Elizabeth felt whole for the first time since she could remember. His bare skin touched hers all over, and she felt loved and happy.

Eventually, Darcy heaved a huge sigh and kissed her sweaty forehead. "Why is sex with you so amazing?" he asked, his voice warm, loving, and exhausted.

Elizabeth lifted her head and chuckled at him. "I thought it was you that was making it amazing."

Darcy grinned back at her and they pressed their foreheads together. "Are you okay?" he asked.

Elizabeth nodded and then answered, "Tired." She relaxed in the warm circle of his arms, resting her head on his shoulder, and found herself crying.

"Love?" Darcy gasped.

"I'm sorry." She smiled brokenly through her tears. "I've just been longing for this and trying to duplicate the feeling of sleeping in your arms for the last two weeks, and now I'm here—" She broke off as the sobs overwhelmed her.

Darcy pulled her close and let her cry out her pain as he gently stroked her back, kissing her hair and murmuring soft words of love in her ear. "It's okay, Lizzy, it's okay," he soothed her. His words were slow, as if unwilling to admit them. "I understand. The pain you suffered is too strong to face alone. But you can face it now, because we're together. We can both face it now."

Elizabeth looked up at him and touched his cheek tenderly, sharing the pain they both felt, even as it ebbed away. When she stopped crying, he gently kissed her flushed hot cheeks, then her full, sweet lips, and told her, "This is our space, right here. It's where we both belong, and we're not going anywhere. Either of us, all right?" his eyes gently questioned hers, while promising himself.

"I'm staying. This is where I want to be more than anyplace else in the world." Elizabeth smiled sleepily. "You do give me the most gorgeous sleep, Fitzwilliam."

"And you me, Elizabeth," he whispered in her ear. By the time her head reached the pillow, she was asleep and he immediately followed her.

CHAPTER 17

Elizabeth awoke feeling warm and happy. The bright morning sunlight streamed in through large windows, filtered by the white linen curtains, diffusing the light as it illuminated the room. She traced a soft sound to a fountain bubbling against one wall.

She could tell by his soft breathing that Darcy was still asleep, and she kept still to make the moment last. She inventoried all the places their flesh touched: his chest against her back, his arm draped over her middle, his hand cupping her breast, his cock firm against her ass, his legs intertwined with hers, and even her one foot resting on his. She couldn't see him from her position, but she could visualize each part in her mind, and she was moved by his great strength and beauty.

As she observed the part of the room she could see, she carefully recalled each part of the previous day, reliving every memory and carefully storing it away, like a beloved keepsake.

It had been some kind of miracle that they had found each other again. But that they had forgiven each other and professed their love, that was no miracle, that was destiny; it was fate.

She had concluded before they were perfect for each other, and now, in his arms, she found her conclusion was correct. A wave of tender emotion washed over her, and she couldn't keep from rolling over in his arms to see his dear face again.

His face was relaxed, even as he stirred slightly. Elizabeth pressed light kisses over his forehead and nose, feeling giddy with love for him. His hand moved up and captured her head, holding her still as his lips met hers.

"Good morning," he intoned when he released her.

Elizabeth smiled joyfully. "Good morning." She kissed his lips then snuggled close, nuzzling her lips on the soft skin near his ear and telling him, "I adore you."

Darcy stretched his long frame out then caught her up in his arms and kissed her soundly. Elizabeth could feel his erection growing against her belly, and with a happy wantonness, she craved it. Her hands slipped down to touch and play with him.

Darcy lifted a questioning eyebrow to her. "You are certainly in a playful mood this morning."

Elizabeth giggled. "I guess I am." She looked up at him with uncertain happiness. "I love you," she said simply. "I never really had a chance to tell you that before, and now I need you to know it, to feel it."

Darcy drew her into his embrace and gently kissed her hair and ears. Elizabeth closed her eyes and moved herself against his mouth, her desire increasing with each touch. She lifted her head to his and kissed him hard. She was relieved, then excited when he returned her kiss with equal passion.

As they kissed, they repositioned themselves, moving as if with one mind. Darcy lay on his back and Elizabeth mounted him, her knees resting on either side of his hips, his erection pressed between their bellies.

Elizabeth broke away from his mouth and gasped, "I'm sorry to rush, I just need you."

Darcy quieted her and leaned back. "I want to watch you pleasure yourself on me. I want to feel you on me."

The softest sigh escaped his lips as she impaled herself on his hard shaft. He watched as she rode him, her lips full and puffy from kissing, her eyes large and wild with desire, her expression full of pleasure and longing.

His hands slid up her thighs to grasp her ass. He squeezed and caressed those heavenly curves, which had fascinated him almost from the start, and Elizabeth's thrusts became more and more forceful.

He looked into her eyes and saw that she was deep in her own sensations now. The tightening of her body around him confirmed that fact. He was bewitched by her actions. She shed all her inhibitions and was completely bare to him. Even her emotions were ripped away and she was driven by pure sensation. She was naked, raw, and powerful, and Darcy understood in a flash that she could never be this free if she didn't have complete trust in him.

With that realization, he lost control to the impossibly erotic vision above him and the waves of sweet pleasure she brought him. The fiery tension in his body took over and he grasped her hips hard as he made the final push toward ecstasy.

Their voices cried out in ardor beyond knowledge or caring. The world was gone and they were lost in sweet pleasure, built off each other, climbing to levels neither imagined before.

It was Elizabeth who peaked first, her body tightening as waves of orgasm enveloped her and she cried out with each contraction. Darcy, completely lost in the worship of her body, emptied himself into her.

They collapsed, exhausted, onto each other, their limbs weak and trembling. With shuddering breaths, they reached for each other, to anchor and ground themselves. As one, they rested.

When her awareness returned, Elizabeth kissed the part of him closest to her lips, his heart. She felt him squeeze her tight in wordless response, and her heart cherished him with such intensity, it was painful.

She closed her eyes and basked in the sensations of his adoration, feeling happiness she had never known. When she spoke, her voice was rough with emotion and wonder. "Will, I can never leave you now." She trembled as she spoke new truths that were as life changing as they were undeniable. "I'm yours. I understand now. Oh God. I love you so much and I'm yours now."

Darcy held her tenderly. Her body more precious to him than anything he had ever known, and he felt an instinctive need to protect her. He didn't understand how it had happened so quickly, but she was right. They were bonded together, their lives linked. It was amazing and frightening and wonderful all at the same time; yet it was as certain and as undeniable as the sunrise.

When the wave of heady emotion passed, Darcy watched as her eyes opened again and smiled with all the love in his heart. She smiled back and relaxed with a sigh, her emotions already exhausted. "It's hard work being in love, isn't it?"

Elizabeth grinned and nodded. "Can we take it easy today?"

Darcy's hand absently traced the muscles of her biceps as he stroked her arm. "Sounds good to me. I have no plans."

Elizabeth nodded contentedly. "I should probably get my stuff from the hotel."

Darcy nodded, and a part of him observed with amazement at how easy this was. Yet it felt so right, there was no doubt. They had both found their place, and that was with each other.

Thinking of the world outside of Pemberley reminded her of something she needed to say, but she was loathe to mention it. Her heart lurched and she prayed for just a few moments of peace with him. She wanted to shut out the world beyond their bed and protect him, but it was hopeless.

"What's wrong?" he asked, seeing through her.

With a heavy sigh, she took his hand and laced her fingers between his. "I wish the timing was better, but I have to tell you something, about Wickham."

Darcy grew very still, but said nothing.

"On Tuesday, I have to go and shoot the second video with him," she announced dully.

Darcy felt a twinge of relief that it was not something far worse, then set his mind to her problem.

"Elizabeth, you don't have to do this," he told her with calm certainty.

Elizabeth looked at him, surprised by his reaction, and tears welled up in her eyes. "Will, I have to," she breathed. "I don't want to. Now that I know what he is, I could very happily live the rest of my life without ever seeing George again. I hate the very idea, but I don't have a choice. If I cancel, how will I explain it? What will I tell everyone? I can't reveal Georgie's secret. We would lose all that money and de Bourgh would fire us so fast. It would be the end of our careers."

"If you really don't want to, you don't have to." He sat up and took her into his arms. "If it's a question of money, I will take care of that."

Elizabeth looked at him sadly. "I can't ask you to do that."

Darcy smiled, taking a moment to regard the face he adored. "Of course you can, Elizabeth." His smile faded as he continued. "I know it's not really about the money, but I need you to know that, at least, that is not a problem."

Elizabeth felt relief that this was going so well. She had feared he would grow angry or not understand. They were so new, so fragile. They could hurt each other so easily. She looked at him questioningly. "You are taking this much better than I expected."

He sighed heavily and leaned against her. "That's because I have to tell you something, and I know you are not going to like it." She looked at him, waiting. "It's about De Bourgh and what happened at the VMAs."

"Oh, we were surprised about that. We figured Anne was going to terminate our contract for sure."

Darcy nodded. "She almost did. The only reason she didn't is that while you were performing, I was on the phone with Lady Catherine, asking her not to."

"You were?"

Darcy nodded sadly. "Elizabeth, the moment you walked out of the theater during rehearsal I felt guilty for what I had done. And then when Jane started to sing, I knew exactly what you were saying. We all did. But I couldn't let you destroy your career over my acting like an idiot."

"I don't understand. What did you do?"

"I promised Lady Catherine she wouldn't lose money over you."

"Did you buy our contract?" She looked suddenly uncomfortable.

"No, no," he assured her. "We guaranteed it, like an insurance policy. So that if you were a flop, we would cover all of De Bourgh's losses."

"We?"

"Charles, Richard, and I all signed the deal." He looked miserable. "I know you hate anyone interfering in your career, especially me, but you were destroying yourselves over something I did, and I had to try to stop it."

Elizabeth looked away. "It wasn't just what you did," she said numbly.

"I know. I know, and that is why we all signed the deal. But I can't speak for the others. I can only speak for myself, and I did it because I love you, Elizabeth. Please understand."

Elizabeth laid her head down on his shoulder. She was shocked by what he said, but she still reached instinctively to him for comfort.

"Lizzy?" he said tentatively as he stroked her hair. "Tell me what you are feeling."

Elizabeth smiled at his question. "Mostly surprised. I had no idea you were so generous, or so caring. But I guess I should have seen it all before."

Darcy kissed her head desperately. "Are you mad?"

"No," she shook her head. "I'm just very lucky I have you." She lifted her face to him. "Hold me," she breathed and he pulled her tight, settling her in his lap as he covered her with kisses and soft words.

She was stunned by what he had told her. She never realized that someone could care so much for her, protect her the way he did. She felt something new inside of herself, a sense of belonging, of safety she hadn't felt before. Even as she was warmed by it, she was appalled at the same time at her own stupidity. How could she have misjudged him so?

After a minute, she pulled herself together. "Are you sure you want to love someone who is so blind?" she asked him archly.

Darcy smiled. "Are you sure you want to love someone who brings nothing but trouble to you?"

They kissed and held each other tightly, until a knock came at the door. Darcy put on his robe and answered it, returning a moment later. "Georgie's home."

"Then I guess we had better get cleaned up and have some—" she looked at the clock and was surprised at how late it was, "oh, lunch."

Darcy smiled and led her to the bathroom. Elizabeth stopped dead in her tracks as she examined the room. "Fitzwilliam, there is a swimming pool in your bathroom!"

Darcy handed her a toothbrush. "Don't be silly. The pool is outside. That's just the spa." He kissed her lightly on the nose and started brushing his teeth as Elizabeth moved closer to the spa. It was either very large for a spa or small for a pool. It had been built into the floor, with steps going down into it and rough stonework along the outside wall. "You like it?" Darcy asked.

"It's beautiful!"

"My parents' nicknames for each other were 'Water' and 'Stone.'"

Elizabeth flashed him a doubtful look and he shrugged. "It was the eighties, they were rich New Agers, whatever. Anyway, they used the element of water or glass and stone throughout the design of the house. The spa was custom built for them and from hints my relatives have dropped, I think I was conceived in there."

Elizabeth's eyebrows shot up. "Oh really!"

He smiled at her around his toothbrush and nodded, then moved away to the sink.

Elizabeth gave the spa an appraising "hmm" and moved to the sink as well.

They spent a quiet afternoon with each other, returning to Tanglewood to see Mary again, hear the two o'clock concert, and then pick up Elizabeth's luggage. Darcy found his attention wandered constantly to Elizabeth. His eyes could not get enough of her. She was dressed in a simple red tank dress that complemented her coloring and her delicious curves. And while he would have normally been mortified by his inattentiveness to the others, he found he couldn't stop himself when Elizabeth met his eyes and stared back at him so often.

Elizabeth left Mary with a loving hug and traveled with the Darcys back to Pemberley. As soon as they got in, Georgiana announced her intention to spend the evening with her girlfriend. Darcy stopped her and the two shared a brief conversation. Darcy questioned her motives and Georgiana assured him that she was all right. Elizabeth politely pretended not to hear them.

When Georgiana had left, Darcy handed Elizabeth a cordless phone and kissed her. "Call your parents. I don't want them to worry." Elizabeth blushed and looked away, still not comfortable with the idea of Darcy and her parents.

"Wait," Darcy countermanded. "What's wrong?"

"Oh, I just know you don't like my family. Not that I don't understand," she quickly assured him, "I know we can be overwhelming at first."

Darcy took the phone from her hand, led her to the couch, and made her sit with him. "Tell me why you think I don't like your family," he said with an expression of disbelief.

Elizabeth wished she had never said anything. "It's okay. You don't have to hide it. I could see by the way you acted at my house you disliked them."

Darcy sighed and rubbed his forehead. "Dearest, I don't dislike your family." He frowned, clearly impatient with himself. "I'm sorry. I'm not really comfortable around new people, and it comes off as my being arrogant and not liking them."

Elizabeth's expression turned uneasy as she recognized her own initial reaction to him.

"Elizabeth, the truth is, I like your family very much." He smiled slightly. "If anything, I'm envious of how close you all are."

Elizabeth felt horrible. "Oh, I'm so sorry. I totally misunderstood."

She wrapped her arms around him and he kissed her. "I feel kinda stupid now."

"You're not stupid, Elizabeth. I'm sorry I acted like such a jerk."

Elizabeth tried to tell him he hadn't, but Darcy wouldn't let her. "I'm quite sure I did. But I hope you are clear on it now?"

Elizabeth nodded and kissed him again. They exchanged words of love, and Darcy got up, saying he would leave her alone to make her call, and went to his studio.

By the time Elizabeth was done talking to her mother, she wasn't sure if she shared Darcy's affection for her parents. Elizabeth couldn't believe how mercenary her mother could be, and it was a relief when her father took the phone.

"Hello, pumpkin," he said calmly. "What is all this I hear about you and the big-shot rock star?"

Elizabeth smiled. Most other people would be offended, but she recognized her father's dry sense of humor. "He's made me his love slave," she answered casually.

"Very good," he replied. "Tell me, is being a love slave to a rock star a well-paid position?"

Elizabeth laughed. "You know, I think there might just be a 'room and board' clause to this. I'll have to check on that."

"Lizzy?" His voice had turned serious. "Are you sure you are making the right decision?"

Elizabeth was touched. This was how she knew that under all his bluff, he loved her dearly. "I am, Dad. He's wonderful. I know this seemed to happen quickly, but it's actually been building for a while and I've never been so happy in my life," she told him confidently. "Listen, we're all off next Sunday, maybe we could come up for dinner and you can give him a hard time."

"Oh, no! The man is taking one of my daughters off my hands. I'm not going to give him a hard time. He might send you back!"

Elizabeth giggled.

"But it would be nice to spend a bit more time with the man. Perhaps Jane could bring her Romeo too?"

"I think that could be arranged," Elizabeth replied, pleased.

"Very good, Lizzy, your mother just passed me a note that says 'Tell Lizzy to call Alex.' Well, now you have been told."

"I have; thank Mom for me."

"Take care of yourself, Lizzy." His voice had a note of tenderness. "I've missed you around here. The house has suddenly gotten very quiet."

"I will, Daddy. I love you."

"All right. I'll see you next week. Bye, Lizzy."

Elizabeth turned off the phone and sat still for a moment, staring out the window at the trees. She had always been her father's favorite but had never realized how painful her leaving would be to him. She resolved to be more faithful in her phone calls to him, even if it meant she would have to listen to her mother's silliness.

With a shrug she turned to the phone and dialed Alex's number. He answered with a doubtful, "Hello?"

"Hey, it's me. Mom said you called?"

"Lizzy? Where are you calling from? I thought you'd be back home by now."

"Oh, that," she grinned. "Slight change in plans. I'm at Darcy's."

"Oh?"

"Yes, I ran into him at Tanglewood and we talked and, well, here I am." Elizabeth looked up to see Darcy coming up the short flight of steps from the studio, his mother's guitar in his hands. She flashed him a bright smile and a wink.

"So now you're fucking him, you mean?"

"*What?*"

"Oh, please, Lizzy. I've seen the way you two have been staring at each other for the whole tour." His tone was ugly. "I'm just surprised you were willing to take him back after the VMAs. He must be damn good."

"How. Dare. You." Elizabeth was shocked and revolted. "I can't believe you just said that."

Silence was her only answer. Elizabeth was about to hang up when Alex said in a low voice, "I'm sorry, Lizzy. I just hate to see him treat you like that."

"Alex, you have no idea how he treats me or what's going on between us, and frankly, it's none of your business."

"Elizabeth, if it affects you or the band, it's my business. That's a manager's job: keeping his band together. And frankly, I don't like what that man and his friends have been doing to you."

Elizabeth wished then that she had never said anything about Darcy to the others. She could see for herself how dubious her admission of love must look to the others, especially after she had been so vehement in her disdain for him. "Look, Alex, I'm sorry you don't like him, but the fact of the matter is we are now a package deal. You want to deal with me, you deal with him." Her nerve broke and her voice softened. "I don't want to fight about this, Alex. I want you to be happy for me."

Again, there was a long pause. "Are you sure?"

"Yes."

"Then I'll be happy for you, Lizzy. And if you're wrong, and I'm right, I'll be there for you too."

"I'm not wrong, Alex. Trust me."

"All right. I just called to see how you were, Lizzy. Are you all set for Tuesday?"

"Yes, I'll meet you at the airport."

"You have all the details for that?"

"It's on my email."

"Good. I'll see you then. Take care, baby girl."

"Bye," she whispered. He hadn't called her that in a year and the words still had power over her.

Elizabeth looked up to see that Darcy was gone. She frowned and went to the bedroom, following the sound of furious strumming. She found Darcy sitting on a chair in his room, playing angrily.

Elizabeth crossed the large room to him and stopped his hands with her own. She looked at him, questioning him.

Darcy put the guitar down on a table next to him carefully and then turned to Elizabeth. "What is he to you?" he asked in a low, deliberate voice.

Elizabeth felt her mouth go dry. "He's my manager. Nothing more."

Darcy shook his head and waited, his eyes staring into hers.

"Does it show?" Elizabeth asked uncomfortably, realizing she needed to tell him; she owed him that.

Darcy shook his head. "Not on your side. But looking at him? Hell, yeah. There's clearly some history between you." He sighed and dropped his shoulders. "Elizabeth?" he asked.

She held up a hand in defeat and nodded. "Okay. It's just, um, I'm not... It's not a pretty story and I'm going to need your help telling it."

Without another word, Darcy stood and took her into his arms. She held him tightly, anchoring herself in his embrace. A few moments later found them stretched out on the bed together.

"It happened a long time ago. I was seventeen and had just graduated from high school. We were very busy that summer, mostly because for the first time I could work past eleven o'clock." She laughed lightly. "But we were traveling around the area, playing everywhere and starting to take off as a band."

"I found myself wanting a boyfriend. Both Jane and Charlotte had serious relationships with guys and I was kind of feeling left out, so I started paying attention to Alex. He was older, and not bad looking, and, well, *there*." She looked down and moved her hair out of her face. "I didn't know that I could be attractive to a man. I was used to being compared to Jane and ignored, and I didn't know that I could affect someone.

"So when I started flirting with Alex, I got really excited when he started flirting back. Looking at it now, I can see that most men would have trouble resisting a horny seventeen-year-old girl, but then I thought I was plain and unsexy." She looked at him unhappily and Darcy kissed her lightly, encouraging her to go on.

"I don't know what more there is to say. I started kissing him, and that felt good, so I started petting with him, and that felt good, and before I knew it, we were having sex."

"Do you feel bad about that?" Darcy asked gently.

"No, well, in a way." She shook her head. "I wished I had really been in love."

"Weren't you?"

"No. I thought I was, but I wasn't," she sighed. "September came and I started college, and between school, rehearsals, and work, something had to give, and that was Alex." She shrugged. "I realized in November that we hadn't had sex in over a month and that I didn't miss him. That was when I knew I didn't love him. I found out soon afterward that he had moved on. While that hurt, I couldn't blame him."

"That's not all," Darcy said, calmly knowing there was more.

"Nope. Fast forward to last summer. We were recording 'First Impressions' then and it was horrible." Elizabeth frowned at the memory. "It was beastly hot and we were in the studio every day for almost two months. And we couldn't even work at our day jobs because we were recording every day, so we were all getting really short on cash and stressed. I was going on almost no sleep because any time I was out of the studio, I was trying to keep my computer network business going. It was just the worst time in my life.

"Finally, I remember one night I was there alone, laying down guitar tracks, and finally the engineer looked up at me and said, 'Lizzy, you're done.'" She looked at Darcy and smiled. "I can't tell you the relief I felt at that moment. You know what it's like. Studio work is nothing like performing. It's so repetitive and long and boring and we had no idea what we were doing. And then that man said I was done, and I put my guitar down and walked out of the room to Alex and he gave me a huge hug. I wasn't even thinking, I just instinctively kissed him. And then he kissed me, and all of a sudden we were making out and rushing off to his apartment."

Her voice had grown very soft with embarrassment and Darcy could see this was hard for her. His hands gently offered his support to her. "Neither of us had been in a relationship for a long time, and I don't know, I think it was just dumb horniness at first. The first week, nobody knew about it, mostly 'cause we never got out of bed except to work. The second week, Jane and Char found out, but they kept quiet about it. It was the middle of the third week before we even had a conversation about what was going on."

"What did he say?" Darcy prompted her.

"He told me I was special and beautiful and he had always had strong feelings for me." Elizabeth bit her lip. "And I knew I was in trouble then, because I didn't feel that way. I was enjoying it, the sex, and I liked Alex, but I still didn't love him, and I knew I couldn't love him." She looked out the window and continued her story. "I knew it wouldn't last, and it didn't.

"We were used to having Alex tell us what to do. He had worked in the music business before, and we hadn't, so we trusted him. It became second nature to do what he told us." She sighed. "But he was starting to get very personal about what he was telling me to do. The next week of the affair, he started telling me how I should look when I sang, what expressions I should use, and how I should wear my hair—even how I should greet people when I met them."

Darcy massaged her back softly, letting her get it out. "It happened during the fifth week." Her voice was low and brittle. "We were in bed together and he was... touching me, and he said, 'Lizzy, you would be so sexy if you just lost weight.'" Her voice cracked and a single tear ran down her cheek.

Darcy held her, comforting her and murmuring soft words to her as she finally broke down and cried, releasing a hurt she had never shared before.

When her tears were done, Darcy pushed her back just enough so he could see her eyes and firmly said, "He's wrong. You are the most beautiful, most sexy woman I have *ever* seen, and he was wrong."

"You're biased," she said, looking away. "I admit my thighs and ass—"

"Stop!" he interrupted her. "I will not listen to this. Your ass is amazing. I've caught myself staring at it—hell! You've caught me staring at it more times than I can count." He tilted his head. "And don't tell me you haven't."

Elizabeth smiled. "I have, even back at my house."

Darcy nodded. "And I love your thighs." His hand touched them for emphasis. "They're strong, because you're strong. You're a swimmer, just like me, and I love the way your body is shaped. It's perfect, and I need you to know it."

She looked at him and nodded, and he pulled her close again. She spoke softly into the crook of his neck. "So, now you know all about Alex. I walked out on him when he said that right in the middle of having sex." She grinned ruefully. "But I guess that's why I'm a little oversensitive about people telling me what to do and why I thought you were negative when you were looking at my body."

Darcy slowly rolled her onto her back. "For the rest of my life, I'm going to make sure you know exactly how sexy and beautiful your body is, Elizabeth," he said with a low, determined voice that made her insides tighten.

He took off his shirt and pushed her dress up to her hips, revealing the red cotton panties she was wearing. Smiling with approval, he placed his lips over her mound and kissed her once, lightly. His hand slowly trailed up and down her outer thigh, over her rounded hip. Elizabeth's head tipped back as she relaxed in his touch, and Darcy felt again the trust she placed in him.

"Roll over, Elizabeth," he growled.

With a sexy smile she followed his direction, turning her ass to him. She moaned slightly as his hands caressed and squeezed her through the thin cotton.

Elizabeth felt herself growing hot under his ministrations. She let herself go and enjoyed the feelings he was giving her, forgetting to worry about how she might look.

Darcy enjoyed the sight of her unashamedly taking her pleasure and he stopped to remove his pants, all the while telling her how he had stared at her ass for so long, wanting to touch it.

"Can I see it now, Lizzy, please?" he asked as he crawled back on the bed. Elizabeth lifted her hips and let him draw down her panties, gasping slightly at what he saw. "You're so beautiful, Elizabeth. I need to taste you."

Slowly Darcy dragged his tongue over the twin curves he found there, stopping only to nibble lightly with his teeth. Elizabeth yelped and wiggled and he slipped his fingers between her legs to find her center wet and open. Carefully he inserted a finger with a second nip, startling her with the sensation. He continued to stimulate her, licking, nipping, and inserting a second finger, until she was crying out in earnest.

Then he stretched himself on top of her, resting on his elbows and cupping her breasts with his hands. "Did you want something more, my love?" he asked as he slid into her.

"Oooooohhhhhh," Elizabeth sighed as her eyes closed in pure bliss. "Yes, please."

Darcy found the depth he could achieve in this position was a pleasant surprise. Elizabeth was purring sensuously as he thrust himself in and out of her. "Do you feel this, love?" he asked as he forced himself completely inside of her. "That's what your sexy ass does to me. You never even touched me."

Elizabeth moaned, lost to the feeling of him. She had never been pleasured so deeply, and with the way he was kissing and sucking on her neck, she thought she would explode, but she couldn't move due to his weight pinning her down. She had to endure every touch, her tension and excitement building. Darcy let go of her breasts to place his hands on the bed and changed the angle of his attack. Elizabeth cried out as his thrusts were then deeper and harder against her.

"Oh God, Lizzy," his voice was shaking with effort as he neared his climax. Elizabeth lost herself in the sensations, crying out her release, and he came with her, her body grasping him tightly and forcing every drop from him.

They sank into the bed, glad no one else was at home to hear them. Then Elizabeth rolled into his arms and smiled brilliantly. Darcy smiled back and kissed her tenderly. "What are you thinking?" she asked, breaking the quiet of the room.

"I'm just amazed at how sure I feel about you. There is no doubt at all, even when I hear you talking about your old lovers, and you are leaving in two days with two men I would cheerfully strangle. There is no question, no uncertainty in my heart or my mind at all." He laced his fingers with hers, their palms pressed together. "I'm yours and you are mine. We are one."

Elizabeth nodded, smiling bemusedly at how accurately he had described her own feelings. "I know. I couldn't explain it to Alex or my dad, but it's absolutely true. It makes no sense at all, but I don't really care." She smiled brightly then. "What is this about happily strangling Alex?"

Darcy looked at her sadly. "He hurt you, Elizabeth. I don't know if I can ever forgive that."

Elizabeth drew his hand to her lips and kissed his knuckles. "Can you forgive me for hurting you?"

"I already have."

She leveled her large, expressive eyes at him. "Can you forgive yourself for hurting me?" She knew this was the crucial question.

"No," he whispered with a shake of his head.

Elizabeth had been afraid of that. She kissed his temple, holding her mouth against him. "You are going to have to forget it then, my love, because I have forgiven you."

He pulled her close. "I hate the part of me that hurt you."

"And I hate the part of me that hurt you, but it's going to happen. No matter how much we love each other, we are going to have misunderstandings and missteps. That's what happens when you let someone in that close." She turned his face to hers. "That's why we have to be able to forgive."

"I do forgive you, Lizzy," he said, an impertinent smile coming to his face.

Elizabeth sighed noisily. "That's it! I give up!" They laughed together, their closeness easing the tension in the room. "Hmm, you know what? I'm hungry."

Darcy rolled off the bed and offered her his hand. "Then let's get you some dinner." He quickly pulled on a pair of faded jeans, sitting low across his hips, and a clingy T-shirt, as Elizabeth fixed the dress she was still wearing. Together they went to the kitchen, Darcy giving her an informal tour along the way. Once there, Darcy pulled out two covered plates from the refrigerator, revealing cold dinners on each.

They sat at the table and Elizabeth asked where the meals had come from. "We have a housekeeper and cook, Mrs. Reynolds. This is her day off, but she always leaves meals for Georgie and me."

"I see," Elizabeth said, as she digested this information. "My father asked if we could go up to their house for Sunday dinner next week."

"That should be fine. I'd like to see your family again."

"It will just be Mom and Dad. Mary'll still be at Tanglewood and Kitty and Lydia are at the Gardiners'. Dad also asked for Jane and Charles to come."

Darcy put down his fork. "What?"

"Jane and Charles," Elizabeth repeated. Then her shoulders dropped. "Oh my God, you don't know?"

Darcy just looked at her questioningly.

"Oh, I should've told you. They've reconciled." She smiled. "They've been at his place in California for the last few days."

"Really?" Darcy smiled slowly. "That's good news. I'm happy for them."

Elizabeth reached across the table to take his hand. "Char told me that you and Charles weren't talking. I should have remembered. Sorry."

"How did Charlotte know?"

Elizabeth blushed at her forgetfulness. "Richard and Char have been talking. He's been calling her almost every night."

"Have they reconciled?"

"No. Char said they are just talking, but she sounded happy." She looked at Darcy, realizing for the first time how alone he had been. She walked around the table and took him into her arms. "I'm sorry," she breathed.

"I'm just happy they are able to get themselves back together," he said, his voice humble. "I'm sorry I ever interfered."

Elizabeth shrugged. "I don't see how you really interfered with Richard and Charlotte. They got themselves into their own trouble. And as for Charles, I know you were only trying to do the right thing, trying to protect your friend."

"Protecting Charles from what? Jane? I should have realized long ago that Charles doesn't need protecting," Darcy said in a frustrated voice. He looked up at Elizabeth. "I seem to owe a lot of people apologies."

"They're your friends, Will," she smiled. "They know how you are and they love you anyway. I know they'll forgive you."

Darcy pulled her into his lap and kissed her thoroughly. When he stopped, Elizabeth noticed a determined look in his eyes. "When did you say Charles and Jane are coming back?"

"They should be back now. Would you like me to call and see if they would be willing to come over to the loft tomorrow? Maybe you two could work things out?"

Darcy nodded. "Would you?"

Elizabeth got the phone from the other room and dialed the number Darcy gave her. She was glad when Jane picked up and she spent a few minutes telling her sister about herself and Darcy.

Jane was delighted with the news, and after a brief conference with Charles a date was set for tomorrow afternoon.

When she hung up, Darcy thanked her with a kiss. "You know, life is much better with you."

"You mean the frequent sex?"

"Well, that too, but I mean hearing your voice and seeing your smile. It just makes me feel happy all over."

Elizabeth smiled glowingly at him and kissed him deeply. "I know exactly what you mean."

They spent a few more minutes kissing until Darcy asked what she would like to do.

"Did you say something about a pool?"

"I did. Right this way," he led her toward the French doors.

"I don't have my suit."

"I never said anything about a suit."

He walked Elizabeth down a stone walkway to the back of the house. It was amazing. Twin waterfalls fell gracefully over piles of rocks into the large, rounded body of water. It looked completely natural, with flowers growing all around it. It was unlike anything Elizabeth had ever seen before.

As she stared, Darcy shucked off his clothes and then started undressing Elizabeth. Elizabeth finally came out of her pool-induced trance and smiled. "Water and Stone, right?"

Darcy nodded.

Moments later they were both naked and relaxing in the cool water. Despite the elevation of the house on a mountain, it was still well into the nineties. Elizabeth's only complaint with the pool was that she couldn't do laps, but sitting naked in Darcy's lap, she had to admit that swimming was really the last thing on her mind.

She leaned back in his arms, resting her head on his shoulder as he played with the buoyancy of her breasts. "This is so beautiful, Will."

"I'm glad you approve," he said warmly. "I mostly grew up in the loft, but this was where I always thought of when I said home when I was growing up. I guess that's because it was here when both my parents would relax and we could all be together." He kissed her neck. "I can't tell you what it means to share this with you."

Elizabeth arched herself against him, feeling his erection once again. She smiled, looking forward to more amazing sex, when a thought hit her with warp speed. "Will!"

"What?"

"I just realized something." She spun so she could see him. "Water and Stone! Slurry is a mixture of crushed stone in a solution. Water and stone! Will, it's you!"

Darcy beamed at her, confirming her guess. "Yes, Water and Stone make a Slurry when put together."

"Just like Fitzwilliam and Darcy." Elizabeth covered her mouth with excitement, her eyes huge. She felt like she had just solved a puzzle, which in fact she had.

"Do you know that *no one*, not Richard, not even Georgiana, has figured that out?" He looked at her almost shyly.

"That's because no one knows you like I do, Fitzwilliam," said Elizabeth, her eyes flashing.

They surged into each other's arms, their mouths eager to share each other. Elizabeth relished the slipperiness of his hard body touching hers. She sank down in the water, letting it surround and touch her everywhere as her lips remained locked with his.

His hands played lightly over her skin, teasing it to full sensitivity. He positioned them under one of the waterfalls, the falling water adding yet another sensation to their kissing.

When he felt she was ready, he gathered her in his arms and carried her to the edge of the pool. "Rest on me," he told her as he supported her weight in his arms. He eased her legs apart and turned her so she faced the wall. Squeezing her ass, he moved to just the right place, watching her face as she felt the jets of water touching her.

Her eyes flew open then closed with a blissful sigh, as her body adjusted to the rushing water that was passing over her most sensitive spot. Darcy watched her nipples harden as her hands tightened on his arms. He tried to follow her leanings, moving her ever so slightly to increase her pleasure. He loved watching her. Her face, expressive as always, told him all he wanted to know. When she finally tensed in his arms, then drew a shuddering breath, he knew he had pleased her by the look of pure contentment on her face. He shifted her in his arms, cradling her as she recovered.

It didn't take long. Soon the wanton grin he had come to anticipate as a forecast of intense pleasure flashed at him as she eased herself out of his arms. "What are you doing, Lizzy?"

Elizabeth only smiled sexily as her hands slid down the length of his body, under the water, to his erection. Her hands closed on his shaft, and she watched his eyes close as the pleasure came over him. Slowly she stroked him, lingering at times at his velvety tip or playing with the softness of his balls.

When Darcy thought he could take no more, he watched in wonder as Elizabeth took a deep breath and submerged. The feeling of her hot mouth on his length against the cool water of the pool was so intense he cried out. She sucked on him hard, her tongue wiggling on him like a tiny fish, then she released him and her face broke the surface. He watched the water stream down her face and hair as she drew another deep breath and sank down again.

Darcy knew that she could never hold her breath long enough for him to come, nor did he want to, so he relaxed and let the sweet tension of Elizabeth's talented mouth work on him. He wondered if she enjoyed the taste of him as much as he did her. He smiled again at the feeling of control he had over her when he had licked her the night before.

When she surfaced again, he decided he wanted something else and he pulled her up. The water was waist deep and after kissing her hard, he asked her to float on her back. She seemed pleased with the suggestion and slowly raised her arms into the air as she lay back on the water.

Darcy enjoyed the view that he knew was only for him. His hands slid down her body to her hips and he pulled them close to himself. Elizabeth understood exactly where this was going and opened her legs to him, allowing him to enter her and wrapping her legs around him.

Elizabeth held his eyes with her own as he thrust into her. She encouraged him to watch her body, her hands trailing to her nipples, which she teased to hard points. Darcy luxuriated in the vision before him even as he enjoyed the sensation of thrusting out of the cool pool water and into Lizzy's hot depths and back out again.

He could feel his own release building but saw she wasn't there yet. He slid his hands up to her sides and walked her into the deeper water, so that it came up to his shoulders. Elizabeth sat up with the water, and he supported her ass in his hands.

"Is that better?" he asked, panting.

"Oh God, yes!" Elizabeth moaned and they were at it again, Elizabeth clutching his shoulders with her hands as Darcy moved her up and down on top of him. "Oh Gooooood!" she wailed as she tightened in his arms, coming against him. Darcy pushed her up against the pool wall and rode her for all he was worth, his body struggling until it reached its climax and found its release. Elizabeth's eyes flared as she felt his hot come pour into her.

Panting, they sprawled on the broad steps of the pool, their hands tightly linked. "Thank you," Darcy huffed. "I can't tell you" (breath) "how long" (breath) "I've wanted to do that."

Elizabeth looked at him and laughed breathlessly. "Me too!" Smiling, they snuggled close, holding each other and talking softly as the summer sun set and the light faded.

❧

Elizabeth woke up to the sound of music. She rolled over to a sight that would stay with her for the rest of her life: Darcy, sitting naked in a chair, his guitar in his lap as he softly played. She watched the concentration on his face and knew he didn't see her. A few more moments of observation told her why; he was composing. She could tell from the tune that he was playing. It was clearly lacking a melody line. Once she even caught him humming, but his voice was too soft for her to make it out clearly.

He stopped to write something on the table next to him and that's when he saw her. She smiled warmly at him.

"You're not supposed to be hearing this."

"Why not?"

"Because," he said as he rose to his feet, "it's not finished yet." He walked to the bed and sat beside her, his hand gently tracing the curve of her cheek and down to her throat, and between her breasts, which were shamelessly uncovered.

"Will I get to hear it when it's done?" she asked, her large eyes caressing him.

"Oh yes," he assured her, as he leaned down and kissed her.

Elizabeth wrapped her arms around his neck in a slow and lazy fashion; being near Darcy made her feel sexy and seductive. "I think I deserve something for waking up alone, don't you?" she asked teasingly.

Darcy smiled and lifted an eyebrow. "If you wish." He settled himself on the bed and raised the neck of the guitar. Elizabeth watched, fascinated, as he played for her. His fingers coaxed a high vibrato out of the guitar while he plucked a simple melody out of the lower register.

She lay back on the pillows, watching all of him: the profile of his face, his hands, his arms and shoulders, his legs. She was struck again by his beauty and by the intimacy of the moment. There was no one else. This was only for her.

The message of the music was different this time as well. In the past, he had played to win her, to prove himself. This time it was more about sharing, an expression of how he was feeling: the contentment, the joy, the awe. Elizabeth shared every one of those emotions.

When he finished, she reached for him and expressed with her body all that she felt for him.

❧

The drive back to the Village felt like a triumph for them. They had both traveled to Massachusetts in a state of depression, and there, to their utter surprise, they found bliss. They spent the drive talking easily about the tiny details of their past, sharing the events of their lives, and coming to know each other better.

Elizabeth was astonished, when they reached the building on Broome Street, to learn the first floor was actually a garage. Darcy unlocked the large door with a key and brought them in, parking his car in one of the two spaces labeled "seven."

"That space is for you," he said, indicating the empty space beside it.

Elizabeth nodded and took inventory of the other cars there. A healthy mixture of Mercedes, BMWs, and Saabs greeted her, along with Darcy's limo resting along one wall. She tried to picture her beat-up truck here and frowned. The warm feeling of easy comfort that had filled her in the car ebbed away, and instead she felt intimidated and out of place.

"What?" he asked, looking at her with concern.

Elizabeth laughed in embarrassment. "I'm not sure my truck is ready for this kind of company."

Darcy stopped and looked at her. Her troubles had become his, as he saw at once the enormous change he was asking her to make. He took her hand and asked, "Would it help if I bought you a new truck?"

Elizabeth laughed with genuine affection and she stepped into his arms. "No, I can buy my own truck now. This success takes a little while to get used to."

"Take your time," Darcy told her. "There is no rush. I'll give you whatever you need."

Elizabeth knew he was speaking of support and patience, not material goods, and she kissed him slowly, her lips lingering on his. "Thank you."

Together they passed through the door and into the lobby. The doorman greeted them, recognizing Elizabeth, and commented that she had found Mr. Darcy.

Elizabeth acknowledged that she had, and with a happy smile they entered the elevator, Darcy holding Elizabeth's bags while Elizabeth carried her guitars.

Entering the loft again, Elizabeth expected to feel pain or regret over the way she had left or a fluttering of her pulse, remembering their first time together, but strangely, she felt peaceful and at ease.

Darcy led her into the bedroom and placed her bags by the closet. Neither one of them was ready to discuss her moving in. It was a certainty, but at the same time, it was too soon. They had each privately made the decision not to deal with it until after the tour.

Elizabeth stood as if uncertain with her guitars in the middle of the room. Darcy looked at her and with a quiet "oh," he took her to the library at the far end of the large living room, where his own instruments were stored.

Once her babies were safe and away, Elizabeth eased herself into Darcy's arms. She rubbed his back with her hand, trying to reassure herself with his body, his scent. She felt Darcy doing the same, and that knowledge, that she was not alone in her uneasiness, helped her tension to fall away. Darcy drew his hands up and cupped her face, kissing her lovingly.

She saw in his eyes the quiet power that was inside of him, telling her with complete certainty that it would be all right, and she put her trust in him.

❧

The sound of the elevator roused them from their silent repose on the couch. Elizabeth stood with Darcy, seeing the increased tension on his features. She moved forward, determined to try to ease his way.

She met Jane in the gallery and hugged her tightly. It was difficult to believe it had only been a week since she had seen her last. Jane looked tan, her hair even whiter, but more than that, she looked happy. Elizabeth hoped her own happiness was as evident.

As if by plan, Elizabeth moved to hug Charles, and Jane embraced Darcy. The women both remarked how good it was to see them and how much they had missed them. Then they moved aside, allowing Darcy and Charles to meet.

The two men acknowledged each other warily. "Would you like to sit?" Darcy asked, opening up the conversation.

"Yeah," Charles nodded.

The party moved down the long hall to the dining area, the sisters having a hushed conversation about the loft while the men kept silent. Darcy served his guests drinks and once everyone was seated, he began his apology.

"Charles, I'm very sorry for what happened. I should have never interfered with your relationship with Jane, and I can't tell you how much I regret that stunt we played at the VMAs. I have no excuse, and I hope you can forgive me."

Charles looked at Jane for a moment before turning a regretful face to Darcy. "Will, it's okay. I was screwing up with Jane at the VMAs and

I knew it, and I just took my anger out on you instead of placing it on myself where it belonged. I'm sorry for that."

Darcy's expression lifted. "I'm really happy that you have worked things out. Lizzy told me you went home?"

Charles and Jane flashed matching grins and joined hands. "Yeah, I introduced her to Dad."

"Lizzy, you should see the house; it's so beautiful, right on the ocean," Jane added.

Elizabeth smiled brightly.

"It's clear that you two have come to an understanding as well," Charles observed. "Jane said you met up at Tanglewood?"

Darcy found himself holding Elizabeth's hand as he nodded. "We were lucky," he said, looking at Elizabeth.

"But I think we would have gotten together even if we had to wait another week," Elizabeth added, her eyes on her lover.

The two couples spent the rest of the day talking and relaxing in the comfortable loft. Despite the easy atmosphere of the setting, it was clear that all of them had tomorrow's separation on their minds, as the lovers never moved more than a few yards from each other.

They were just discussing getting dinner when the phone rang, breaking the cozy mood. Darcy answered it, his expression hardening as he listened to the voice on the other end of the line.

"Yes, she's here. Hold on." He handed the phone to Elizabeth, who took it with a questioning look.

"Hello."

"Lizzy, it's me. I couldn't reach you on your cell."

"Oh, hi, Alex." Elizabeth was relieved that it was someone familiar, but she hadn't fully forgiven him for the incident yesterday. "What's up?"

"I've been trying to reach you all over. George Wickham wants you to call about tomorrow."

Elizabeth felt her stomach drop. "Can't it wait till we get there?" she asked unhappily.

"No, he wants to talk to you today, so he can get things set up for tomorrow. Just call him, Lizzy."

"All right," she answered softly. Elizabeth dutifully took down the number and read it back to him. Promising to see him tomorrow, Elizabeth hung up.

She looked up at Darcy, not needing to say anything. Darcy appeared to be made of stone, his face expressionless. Finally Elizabeth said, "I have to call."

Darcy nodded tightly. "I'll be back." He kissed her hair and walked to the elevator, a puzzled-looking Charles running after him to catch up.

When the elevator door shut, Elizabeth found herself alone with her sister. Her finger trembling, she called George Wickham. She tried to keep her voice as calm and as normal as possible as she talked with him, discussing the plans for the video shoot and details that involved her, such as costume. When George was through discussing the shoot, his voice changed and he asked her if she missed him. Elizabeth rushed to get off the phone, claiming that her mother was calling her for dinner.

When she hung up, Jane was looking at her expectantly. Elizabeth sighed tiredly and dropped down onto the couch and let her sister put her arms around her. When Elizabeth had sufficiently regained control of herself, she started talking and told Jane everything. She worried about betraying Darcy's confidence, but she trusted Jane like no one else, and Elizabeth had to tell someone or she would burst.

Jane watched her sister, listening with growing horror as Elizabeth told the story. "Oh my God," she said finally. "Lizzy, I had no idea!"

Elizabeth shook her head. "No one had any idea. He's a con man, and he's very good at it."

"You must have been so upset."

Elizabeth nodded, her eyes closed against that memory. "Oh, yeah," she sighed. "That was not one of my best moments."

"And Will?"

Elizabeth found herself tearing up. "Will understood. He understood everything and he forgave me. Hell, he even blamed himself." She looked at her sister as she tried to hold back her feelings. "Jane, he's so good. I was so wrong about him. And I love him so much."

Jane smiled and hugged her tight. "Does he know you love him?"

"Yes."

"Then I think everything will be okay, Lizzy. I'm pleased for you. I never could have been completely happy with Charles if you weren't okay with Will."

Elizabeth smiled. "You look very happy."

Jane nodded. "I am."

The sisters smiled as they heard the elevator arriving. But instead of their lovers, Richard Fitzwilliam walked out.

Elizabeth smiled in welcome. "Hi, Richard."

"Hey," Richard looked puzzled as he surveyed the Bennets in the otherwise empty loft.

"Charles and Will ran out. They'll be back soon."

"Oh, good," he nodded. "How are you both doing?"

Elizabeth grinned at his obvious confusion. "We're doing great, Richard. How are you?"

"I'm good. Um, Charlotte wouldn't happen to be down with you, would she?"

Jane refrained from laughing. "No, she's still up in Meryton. She'll come down tomorrow, and we're meeting her at the airport."

Richard's expression darkened. "Right, the video shoot. I hope you are both very careful down there."

Elizabeth shared a look with Jane. "Richard, we know about what happened with George. Don't worry, we just want to get this over and be done with him."

Richard set his jaw. "That's probably for the best. But be careful anyway."

The elevator hummed into life again, and Charles and Darcy returned to the loft. Darcy took a long look at his cousin, remembering the last time the three of them were in the building together. He walked over to Elizabeth and kissed her passionately.

When he released the slightly breathless woman, Darcy looked at Richard dead on with an arched eyebrow.

"I get it," Richard said, holding up his hands. He grinned good-naturedly. "Enjoy the irony, Will."

"Oh, I do," he said smugly and leaned down to kiss a laughing Elizabeth again.

CHAPTER 18

ELIZABETH DIDN'T NOTICE HIM when she came out of the shower, as she dried herself off and studied her reflection in the mirror, the high-powered ventilation system keeping the mirror from being fogged. Darcy watched mesmerized as she studied her reflection: her face, her breasts, both head-on and in profile, then her waist, and with a dreamy smile, she even twisted to look at her rear in the mirror.

"Very nice."

She started and smiled at him, even as she blushed. "You aren't supposed to be up yet. Did I wake you?"

He shook his head, all traces of sleep gone. "I heard the shower." He walked up behind her, his eyes meeting hers in the mirror. "Besides," he told her, planting soft kisses on her bare neck, "I'm not going to let you go without a proper good-bye."

Elizabeth purred low in her throat as his hands brushed her sides. Encouraged by her response, he moved his hands upward, cupping her breasts and massaging the softness he found there.

Elizabeth instinctively rubbed her ass against his erection and found him delightfully hard. She didn't know if he always slept naked, but he had every time they had been together and she found it particularly pleasing. His hands were making her crazy, stimulating a response that surprised her with its strength. She was shocked at the low moans that were coming out of her mouth, yet she couldn't seem to hold them back. He felt so good.

"Turn around," he told her in that low voice that made her burn.

She complied, kissing him hungrily as his hands traveled down to her hips. He lifted her up so she sat on the edge of the vanity, where Elizabeth spread her legs eagerly.

He seemed to share her eagerness, as he entered her immediately, sliding into her hot depths as he lifted her legs so that her feet rested on either side of him on the counter. Grasping her knees, he began thrusting into her as she leaned back, her arms propping her up, to enjoy the sensation and the amazing sight before her.

He watched as her excitement built, the tension in her body matching his own. Her nipples grew hard and pointed and he felt his excitement soar. He needed her urgently to be closer to him.

With a growl he snatched her body up in his arms, pulling her chest against his. Elizabeth's arms slid under his, her hands on his back, pulling him even closer.

She cried out as his hips worked like a piston, pushing harder and faster into her with every second. The violence of their joining became frantic as they lost themselves to the sensations that were flooding them. Darcy heard her howl even as her fingernails dug into his skin. The tightening of her body in its orgasm was the push he needed, and he felt the pressure in him shoot into her with his ejaculation.

He held her close, kissing her damp hair lightly as they recovered their breath. When she finally looked at him, her face red and sweaty, her smile blissfully happy, her eyes glowing with satisfaction, it was an image that imprinted upon his heart, filling him with an intensity of love he never knew was possible. He hugged her tight, kissing her, before releasing her and helping her off the counter.

Elizabeth giggled, feeling light-headed from her orgasm. She held on to Darcy's hand, as she took stock of her situation. Then she heard a light knock on the bedroom door.

"Darcy, Lizzy, we're here," Rebecca's voice called to them.

Elizabeth looked at him in shock, instantly clearheaded. "Shit!" She looked at the clock and swore again. "Damn! I don't have time to shower again. I'm going to smell like sex all day." She hurried to her clothes but not without seeing the guilty expression on her lover's face. She was half-way dressed before the meaning of the expression dawned on her. "Did you do that on purpose?" she asked, turning toward him.

Darcy had been pulling on a T-shirt and shorts as Elizabeth rushed. "No." A look from Elizabeth forced him to continue. "I didn't plan it, but I will admit that a part of me is glad it happened."

Elizabeth stopped what she was doing and went into his arms, squeezing him tight. "You know I love you, don't you?"

He hugged her back, rubbing his forehead against hers. "I know. And

I do trust you. It's just a part of me is pleased he's going to know you came from my bed." He looked at her, expecting a backlash.

Elizabeth closed her eyes and kissed him thoroughly. "I'm coming from your bed and tomorrow I will be returning to your bed," she smiled painfully. "I don't like leaving like this either. But trust me, nothing Wickham can say will change my feelings about you."

Darcy smiled and looked away. "I actually meant Alex," he admitted with embarrassed humor.

Elizabeth laughed. "Well, that's just being petty." She stopped to kiss him, softening her words. "We are going to have to do something about this possessive streak of yours."

He looked at her with dry amusement. "I have a few ideas about that."
"Oh?"

He kissed her slowly. "I'll tell you when you come back."

"Bastard," she swore, before kissing him again and releasing him to finish dressing. She was going to the bedroom when she heard the elevator stop and Jane's voice reached her. "Fuck!" she muttered as she rushed into the bathroom.

Darcy smiled as the blow-dryer started and he left his room to greet his guests. "Good morning. Lizzy is running a little late. She'll be ready in a moment."

"Umm hmm," Rebecca said knowingly. "Tommy has the limo ready out front."

Darcy suspected that it was only her respect for him as her employer that kept Rebecca from telling Jane and Charles why Elizabeth was running late. He walked to the kitchen and started making coffee and tea.

A moment later Charles joined him. Darcy could see the concern on his face. "Will," he paused, uncertain how to continue.

"Did Jane tell you?" Darcy asked flatly, solving his friend's dilemma.

Charles nodded. "She didn't want to, but she was so upset, I made her." He looked uncomfortable.

"I'm glad she did." Darcy's eyes left his friends, and he focused instead on the cups before him. "I'm sorry I never told you, Charles. It was just too hard to talk about."

Darcy stopped when he felt a hand on his shoulder. He looked up to see Charles's face looking at him with understanding and support.

"Thanks," he said sincerely. "I'd hug you but, you know, rock gods don't hug."

Charles laughed softly, understanding his friend's need to release the tension between them. "So, now that I know, I'm worried about sending Jane and Lizzy to him."

Darcy sighed. "If you are asking me if we can trust Wickham, the answer is no, not at all. But I do trust Lizzy, and I know you trust Jane," he shrugged. "That's going to have to do."

Darcy finished with the drinks and checked Lizzy's cell phone, which had been charging on the countertop. He dialed a number on it, and the landline to the loft rang, then he used the landline to call the cell. "I offered to buy Lizzy out of this, but she feels she needs to do it, and I respect that."

"I offered to do the same for Jane," Charles admitted. "I just hate this. They're our lovers, and we are sending them to this—"

"Don't go there," Darcy interrupted. "Thinking like that will only make you insane." He frowned, trying to cope with his own worries. "Besides, what's the worst he could do? Wickham is not aggressive. He's lazy. He's an opportunist. He's not going to attack or rape them; it would put him at too much risk. The worst he can do is try to seduce them, which won't work, or fuck up their video, which will ruin his reputation."

Charles exhaled sharply. "Damn straight it would."

"And I don't think he'd bother Jane anyway," Darcy continued. "It's me he wants to hurt, and hopefully he doesn't know about Lizzy and me."

Charles studied the bitter expression on Darcy's face. "You hate this, don't you?"

Darcy's eyes flashed. "'Course I do," he said darkly.

"Well, like you said, it'll be fine. They are going to fly down this morning and be back tomorrow night." Charles smiled reassuringly. "What's the worst that could happen?"

Darcy rolled his eyes, hearing his own words used on himself and realizing how weak they sounded. "You want to hang out here today?" he asked his friend.

"Yeah. Maybe we could do some work in the studio."

Jane and Elizabeth emerging from the master bedroom ended their conversation. Darcy brought Elizabeth her coffee and the cell phone, which she tucked into her bag.

"Is that all you are bringing?"

Elizabeth shrugged. "It's just an overnight. I'd rather leave my guitars here where I know they'll be safe." She shared a look with Darcy that spoke of her trust in him.

"They will be," he said, kissing her deeply. He looked up to see Jane and Charles embracing and returned to Elizabeth's lips, knowing he still had time. He kissed her, gathering the sweet taste of her to him and touching every part of her mouth that he could. He wanted to feel her, to lock this moment in his memory. She seemed to share his intent, holding him closely as her mouth made love to his.

All too soon, Rebecca cleared her throat and announced, "We really have to leave if we are going to catch that plane."

With final words and kisses, the women stepped into the elevator, leaving the two men unhappily behind. Rebecca escorted them out through the lobby and to the limo waiting in the street below.

Elizabeth sighed as she settled into the car beside her sister. She hated doing this, but there was really no choice. She sipped the coffee he had made for her as she thought. Sighing, she told herself that she was just going to do this quickly and professionally and hope that Wickham didn't know about her relationship with Darcy.

◦◦◦

They met up as scheduled with Alex and Charlotte by the security gate. Charlotte rushed forward to embrace them, all the time teasing them about how good the sisters looked.

"It's vitamin P," Lizzy explained with a wink.

Charlotte grinned. "Are you finally getting your recommended daily allowance?"

"Oh yeah," Elizabeth laughed.

"She was deprived of it for so long, Will is making sure she gets extra doses," Jane piped in, with a wicked grin.

"You're not looking so deprived yourself, Jane," Charlotte observed.

Jane blushed a fiery red, causing the other two to erupt with laughter.

They said good-bye to Rebecca and moved through security. Finding their gate, they settled in to wait for their plane. Elizabeth could tell Alex wanted to talk to her. He was sitting on her right side and seemed to be waiting to say something.

"So, where exactly are we going, Alex?" Elizabeth had to admit that since learning the truth about Wickham, she had lost all enthusiasm for this project.

"We're flying to Tampa. The shoot is taking place on a small island nearby."

Elizabeth nodded as she absently flipped through a magazine. She could feel his eyes on her. "What?"

"Nothing." But before Elizabeth could protest, he quickly asked, "Do you love him?"

"Didn't we already have this conversation? I told you what I felt over the phone." Her voice was unusually cool.

"He just doesn't seem to be your type," Alex replied sullenly. "I would hate to have you selling out because of the money or something."

"Alex, do I need to find another manager? Is this too much?" Elizabeth asked, her voice flat, her eyes narrowed. "It was never a question of choosing him over you. We were never going to work. You knew that, didn't you?"

Alex swallowed and nodded. "I know, Lizzy, and you don't have to get a new manager. I'm okay with it."

Elizabeth nodded, not completely convinced but willing to let it go. It was only then that she realized that she had chosen her relationship with Darcy over her professional relationship with Alex. As they waited, she studied him, weighing the emotional distance between them. It had been a long time since she had felt affection for him, but now she realized how little she had shared with Alex and how much she could have with Darcy. She was a little sad to acknowledge it, but she also knew she was much better off.

❧

A ferry took them to an island a couple of miles offshore. It was owned by a luxury resort, which is where they would be staying overnight. The resort complex used up only about a quarter of the land, with a small airstrip the only other structure. The remainder of the land was left open and undeveloped. Elizabeth had to admit it was beautiful, and a part of her wished that Darcy had come down.

The warm smile on her face was wiped away as they drove to the set and Wickham met their cars. George was looking good. His hair had been further lightened and his skin was deeply tanned. He was wearing a beige shirt and crisp white linen shorts. He greeted the women warmly, giving Elizabeth the same extra attention he had the last time.

He explained that today they would be doing action shots in the water, and then they would have a night shot on the beach, and tomorrow they would finish up with the concert shots.

As Jane and Charlotte were led away to wardrobe, George stopped Elizabeth. She forced herself to smile at George. "What's up?"

"I wanted to know how you are doing. It's been awhile."

"Not that long," she teased. "I've been good."

"Yeah, you look great."

"Thanks."

"So, have you been busy?" he asked hopefully.

"Actually, I have. I'm in a new relationship now."

"Oh?" his eyebrows peeked out over his sunglasses. "Lucky guy. Anyone I know?"

Elizabeth shook her head. "I don't think so. He's a classical musician."

His expression was hidden behind his sunglasses. "That's great, Lizzy. I'm happy for you."

Elizabeth smiled and left for wardrobe, pleased that the initial confrontation was over.

❧

Darcy looked down at his guitar, carefully strumming the new melody. A few bars later he heard Richard's voice singing. It was different; Richard's voice was gravelly compared to Charles, but it was his song. As soon as they read the words, they understood that Richard had to sing it.

They stood in their studio, playing together, the way they had for years. The differences, Richard singing and a studio musician, Mike Hurst, on drums, were of no consequence as the men lost themselves in the creative process.

"You know, we could thicken this up with some keyboards," Charles observed when they finished.

Darcy and Richard shared a grin, knowing full well the pretty keyboard player on Charles's mind. It was a gentle grin. Each one of them was in the same place, thinking about a lady far away.

"I've got something else I'd like to work on," Darcy told them, pulling out sheets of music.

And so the day passed into evening. The three members of Slurry found themselves easy in each other's company, quitting the studio and returning to the loft, eating pizza and watching movies. Around eleven they began to grow quiet, then fidgety. Charles extracted his cell phone and checked that it was on and charged, resting it on the couch beside him. Darcy got his cordless and placed it on the floor next to him.

Richard frowned. "Did you give Lizzy your cell number or the loft's?"

"The loft's," Darcy said darkly.

"Why didn't you give her your cell? Charlotte is calling the loft."

"Because it's my house!" Darcy replied. "Why didn't you tell Charlotte to call your cell?"

The ringing of Charles's phone interrupted the fight; Darcy and Richard watched, eyes wide, until Charles said, "Hi, Jane," loudly, for their benefit. Charles got up and moved into the library as the landline rang.

"Lizzy?" Darcy answered.

"No," a laughing voice answered, "it's Charlotte."

"Hi, Charlotte, hang on." Darcy said sullenly, passing the phone to Richard.

Richard took the phone and, covering the mouthpiece with his hand, told Darcy, "Call Liz on your cell," before speaking into the phone.

Darcy was up in a heartbeat, grabbing his cell and dialing Elizabeth's number as he went into his bedroom and closed the door.

"Hello?" a very confused-sounding Elizabeth answered.

"It's me. Charlotte and Richard are on the landline."

"Oh good. I tried calling and couldn't get through." He could hear the relief in her voice. "How are you doing?"

❧

"Terrible," Jane moaned. "I'm bruised all over."

"Baby, what happened?" Charles asked imploringly.

"Promise you won't hate me?"

❧

"She can't surf!" Charlotte replied. "Oh my God, I lost count how many times she fell off the dumb surfboard just paddling out."

Richard laughed. "And how did you do?"

"I'm a surfing natural," she grinned.

"That's my girl."

❧

"So then what happened?" Charles asked.

"Oh, George finally gave up on the surfing thing and had us cliff diving instead," Jane said wearily.

"How did that go?" Charles sounded dubious.

❧

"Well, it was more jumping off rocks than actually diving. I tried to do a
real dive, but then George said they couldn't see my face."

Darcy smiled, warmed by her voice. "I hate to admit it, but he's right
about that. How has he been treating you?"

"Fine," Elizabeth shrugged. "I told him I was in a new relationship
and he's totally left me alone."

❧

"Good, I'm glad that's all over. So how was the night shoot?"

"Boring," Jane said tiredly. "They got a bunch of guests from the
resort to be extras and had us playing around a bonfire on the beach."

❧

"Oh, that sounds lame," Richard scoffed.

"Tell me about it," Charlotte agreed. "George has changed. You can tell."

"How?" he demanded.

"It's like he doesn't care. He wasn't paying much attention to the
shooting, and the crew clearly had no respect for him."

❧

"It's like everyone is just going through the motions here. I don't think
the video will be very good."

Darcy sighed. "Just get it done and come home, Lizzy."

Elizabeth smiled. "That's what I'm doing, my love. What did you
do today?"

❧

"We worked on some new songs today."

Jane sounded pleased. "Will we get to hear them when we get back?"

Charles smiled, recalling the content of the two love songs. "I guarantee it."

"When?"

⁂

"So, um, tomorrow night."

Charlotte was puzzled by Richard's tone. If she didn't know better, she would swear he was almost shy. But that was ridiculous, she told herself. Richard Fitzwilliam had never had a shy day in his life.

"Yes?" she said encouragingly.

"Do you think we could get together and, um, talk?"

Charlotte stopped breathing. Struggling, she laughed weakly. "Richard, we've been talking every night."

"I meant face-to-face. I want to see you, Char."

⁂

"I'm never going to sleep tonight," Darcy complained.

"I know. Why do they make these beds so huge?"

"Do you forgive me for this morning?"

Elizabeth had to think a moment to remember what he was referring to, and then she smiled brightly. "Of course I do." She laughed. "Can I tell you something?"

Darcy's voice warmed. "Anything."

"Well, this is a little gross, but I um, I kind of liked it. All morning long I would catch little whiffs of you in my hair. It was nice," she said in a very small voice.

Darcy grinned. "I found one of your long Lizzy hairs on my guitar today."

Elizabeth laughed. "How did it get there?"

"I don't know, but I liked it. It's like having a 'Property of Elizabeth' sign on me."

⁂

"I love you," Jane cooed.

"I love you too, angel." Charles sounded lonely. "I wish you were here. Let's not ever do anything stupid, like go on separate tours, all right?"

"Charles, I could never do that," Jane answered without thinking. She paused, realizing what she said and was stunned by the implications. "Oh!"

"Jane?" He was concerned by the emotion in her voice. He wished he were there with her. "Jane, it's okay. We'll talk about it when you get back, but it's okay."

"Are you sure?" Her voice was a weak whisper.

"Darling, I'm certain. I lost you once and I am not going to do that again. We'll work it out. We always do."

Jane closed her eyes to the sound of his voice and let it soothe her.

≈

"I'll meet you at the airport?"

Charlotte looked down to see her fingers trembling. She clenched her fist to stop them. "Yes," she answered, wishing her voice was stronger.

"Great." He sounded relieved.

"Richard?" she called out plaintively.

"Yes?" His answer was quick and ready.

"I… I miss you."

He closed his eyes against the desperation in her voice. "I miss you too, Char. I've missed you so much. There are so many things I want to tell you." He made a conscious decision to stop talking. He longed to say those three little words to her, but he wanted to see her face, to hold her when he said it. Instead he told her, "I'll see you tomorrow, Char."

≈

"I can't wait."

"I never knew one night could be so long, Elizabeth."

"Me neither. I love you."

"I love you, too."

"Sleep well, angel."

"You too, love."

"Bye."

"Bye."

≈

Elizabeth found herself in the strange position of growing tired of her own song as she heard the playback once again.

While the previous video was filmed with a sense of order and precision, this one seemed to be thrown together in a haphazard fashion. The day had started out well enough, with filming Elizabeth in an RV. But it had since gone downhill. After a half-dozen takes of the band playing together while sitting on the sand, Elizabeth was now being asked to writhe about on the beach while a camera filmed her from overhead. She was quickly losing patience with it all.

She found her attention drifting back to Darcy and all the things she wanted to do with him back in New York. This would be the last night of the break. Tomorrow they were scheduled for the first of three nights at Madison Square Garden, then a day off, and then they were back on the road.

Elizabeth's eyes drifted over to Charlotte, who was smoking again. Elizabeth realized that she had been smoking every time Elizabeth had seen her today, except when they were filming, and wondered what was wrong. Charlotte was being uncharacteristically quiet and withdrawn, and Elizabeth strongly suspected that returning to the tour was weighing heavily on her mind as well.

Elizabeth sighed. No matter what happened, Elizabeth couldn't see a happy course for her. With a flash, she realized that Charlotte was now in the same boat she had been in for most of the tour—the only one not in a relationship—and Elizabeth's heart filled with empathy for her friend.

◈

The pleasant creativity that had prevailed the day before for Slurry was long gone by the next morning. In a strange twist of behavior, Richard was the first one up. Darcy woke to the smell of coffee and was surprised to find his cousin up and dressed.

With a puzzled look, Darcy sat on the bar stool beside his cousin and poured the tea that Richard had thoughtfully made.

"Okay, spill," Darcy said shortly.

"What? It's after ten already. What's the problem with a man not wanting to sleep the day away?"

Darcy studied him impassively, took a sip of his tea, and said, "So, it's Charlotte then?"

"Jesus *Christ*!" he swore sharply, putting his elbow on the counter and resting his forehead in his hand. "Fuck," he muttered under his breath.

"What did she say last night?" Darcy asked calmly.

"She said she missed me," Richard answered automatically. "And I almost blew it." He closed his eyes and slammed his fist on the counter. "What if I screw up?" he demanded, his voice bordering on desperate.

Darcy lifted an eyebrow. "Richard, you already screwed up. What you really mean is 'What if Charlotte doesn't want to love an alcoholic and sex addict,' right?"

Richard gave him a black look. "I hate it when you're like this."

Darcy nodded once. "I know." He took another sip and continued impassively. "What are you going to do?"

"I'm meeting her at the airport, and I'm going to take her to my place."

"Does she know this?"

"Yes, I asked her last night if we could have a date tonight to talk." He slammed his fist down again, rattling the cups. "I can't believe I asked her for a fucking date! I'm acting like a high school kid!"

"No, you are just nervous because you are planning on admitting some important stuff to someone who could really hurt you deeply."

Richard glared at his cousin. "I fucking hate you."

One corner of Darcy's mouth turned up. "If it's any comfort, I can tell you I've been there, and I think you're doing the right thing."

Richard took a long sip of his coffee and grumbled before saying, "How did you tell Elizabeth that you loved her?" His eyes, when he looked at Darcy, held his vulnerability, despite his light tone of voice.

"Well, you heard the first time I told her and witnessed how successful that was. When we met again at Tanglewood, we couldn't really be alone all day, and while that was making me crazy at the time, it was actually kind of a good thing because we didn't have a chance to let words trip us up." Darcy frowned thoughtfully. "Words have always been hard for Lizzy and me."

"You seemed to have worked that out," Richard observed.

"Yeah," Darcy grinned, "but we still do better communicating with our music or nonverbally." He looked over at his cousin. "You and Charlotte are different, though. You two have never had a problem with words."

Richard smiled for the first time that morning, as he thought about all of their interactions. "That's true. We're really good at talking to each other. I'm just not sure how good we are at loving each other."

"From the point of view of a neutral third party, I'd say you are both better at that than you give yourself credit for."

Richard stared at the man who knew him better than any other. "You think?"

Darcy nodded with calm certainty. "Tell her, Richard; you owe her at least that."

"I'm going to."

"Good," Darcy said as he put down his cup and headed back to his bedroom to shower and dress, leaving a thoughtful Richard sitting at the bar.

❧

It was almost four when George announced that filming was over. Elizabeth shared a look of relief with Jane and then noticed Charlotte biting her nails. The girls had packed their bags that morning, so they were ready to leave right away for the airport.

As they were getting into the limos, George walked up to them with a bag over his shoulder. "Can I hitch a ride to the airport?"

Elizabeth was surprised. "Don't you have to stay here and clean up?"

George shook his head. "No, the producer takes care of all that. I have to go back to New York to oversee the editing."

"Oh."

"Sure, George, we've got room," Winnie volunteered. Jane, Charlotte, and Alex rode in one limo, while Winnie and Elizabeth rode with George.

"How's Darcy doing?" George asked conversationally.

"He's good," Elizabeth answered with forced indifference. "I haven't really seen him, but I've heard he's good."

"I'm glad to hear that," George said smoothly and changed topics to talk about the videos he had recently made.

When they reached the airport, George casually reminded Elizabeth to have her ID ready, which prompted a pause as all three members of LBS had to search through their bags to find their driver's licenses. A full two minutes later, they were ready and moved on to their gate.

❧

Darcy followed Rebecca through the crowded airport. He was glad she was there, because it meant he couldn't rush the way he wanted to, and it guaranteed that he would find the right terminal. In his current frame of mind, he suspected he would have trouble finding his own house. He was in a state of happy anticipation like he hadn't felt since he was a child.

They reached the security checkpoint and had to stop. The security regulations prevented them from going to the actual gate. Darcy wasn't surprised to find the other members of Slurry waiting there as well.

Charles looked at him and laughed. "I've got tulips," he said, holding up the bouquet in his hand. "What have you got?"

Darcy smiled smugly. "Red roses."

"I've got you both beat," Richard boasted, holding out a white box with a cellophane window. Inside was an exotic orchid in deep black with a slight purple undertone. "Candor Kohl," he announced proudly.

Charles whistled appreciatively.

"You didn't get that at a florist shop," Darcy quipped.

"No," Richard replied, looking at the flower. "This was almost as rare and hard to come by as she is."

Charles shook his head. "Good luck, man."

"Thanks."

A group of people started coming through the gate and captured their attention. Darcy's significant height gave him an advantage and he smiled as he recognized Elizabeth in the crowd.

She smiled and waved across the distance until she was stopped by a police officer. Darcy saw her frown in confusion and then she was gone. He spoke her name as his eyes searched for her, growing more frantic with each second.

"Well, well, the gang's all here."

Darcy's attention snapped to the last person he ever wanted to see again. George Wickham was standing in front of him.

"What are you doing here?" Darcy hissed.

"Will," George chided, "is that any way to talk to your old buddy? Hey, Richard, good to see you."

Richard glared dangerously.

"And you must be Charles. George Wickham, nice to meet you."

"I know who you are. Leave. Now."

George lifted his eyebrows to Charles in surprise and laughed. "I was just going to tell Will that I'm afraid Lizzy might be a little late. After all, that is who you're waiting for, isn't it, Will?" His tone was mocking. "She's nice, but you know, she really is a horrible liar." He shrugged and grinned. "But a few years of prison should fix that. She'll learn all sorts of things there."

Darcy stood frozen, as his blood turned to ice. "What are you talking about?" he demanded in a harsh and choked voice.

"I just wanted you to know who had taken her away from you. So that makes it George two, Darcy zero."

Darcy felt himself rooted to the ground, unable to move. He watched, stunned as Richard's fist smashed into Wickham's jaw.

"What did you do?" Richard snarled, his face transformed by hate, as he held Wickham by the shirt.

"Darcy, Richard!" Charlotte's voice cried out, twisted by fear. "Lizzy's been arrested!"

CHAPTER 19

RICHARD'S EYES NARROWED, "WHAT did you do to her? What the *hell* did you do?" he shouted into the man's face, oblivious to the crowd gathering around him.

Darcy moved forward, trying to get to Elizabeth beyond the security gate, when Rebecca stopped him. "Will, you can't go in there. It's no good. They won't let you by."

Darcy stared, as if he couldn't understand her. "No. No, she needs me."

Rebecca stopped him from going any farther, using his shock as an advantage in turning him around. Two policemen were hurrying to Richard and Wickham. Richard heard their shouts and released Wickham, holding his hands up in the air. "Search him! He's carrying something."

One of the officers put his hands on Richard while the other helped Wickham to his feet. "Are you okay, sir?"

Wickham smiled evilly. "I'm fine."

"Search him!" Richard insisted. "You just arrested a woman, Lizzy Bennet. Whatever you found on her, he planted it. Search him!"

The officers exchanged looks as two more ran up to the group. "Sir," one of them said, "we can't just search someone. That's a violation of their rights."

While he was talking, Rebecca made eye contact with one of the officers and nodded. The officer pulled his walkie-talkie out and spoke softly into it. A minute later, as Richard argued, a police dog was escorted to the scene.

"Watch," Rebecca told Darcy discreetly in a low voice. As they watched, the beagle pointed to the bag and made a whining noise in her throat. "That's an alert."

"Sir?" the officer who was holding Wickham said, "could you come with us?"

Wickham looked at the small dog, as if seeing it for the first time. "Of course," he said smoothly.

Rebecca set her jaw. "He's clean."

"How do you know?"

"He would have never agreed to the search otherwise. Whatever he had, he planted it on Lizzy. It's a setup."

Darcy's hands began to shake. "How bad is this?"

Rebecca shook her head. "I don't know. It could be real bad."

It was then that Jane and Alex caught up with the group. Jane flew into Charles's arms and he held her tightly for a moment, his face expressing relief.

"What happened to Lizzy?" Darcy demanded of Alex.

Alex glared. "I don't know," he replied sullenly. "We were walking through the gate when a cop asked her to come with him. A few minutes later we were informed she'd been arrested."

Darcy closed his eyes, as his face became a hard mask. "For what?" he growled between clenched teeth.

"I don't know," Alex answered softly.

Darcy opened his eyes to reveal the desolation he felt at that moment. Charles stepped forward and put his hand on his shoulder, subtly indicating the photographer who had appeared in the crowd watching them. "Hang on," he said softly. "This isn't the place."

Darcy looked at his friend. "I can't leave her."

"She's probably already gone," Charles replied calmly. "You can't help her by making a scene here. Let's go to the loft now, all of us. We can do something there."

The walkie-talkie at the belt of the officer holding Richard squawked, and a moment later Richard was free to go. Charles and Rebecca directed the group to the doors, informing everyone they were to meet at the loft. Charles pulled out his cell phone as he kept one arm around a shaken Jane and pressed a button.

"Caro? Caro, damn it! Pick up, now! It's an—It's me. I'm at the airport. Lizzy's been arrested... We're not sure... He—" Charles stopped and looked at Darcy, who was moving as if he was sleepwalking. "He needs our help. Get Rachel and meet us at the loft... okay, bye."

Charlotte sat quietly in the passenger seat of Richard's car. She was in a state of shock, barely noticing the way Richard had carefully fastened her seat belt. She felt rather than saw him get in on the driver's side.

"Char?"

Slowly she turned her head to him. She opened her mouth once, but no words came out.

Richard took her hand and squeezed it. "It's going to be okay, Char," he told her gently. "It's okay."

The gentle kindness in his voice was almost her undoing. She felt herself losing it and forced all her upset down, into her stomach. Calming her expression, she stared at her hands until she was sure they wouldn't shake and nodded her head slowly.

Richard watched her, able to read her emotions perfectly. What he wasn't certain of was if she didn't trust herself to break down, or if she didn't trust him. He remembered their last time alone, when she held herself back from him, and it cut him deeply.

Richard looked down, surprised to see the small white box in his free hand. Jane gave it back to him when the cop released him. He smirked at the way all his great plans for this night had been destroyed in an instant.

Slowly he turned to Charlotte, who was still in a daze and held out the box to her. "This isn't how I planned your homecoming," the irony was thick in his voice, "but I got this especially for you."

Charlotte's eyes met his with a look of disbelief and confusion.

"Open it," Richard said gently.

Slowly Charlotte opened the box and saw the single perfect blossom resting there. It was shiny and delicate, dark black with purple under-tones that matched Charlotte's hair perfectly.

"The black orchid is one of the rarest and most treasured flowers known. It's exotic and precious." Richard squeezed the hand he was holding and with his other hand lightly touched Charlotte's cheek. "That's how I feel about you, Charlotte."

Charlotte looked from the flower to Richard, and he watched as her carefully constructed wall disintegrated, revealing the fragile woman underneath. "Richard," she gasped.

He pulled her close, pressing her face into his shoulder and holding her as sobs began to rack her slender frame. He rubbed his face against her hair, murmuring softly, "Charlotte, my beautiful, beautiful Charlotte, it's okay. It's okay."

She clung to him, suddenly weak, overwhelmed by the conflicting emotions ripping through her. She didn't know if she should feel happy or sad or afraid, and her heart was heavy and sore.

When her tears subsided and she was still, Richard gently pressed her back so he could look in her eyes. When he spoke it was in a low earnest tone. "Char? We're going to go to the loft now. Lizzy and Darcy need us, but I promise you we will talk. We need to talk." He grinned to himself. "I need to talk to you, Char."

Charlotte nodded, her short hair swinging back and forth. "I'm not normally like this," she told him, her voice trying to sound normal.

"I know," Richard smiled, giving her hand a final squeeze before turning to start his car. The vintage Mustang came to life with a roar and Richard took off toward the Village.

He knew she was feeling better when fifteen minutes into the trip she looked around the car, as if seeing it for the first time, and asked, "What year is this?"

"Sixty-seven," he answered lightly.

"Damn," she replied, drawing the word out.

Richard's warm laugh bubbled up and filled the small car.

❧

Elizabeth sat in a daze, completely at a loss. Never before had she dealt with the police beyond a speeding ticket, and now she was sitting in the station house, hands cuffed together.

Now it all seemed clear. Wickham must have put something in her bag. Elizabeth assumed it was cocaine, but the fact of the matter was she didn't have a clue what was in that tiny packet they showed her. She had certainly never seen it before, and she could only guess how it had gotten in there.

She felt sick with the knowledge that while all those things were true, they were also what every single person, guilty or innocent, said when confronted by the police.

She couldn't believe this was happening. Everything seemed so surreal, and a part of her kept expecting someone to walk out and tell her it was all just a mix-up and she could go home. Every second she wore the handcuffs, she realized that this was real, and she was in a great deal of trouble.

She trembled with fear, not knowing what she was going to do. She needed a lawyer, that much was clear, but the only attorneys she knew were her uncle and the lawyer for LBS. She didn't even know if she could afford a lawyer. Then she remembered with a pathetic chuckle what the police at the airport had recited to her: "if you cannot afford a lawyer, one will be provided to you." Elizabeth felt tears pricking her eyes and she bit her lip hard, trying to keep control.

A bored-looking officer calling her name interrupted her thoughts. She followed the woman to another room where she was photographed and fingerprinted.

⌘

As the elevator doors shut, Charles drew his love into his arms. He needed the reassurance of her touch as much as she needed his. Gently he lifted her chin up and softly kissed her, savoring the taste and feeling of the one he loved best.

"It's going to get wild for a little while, baby. Are you going to be okay?" He looked at her carefully, studying her and measuring her distress.

"Charles." Her voice was weak and frantic.

"I know, I know, angel." He soothed her as he rested his large hands on either side of her head, his thumbs rubbing her cheeks. "I know. And I'm going to do everything I can to get her back. Try not to worry."

Jane responded to the strength and authority in his voice. Instinctively she trusted him to know what to do. She nodded, pulling herself together.

"I'm going to be busy, but if you start to lose it or need me to hold you, tell me. Don't wait. I'm going to be there for you."

Jane nodded again, even managing a weak smile. Charles made her feel infinitely better. She now had someone to trust and something to hope for. As Charles released her with a final kiss, she watched him turn toward the doors and square his shoulders, preparing for the emergency waiting for them. She couldn't help but smile to herself, knowing with sudden clarity that this was the man she would spend the rest of her life with and that she had made the right choice.

As the doors opened, the first thing Charles saw was Tommy. He was waiting at the end of the gallery, clearly functioning as gatekeeper, providing security as he always did. Charles nodded and was informed that Alex was in the kitchen and the rest were in the living room.

Charles nodded his thanks and stepped forward, Jane's hand in his own.

Alex was talking on his cell as they passed by the bar, and Charles gave him a nod and moved on. In the main room, he found Caro and Rebecca both on their phones while Rachel sat at the table next to Darcy, pale and staring into oblivion. Faust was standing by the kitchen entrance, watching and ready to help where needed.

Charles caught Caroline's eye and gave her a nod. She returned it while speaking into the phone. Jane let go of Charles's hand, sitting down on Darcy's other side, and gave him a hug. Darcy's awareness seemed to return and he hugged Jane back, exchanging a few low words with her.

"I found her," Rebecca announced as she hung up the phone. The room stilled and Alex appeared. "She's been turned over to NYPD and they have her at the 114th in Queens." Rebecca seemed pleased with her discovery until she noticed the look of distress on the others, and her mood sobered.

Caroline relayed the information to whoever she was talking to and hung up. "We're in luck. Linda was nearby for a seminar or something. She's on her way here."

"Do we know what she was arrested for?"

"They found 500 grams of cocaine in her bag," Rebecca announced in a professionally indifferent tone. "A dog sniffed it and Elizabeth probably never thought to refuse the search because she thought she was clean." She shrugged. "Actually, that may help her case. She doesn't have any previous convictions, does she?"

Jane shook her head no.

"That'll help too."

Darcy went even paler at her words.

The shrill of Darcy's phone shattered the silence. He answered it quickly, exclaiming, "Lizzy!" when he recognized the voice at the other end.

"Will," Elizabeth said in a calm yet brittle voice. "I need help."

"Are you okay?"

"They found drugs in my bag. I have no idea how they got there. It's a mistake. I'm so scared."

Darcy's heart was breaking at the terror in her voice. "I know, love. We think George planted them on you. Listen, the best lawyer I know is going to be there soon. Her name is Linda St. Andrews. She's going to help you." His voice ran down. "I love you, Elizabeth."

"What's going to happen?"

"We're going to get you out, Lizzy. You're going to be released and you'll be all right." Neither of them was convinced by his words.

"Oh God, Will," she whispered.

"Lizzy, listen to me. You have to be tough. I'm going to get you out of there. No matter what I have to do. Do you understand?"

"Okay, I'll be tough." Her voice sounded more like her usual self. "But please hurry."

"I will. I love you!"

There was a pause, and then Elizabeth said, "I have to go. Bye."

"Bye." He turned to see Richard watching him. He had clearly just arrived with Charlotte.

"Lizzy?"

Darcy nodded.

"Is she okay?"

Darcy nodded once, then shrugged and turned away.

Charlotte passed by her brother, touching his arm supportively, and placed her flower in the refrigerator. She noticed the bouquet of roses intended for Elizabeth lying forgotten on the counter and began unwrapping them. Silently Richard joined her, reached into a cabinet, and brought down a crystal vase.

"That's lovely," she said softly.

Richard gave her a slight smile as he put some water in it. "Aunt Anne always had great taste."

Charlotte smiled gently back to him and began arranging the roses. She longed to do something more, but recognized that she couldn't and was grateful she could occupy herself with this simple task.

The elevator rumbled and opened and a woman entered the loft, talking on a phone. She was tall and slender, in her midthirties, with blonde hair that was wrapped in a neat twist at the back of her head. She was the top criminal attorney in the law firm that handled De Bourgh Records and had a long history with Slurry. She hung up as she reached the living room and walked right into Darcy's arms.

"Damn, Will. What happened to you? You look horrible," she commented after releasing him.

"Linda, thanks for coming." His eyes were haunted. "You have to help her."

Linda nodded. "I've been talking to my friends downtown; I'm on it. The deputy DA who's been assigned is a good guy. It'll be okay." She smiled and looked around. "Charles, could you introduce me to the people I don't know?"

Charles quickly took care of the introductions. Linda nodded to LBS, making a silent observation on the pairing-up that was going on. "It's nice to meet you all." She walked Darcy to the table and pulled out a chair. "Now, I want you to sit down and tell me what you know."

Darcy settled into a chair, with Charles joining him. Linda sat across from them and crossed her legs, waiting.

"It was Wickham," Darcy said without preamble.

Linda's face changed in a flash. "That asshole?! How the hell did he get involved? I thought it was part of your contract that he got nowhere near you?"

"Lizzy is a part of Long Borne Suffering, the warm-up band on our tour. The Wickham rule doesn't apply to them," Charles explained quietly.

"What happened?"

"Wickham was hired to direct LBS's video."

"And why don't I believe that was a coincidence?" Linda interrupted "Oh, wait, I know! It's because he's a scumbag who would do anything he could to screw you over."

Charles hid the smile he couldn't repress behind his hand. "We suspect Wickham learned about Lizzy and Will's relationship, but that's just a guess based on what he told us."

"Go on."

"LBS flew down to Tampa yesterday to shoot a video. Everything was fine until today, when Elizabeth was stopped at the airport, searched, and found with drugs."

"Help me out here; is there any chance the drugs were hers?"

Darcy's eyes narrowed as Charles answered, "None at all. She's clean."

"And Wickham?"

"Wickham was on the flight back to New York with them."

"He rode with Lizzy to the airport as well," Jane volunteered.

"Why was she in the same car as him?" Darcy hissed.

"Winnie was there as well," Jane answered softly.

Linda continued. "Now, we know that Wickham was in the car and on the flight with Lizzy. Do we have any other reason to suspect him?

"He said some pretty provocative things at the airport," Richard answered.

Linda was making notes on a legal pad. "What kind of comments, how provocative?"

Richard shrugged. "Enough that I punched him in the jaw."

Linda looked up and held out her palm to Richard, who slapped it. "Wish I was there."

"He said she would be going to prison," Darcy said quietly.

Linda looked at Darcy and lifted her eyebrows. "Well, that's pretty telling, isn't it?"

"Wickham was searched but he was clean."

"Sadly, he's not that stupid. If he was, my job would be a lot easier." Linda looked at her notes. "Okay, I think I have enough. I'm going to go over there now."

"I'm going with you," Darcy announced firmly.

Linda looked at Caroline, then Charles.

"No, Darcy. You can't do that," said Caroline.

"Why not?"

"Because, they won't let you. She only gets to see her lawyer, and besides, Will, right now this is nothing. It's probably not even going to be picked up by the press. But if you go, it's going to be news. Big news."

"Charles is right," Linda added. "Write her a letter, and I'll slip it to her."

Darcy looked from Linda to Charles. Charles nodded and, frowning, Darcy walked to his library.

"Okay," Linda said, turning to Charles, "who is she to him?"

Charles smiled. "She's the love of his life. Can't you tell?"

Linda sighed. "She must be to make him act like this."

"I better check on him," Charles said as he followed Darcy into the library.

Darcy sat at a desk, staring into space, a blank sheet of paper in front of him. "I don't know what to write. What do you say in a situation like this? I want to apologize and beg her forgiveness, but..." He sighed, disgusted with himself.

"Don't beg for her forgiveness."

Darcy ran his hands through his hair and sighed. "You're right."

"Good. Now, write this down."

Dearest Elizabeth,

I wish I could be there with you, but I can't. This note is all I can do. Linda is the best lawyer I know. I trust her completely and you can trust her too. I will not rest until you are back here, safe in my arms. Please be brave, and know that I'm with you in my heart.

All my love,
Fitzwilliam

Darcy handed the note to Charles, who read it, sealed it in an envelope, and gave it to Linda, who was waiting in the living room. He then returned to Darcy and shut the living room door.

"Will, let me help. I know what you're feeling."

Darcy looked at him in disbelief. "How? How can you know?"

"Because I've been there. Remember? My dad? I went through all of this. You're feeling angry, terrified, guilty, and helpless."

Darcy looked down at his desk and his hands began trembling. "She trusted me, Charles. She trusted me, and I let that monster destroy her." His voice was a harsh whisper. "I'm so afraid. She's in jail, all alone. I would give anything for her to be here, and safe. What if, what if she's…"

Charles could see what Darcy was so afraid of that he couldn't even say it. Charles put his hand on Darcy's shoulder. "I know. It's hard. Get it out. Tell me what you're thinking."

"I'm afraid that she'll be convicted, that she's going to prison. What if Wickham is right? What if she does go to jail and it changes her? What if she blames me?"

Charles nodded. "Those are all reasonable fears and I don't blame you for being terrified. It sounds like you are afraid of losing her as well."

"I am going to lose her," he said in a dead voice. "I can't expect her to forgive me for this. It's just like before. I just got a chance to love her, and she's being ripped away."

"Do me a favor. Try to reverse the situations. Imagine that an old enemy of hers framed you. Would you hate her? Would you even blame her?"

Darcy looked at Charles incredulously. "Never. I love her. I will always love her."

"There's your answer, Will. If I know Lizzy, she probably just wants to get back to you, not to hate you."

Darcy put his head in his hands and thought. "All right."

"Are you going to deal? 'Cause Elizabeth needs your help."

Darcy nodded. "I don't know how I'm going to cope if she's not released."

Charles nodded. "Fair enough. We'll deal with that if it happens. One step at a time."

❦

Elizabeth had been waiting in the interrogation room for almost an hour by the big clock that hung on the wall, an hour with nothing to keep her company but her own thoughts.

Talking to Darcy had been a mixed blessing. It was good to know he was helping her, but the pain and fear in his voice had made her all the more frightened.

She started when the door opened and a tall blonde woman walked in. "Ms. Bennet? I'm Linda St. Andrews. I believe Will told you about me?"

Elizabeth felt her heart lift with Darcy's name. "Yes, yes he did," she said quickly.

Linda smiled and held out an envelope. "This is for you."

Elizabeth took the blank envelope and opened it, pulling out Darcy's letter. She gasped as she recognized the handwriting and read it, eagerly devouring each word. She looked tearfully up at Linda and said, "Thank you," in a tremulous voice.

Linda gave Elizabeth a reassuring smile and a tissue. "Feeling better? Now, let's get down to work."

A half hour later found them sitting with the police, going over questions. Elizabeth answered them all honestly, but it was clear the police were growing annoyed. After another fifteen minutes, the two detectives left in a huff.

"What did I do?" Elizabeth asked.

"Nothing." Linda shrugged, going over her notes. "Cops hate that. They want you to trip up and be guilty. Innocent people make them nuts."

"What's going to happen?"

Linda looked up and squeezed Elizabeth's hand sympathetically. It was clear that she was terrified. "They're probably going to move you to a holding cell, where you get to spend the night."

"Tomorrow you will be arraigned before a judge. That is when you will plead not guilty and bail will be set. Then you can go home to that man who is missing you so bad."

"Will? Is he okay?" The color drained from Elizabeth's face.

"He's very concerned. Didn't he tell you that in the letter?" She gestured to the paper in Elizabeth's hands and Elizabeth nodded. "What about the trial?" she asked fearfully.

"Well, we will have to see about that," Linda said in a businesslike tone. "I'm going to try to get the charges dropped, but that's going to be tricky. The good news is that your fingerprints aren't on the packet, there were no traces of residue on your hands, and with any luck Wickham's prints will be on the packet. Add the fact that you have agreed to drug testing and that you agreed to let your bag be searched and I say we have a pretty strong case."

"But what if…"

"Lizzy, don't think about that now. I'm going to do my best to see this never gets to trial, and they don't tremble when my name is spoken in the DA's office for nothing." She grinned. "I'm good. Have some faith."

Elizabeth nodded, her faith stretched to its limits.

Linda smiled. "Good." She turned to her papers and started working.

Elizabeth sat puzzled in silence for a few minutes and then asked, "What are you doing?"

"Very boring paperwork. But every minute you spend with me is one less minute you spend in the holding cell, right?"

Elizabeth smiled and nodded.

"Now, listen to me. You are semifamous, so the cops are going to be careful with you, but there might be other people in the holding cell. If at any time you feel afraid, demand to see me. I'll be nearby so I can get here quickly. We'll get you out of the cell and you can hang out in the interrogation room for a few hours. Understand?"

Elizabeth nodded.

"You'll get through this, Lizzy."

Darcy came out of the library when he heard Caroline swearing loudly. The large-screen TV was on and showing a picture of Elizabeth as an MTV News announcer said,

"Bennet is the singer for the girl group Long Borne Suffering, which is currently on tour with Slurry. In possibly related news, Slurry drummer Richard Fitzwilliam was also at LaGuardia Airport at the same time and was seen having an altercation with former Slurry lead singer George Wickham. Wickham now directs music videos after leaving Slurry in 2006."

"Turn it off," Darcy said disgustedly as he turned away.

"Well, there goes her reputation. I hope you're happy," Alex commented savagely at Darcy.

Darcy felt something inside of him snap. "Do I look happy? Elizabeth is being held by the police. Why do you think I would be happy about that?"

The room grew silent as every eye fixed on the two men.

"Well, you sure seem to be doing your best to mess her up."

Darcy slowly closed his hands into fists. "You were the one with her when she was arrested," he said in a dangerously low voice. "I trusted that you would bring her home safely, but you didn't, did you? What were you doing, letting her out of your sight? Leaving her alone with him?"

Alex took a step forward, his eyes cold with disdain. "We both know Wickham would never have even looked at Lizzy if you weren't involved. She was safe before she got messed up with you."

Darcy took a step forward right at the same moment Richard used his strength and bulk to move Darcy away. Charlotte took that moment to grab her brother and drag him in the opposite direction. They ended up in Richard's bedroom, which was at the far end of the loft.

"What the fuck was that about?" Charlotte asked incredulously. "Why did you do that?"

"He's a jerk," Alex sulked.

"That is no reason to attack the man like that. My God. Don't you have any feelings? How would you feel if your lover was dragged away like that?"

"You wouldn't understand."

"Probably not, but try me."

"It's just…" He stopped, unable to find the words.

"Don't tell me you still love her?"

"No, at least not like that. I know that it's over between us and has been for a long time, but... it's hard, you know. Watching them. Even when they were fighting like cats and dogs, they would stare at each other. All the time. You had to notice."

Charlotte nodded.

"She never looked at me like that, never."

Charlotte put her arm around him and leaned her head against his. "I got bad news for you, Bro; you're not Fitzwilliam Darcy."

"Nope, I'm sure not," he agreed resignedly.

Charlotte sat up and studied him. "You lied the other day at the airport. You aren't okay with this, are you?"

"Char—"

"No, just admit it. For whatever reason, a part of you just can't handle Lizzy being with Darcy."

Alex stared at the floor.

"You can't," Charlotte said in a low voice that indicated she was thinking out loud, "and you won't leave, and Lizzy won't fire you." She paused for a moment then said in a calm, resolved voice, "Alex, you're fired."

"What?"

"You're fired. I'll discuss it with Jane, but I'm sure she will agree with me."

"You can't do that."

"Yeah, I can. When Lizzy gets back, we'll finalize it, but we're going to have to sever our professional relationship."

Alex stared into the eyes that matched his own and saw there was no room for change in Charlotte's mind.

"All right," he conceded. "But I'm staying to help Lizzy."

Charlotte shrugged. "Not a problem. Just stop pissing off Will."

❦

Richard dragged and pushed Will into his bedroom and shut the door. "Okay, take a moment and calm down. Punching Alex's lights out isn't going to help matters."

"Oh, like punching George's did?"

"I didn't say it wouldn't feel good," Richard said. "And I'm sorry about that. I lost my temper. Besides, he was asking for it and I knew you weren't going to hit him."

"You're right." Darcy sank down on his bed. "What's going to happen, Richard?"

Richard shrugged. "Lizzy's going to be released on bail in the morning. We'll take it from there."

"And the press?"

"I wouldn't worry about it. It's probably going to die down. After all, I was the one who punched Wickham. There isn't anything to connect Lizzy and you other than the tour. The fact is she's not a big enough star to stay in the news long for a drug bust."

"Actually, there is."

"What?"

"When Jane was hit by that bottle, Lizzy and I created a diversion so Jane and Charles could get into the hotel. We... acted for the press in the lobby."

"Oh hell, Will." His eyes widened. "Christ, you were in love with her even back then, weren't you?"

Darcy looked at him from where he was lying on the bed and nodded.

Richard sighed. "And they've got those pictures somewhere, don't they?"

Again Darcy nodded.

"Well, then I'm guessing you're going to be on the front page of the *Enquirer* again, my friend. Won't be the first time."

"But it will be the first time it's true," Darcy growled.

Richard looked on sympathetically. "I know. It sucks all around. Wickham really got us good."

Darcy sat up and sighed. "I can't help but feel like I've failed her. I should have never let her go down there. And now she is gone, forever. I've destroyed her."

Richard stared, not believing his ears. "Will, will you listen to yourself? Christ, she's just being held until her arraignment. It's just one night. She's not dead!" He lifted up his hands in frustration and dropped them again. "Try to stay based in reality, okay?

"Oh, and you're one to talk," Darcy hissed. "What kind of fantasy have you got planned? You and Charlotte living happily ever after?"

Richard set his jaw. Darcy was just lashing out, but he had hit a painful target. "I know. I've got a lot of work ahead of me. But at least I'm facing it." He took a deep breath and released it. "I just don't know what to do about it."

Darcy stared, his dark eyes piercing Richard's. "Talk to her," he said. "That's where you have to start."

Richard nodded, and left the room.

❦

Richard found Charlotte shaking her head from her encounter with her brother. He held out his hand. "Come on," he said and drew her up a wooden and steel stair, through a doorway onto the roof.

"Oh!" she gasped in surprise. Before her was a beautiful garden. It was made of long, raised beds that were arranged with wooden screens to form a sort of maze. From the center, a visitor would be completely enclosed, shielded from any sight of the city. On the perimeter were lovely vistas, with benches to take in the spectacular views.

The beds were filled with a riot of bright colors, flowers of every type, blooming wantonly. The heat from the day was just starting to abate, and a cooling wind was blowing, carrying with it lush perfume from the flowers. "It's beautiful."

Richard nodded. "My aunt had it made. She loved having a sanctuary in the middle of the city that she could escape to." He led her along the edge of the garden, stopping with her to watch the sun setting low in the sky. He lightly placed his arms around her as he gathered his thoughts. Absently he noted the way the sunlight brought out the highlights in her hair, reminding him of the orchid he had given her.

After a minute, Charlotte asked, "What are we doing?"

All of Richard's worry and concerns broke away with the smile that warmed his face. "We're watching the sunset. Shhh. It's romantic."

"I'm not seeing the romance here," Charlotte disagreed. "I see New Jersey."

Richard laughed as he turned her in his arms to face him. "You're not going to make this easy, are you?"

"I'm not really the romance type," Charlotte stated. "And you know that."

Richard sighed dramatically. "Come over here then, my nonromantic one." They walked into the maze to the elegant wooden benches at the center there. He took her to one that was covered with a large, plain, dark green cushion. "I was going to put out some candles but—" He stopped at the expression on her face.

They sat comfortably side by side in silence. Finally Charlotte pulled out her cigarettes. "I need this," she murmured before offering one to him. Sitting together, smoking, brought them both a flood of memories, both good and bad. Gently, Charlotte explored them, evaluating again her feelings for the complex man beside her.

Richard struggled for a moment, and Charlotte let him, waiting silently to see what he was going to say. Finally he began, "Char, I don't know why this is so hard. I can talk to you about anything, but when it comes to us? I'm tongue-tied. What I want to say is I want you, and I want us to be better."

"Better?"

"I know," he sighed, dropping his head into his hands for a moment. "That's not very good. Sorry. What I mean is, I don't want us to go back to how we were. I want us to be better."

Charlotte crossed her arms and then started rubbing her forehead with her hand. She sighed. "Richard, you're the only one who's keeping us from being better." She dropped her hand and looked up at him. "I was doing what people usually do, moving from nonexclusive dating toward exclusive dating." She tilted her head a little. "You, being the creative soul that you are, went from nonexclusive dating to not dating me, to not dating at all—if your phone calls are to be believed. I think the next step would be to reverse puberty." She stopped herself, wondering if she had gone too far, and regrouped her thoughts. "My point is, if you want us to be better, then *be better.*" She touched his arms to emphasize her words. "I don't need the orchid and candles in the middle of the day and the view of beautiful New Jersey. I haven't suddenly morphed into Jane. I want us. You and me. That's all I've ever wanted."

Richard put out his cigarette and slowly wrapped his arms around her. "Are you sure?"

She nodded. "Yes."

His expression carried the uncertainty he felt. "You know I'm not cured, right? I mean, I want to be. I want to be with you and only with you, but," his voice dropped, "I might stumble."

"I know. All I'm asking is that you be honest with me." She put out her cigarette and placed her hands on his chest. "I can handle stumbles. I won't like it, but as long as you're sure that you want to be with me, I can handle it. But I need you to promise to tell me. And if you ever change your mind, and you don't want to be with me, you have to tell me that too."

Richard considered her words solemnly. "That's actually a really big promise."

Charlotte nodded. "I know it. It just came out, I didn't mean to…" She ran out of words. Then she took a deep breath and continued, "It's what I need to be able to trust you again."

"Can you promise the same to me? Full honesty? No keeping things secret to 'protect' my feelings?"

Charlotte paused and thought about what he was saying. "I can promise to do my best. That's about all."

"I think that will be enough," he agreed. "We do pretty well when we're honest with each other." He took a deep breath, "And I promise to be honest with you, Charlotte." He smiled and kissed her, slowly, sealing himself to her.

Charlotte felt like a tight band that had been wrapped around her chest was being removed. She felt like she could breathe again. All the grief and anxiety left her, leaving her rejuvenated. She wrapped her arms around his neck and stretched luxuriously against him, as if her body was responding to the relief in her heart. A smile of deepest joy graced her features. "Thank you," she breathed softly as she leaned against him, lifting her lips to his.

Richard opened all his senses to her: her beautiful dark eyes against her luminous pale skin, her scent, her taste, the feel of her slender body in his arms, and he was transfixed by what he beheld. "Charlotte," he whispered in awe. It had been a long time since he had thought of her as anything but beautiful, but in this moment, she was transformed again, almost like magic, to magnificent.

He kissed her, trying to express all the love and wonder that he felt for her. "I love you."

She kissed him back, long and deep. Smiling, she said, "I got that. I love you too." She threaded her fingers in his long dark hair, enjoying the silkiness of it. "Promise me you'll stop being so stupid?"

He kissed her again, longer, using all his skill to pleasure her. "I'm trying." He kissed her until she moaned. "I was trying to save you from me."

She hit him, hard, on the shoulder. "Ow!"

"That's what I mean. Stop being so stupid!" She kissed him again, sucking hard on his tongue as she worked at the buttons of his shirt.

"Okay," he grinned before kissing her again, his hands slipping under her shirt.

She moaned as she felt his hands on her bare skin. "Ooooooooooh God! It's been so long." She hit him again. "Don't ever keep yourself from me again." She kissed him again, hungrily, trying to touch all of his mouth with hers.

He grinned wickedly. "You like hitting me, don't you?" he asked as he nipped lightly along the length of her jaw, before moving to the sensitive curve of her neck.

She cried out as the new sensations assaulted her. "Maybe I do. But I think you deserve it." She found his hand and placed it on her breast, squeezing hard. "You've been a very bad—oh!—man and you should be punished." She put both of her hands on the sides of his head and pulled him away. "Are we alone here? No one else has access to the roof, right?"

"We're fine. It's all ours," he answered as she quickly removed her top. "Oh Char!" he whispered as he pulled her to him, needing to taste the newly revealed skin.

She curled her arms around his head as his mouth pleasured her, finding a hard nipple and suckling it eagerly. Longing that had been denied for so long flamed, causing an almost physical pain, driving her on like the lash of a whip. Her skin was on fire every place he touched. He was hers, finally, and she intended to possess every inch of him.

She pulled away from him and stood up to quickly remove every last remnant of clothing, until she stood before him, proud, her body throbbing.

Richard watched. His eyes were filled with her beauty, but his mind was stunned at what her eyes were telling him. This was completely different from any woman wanting him before; this was his mate demanding him. This was primitive, primal, and yet he was fully aware of the commitment he was making. This wasn't a promise of words, or even of his heart; this was a promise of his soul. He removed his clothing and prepared himself until he stood like her, naked in that improbable garden, and he held out his hand to her.

With one step she grasped his hand, and with another step she was in his arms, skin to skin, heart to heart. "Take me, now," she commanded, her voice clear and certain, as she sealed her mouth to his. Holding her close, he sat on the bench, drawing her up into his lap, her legs straddling his thighs. His mouth broke away from hers to find a breast, red, full, and swollen. As he drew her nipple into his mouth, his hand slipped between her legs, stroking her there.

She moaned low in her throat, dizzy with the pleasure that was filling her. His touch was teasing, pleasuring, but leaving her wanting more. "Richard," she cried, her voice shrill with need. Balancing with her hands on his shoulders, she found him pressed against her, his cock hard and ready. Her nails dug into his shoulders as he drew his tip across her, playing with her clit, making her scream. "Please," she begged as she ground mindlessly against him.

"Open your eyes, Char," he said, and once she did, he guided himself to her, watching as she sank down on him, slowly, inch by delicious inch, until he filled her completely. Her body shook equally from both the need for release and from the relief of having him again. Closing her eyes again, she rose and fell on him, savoring every sensation, the sweet fullness that seemed to be growing with each second. She felt wicked and dirty, and she adored it. With every stroke, she worked out every ache and scar that had pained her heart, grinding and polishing every defect from it, until she glowed, bright and hot.

She opened her eyes and took in his expression of wonder and amazement, owning the compliment that it was, even as a deep, aching need filled her. "Richard," she prayed through swollen lips just as the circuit closed and every muscle tensed and molten pleasure exploded throughout her body. Again and again she throbbed, fresh pleasure filling her each time.

Richard's voice was frantic as he called her name, pleading, as if for his life. Quick as a thought, he pulled her close and rolled on the bench, drawing his knees up and clasping her hips. "Charlotte, my God, Char!" he roared. "That was so hot. God, Char, that was so hot." His hips pistoned in and out.

Charlotte smiled wantonly as her hands played at her own breasts, pinching her nipples as her desire rose again. Richard's thrusts were becoming violent as he lost control he didn't even know he had and she drew in each thrust and demanded more. She was distantly aware of boundaries of pleasure she had never crossed before. She demanded more than she had ever dared, risking more, taking more.

"Richard," she said, low and urgent. "You're mine. Do you understand?" She waited for him to nod, her words breaking through his lust. "You are going to fuck me any time I want, any way I want. Understand?" His eyes rounded in amazement even as he nodded and moaned desperately.

"If I want to spank you, I can. If I want to tie you down and use you like a toy, I can. If I want to watch porn while you lick me off, I can! Understand?"

He nodded rapidly, almost unable to believe what was happening. "Now, I want you to fuck me hard and come like you've never come before." Even before the words were out of her mouth, he was shouting as his release overtook him. Charlotte came with him, her cries joining his as their bodies violently shook and then slowed before coming to an exhausted stop.

Richard rolled to his side to take his weight off her, holding her tight to him. "Char?" he said when his breath returned to him.

"Yes?" she panted.

"That was amazing." He laughed. "And kinda scary."

"Want me to do it again?"

"Oh God, yes."

Charlotte smiled to herself and kissed him. "I love you."

"And I adore you, my Charlotte," he said as his eyes studied her face, contemplating all that had happened. "I've lived most of my life being a monster in bed. It's been my identity." He voice was soft with wonder. "And here I find you, and you've not only matched me but completely overtaken me. You're a wonder, Charlotte."

She lifted an eyebrow. "I know." She kissed him sweetly. "I've resolved that if you ever stumble, it won't be because you're bored or wondering if someone else could be better."

"There's anyone else?" he asked disbelievingly. "Honestly, Char, you keep this up and I don't think I'll have the energy to stumble."

She ruefully shook her head and sat up. "Come on; it's been a long day and I need to get some sleep."

"You're sleeping with me."

"Where else would I sleep?" she asked as she started dressing.

Without rushing, they dressed, pausing now and then to kiss or simply hold each other close. They stopped a long moment before moving from the area around the bench, each wishing to protect the other from the pain and conflict that was waiting for them back in the loft.

"We're a team now, right?" he asked.

"I'm yours and you're mine," she answered. Satisfied, they joined hands and walked back to the doorway and into the loft. Wordlessly they descended the staircase, and after ensuring that there had been no change, Richard led them to his room.

Charlotte sat on the bed and as he watched, her eyes filled with worry for her friend, like water in a jar.

"Have you ever been arrested?"

She nodded. "Twice." She smiled deprecatingly. "I'm a bit of a brawler when I'm drunk."

"Oh, I'd never have guessed that," he joked lightly as he sat down beside her. "I've done the same, plus the DWI," he admitted. "We've been through it and know what's involved, so why am I so nervous for Lizzy?"

"Because we were guilty?" Charlotte guessed. "Because poor Lizzy didn't do anything, so just being arrested is wronging her, and because, well, she's not like us." She reached out and drew him close to her. "I am worried for her. And I'm glad you punched that asshole."

Richard kissed her lightly. "So am I." They lay down together and he cuddled her close, pillowing her head with his shoulder and covering her lightly with a sheet. "Try to rest now, Char. We've done enough today."

She snuggled closer, content to leave her worries until morning, and soon fell asleep in his arms.

Sleep took much longer to come to Richard as he struggled to understand all that had happened, what he had promised and been promised, the new opportunities that had opened to him, and the astonishing woman in his arms.

CHAPTER 20

ELIZABETH WAITED IN THE tiny room, puzzled at how long she had been there. Almost an hour had passed since the two detectives left, promising to "be back in a few minutes." She wasn't complaining; she certainly didn't want to go to a holding cell, but she wanted to know what was going on.

She looked up at Linda, a question in her eyes, and Linda frowned and nodded. "The DA's office should have called me by now." Linda stood up. "Let me go and place a call and see—" Her words were interrupted when the door opened and three people entered the room.

There were two large burly men wearing suits, followed by someone Elizabeth knew. "Winnie!"

The woman smiled in recognition. "Hi, Lizzy."

"Miss Bennet," the man with lighter-colored hair said, "I'm Agent Austen of the DEA, and this is my partner, Agent Holmes. We would like to have a word with you," he looked squarely at Linda, "in private."

Elizabeth drew in a breath to speak, but the sound of Linda's deep-throated laughter interrupted her.

"You don't really think I'm going to let you speak to her without counsel, do you?" Linda asked disbelievingly, her eyes locked with Agent Austen's.

Agent Austen bit back a retort. "Ms. St. Andrews?" Agent Holmes said in a calmer voice. "Miss Bennet is no longer under arrest. She's free to go."

"*What?*" Elizabeth gasped. Linda's face was more composed, but she was clearly astonished.

"I saw Wickham place the drugs in your bag, Lizzy. The police know that you are innocent," Winnie said gently.

Elizabeth struggled to comprehend her words. Innocent? Free to go? Just like that? It was what she was praying for, but it didn't seem possible.

"You're free, Miss Bennet," Agent Holmes began, "but we would like to ask a favor of you." His eyes flicked to Linda's.

Elizabeth became aware she needed to speak. "I would like Linda to stay, if that's possible."

Agent Holmes, a tall man with very dark curly hair, lifted an eyebrow at Linda and said, "Of course. May we sit down?"

The newcomers joined them at the table and had a quick, silent conference with their eyes. Linda leaned back in her seat, clearly waiting to hear what was coming.

Winnie finally spoke. "Lizzy, what we are going to tell you is going to have to stay confidential. It's vitally important. Do you understand?"

Elizabeth nodded, still puzzled.

"Winnie isn't my real name. I'm actually Agent Wendy Yee. The DEA has been investigating George Wickham, and I've been working undercover."

Elizabeth's jaw dropped. "But…" She was filled with so many questions that she didn't know where to begin. Instead, she kept quiet, allowing Winnie—that is, *Wendy*—explain.

Linda clearly had other plans. Her chair slid back and she sprang to her feet. "You're a Fed?!?" she demanded angrily. "And you let them take her in when you knew she was innocent? How dare you? Do you know this is going to affect her career?"

Wendy fixed Linda with a hard stare, and Elizabeth could see the sparks coming off both of them. "Ms. St. Andrews, if you would just sit down, I will explain," she said icily.

Linda sat down and glared.

"Wickham is a major player in the cocaine trade in New York City. He receives shipments from South America and arranges for their transport to New York, and then he cuts and distributes them throughout his network of dealers. He also launders the money."

Wendy turned to Lizzy. "I've been following Wickham for several months now. When we first met, I didn't know if you knew about Wickham's illegal business transactions and I didn't want to discourage you. When you came down to Tampa yesterday, I knew by then who was clean and who wasn't."

"Miss Bennet, George Wickham went to a great deal of trouble and expense to set you up. Do you have any idea why he would have a personal grudge against you?" Agent Austen asked.

Elizabeth looked to Linda, who rolled her eyes and nodded. The

DEA had shown Elizabeth their hand; it was time to reveal hers. "He has a long-standing dispute with my… um, boyfriend, Will Darcy." She felt her cheeks warm from the inelegance of the title.

"Fitzwilliam Darcy?"

Elizabeth nodded. "I'll admit this seems extreme," she attempted to explain.

"Don't worry about it, Lizzy," Wendy stopped her. "We know George is unstable. He's becoming paranoid from the cocaine and soon he will be too far gone for his higher-ups to use him. That is why we want to arrest him now."

"You said you need my help? I don't understand. I don't know anything about drugs."

"Yes," Linda said in a slow, careful voice, "what exactly are you offering?"

"As Austen said, Wickham blew a lot of money to get you framed, and he did a good job of it. The deputy DA did not want to let you go," Agent Holmes explained. "Wickham is going to be watching you to enjoy his revenge. If you are released now, he will know it and he'll suspect something is wrong."

"Lizzy, George received a major shipment of drugs while on the island," Wendy continued. "He has it coming up north overland by way of three couriers, called mules, arriving through the night. Tomorrow morning, we plan to arrest him and the whole operation. We're very close to nailing him. We want you to play along with the arrest and stay at the station house tonight. You don't have to go to a holding cell or anything; you can stay here. In the morning, you can leave when you normally would, after a mock arraignment."

"Once we have Wickham, we will make a public announcement, clearing you of all charges," Holmes added.

Elizabeth frowned. "When do you expect to arrest George?"

"Before noon," Wendy answered.

Elizabeth sagged in her seat. She felt like she was on a roller coaster. It was difficult enough to accept that she was free and that the charges would be dropped. Now she was struggling with a new request: to stay when all she wanted was to go home to Darcy. She sat stunned as she heard Linda firing off question after question to make sure the deal was fair. Elizabeth didn't understand half of what she said, and frankly, she was too tired to care.

"Can I call Will? I'd like to discuss this with him," she asked numbly, when there was a break in the conversation.

"No," Austen snapped.

Wendy leaned forward. "Elizabeth, I know Will is special to you, but he has a history with Wickham and there are a lot of rumors about him being a drug user. We have to insist that you not tell him about this until George is in custody."

Elizabeth felt as if she had been slapped. Shock and embarrassment were quickly followed by hurt and anger. "But he's not like that. He hates Wickham." Elizabeth felt Linda's hand on her arm, gently squeezing her, and she stopped.

"He deserves to be consulted. If Lizzy and Darcy are connected by the media, it will affect his reputation," Linda pointed out coolly.

"You're worried about *Fitzwilliam Darcy's* reputation?" Agent Austen scoffed.

Wendy rolled her eyes and spoke up before another argument could break out. "It's too late for that. MTV News covered the arrest and there was an altercation between George and Richard Fitzwilliam at the airport. They're reporting that as well. It won't take long for them to connect you two. I'm sorry, Lizzy. We have to insist on that. You can take a moment to think about it, if you want."

Elizabeth nodded. "Please."

The three agents looked at each other and filed out of the room. Elizabeth put her elbows on the table and rested her head in her hands. Sighing, she looked up at Linda. "I just want to get out of here, and now this. Damn it. Why doesn't the universe want me to be happy?"

Linda shrugged. "Maybe the universe does." She took a deep breath and continued. "Look, Lizzy, I hate this too, but I was there three years ago. I was the one who told Will not to press charges against George after Ramsgate. Looking at it now, that might have been the wrong decision, but I was trying to protect Georgie. Believe me, I still feel guilt over that one. My point is that you have a chance now to really help Will, and yourself. If Wickham wiggles out of this, he's not going to go away. He's going to find another way to hurt Will and you."

Elizabeth nodded thoughtfully. "Okay. I guess I can stand a few more hours in this place."

"Lizzy? You know that there are going to be people who won't believe that you are innocent if you do this."

Elizabeth smirked. "I know. It sucks, but frankly, it's nothing new. Ever since I joined this tour, people have been dragging my name through the mud. 'Slurry's Bitches' they call us." She smiled ruefully at the memory.

"So you are going to do it?"

"Yeah, what choice do I have? I just wish I could get some word to Will. This is going to kill him."

Linda pursed her lips thoughtfully. "I'll call him."

Elizabeth's eyes lit up.

"Don't get all excited. I'm not going to tell him about Wickham. There are too many chances that someone might monitor the call, but I'll tell him you are safe and all right."

Elizabeth frowned even as she agreed. "Make it good, Linda. And tell him I love him."

Linda nodded. Within minutes the deal was set. Elizabeth would spend the night in the interrogation room. Hot coffee and snacks were provided, and she was allowed to call her parents and relieve their worries. Linda departed, promising to return in the morning, and Elizabeth settled in to wait out the night, alone with her thoughts.

❧

It was almost midnight when the phone rang. Darcy pounced on it like a cat and answered. "Darcy," he snapped.

"It's Linda."

"What's going on?"

Linda could hear the tension in his voice. "Elizabeth is okay. She's being held overnight until her arraignment in the morning."

"Is she safe?"

"Yes, they are handling her with kid gloves and even gave her a separate cell." Linda waited, but heard nothing in response. "Darcy? Will?"

"I'm here," he replied automatically.

"Will, she's as safe as she can be. And I have good news: a witness came forward. I think I can get the charges dropped tomorrow."

Darcy felt his heart start beating again with her words. "Linda, I love you."

"Yeah, yeah."

"If they know she is innocent, why can't she be released now?"

"Procedure, Will. There is no way to get her out before the arraignment. You are just going to have to accept that and try not to worry. She's safe."

Darcy wished it were that easy. "How is she doing? Is she very upset?"

"She's upset, but she's hanging tough. She's mostly worried about you."

"Really?"

"She wanted me to tell you that she loves you."

For a moment, Darcy was speechless. When he spoke again, his voice was rough. "Linda, whatever it takes tomorrow—bail, bribe, I don't care—you have got to get her out!"

"I will, I will. They told me the news has grabbed this?"

"Yes," Darcy said tiredly.

"That means that the press is going to be all over her after the arraignment tomorrow. How are we going to get her out of there and where is she going?"

Darcy's voice changed, from depressed and defeated to hard and businesslike. "Linda, this is her home. My limo and my security will pick her up and bring her here."

Linda smiled to herself. "That means the press will be all over you too."

"Fuck the press."

"I just wanted to be sure where we stand."

"Just bring her home. That's all I care about."

❧

Darcy looked at the phone he just turned off. Georgiana had called when she saw the news report on television. The first part of their conversation was a simple recounting of the facts. Darcy did his best to keep Wickham's name out of it, but it was unavoidable.

Georgiana surprised him by handling it better than he expected. He wondered, as he walked through the quiet of the loft, if it was helpful for her to see Wickham doing his thing on someone else. From a distance, it was easier to see that he was a villain and to evaluate his actions.

Darcy smiled mirthlessly as he got himself a bottle of water. It would be ironic if the one good thing that came out of this ordeal were for Georgie to do better.

Darcy told his sister what Linda told him: it was likely that the charges against Elizabeth would be dropped, and in any case she would be released tomorrow. He wished he believed it.

Oh, he trusted Linda; there was no better lawyer that money could buy. It was his luck he feared. He occupied himself for almost an hour, thinking of ways and reasons that Elizabeth wouldn't be released, that she would be taken away from him, or that, worse yet, she would hate him for what Wickham did.

Memories were triggered by these thoughts and he went noiselessly to his library. He said a silent prayer as he booted up his computer and opened his email. His breath rushed out as he found what he was hoping for: Elizabeth's song.

He plugged in headphones to avoid waking the others and quietly, with a tear running down his cheek, he listened to the song she had written just for him.

He sang along with her voice, picturing her in his mind. He realized that he had to believe. Faith was all he had, faith that had not served him well in the past. Talking to Georgiana had brought it all back to him; he was terrified of losing Elizabeth at the moment when he drew closer to her, just as he had lost his parents. Was his life destined to follow the same script again and again?

It was almost too much to face, and he took refuge in Elizabeth's song. Tenderly, he recalled the night he first heard it: the night she gave him her love. Oh, he believed she had loved him that first time, before the VMAs, but she wasn't aware of it then. At Pemberley, she knew. She knew exactly how she felt about him and she offered herself to him completely.

He felt warmed by the memory, and a sudden realization dawned on him: no matter what happened, the situation with Elizabeth was different from his parents. Richard and Georgiana had hinted at it, but only at that moment did he see it clearly.

He would never lose Elizabeth as he lost his parents. His parents never freely gave their love. He always had to win it, to earn their approval. His mother had never focused on him until his child prodigy status deemed him worthy, and his father had only accepted him as a replacement for his mother.

Darcy had been so hurt by this he had lived his life trying to still win their approval, long past their deaths. His parents were his reason to push himself so hard, trying to be an industrial leader and a classical musician, as well as the driving force behind Slurry. They were the reason he never gave himself permission to make a mistake.

Elizabeth, on the other hand, didn't care about that. She never required him to be something he wasn't. She had offered her song and her love to him not because of what he did but because she knew who he was and she loved him. Him! Not some figure and not some achievement. She had seen the most awful he could be and still she loved him.

Suddenly everything was so clear. He felt like he had a new freedom he had never known before. Elizabeth proved that he was worthy of being loved, and even if his worst fears came to pass, and he never saw her again, nothing would ever take that away.

He couldn't express it yet, not even to Elizabeth, but he had turned a corner somehow. The power his grief had over him was gone. He now knew he didn't have to prove himself to his parents, or to anyone, anymore.

❧

It was after six in the morning when the soft rumble of the elevator motor drew Darcy out of his thoughts. As he walked toward it, Richard and Charlotte, Jane and Charles, and Caroline and Faust exited from their rooms.

"Hey, Darcy, I've got some bad news," Rebecca announced as the elevator doors opened and she walked out with an armful of newspapers.

"Rebecca?" Darcy said in a puzzled voice. "What are you talking about?"

"This," she sighed, holding up the *New York Post*. On the front page of the tabloid was Elizabeth's mug shot with the headline: *Slurry's Bad Girl.*

"Fuck," Darcy swore and his band mates echoed him.

"The media knows you and Lizzy are an item, too," Rebecca continued. She walked into the loft and deposited the pile of newspapers on the bar.

Darcy picked up one and was grieved to read about *Fitzwilliam Darcy and Black Lizzy: A Match Made in Hell!* Pictures of Darcy and Elizabeth were everywhere. He was not surprised to see one from the night Jane was injured, with Darcy tenderly kissing Elizabeth's head in the elevator. He went through them all, reading the tacky headlines. (*Do Jailbirds Sing?*) When he finished, he looked up to see the others watching him and waiting for instructions.

Darcy might have been feeling released from his obligations to his parents, but he gladly took responsibility for Elizabeth. "Where's Tommy?" he asked, his voice soft yet commanding.

"In the lobby," Rebecca answered quickly. "I felt it would be a good idea for the doorman to have some back up."

"Good. Here's what we are going to do. Our first priority is to get Elizabeth back. Rebecca, get some extra people ready. I want you to pick her up when Linda calls. Rachel?"

"Yes, Will?"

"I want you managing the phone. We are not giving out interviews or making comments." He turned to the others. "What about tonight?"

Caroline looked around. "If we are going to cancel, we better do it soon."

"Will," Charles said, "this affects you the most. You have to make the call for Slurry." Charles's hands rested protectively on Jane's arms.

Darcy took a deep breath and thought. "At this point, I say we go, but I won't confirm anything until Lizzy's free." He looked at Jane and Charlotte sympathetically. "What do you want to do?"

Jane looked miserably at Charlotte. "I don't know," she whispered, clearly hurt by what she had read. "I can't believe they said this about Lizzy. None of it is true."

"We know, angel, we know," Charles comforted her.

"Jane, why don't we plan on LBS not performing tonight?" Darcy said. "We don't know how tired Lizzy is going to be and we can always change our minds if things go better than expected."

Jane nodded from Charles's embrace. Darcy looked to Charlotte, who was glaring at the newspapers and smoking with trembling hands. "Char?"

Charlotte nodded and turned away, pressing her forehead against Richard's chest.

"Okay, let's do it then." The group moved into action, Caroline, Rebecca, and Rachel handling the phones, Faust moving the offensive newspapers away while Charles and Richard comforted their lovers and Darcy made coffee and tea for everyone.

꧁꧂

It was almost 8:00 a.m. when Linda returned to Elizabeth. She entered the tiny room grinning and carrying a Starbucks bag. "How is the hero today?"

Elizabeth did not share Linda's cheerfulness. She simply wanted to be out of there. "Badly in need of a shower, thanks."

"Here, coffee will make a new woman out of you." Elizabeth gladly accepted the cup. "I had some interesting phone calls," Linda continued.

"From whom?"

"Deputy DA Rodgers and I had a nice little chat."

"Oh?" The coffee was helping and Elizabeth looked at her with new alertness.

"Yes, he's not a happy camper to let you go. He thought he had a nice, high-profile drug bust all nailed up tight."

Elizabeth shrugged. "So sorry to disappoint him."

"He'll get over it." She paused a moment. Her voice had lost all its light tone when she spoke again. "Lizzy, you need to know; this has become very high profile. It's a slow news day, so you and Will are on the front page."

Elizabeth received this news without visible reaction. "Have you spoken to Will?" Her voice was soft, yet firm.

"Oh yeah." She laughed. "I asked him what we were going to do once you were released and he said, quote: 'This is her home. My limo and my security will pick her up and bring her here,' unquote."

Elizabeth smiled brightly, covering her face with one hand, and then a second, as she fought to keep control over her emotions. She was exhausted and overwrought and just needed to hold it together a little while longer.

Linda pretended not to notice. When Elizabeth dropped her hands and surreptitiously wiped her eyes with a napkin, she asked, "I take it you have heard that before?"

"Oh yeah," she smiled and nodded, remembering. "So, what is the plan for this morning? Do I have to go to the courthouse?"

"Yep. We get to drive over, lots of flashing lights and whatnot, and then you get to leave, no doubt in a big media blitz."

"I wish I could call Will and get his advice on how to handle this. He's much better at playing the bad boy than I am."

"Well, what did he tell you before?"

"He said to hang tough."

"Then do it. You have been falsely accused. Let it show."

Elizabeth nodded thoughtfully. "Yep, I guess I better get used to this. It's not like we'll ever have a life without the media."

"Ah, the price of fame," Linda sighed.

Elizabeth smiled. "When will I know that they have Wickham?"

"Paul is going to call me and I'll call you."

"Paul?"

Linda giggled. "Agent Holmes."

Elizabeth rolled her eyes and sipped her coffee. She was grateful for the chance to think about something other than what she would tell Darcy and how he would take it.

⤜⤚

In the end, it was easier than Elizabeth ever expected. Transported to the courthouse in a police car, she was spared a media gauntlet by entering the courthouse through an underground garage. Linda was waiting when she arrived. They were escorted into a small room and waited there for twenty minutes before being informed that they could leave. The Feds wanted a certain amount of media attention, so they asked Elizabeth to go out through the front when she left.

There was a knock on the door and Rebecca entered. Elizabeth was flooded with relief at the sight of her face. "Oh my God. It's so good to see you."

Rebecca dropped her professional scowl for a moment and smiled. "Are you ready to go?" she asked warmly.

"Oh yeah. More than ready."

"Good. There is a gang of photographers out there, so I've got two of my people to help with security. Linda, you'll walk with us to the limo, right?"

Linda nodded.

"I don't know why they wouldn't let us use the underground lot. It would be so much easier," Rebecca complained.

Elizabeth feigned ignorance, and the three women exited the room. Waiting outside were two large burly-looking men, reeking of body-guard. Rebecca took point and whipped out her cell. "Tommy, we're coming out."

Elizabeth walked with Linda, a bodyguard on either side. She felt like she was playacting. Surely there had to be a mistake. Famous people got this kind of treatment, not her. She was just... somebody?

Rebecca parted the crowd like Moses at the Red Sea. Elizabeth wore the dark sunglasses Linda gave her and tried to keep her expression calm. She focused on simply walking, knowing the last thing she wanted to do was trip and fall on the courthouse steps.

On the street, the long black limousine was waiting. Tommy opened the door and Elizabeth slid in, followed by Rebecca and one of the bodyguards.

Elizabeth was surprised to find the limo wasn't empty. Sitting silently in the far corner, dressed in dark clothing, was the tall figure of a man. "*Will!*" she cried.

As soon as the door was shut, there was a quick rearranging of seats and Elizabeth found herself ensconced in his arms. "Will? Will?" she repeated, touching him to be certain he was real.

Darcy's face held an expression of heartfelt relief as he held her close. "It's okay, it's all right," he murmured softly to her. "How are you?" he asked as the car moved forward, his eyes carefully examining her.

Elizabeth felt all her hard-won control dissolve, and tears slipped from her eyes. "I'm okay," she choked out before her face bunched up and she began sobbing in his arms.

Darcy held her tight, stroking her hair and back and hating himself. Every tear, sob, and gasp was his fault. Elizabeth's sobs subsided by the time they reached Manhattan, and she sat in a daze for the rest of the ride to the Village, her head pillowed by his chest, his heartbeat reassuring in her ear.

The limo drove past the reporters and straight into the garage. Rebecca and the bodyguards exited first and then gave the signal for Darcy and Elizabeth to exit. They walked smartly as a group to the elevator and when the door shut, Elizabeth felt as if she was going to drop to the floor. Darcy squeezed her hand tightly, his eyes never leaving hers, giving her his strength.

They entered the loft to find everyone waiting for them. Jane quickly snatched Elizabeth up into a hug, and she was passed like a hot potato to everyone there, receiving hugs and words of encouragement.

"Thank you," Elizabeth said, smiling through teary eyes. "I'm sorry. I'm just really tired." A soft murmur of understanding passed through the group.

"Elizabeth needs to rest," Darcy announced. "I think it would be best if everyone went home now, and we'll meet later. Caro, when do we need to be at the Garden?"

"Well, we," she indicated Faust and herself, "have to be there around noon, but you artists," she smiled at the word, "can lounge about until four or five."

Darcy nodded. "Rebecca, help everyone get out. Rachel, I'd like you to stick around in case I need you."

With that, everyone began to depart, each giving Elizabeth at least one more hug. Elizabeth fled as quickly as she could to Darcy's bedroom, and she wasn't surprised to see him enter a minute later.

"I thought you would be in the shower already," he said lightly.

Elizabeth smiled weakly and then her expression drooped. "Will, I have to tell you something."

Darcy felt himself go numb. He was certain that this was it. The experience had been too much and Elizabeth was going to break up with him now. He sat carefully on the bed, close, but not touching her. "What?"

Elizabeth sighed. "The charges against me have been dropped."

Darcy eyes widened. "Already? Lizzy, that's great news!"

Elizabeth held up her hand. "Wait, there's more." Slowly she told him the whole story, her hands moving restlessly in her lap the whole time.

Darcy listened without interrupting until she was finished. "You were never in jail?" he asked weakly, trying to understand.

"No," Elizabeth shook her head and smiled sadly. "I'm sorry I couldn't tell you, Will. I wanted to. I wanted to so badly." She drew up her knees and wrapped her arms around them, resting her head there.

Darcy struggled to understand what had happened. He laced his fingers together and touched his index fingers to his lips. "I didn't sleep at all last night, I was so worried about you."

"That makes two of us," Elizabeth replied gently. "I know you blame yourself for what has happened, but I need you to know that I don't. Wickham's actions are his own, and I don't feel anything but love for you. I'm sorry you were so scared last night, and believe me, if there had been another way, I would have taken it, but I had to do it. I love you too much to not do everything I can to get that bastard out of your life."

Darcy roughly pulled her to him and held her as tightly as he could. "Elizabeth, you're so brave. I can't believe you did that for me," he whispered.

"Well, I did it for me too," she added. "I can't believe he tried to frame me like that."

They rocked together, comforting and soothing each other, until Darcy pulled back and gently cupping her face in his hands, he kissed her lips with soft, loving kisses. "Are you ready to get cleaned up?"

Elizabeth nodded tiredly and let him help her off the bed and lead her to the bathroom.

There he gently undressed her, then himself, and turned on the shower. Elizabeth stood numbly still, letting him care for her.

"Will," she whispered when he brought her under the hot water.

"Shhh, it's all over now, Elizabeth," he told her firmly as he gently began washing her body. "Just try to forget about it for now."

Elizabeth let him wash her all over. By the time he was finished, she was trembling. He drew her close and let her weep, giving her the primal comfort of skin against skin. Finally she lifted her drained eyes to him.

"I've got you now; you're safe."

Elizabeth lifted her trembling lips to his and kissed him deeply, desperate for the succor she found in his mouth. They kissed until their exhausted bodies could take no more, then Darcy gently dried her off and led her to the darkened bedroom. There they snuggled together under the coverlet, the sheets cool against their tired skin.

Elizabeth was uniquely comforted by finally being in the place that she had needed for so long. Her mind wandered freely as her body sank heavily into the soft mattress. She realized something and giggled softly. "So, Char and Richard?"

Darcy's voice was warmed with relief. His heart was lightened to hear her sounding something like her old self again. "I don't know exactly what happened, but they talked."

Elizabeth laughed. "Knowing them, I can guess what happened." Darcy laughed softly with her, and they relaxed in the comfort and familiarity of the moment. Elizabeth wanted to ask him about playing her song, but she drifted to sleep before she could, exhaustion finally overcoming her.

❧

Elizabeth awoke disoriented. The cause was immediately clear: she was alone. If Darcy had been there, she would have known exactly where she was, but he was missing, so it took a minute for her brain to piece her location together. She sat up and saw by the clock on the bedside table (the same one that had awoken her for that flight a lifetime ago) that it was 7:19 p.m. She puzzled at Darcy's absence until she saw a note and a cell phone on his pillow.

Opening the note, she read:

My dearest, loveliest Elizabeth,
  Call me.
  Your Fitzwilliam

Elizabeth hit the button that was programmed with Darcy's number and waited for him to answer, her lips curling into a smile.

"Lizzy?"

"Hi."

"Hang on a moment." She could hear him moving. His voice was relaxed, warm, and touchable. "I had to get away from the meet-and-greet. How are you, Sleeping Beauty?"

Elizabeth smiled. "Missing my prince."

"Well, I tried kissing you back to life, but you just rolled over."

Elizabeth laughed.

"I'd like for you to come down for the show. I understand if you are too wiped out to perform, but I want you here."

Elizabeth was touched by the earnestness in his voice. "Then I'll be there."

She could hear him smile. "Great. Rachel is there and I'll send Tommy up with the limo. They have instructions."

Elizabeth suddenly had the sensation that he was planning something and her stomach tightened in anticipation. "I'll see you soon."

"I love you."

"I love you."

She hung up and found a robe draped across the bottom of the bed, clearly for her. He had planned for her, just like he always would. For once she found this didn't offend her; instead, she was touched by his thoughtfulness and love. She realized that the two biggest control freaks she knew had accepted, with surprising ease, letting someone else have control. Smiling to herself, she put the robe on, opened the door, and called out to Rachel, "So, what would you suggest I wear?"

CHAPTER 21

DARCY TURNED OFF HIS cell with a smile. Inside, he felt a sense of deep contentment. He loved the sound of her voice, thick with sleep, knowing she was in his bed. A part of him was appalled at his possessive feelings, and there was no way he would tell Elizabeth about them, but he couldn't deny them either.

He was pleased and comforted to know she was safe and well, in his home. Having lost that simple blessing for even a few hours had magnified its value to him. And that value wasn't going to recede for quite a while.

"Hey." Charles's voice arrested his meditations. "Time to get ready." Charles looked at the phone in Darcy's hand. "Is she coming?"

Darcy smiled and nodded, not needing to explain anything more.

Charles looked pleased. "Good. Are you sure you want to do this?"

"What? You think I can't?" Darcy's tone was playful, not defensive.

Charles matched his mocking tone. "I just wouldn't want to see you choke." He tilted his head. "That would suck."

Darcy smiled. "You just play your bass. I'll be fine."

Charles smiled back. He knew that Darcy would never have taken him up on his offer, but friendship had demanded that he make it.

⤳

Darcy collected his acoustic guitar from the instrument area and joined Jane and Charlotte, being mic'ed in preparation for the concert. Richard and Charles stood nearby.

Darcy wore his leather pants and a black clingy T-shirt. He didn't want to take anything away from Jane tonight. Jane stood quietly, letting the sound technician wire her and test her equipment, her expression calm and distant.

Charles studied her, reflecting on how easily someone else could look at her and believe her indifferent. He knew that was far from the truth.

Behind Jane's still blue eyes, he knew she was distressed. The news that the charges against Elizabeth had been dropped had reached them the same way it had reached the rest of the world: on the television, flickering in the darkness of his bedroom. There, in their private cocoon, she expressed her feelings of relief, crying on him, and then finding comfort in his body.

After they learned the details, first from Rachel, and later from Darcy, she became defiant. Long Borne Suffering were not victims and they would perform that night. Charlotte's fearlessness matched Jane's, and Darcy immediately volunteered to take Elizabeth's place. They spent little more than an hour rehearsing the three songs they would perform. It wasn't a full set, but it was a statement.

Now, as Jane prepared to go onstage for the first time without her sister or her manager, Charles knew the apprehension that filled her, yet he was impressed by her cool resolve. He felt deeply touched and honored to know that he was one of the few whom his private Jane would trust with her feelings. She was like a beautiful work of art only exhibited to a very select few. He found it was yet another reason to love her, his heart won over once again.

She looked up and her eyes met his. He stepped forward and took her into his arms, holding her close and shielding her for a moment with his body. As he embraced her, letting her ground her fears in him, he was struck by the memory of the first time he held her, on that jet so long ago. He realized that while Jane might not have trusted her heart to know she loved Charles until much later, the way she trusted him with her fears was all the reassurance he should have needed.

He kissed her lips lightly, careful of her makeup, and his eyes spoke comfortingly to her.

Charlotte couldn't help but look around, her eyes seeking people she knew wouldn't be there, as her hands rhythmically moved in their mindless dance.

"You okay, beautiful?"

Charlotte focused on her lover, and she couldn't repress the smile that came to her. Love, the experience of being in it, continued to surprise her, with tiny and immeasurable delights that she had never known before. Hearing Richard call her beautiful and knowing now what it meant, sent a tiny electric shiver up her back, interrupting her thoughts and playing havoc with her senses. She was goofy with love and relished it.

She laughed, her emotions too high to bottle up, and nodded. Richard took her hands in his and brought them up to his lips.

"Big house tonight."

Charlotte voiced a sound of agreement. "We've played bigger."

Richard's eyes crinkled. "You're not going to do it, are you?"

"What?"

"Let me play the big strong man while you swoon in my arms."

Charlotte laughed again. "No." She took her hands out of his and wrapped her arms around his neck. "But if you want, I'll be happy to swoon in your arms when we get back home." She lifted her eyebrows seductively and Richard kissed the rich sweetness of her lips, pressing her slight body to his.

She was amazing, growing in beauty and confidence by the moment, each second becoming more and more desirable and beloved to him. He was awestruck with the knowledge that his love had effected this change in her. And while he knew his demons might return, he believed that he would never stop craving the remarkable woman in his arms.

"I love you, Char," he whispered in her ear, delighting in the response he provoked with his words. She purred happily before kissing him. As he tasted her once again, he knew he was lost. Gone. Done. Take him off the market and put him out to pasture. This smart, sassy, beautiful, sexy woman wanted him, and he would be happy to follow her around for the rest of his life.

Caroline approached the group and shared a smile with Darcy at the two couples. "She's coming?" she asked softly. Darcy nodded and Caroline found herself pleased for him. "Good." Then she raised her voice. "Jane, Char, it's time."

The two couples released each other and the women shared an awkward smile. Their routine was broken and they were uncertain what to do next.

Charles stepped up and said, "Come on," in a low, easy voice, leading them along the dark path to the stage edge. Charlotte had earlier explained her discussion with Alex to Jane, who accepted it, both of them knowing nothing would be final until they had conferred with Elizabeth. But it did leave them in an uneasy position on this night.

The trio was surprised when Charles walked boldly out to center stage, after stopping them offstage. The audience roared with recognition. He waited a moment and then held up his hands.

"Hey," he said as easily as if he was talking to a single person instead of a crowd of twenty thousand. He waited while they responded and then continued. Offstage Jane and Darcy shared an amused look. This was Charles at his best. "You might've heard, we've had a busy day," he told the crowd conversationally, intimacy building with each word and expression.

The audience puzzled for a moment, then responded with a loud building cheer.

"Yeah," Charles shrugged, "but that's not gonna stop us."

Screams followed.

"Are you ready for this?" he asked, his voice deep and sexy. "Long Borne Suffering."

The trio moved out as the crowd climbed to an even higher pitch, not a seated person in the house. All the audience's doubts and concerns about the night's performance had been dashed by Charles's confidence. They knew they were in for one hell of a show.

Darcy started the familiar riff of "Everything You Are" and they were off. After "Wanted" Jane took the entirely redundant step of introducing and thanking Darcy for playing for Elizabeth. They finished with "The Longest Good-bye," Jane singing that night for someone she had never sung to before, who wasn't even there.

Charles was waiting to lead them back when they came off the stage and Richard met them at the green room, full of praise for all of them. The three men came together fully prepared to show everyone why Slurry was one of the top names in the business. They moved with a precision founded on confidence and long practice. Charles was wired for sound while Darcy removed his shirt and warmed up his Paul Reid Smith. The stage was done over for them, with an additional monitor set up for Darcy.

When Caroline came over, Darcy asked her, "You know what to do?"

Caroline smiled. "I've been briefed." They found themselves together as once again the others were locked in passionate embraces. Darcy looked charmingly embarrassed. "So, um, how's Faust?"

Caroline struggled to keep her countenance. "He's great," she answered warmly, trying to reassure him. "It'll be fine. Don't worry."

Darcy nodded, relieved that once again, Caroline always knew what he was thinking. They took the stage, and all of their distractions fell away. Darcy lost himself in his music, Charles giving voice to his thoughts, and Richard pounding out his heartbeat.

And the crowd responded to *him*. He was reaching them through his music and he felt a sense of acceptance that Darcy hadn't recognized before.

⤜⤛

Elizabeth declined Rachel's offer to go shopping for an outfit for the night. She couldn't help but suspect Rachel was trying to torment her employer by keeping Elizabeth away from the show as long as possible. She dressed in one of her concert outfits, finding that it felt natural to wear, even though she didn't expect to perform.

She was hungry and did stop to eat when Rachel had some wonderful-smelling take-out delivered. She was finishing her makeup when the phone rang, with Tommy announcing he was waiting for them downstairs.

When they were safely in the limo, Rachel gave Elizabeth her backstage pass and put on her own. Elizabeth followed Rachel into the building as Tommy hurried them past the security points. They walked down a long corridor, the sound of Slurry passing through the walls. Elizabeth smiled, hearing her lover's playing and finding herself warmed by it.

They emerged backstage and Rachel took Elizabeth directly to the control center. Caroline greeted her warmly, giving her a hug and expressing her happiness at Elizabeth's good news.

"Darcy asked for you to stand here," Caroline told her, leading her to the bank of monitors, which showed Slurry rocking out onstage. Elizabeth stood where Caroline placed her, not even noticing the small camera aimed at her. Caroline took a moment to stand at Elizabeth's side, enjoying the spectacle on screen before going back to the console.

⤜⤛

Darcy was relaxed, playing "Taking Control," a song he had written with Charles. It was loud and vigorous with a challenging, syncopated beat. Darcy enjoyed himself, his guitar riding low over his groin as he played powerfully, relishing the pleasure of mastery, of doing something difficult well.

Caroline's voice came to him over the headset. "She's here."

Darcy looked up to Charles, who nodded that he had received that same message, and then to Richard.

"Look at your monitor, Darcy," Caroline instructed. There stood Elizabeth, watching them with a smile for him alone.

❧

Elizabeth watched with Jane and Charlotte as Slurry's song ended and surprisingly, Darcy moved to center stage. Charles stepped away and the full light was on Darcy.

Elizabeth looked to her band mates, who both shook their head in confusion. They knew Slurry's sets as well as their own, and this was completely new to them.

Their jaws dropped as they saw Darcy remove his sunglasses before he began to speak.

"This is for Elizabeth," he said, then stopped, looking like he wanted to say more but instead nodded to Charles and began the riff that Elizabeth recognized from that morning a week ago at Pemberley. Her astonishment was complete when he started singing, his voice deep and rich.

> It was a long, dark, lonely night,
> And I thought you were gone.
> I didn't know how I'd get through.
> I had to look inside.
> I found a trust I never knew.

Elizabeth's jaw quivered, her eyes locked on his, as he looked right into the camera and her.

> But somehow my luck turned around
> The fate that was overdue,
> And suddenly you're right by my side.
> And now everything is new.

Darcy looked up at the monitor and was confused to find it empty. He turned to look offstage and found Elizabeth there, watching him.

Her eyes were huge and shiny; her face pale, but a huge, heartfelt smile illuminated her features.

Smiling back, Darcy sang the chorus:

> *You changed me,*
> *You broke through all the pain that there was.*
> *You changed me*
> *And made me brand new.*
> *You changed me.*
> *And now that I am free I know*
> *I want to spend my life with you.*

Turning, he sang to her, expressing everything he felt in his heart, ignoring the crowd that was screaming wildly at what it was witnessing.

When he finished the final repeat of the chorus he moved offstage, completely mindless of the audience. Charles took over, announcing they would have a break, while Caroline made sure Darcy's microphone was turned off.

—❧—

They found themselves in the instrument area, the one place they had met so many times on the tour, the place that was always the same, no matter where they played. He released the strap on his guitar and lowered it to its stand, all the while his eyes never leaving hers.

She stared at him, moved beyond words. Her eyes alone expressed the fierce love she felt.

As soon as the guitar was down, he snatched her up, unable to be another second from her embrace. As she felt his hands tangling in her hair, pulling her close, fresh tears formed in her eyes. She had never felt so loved before, and her heart broke and was remade with each tear.

His mouth was upon hers, starting with gentle tender kisses that soon exploded in their mutual need. Her mouth opened and he explored the depths, his tongue probing and possessing. Her hands touched his bare back, feeling the strength of his body and the slickness of the sweat on his skin.

She was lost to everything but desire. The delicious pleasure of his mouth ignited a fire inside her. She needed more. Her hands stole around him to rest on his chest, where she stroked him, from his shoulders to the waistband of his pants.

Darcy was fumbling with the hooks of her bra when he realized where they were. He didn't know how his hands had gotten under her shirt, which was pushed up, her skin against his own, but he knew this was not the place for what he wanted, needed to do to her. With trembling hands he lowered her shirt, her eyes showing first confusion, then surprise and understanding as she returned to awareness.

He grabbed her hand and led her to the dressing rooms. They entered the first open door they found, stopping only long enough to make sure it was empty and to lock the door, then they surged back into each other's arms, kissing each other frantically to make up for their brief pause. Elizabeth's shirt and bra fell to the floor, and neither could recall removing it. Darcy soon found himself opening the zipper and button of his pants to prevent injuring himself.

Elizabeth relished the sensation of her bare chest against his. She writhed against him as her mouth hungrily devoured him. Darcy was once again surprised to find his hands attempting to remove Elizabeth's jeans without his knowledge. He stopped to look at her, his eyes questioning hers.

She undid her pants and pushed the remains of her clothes to the floor in response. Darcy shivered at the desire he found in her eyes and snatched her up again, not wanting to see anymore, only to feel.

Their mouths locked, he held her close with one hand while the other touched her breasts. They were full, her nipples tight and pointed. Moaning, he placed her on the nearby counter and lowered himself, so he could suckle at her sweet tit.

Elizabeth clutched his head to her as she leaned back, exposing herself. Darcy understood and his hand slid down to her sex. Elizabeth's breath came in short bursts as he touched her, fulfilling the need that had been burning within her. She cried out, pushing herself against him as he penetrated her with one finger, then two, his thumb skillfully massaging her as she moaned softly against him. He was sucking on her nipple, making her dizzy with the pleasure that was quickly overpowering her. With a sudden gasp and a scream, she came against him, her body going limp against his.

"Oh God," she panted.

Darcy stood up and stared down at her, his expression one of pleasure and satisfaction at what he was able to do for her. "You're beautiful when you come."

Elizabeth gazed at him, her breath passing through her tingling, swollen lips. She wanted more. She wanted him, and she let it show in her eyes.

Grasping the back of her skull in his large hand, he crushed her mouth to his, her hot body pressed against his.

"Not here," she gasped between long, hot kisses. "I want to—" Words became simply too difficult and she gave up trying to speak.

In any case, Darcy had gotten her message and eased her off the counter and onto the couch. "Here?" he asked as he licked and nibbled her throat, making her tremble as he found the sensitive spot just below and behind her ear.

"Yes," she breathed, her need becoming urgent. When he released her, she lay down on the couch, her hands behind her head as she stretched luxuriously, fully aware of the vision she was presenting him.

Darcy stared, his eyes dark with hunger. Unconsciously his tongue moistened his lips as he worked the tight-fitting pants off his hips.

Elizabeth opened her eyes, wondering what the delay was. "Don't worry about that!" she urged him, one hand dropping to her sex and her fingers resting on the soft curls there.

All thought left Darcy's mind; he climbed on the couch, carefully balancing on his knees, as his height would not allow him to lie down fully.

Elizabeth welcomed him eagerly, her legs splayed apart, one foot on the floor and another in the air. She pulled Darcy close, her lips on his, her arms and legs enfolding around him.

"Oh yes," she moaned as he entered her at last. Wantonly, she lifted her hips to hold him as deeply as she could, her legs caressing the smooth leather that encased his. Darcy struggled to hold back, his body moving against his will, wanting only to find immediate release in her wet, lush depths. They became as one being, their motion having no origin or destination. He was not making love to her, nor she to him. They simply were. One creature, moving with one purpose and goal.

Darcy watched through haze-filled eyes as her hair shifted with each thrust, a living curtain surrounding her lovely face. Elizabeth lost herself in his eyes, eyes that were beyond seeing, only recording sensation after sensation. She felt herself grow larger, deeper, a vessel to be filled by him. Deeper and deeper he filled her, and yet she could hold more. She wanted to hold all of him, inside of her, forever.

The sweet pleasurable tension in her body rose and she found herself shaking all over as white electricity flooded her core and overrode the circuit of her nervous system. She heard screams and knew they were hers, but she couldn't sense herself breathing. All she could do was feel, pulse by pulse, the indescribable pleasure that rocked her. She felt fire burn her inside and knew that he had joined her in bliss, a moment before he fell limply on top of her.

Giddy joy filled her. She tenderly wrapped her arms around him and gently kissed his temple as he caught his breath. She felt loved, empowered by her bond to him. They were beyond closeness; they were intimate: a word that now had new meaning for her. Goals, plans, and priorities had all shifted in a heartbeat. She took this new knowledge and understanding into her heart and cherished it closely as she let her lips lightly caress his face.

He came back to himself and pushed himself up on his elbows. She met him with a look of pure satisfaction that ought to have been illegal. It pleased him to know that he equally affected this amazing woman, who moved him so deeply. With a look of pure adoration, he kissed her lips, lightly nibbling on her sweet flesh.

He opened his mouth to speak when there was a loud banging on the door. "Darcy!" Caroline's voice came to them from the hall. "Sorry to interrupt but there is this concert going on. You might want to finish it?"

Elizabeth giggled, her face blushing prettily.

Darcy kissed her lightly and began carefully getting up. "We'll continue this later?"

Elizabeth nodded as she sat up and began looking for her clothes.

Darcy fastened his pants and, with a last quick kiss, exited the room. Caroline was waiting, looking very put upon.

"Sorry, Caro," he mumbled uncomfortably as he moved toward the instrument area, unable to meet her eyes.

"Don't worry," she said, exasperated. "It's not like I could hear you over the other two."

Darcy looked at her in surprise, and then he noticed Charles coming over from the area of the dressing room, a distinctive smile on his face.

"Hey," he greeted his band mates pleasantly. There was no doubt. Bingley had just been fucked well.

Darcy looked questioningly at Richard, who flashed him a look of disdain. "Not everyone behaves like rabbits in heat, you know."

Charles laughed at this as he picked up his bass and had the sound tech rewire his mic. Darcy found his own sound equipment was gone and was trying to remember where it had come off when Elizabeth walked up with it.

When Darcy turned to the sound tech, he heard Elizabeth gasp and Charles burst out laughing.

"Oh man!" Charles exclaimed.

Darcy looked behind him to see Elizabeth covering her face with both hands. "What?"

"Will, you either have to put a shirt on or not turn your back to the audience."

Richard's eyes widened and he exclaimed, "Whoa, nice work, Lizzy."

"Oh God," Elizabeth moaned, mortified.

Charles could see Darcy was quickly becoming annoyed at not knowing what was going on. "Will, you have an impressive set of claw marks across your back," he explained.

"I'm sorry."

Darcy smiled and laughed at the absurdity of the situation. He put his hands on Elizabeth's waist and kissed her lightly. "It's okay. I'll just be careful how I stand," he assured her.

Elizabeth hid her face against his chest, then looked up and nodded. She kissed him for luck, placed his sunglasses on him, and stood back with Jane and Charlotte as the men left to go back onstage.

"Come on," Charlotte directed, and they moved silently back to their place in front of the monitors where they could watch the show.

The guys were dead on that night, playing flawlessly and engaging the crowd between songs. Even Darcy was more animated than they had ever seen him. When they got to the point where they would normally play "It's All a Joke," he asked Charles, "You think we should play this?"

Charles paused a beat. "I don't know. I think we should check with the bosses."

The audience ate it up.

"You know," Darcy continued, "I thought I was the boss."

Charles grinned. "Well, you were. But you know, Jane…"

"Gives better head?" Richard piped in.

"Exactly."

The house fell apart. Backstage Elizabeth, Charlotte, and Jane were doubled over laughing. A full minute passed before Darcy could continue, partially because the first time he tried to talk, he lost his control and started laughing himself, which set everyone else off again.

When he did regain control, he said, "Okay, let's see what the bosses have to say."

Jane caught her cue and she took a headset from Caroline. "Charles," she drawled, her voice filling the stage.

"Your call, ladies," Charles began. "Do we play it or pass?"

"We wouldn't want to offend you," Darcy added.

Elizabeth gave Jane a thumbs-up. "Oh, you are playing it."

"You're sure?"

"It's your penance," Jane added menacingly. "Don't screw up."

Richard laughed, "You boys are fuuuuucked!"

Laughter erupted again and Darcy nodded, careful not to turn his back. "I think you are right."

Darcy began the riff to the song as Charles started singing to Jane. They didn't screw up. They were electric and exciting and words that had once provoked such pain and hurt now were rendered harmless.

As the girls returned to their usual place before the monitors, Elizabeth asked, "Where's Alex?" noticing him missing for the first time.

Jane's face sobered and she looked at Charlotte. "He's not here," she said uneasily.

Elizabeth faced Charlotte. "What?" she asked.

"Lizzy, you've been through a lot today, maybe we should leave this for tomorrow."

"What's going on?" she demanded.

"Lizzy, Char's right. We're going to have a meeting with him tomorrow," Jane said, her eyes full of affection. "Let it go for now."

Elizabeth looked from Jane to Charlotte and nodded slowly, surprising herself with her ability to trust.

❦

The three men stood together, as close as brothers, their long, lean bodies weary with exertion, shimmering with sweat in the bright stage lights, their long arms hanging at their sides, holding their instruments ready.

Charles talked to the audience with trust and ease, as though they were his best friends. When he called their names, Elizabeth, Jane, and Charlotte moved back onstage, crossing the line from invisibility to visibility. They took their positions near their lovers, to play the song they had all written together.

They decided to perform "The Game of Love" between sets, to celebrate the huge changes that had occurred among all of them and also as a statement of vindication. Elizabeth was free and cleared; Wickham would never trouble them again. That alone was worthy of being acknowledged, and they had no better way than with their music.

The audience roared as Elizabeth playfully took Darcy's dark glasses and put them on, winning a bright smile from him. Jane took Charles's place at center stage, as he stood nearby, and Richard and Charlotte arranged themselves behind a huge percussion display. A look was passed around them, silently communicating, and with Charlotte's cymbal, they were off.

Darcy played for Elizabeth, as he had the last time. The difference was that she was now receptive to him and was in fact playing back to him. The song was like a duet of the two guitars, electric and acoustic, their voices dancing around each other, even as Darcy's and Elizabeth's bodies circled each other.

Elizabeth started singing with Jane, encouraging Darcy to serenade her, which he did, manfully playing to the two sisters as Charles played his bass on their other side. Richard and Charlotte were easily performing their own dance, moving with perfect timing across their instruments, sharing a smile and wink.

The song ended too quickly, yet they were pleased with their performance. They had given something special of themselves to the audience, who thanked them with wild cheering and applause. It was clear to everyone in the crowd that this was much more than two bands simply playing together. This was in fact one entity, a being with six faces.

꿏

Later, after the show and back at the loft, Elizabeth picked up her carton of take-out and her chopsticks and followed Darcy to the bed. She was emotionally exhausted, but her body was still fairly awake. She figured she needed Darcy and bed, in that order.

Darcy was already stretched out on the bed, wearing his black T-shirt and gray shorts, looking delightfully comfy. Elizabeth took off her pants, her shoes long ago discarded, and settled down next to him. They ate, sharing each other's food and talking lightly of the performance.

Shyly, Darcy asked, "You liked your song?"

Elizabeth felt like her face would split, she smiled so hard. "I loved it. Couldn't you tell?"

"Well…" he blushed.

Elizabeth put her food down and reached for him, cuddling close. "I couldn't believe you sang for me."

"I would do anything for you," he told her earnestly. "I wanted everyone to know that I love you, completely and unconditionally." He stopped and took her hand and kissed it. "You have changed me, and I'll always be grateful."

Elizabeth looked into his eyes, seeing more there than words could ever say. "You changed me too, you know."

"Did I? I hadn't noticed. I was too busy discovering how wonderful you are."

Elizabeth blushed at his flattery and lifted her lips to his. He kissed her adoringly, pressing close to her and feeling their legs tangle together. He released her lips to kiss her neck, and she tilted her head absently, her body roiling with sensations while her mind was in a distant place. "Are we going to be okay?" she asked.

"We're going to be fine," he told her, his voice certain, even though he didn't fully understand her question.

"What's going to happen?" she asked, her eyes troubled. Feelings of uncertainty born during her incarceration came back, demanding to be answered.

Darcy didn't understand what prompted her fears, but he perceived them clearly. "We are going to be together, you and me. We're going to finish out this tour, and then we'll do whatever we want to, but," he gripped her hand tightly, "we will do it together."

She closed her eyes. "Hold me," she pleaded.

Darcy pulled her close, cradling her. "Darling, didn't you hear my song? That was for you. I love you, and I always will."

"I know," she whispered, "and I love you. But... what if we are separated? We are both rock stars now and that's not a very good career track for a relationship."

"Then screw the careers," he told her fiercely. "If it's a question of Slurry or you, I pick *you*. I don't need to be a rock star. Hell, I don't ever need to work a day again. But I do need you. I found that out last night." He stopped, his eyes downcast. "Lizzy, I love you, and I don't care if rock star marriages don't work. If the rules don't work for me, I change them, and you and I are going to work." His eyes were burning into hers as he finished.

"Marriage?" Elizabeth gasped.

Darcy's mouth fell open and for a heartbeat he was back at the disastrous morning a month ago. He searched Elizabeth's eyes for a sign of what she was feeling, and then gathering his courage, he spoke. "Elizabeth Bennet, will you please marry me?"

Elizabeth trembled, shocked and speechless. She looked at him questioningly.

"I know," he said in a calmer voice. "It hasn't been very long for us, has it? But I've loved you for so long, I can't even tell you when I started. And I know you, Elizabeth. I've seen you when you are angry, and tired, and bitchy. I've known you when you are sad and upset, and I've known you when you are so happy you literally dance on your feet with joy. I've seen you in every way, and I love you. I know that I don't want to miss a moment of you. I want to spend the rest of my life with you being happy and sad and grumpy because you haven't gotten your coffee yet." He smiled then turned serious again. "Please, Elizabeth. I know you love me, and I can't see living my life without you. Please say yes."

Elizabeth felt her emotions tossed like a tiny boat on the ocean with his words, but in the end, she knew he was right. She did love him and wanted nothing more than to be with him, and she knew he felt the same. It didn't matter to her whether they married or not, but it clearly did to him, and suddenly the answer was easy. "Yes, my love, yes."

He crushed her to him, kissing her like he could never get enough. Elizabeth responded, feeling unexpectedly happy and comforted in his embrace. They made love, slowly and gently, reaffirming their feelings for each other throughout the night, until exhaustion claimed them.

❧

Tuesday morning found them back at JFK Airport, the same place they had left from four months ago. The plane was different; instead of the De Bourgh corporate jet, they had a chartered airliner, and instead of watching Darcy arrive, she sat beside him in their limo. Despite the familiarity of having done this before, Elizabeth was struck by a powerful sense of distance as she climbed the steps to the plane, a pair of sunglasses on her face, her guitars in her hands. She had changed so much and become a new person in so many ways. Gone were the nervous uncertainty and the forceful need to prove herself. Elizabeth walked with a confidence that came from knowing who she was and what her strengths were.

Darcy was right behind her, and this time she did not hesitate to move to the front of the plane. Instead of a group of strangers onboard, Elizabeth was happy to find that she knew almost everyone there. She smiled as people called out greetings to her, and surprisingly, to Darcy as well. As she waved, Elizabeth felt the sense of responsibility for them that Darcy had told her about so long ago. But she didn't find it overwhelming. She knew that they all wanted to be there, to share in their journey and go wherever it might take them.

She passed Richard and Charlotte, who were relaxing with a pair of PSPs plugged into each other. By some rare miracle, Charles and Jane had arrived on time and were holding each other's hands in preparation for takeoff. Elizabeth said good morning and took her seat next to Darcy. As the plane started moving, he laced his fingers with hers and they shared a tender kiss, the light in his eyes telling her how happy he was.

"Are you ready?" he asked, his voice as always soft and strong.

Elizabeth smiled at the question. She was ready for whatever was next. "Let's go," she answered him, as the plane took off.

Epilogue

"For MTV News, I'm Mark Cole.

"It was destined to be the wedding of the season, the widely publicized nuptials of Slurry lead singer Charles Bingley to Long Borne Suffering's Jane Bennet, but it turned into so much more. In this MTV Valentine's Day special we are going to talk to the members of Slurry and Long Borne Suffering about what happened on that day, January 24, 2011. But first, let's watch the video."

The tape first shows Charles, Richard, and Darcy waiting at the front of a tastefully decorated church. They are all wearing dark suits. Flowers are everywhere. The music starts and the congregation stands. All eyes are on Jane as she enters the church on the arm of Mr. Bennet. She is wearing a sleeveless white gown with a pink ombré and carrying a bouquet of white tulips. At the front of the church, she takes Charles's arm, and they move slightly to the left as the congregation murmurs and turns.

Charlotte now enters the church with her father. The crowd is growing louder but Charlotte smiles happily at Richard. She is wearing a slim, white sheath with sheer bell sleeves that reveal her tattoos. She is carrying a modern-looking arrangement of purple and white orchids. She takes her place next to Richard and they move slightly to the right.

The congregation has grown silent as the music plays on and Darcy is waiting alone at the front of the church. Then the doors open once more and Elizabeth emerges with her father, who clearly slipped around to the front of the church again. She wears a classically styled wedding gown in ivory with a full skirt and fitted bodice and carries red roses. She smiles archly at the gasps as she takes her place next to Darcy. The three couples stand together for a long moment and then turn, and the ceremony starts.

Mark Cole: "With me in our Times Square studio, just back from their Hawaiian honeymoon, are Charles and Jane Bingley, Fitzwilliam Darcy and Elizabeth Bennet, and Richard and Charlotte Fitzwilliam."

The camera pans to each couple, who are looking relaxed, tanned, and happy.

"Let me start by congratulating you all, and I have to ask, why a surprise triple wedding?"

The couples laugh.

Darcy: "Well, Charles and Jane were the first ones to set a date, and because of Jane's condition, we felt that would be best."

Quiet laughter as Jane pats a very pregnant tummy.

Richard (interrupting): "Don't believe him. Will was actually dying to get married all through the tour. We kept expecting Will and Lizzy to announce that they had snuck off to a justice of the peace's office at breakfast one morning."

More laughter.

Mark: "Will, is this true?"

Darcy (looking slightly embarrassed, with Elizabeth teasingly looking on): "Yes." *More laughter.* "I'm the kind of person who, once I make up my mind, I want to do something right away." *He looks at Elizabeth.* "Lizzy had other ideas."

Elizabeth: "Oh great! Now millions of women are looking at the TV and calling me an idiot. Thank you very much."

Darcy kisses Elizabeth.

Mark (trying to get them back on topic): "So, when did you decide to have a surprise wedding?"

Charlotte: "We finished touring in December, before the holidays, and we immediately got to work on Jane's wedding."

Mark: "No break?"

Charlotte: "No break. Richard and I saw how much work the wedding was and what a nightmare it was turning into, and at one point we just looked at each other and said, 'We're never gonna do this again.'"

Richard: "So the idea came to us that since Jane and Charles were already doing all the work and since everyone we would want at our wedding would already be at theirs, why not just save ourselves the headache and piggyback onto it?"

Charles (smiling): "Yeah, let us do all the dirty work."

Mark (looking at Darcy and Elizabeth): "And you basically had the same thoughts?"

Elizabeth (nodding): "That was it. It was a funny coincidence of timing, because we all came up with the same idea on the same day. I was talking to Jane about the idea while Char and Richard were talking to Charles."

Darcy: "We decided to keep it a secret because we knew otherwise the news coverage would get out of control."

Mark: "Now, about the timing, is it true that you all met each other on the same night, and you all proposed on the same day?"

Charles: "Within twelve hours of each other, I think."

Mark: "When was that?"

Charles: "That was six months ago, back in August. We were playing at the Garden, here in the city."

Mark (continuing with Jane): "Is it true that you proposed to Charles, Jane?"

Jane (smiling beautifully): "Yes, it is. But in my defense, I have to say it was before I was pregnant."

Charles smiles warmly at her.

Charles: "Not that it would have mattered."

Mark: "You've just completed a heavy four months of touring. During that time, not only were you performing, but you were also starting your own label, Pemberley Records. What can you tell us about that?"

Sighs and laughter from everyone.

Richard: "I'll tell you, it was a great experience that I hope we'll never have to repeat." *Everyone nods.* "There's nothing in the world like touring and performing every night, but it takes a lot out of you. We had the additional complications of Jane's condition and our fairly new relationships, so there was something different every day." *He smiles.* "I will say that we never could have made it without each other's support and the support of an absolutely amazing team of people we have working with us."

Mark: "Richard, your marriage surprised a lot of people. Many people said you would never settle down."

Richard: "My mother being one of them." *Laughter.* "I was actually in a pretty bad place during the first half of the tour. I was doing some really self-destructive things and it was during the break in July that I realized I had to stop and turn myself around or I would lose everything." *His fingers lace with Charlotte's.* "I was lucky in that I found someone who wasn't willing to give up on me and that I have this great group of friends who have helped and stood by me every day."

Charlotte says nothing but squeezes his hand.

Mark (referring to notes): "You all honeymooned together?"

Jane: "Yes, at Richard's condo in Honolulu."

Mark: "It's unusual for people, even members of a group, to be so close."

Charlotte: "Don't get the wrong idea. I've seen department stores smaller than that condo. We didn't see Will and Lizzy for five days straight." *Laughter.*

Darcy (looking cool while Elizabeth blushes): "We're very close."

Richard: "We are all related now, through marriage. We made a chart when we were touring."

Charlotte: "There's a lot of down time on the road."

Richard: "A *lot* of down time. But we made a chart and we figured that Charles and Char were the most distantly related but that we're all one big family."

Elizabeth (to Richard): "How did that go again?"

Richard (pointing): "Charles to Char is my cousin's wife's brother-in-law."

Mark: "So, what is coming next for you?"

Darcy: "We're all going out to California. Both groups have new songs to record."

Mark: "This past year has given you some inspiration?"

Darcy: "You might say that."

Elizabeth: "We, LBS, need to get our next CD recorded before Jane gives birth in May."

Charlotte: "We *hope* we have until May."

Jane: "Speak for yourself." *Laughter.*

Darcy: "We're going to be producing LBS's next CD, and then we'll record our own."

Mark: "Why California?"

Darcy (smiling ruefully): "Because that's what Charles wants."

Charles: "You want to stay in New York in this weather?" *He smiles, then pats Jane's tummy.* "These are West Coast babies; they are going to be born where they belong."

Mark: "Do you know what you are having?"

Jane: "We know one of them is a boy, and the other one is shy."

Elizabeth: "Once we have the next CDs recorded, Richard, Charlotte, Fitzwilliam, and I will return to New York to finish up all the details for

Pemberley and give Charles and Jane some downtime with the babies. Then we'll have the formal launch of Pemberley Records. At that time, we'll be announcing other groups that are signed to the label, but right now we are still working out the legal details."

Mark: "And when will this be happening?"

Darcy: "We anticipate sometime this summer."

Mark: "That sounds like you have quite a bit of work planned."

Charles: "We're really fortunate in the team of people we have working for us, because it's a lot of work. What you see here"—*gestures to indicate the group*—"wouldn't be possible if it weren't for our team."

Mark: "And some of them are family members, too?"

Charlotte (laughing): "That's right, my brother Alex is the general manager at Pemberley and Charles's sister Caroline manages both the bands."

Richard: "We're always busy, but that's good. The worst thing in this business is to do nothing. Right now we're in a really good place, both business-wise and creatively, to do the things we've always wanted to do."

Mark: "Lizzy, Charlotte, Jane, it's been a little over a year since your first CD was released, less than a year since you met Slurry. Some people have called your story a 'modern-day fairy tale.' Did you ever imagine you would be here?"

Jane: "We always knew we had the talent and the drive. And I will admit that before we met Slurry, I didn't know if we were ever going to make it really big. But when I met Charles, and he asked me to sing with him, I knew that our lives would be different."

Charlotte: "It *is* like a fairy tale. I read the news reports and even I can't believe it. I mean, the three members of a girl group marrying the three members of a rock band. That just sounds so hokey. If you tried to sell our story to a movie studio, they'd just laugh, so I try to forget about all that and stay grounded in the here and now. It isn't hard to do when you are living out of a tour bus and wondering when you'll next get a chance to do your laundry."

Elizabeth: "I never thought this would happen, and in truth, I fought it the longest. I wanted LBS to make it on our own, but in the end, I knew that this was the way it was going to go." *Elizabeth smiles at Darcy.* "And I'm glad it did."

Darcy: "Me too."

Mark: "We are almost out of time here, but do you have anything to add on how Slurry has grown?"

Darcy (slowly): "I started Slurry as a way of coping with the loss of my parents. Over time it's not just helped me deal with the loss of my family, but it's become my family, both figuratively and now literally. It's surpassed everything I ever imagined for it, and it just continues to grow. I'm humbled by what we have created and the lives we have touched. It was a long, hard road to get here, but this past year has been very healing, for Slurry as a band and for its individual members. We're now stronger and able to move on to the next level, whatever that may bring."

Mark: "I want to thank you all for coming to talk to us about what is being called the 'wedding of the year' and about what we can expect from Slurry and Long Borne Suffering. I'd like to wish you all good luck with your future and a happy Valentine's Day."

Cut away from the studio and play "Journey to You" video while the credits roll.

THE END

Acknowledgments

This book was written at a breakneck pace requiring not just the energies of myself but also several dear women who proofread and edited, as well as listened to any number of weird songs I threw at them, all without complaint.

My thanks go to Abigail, Dorothy, Elaine, Amy, Jean-Louise, Debbie, and Sylvie.

ABOUT THE AUTHOR

Heather Lynn Rigaud is fascinated by the comparisons between life in earlier times and modern times. Thus, she spends much of her time thinking about how Regency-era characters would exist now and how a wife and mother would have lived in the past. She is a professional writer with degrees in music therapy and teaching who lives with her husband and two sons in Kingston, New York.